Once making her home in [**Luana DaRosa** has since [continents—though her favourite romantic locations remain the tropical places of Latin America. When she's not typing away at her latest romance novel, or reading about love, Luana is either crocheting, buying yarn she doesn't need, or chasing her bunnies around the house. She lives with her partner in a cosy town in the south of England. Find her on Twitter under the handle @LuDaRosaBooks.

THE VET'S CONVENIENT BRIDE

LUANA DaROSA

THE SECRET SHE KEPT FROM DR DELGADO

LUANA DaROSA

MILLS & BOON

First published in Great Britain 2023
by Mills & Boon, an imprint of HarperCollins*Publishers* Ltd,
1 London Bridge Street, London, SE1 9GF

www.harpercollins.co.uk

HarperCollins*Publishers* Macken House, 39/40 Mayor Street Upper,
Dublin 1, D01 C9W8, Ireland

The Vet's Convenient Bride © 2023 Luana DaRosa

The Secret She Kept from Dr Delgado © 2023 Luana DaRosa

ISBN: 978-0-263-30615-6

08/23

THE VET'S
CONVENIENT BRIDE

LUANA DaROSA

MILLS & BOON

For Kery from Durban North Vets,
who is the real-life Maria and adopts any
homeless animal that comes her way.

CHAPTER ONE

A LONG SIGH that spoke of the myriad sleepless nights Maria had struggled through over the last weeks dropped from her lips. Exhaustion sat deep in her bones, and there was no end in sight.

'Looking at the accounts again?'

Maria looked up from her desk and received the cup of coffee her sister Celine held out with a grateful smile.

'*Obrigada*, this was exactly what I needed,' she whispered into the brew as she basked in its aroma streaming up her nose.

'So, what's up?'

Maria took a long sip, avoiding her sister's piercing gaze for a moment as her face vanished behind the coffee mug. 'It's…not looking too good, Celine,' she finally said with a frown she saw reflected on her sister's face.

'Daniel really screwed us over,' Celine mumbled, and drew a scoff from Maria's throat.

'That's putting it mildly.' She would have used much more vulgar language to describe her deadbeat brother. Without his poor decision-making and downright betrayal of the family, she wouldn't struggle to pay the bills so they could keep the doors of their animal sanctuary open.

Their work already didn't pay well, even though their charity was a vital part of the community in Santarém.

Nestled right along the Amazon River and surrounded by swathes of the rainforest, they provided services for the most vulnerable in their society—wild animals. They were the voiceless when it came to the deforestation works happening in the rainforest, so her grandparents had established this charity to help the animals in need. They might not be able to stop deforestation, but at least they could try and help the victims of these works.

They hadn't told anyone they were in financial trouble. The kind-hearted people of Santarém would probably sell their most expensive heirlooms just to keep the charity of Rodrigo and Alma Dias alive. Just as they had done when Gabriela, who ran the local charity shop, had fallen and broken her hip. Or when some vagrants broke into José's store and destroyed all of his machines. Both times the entire community had rallied around their members, giving whatever they could spare—and sometimes even more.

Maria's parents had continued their work because of that sense of belonging and togetherness. When they'd left to live out the rest of their retirement in Switzerland, the responsibility to continue had fallen to Maria, Celine and their brother, Daniel.

Because their animals had no owners and no one to claim them, they relied almost exclusively on donations from different sponsors. The lion's share of their monthly donations had come from a wealthy tech entrepreneur from Minas Gerais—that was until her brother ran off with the donor's wife.

The donations had stopped, and Maria had failed to attract new sponsors to make up what her brother had taken from them. They needed so much money to keep afloat, much more than anyone in Santarém could afford, that she didn't want to ask anyone. Because they wouldn't say no—they would just give. Only one option remained.

'We have to shut down,' Maria said into the quiet spreading between her and Celine. 'Even with the additional income from the vet clinic, we aren't even near to breaking even.'

In a last-ditch effort to keep her family's legacy from shutting down for ever, Maria had hired an additional vet and started offering treatment for a wide range of domestic animals. She looked after any of the exotic and wild animals that needed rehabilitation, while Celine covered the farms in the area as a livestock veterinarian, and three months ago Dr Rafael Pedro had joined their clinic to look after the domestic pets of the area.

Regret constricted her chest when she thought of Rafael. He was a quiet man, not prone to sharing much of himself, yet they had still formed a friendship by co-existing in the same space—both in the practice and at home. Part of the deal for this job included the spare room in the Dias house.

Their areas of responsibility rarely overlapped. Despite that, something between them clicked into place as they worked around each other. A sense of connection, a live wire that crackled and sizzled with the heat and veiled longing.

Their conversations almost always turned flirty, leaving Maria with a sense of unfinished business. That there was something brewing between them was undeniable, yet an invisible boundary had stopped her from acting on the attraction. She was his boss, and though it had been a long time since she'd felt attracted to anyone like that, she couldn't go there with an employee. That would be inviting trouble into her own house. Literally. She didn't even know if he was interested or just being polite. The last time someone had asked her out had taken her by surprise.

Maurice, a *gringo* seeking investments in Brazil and owned of a company providing boat tours up and down parts of the Amazon River, had found an injured snake and instead of simply killing it he'd brought it to her so she could nurse it back to health and release it. After that, he'd come by a couple of times whenever he found something along the river, and eventually he'd asked her out on a date.

Though she had liked him enough, their relationship never went anywhere—her work always taking first place in her life. That much hadn't changed. If she wasn't here, she was at home taking care of her abandoned niece.

That didn't leave any room for romance, no matter what she sensed in the air between her and Rafael.

Celine seemed to have read her mind, for she smirked at her elder sister. 'Maybe if he's not our employee any more, you can finally ask him out.'

Maria rolled her eyes, but her pulse fell out of step at her sister's words, sending her heart tumbling through her body.

She had to admit that Rafael caught her attention. Though the muscled arms and strong chest had drawn her immediate attention when he'd first arrived, it was the warmth in those hazel eyes that had her pulse racing. The way he spoke to distressed animals, handling them with such care as if they were his own family members, opened up something inside her that made her want to consider what Celine had just suggested. But when her brother left with his mistress, he didn't just doom their sanctuary. He also abandoned his daughter, to whom Maria was now a mother figure. She had a hard enough time understanding how Daniel could have done this to them—it got even harder when she tried explaining it to her niece.

'Maybe you should, since you seem so obsessed with him,' Maria deflected, and drew a laugh from her sister's lips.

'I'm legally still married, if you remember. Plus, I'm not the one making doe eyes at him every time I see him.'

'I'm telling you we have to shut our sanctuary down and all you can talk about is the hot vet I hired?' How had they landed on Rafael in the first place? There were so many more important things happening right now.

'Hah, so you *do* think he's hot.'

'Celine! Do you understand what I'm trying to tell you?'

'Of course I do.' Celine sighed. 'But I don't know what you want me to say. I'm devastated to close this place, but we both know you and I have done everything we can to stave off the inevitable.'

Maria sighed as the weariness in her chest grew heavier. 'I'll talk to Rafael first before calling the lawyer. He should know he's about to lose his job.'

Celine walked over to her, giving her a comforting pat on the shoulder. 'Let me know once you've spoken to the lawyer and what our next steps are.'

Maria nodded and when her sister closed the door behind her she let her head fall back onto the top of her office chair. She closed her eyes for a moment, willing her racing heart to slow down.

She needed to admit defeat and focus on rebuilding her niece's life, no matter if that put her own life's plans on hold—again. Her search for love, for a person to start a family with, hardly mattered when Mirabel had had the rug pulled out from under her by the one person who had

sworn to protect her. She had ignored the longing clawing inside her chest for a long time, wanting to focus on
her career first. She had thought there would be a moment where everything came together...or was she living
that moment right now but unaware of it because she had
never really *let* herself get attached to anyone?

Maria shouldn't even be thinking about this. Especially
as she hadn't even asked the target of her attraction if he
felt the same way and wanted to go out some time. But
if they shut down the charity portion of the sanctuary,
the vet clinic was all that remained. And, as much as she
wanted him around, she didn't need another vet and she
certainly couldn't afford it.

Maria would have to fire Rafael today.

Sweet and gorgeous Rafael. The innocent smiles and
stolen glances they exchanged throughout the day sent
jolts of unreserved happiness through a life marred with
hardship. His friendship had become something she trea-
sured, their passion for animals leading to an instant bond.
Giving up on him was adding salt to her already mounting wounds.

If only things were different. That was the dream world
Maria liked to escape to in the quiet moments, where her
traitorous brother and empty bank account couldn't reach
her, only the soft kisses of her would-be lover.

Not that Rafael had ever expressed such a desire for
her, but the looks and the smiles were there, along with
the gentle familiarity that came only from a friend.

Maria sighed again, leaning forward and burying her
face in her hands. Maybe this was for the best. With the
impending closure of the charity she had poured her heart
and soul into, and becoming the full-time legal guardian

of her niece, she had enough going on without needing to add romantic adventures to the mix.

Still, this conversation was going to suck.

Rafael sat behind the counter of the reception typing out his notes when the door to the clinic opened. 'Sorry, we are not open any more,' he said without looking up from the screen in front of him. But the soft shuffling of bare feet on the tiled floor only got louder.

Exhaustion sat deep in Rafael's bones, and he couldn't take on another walk-in. It was already after nine and he'd been woken up by a call from Emanuel, the owner of the local café, at an ungodly hour. The family dog, Rex, had sneaked into the pantry and found some chocolate he wasn't supposed to eat. At least Emanuel knew his regular coffee order by now and had asked his son to deliver it, along with some pastries, as a thank you.

Because of that he had missed dinner with Maria and the Dias sisters' children. Even though he was a tenant and not a family member, Maria had invited him to dinner consistently until it became a habit. Those easy meals they spent together talking about their days in the clinic were a highlight of his days here in Santarém—along with the Sunday markets in the town square that they visited together.

He hated missing any of those occasions to speak to her, but he didn't get to decide when his patients would need him.

Paulo, the ten-year-old son of Irina, who ran the small grocery store in town, held a cardboard box out in front of him and looked somewhat lost. Rafael got off his seat with a furrowed brow. 'Paulo, what's the matter?' he asked as he circled around the reception desk separating them.

'My *mãe* told me to bring this here. She said you look after lost animals,' the boy said, and pushed the box into Rafael's hands.

He took it, placing it on the reception counter, and hissed when he opened the flaps to look inside. A kitten lay among some grass the boy and his mother had collected to make it feel more comfortable. Someone had ripped parts of its fur out from the neck and Rafael saw a deep cut further down. The blood had already congealed, closing the wound, but there was no way of telling if they had hit any vital organs.

'Where did you find it?' he asked, his eyes narrowing on the boy. It wouldn't be the first time he had to treat an animal that fell victim to the cruel whims of humans.

The boy seemed to sense Rafael's apprehension, for he lifted his hands in a gesture proclaiming innocence. 'We found it near the river and my *mãe* asked me to run here so you could take care of it. It was lying on the floor next to a small fire, but there wasn't anyone around when we got there.'

Rafael looked at him for a moment, considering his words. He knew that neither Paulo nor Irina would have hurt a kitten like that. They had their own clowder of cats running around town. Milo, the only black cat out of the bunch, regularly went to the river exploring, and came back with lots of trinkets and baubles. He must have led them there.

He nodded, closed the box again and lifted it off the counter. 'This kitten might have a shot thanks to you,' he said with a small smile and a wave as the boy left, before vanishing into the exam room, where he took the injured animal out of the cardboard box and lay it on the table.

'Okay, let's have a look at you.' He stepped closer, his

hands gentle as he began his exam. He stopped in his tracks when he noticed the markings on the remaining fur, his brow furrowing. 'You're not a domestic cat...'

Rafael placed his hand under the animal, propping it up as he looked at its face, prising the lips open to examine its teeth. 'Are you a baby ocelot?'

With the size of the kitten, it was hard to tell, but the markings on its fur were not ones commonly found in domestic cats, especially not in a rural region like this one where most people kept barn cats.

The ocelot didn't even flinch when he probed at the stab wound. 'You've been hanging in there for quite some time, haven't you?' he mumbled as he picked his patient up and took its temperature, careful to keep it tucked in under his arm to reduce the stress on the already suffering animal.

'Forty point three... Higher than we would like it to be, but that might be from the stress more than anything else.' Rafael set the ocelot down again and frowned. Big cats like ocelots were part of the overall training they received, but he hadn't worked with them since veterinary school. He was pretty sure he knew what to do—ultrasound to check for any internal bleeding and, if everything checked out, bandage the wound and set her to rest.

Were the topical anaesthetics the same as for domestic cats? Doubt crept into his mind and Rafael sighed. He needed to check in with Maria. He glanced at the clock, frowning. Interrupting her this late wasn't something he wanted to do, even though he knew she'd want to know about the ocelot in their care.

Ever since Rafael had started working at the clinic, the gorgeous owner of the charity had invaded every quiet moment afforded to him. Whenever his mind wandered, he'd inevitably think about her, wondering where she was or what she was doing. Missing her when he'd gone a day without seeing her.

A thought that was as ridiculous as they came. How was he so attached to her already, when all they did was talk about animal welfare? Or was it that kind of simplicity that drew him to her?

Because Maria was unlike any of the women who had entered his life. Granted, all of them were fame-hungry socialites who wanted to benefit from the wealth a romantic link to him promised. Through gossip papers and social media they all knew that the person who married Rafael Pedro would finally unlock the trust fund his famous grandparents had set up for him years ago.

One had almost succeeded in tricking him into marriage, setting up everything so perfectly that Rafael hadn't suspected anything until he stumbled upon the truth by accident. That was the moment he had disavowed his family and love altogether, instead dedicating his life to his work as a veterinary surgeon.

And Maria was his *friend*, one he cherished way more than he had originally planned—along with the entire village of Santarém. What had only ever been meant as an escape had become as close to home as he had ever felt. A large part of the credit went to Maria, who had taken the time to befriend him and introduce him to everyone in the village.

He could acknowledge all of that, yet the yearning within him grew louder, hotter, as they spent more time together. Whatever that was blooming in his chest, he needed to stomp it out right now—before it got out of hand.

Rafael picked up the ocelot again, placing her in a little

pen next door to keep her comfortable while he stepped away. The main building was solely dedicated to the sanctuary's rehabilitation efforts. Outside of two small treatment rooms, there was also a bigger surgery and several rooms to house crates with their overnight and long-term patients. Next to this building was a smaller house where the Dias family—and he—lived.

Rafael breathed a sigh of relief when he saw the lights in the kitchen were still on. He opened the door, closing it silently behind him so as not to wake the children, and stepped into the kitchen to find Maria sitting at the table, her delicate fingers wrapped around a steaming mug of tea.

Her look of utter defeat as she glanced up at him stopped him dead in his tracks and, for a moment, he forgot why he was here as a bout of irrational protectiveness surged in his chest.

'What happened?' he asked before he could rethink it.

The shock on her face told him she hadn't realised he knew her well enough to read her expressions. She shook her head. 'Nothing,' she said, somewhat too quickly.

Rafael narrowed his eyes but decided not to pry. There were more pressing things happening in this moment.

'Hey, I need you for a quick consult,' he said, pushing all the unwelcome feelings and reactions towards Maria away.

'What's the matter?' The look of defeat vanished, replaced by concern as she got up from the chair.

'Someone dropped off an ocelot with a strange knife wound. Not sure what that's even about, but I just wanted to double-check my steps since I'm not sure how much wild cats deviate from the treatment of a house cat.'

Maria nodded and walked past him, motioning him to

follow as they crossed the yard to get to the clinic. 'Did they rip out the fur of the ocelot too?'

Rafael nodded. 'It's alert but tired. I was going to suggest an ultrasound before we stitch it up.'

He led Maria through the door and she went onto her knees in front of the pen with the ocelot, stroking its exposed chest. 'Some people in the area ritually kill baby ocelots or monkeys. We occasionally get some of the failed sacrifices here to patch them back up.'

'What? The indigenous communities wouldn't do that, would they?'

Maria shook her head. 'They know the value of an animal's life much better than most of us do. No, it's a strange occult sect terrorising the local animals.'

Rafael swore under his breath, struggling to imagine how anyone could do such a thing. To think this happened often enough that Maria could recognise the injury on sight alone.

'It's breathing okay. Going by the angle, I don't think they hit any of her organs, but her temperature is elevated.'

'Could just be the stress,' Maria mused as she looked at the wound. 'Grab me the ultrasound.'

Rafael went to the storage room and grabbed the handheld device, dabbing some gel on the ocelot's chest before Maria placed the transducer on the skin, scrutinising the image on the screen.

'Doesn't look like there are any internal injuries,' Rafael said.

'The blade just missed this artery here.' She pointed at the screen and Rafael took note as she explained the surrounding organs.

'Should we stitch up the wound?' That was the part

he'd been uncertain about and why he'd gone to look for Maria's advice. He wouldn't have suggested stitches on such a wound on a cat or small dog, but there were potentially other factors with wild cats he didn't know about.

Maria grabbed a sponge and gave the wound a careful wipe. 'No, this wound is a couple of hours' old at this point. We would do more harm than good if we disturb it. Best to observe and intervene if we find any infection.'

She picked up the ocelot and hugged it close to her chest for a moment, cooing as she petted its head. 'You poor thing. We'll get you back out there once you are all healed up.'

Rafael smiled at that small gesture, appreciating the place of compassion it came from. His profession was full of people with incredible drive and passion, yet in the three months since he'd been here, Maria had surpassed all expectations with her level of care for anyone coming through her door—animals and humans alike.

What a shame his parents had schemed and pushed so much that he'd lost any confidence in having a normal relationship with a woman without fearing for both his and her sanity. But after losing the one woman he'd ever loved to his family's plots, trust didn't come easy to him any more. Laura—his ex—had been in league with his parents all along, whispering sweet nothings into his ears and making him believe that he could find love after all. The brutal sting of rejection rose in his chest at the memory, reinforcing his ironclad defences.

Defences that didn't seem fortified enough. Watching Maria work and provide value to her community had such a profound impact on Rafael and the way he worked that he had caught himself fantasising about having this—

her—for the rest of his life, as more than just the friend she was to him now.

The part of him that had been hurt in the past cautioned him to be careful, and it mingled with the fear of losing what he had built for himself here. Was it worth risking the friendship they shared for a shot at something more when he wasn't sure if he was broken beyond repair?

Maria felt the warmth of his stare on the back of her neck, sending a shiver down her spine. She stayed in the adjacent room for a moment and fought to find the strength within her to start the conversation she needed to have with Rafael. It didn't help that he'd stayed longer to help an injured ocelot that had found its way into their clinic— same as it didn't help how much she enjoyed seeing him every day, how much their friendship meant to her.

She bit her lip as she got back to her feet. This was beyond ridiculous. In the three months he'd been here, he'd not made a single move that would signal he wanted more. No, quite the opposite. Whenever they spoke, the sense between them was one of easy familiarity. There was no reason why this sort of heat should lick across her skin from a mere glance.

Taking a deep breath, she stood up straight and walked back into the room. An awkward silence spread between them as they shot each other tentative glances. How did one even start such a conversation?

She swallowed hard before she opened her mouth. 'Listen, while I have you...'

Rafael turned towards her, his hip leaning against the exam table as he looked at her with those hazel eyes that turned her insides into gooey puddles. Oh, God, why had she let the flirting go so far? Now her tongue suddenly felt too large for her mouth, unable to form the words she needed to say.

'The charity isn't doing so well at the moment. It hasn't been in a while if I'm honest.' She took a breath, her lips trembling when genuine concern lit up his eyes.

'Is that what's been bothering you this last week or so?' he asked.

Maria's eyes widened at that question, thinking back to the few moments they had shared since she'd woken up nine days ago and admitted to herself that the charity had to close. Of course he would have noticed.

She closed her eyes, focusing on the task in front of her as her mind drifted and heat rose in her body as she sensed the connection of genuine attraction zing to life between them once more. That was the last thing she needed to concern herself with.

Though when she opened them again Rafael's face was so full of concern for her that the heat pooling in the pit of her stomach exploded, sending sparks all around her body.

'Last year we lost our biggest sponsor. Ever since then we've been struggling to keep our heads above water. Opening the vet clinic was a last effort to see if the revenue would help us make ends meet.' Maria bit down on her lower lip, glad that her voice didn't crack as she delivered this news that she'd been dreading.

Rafael looked down at his feet as he crossed his arms, a sigh expanding his chest. 'Is there anything I can do to help?'

Maria's hand went to her chest as her pulse accelerated. Though she knew already there was nothing he could do, the fact that he'd bothered to ask opened something inside her that she wanted to remain closed. Now that they'd started this conversation, he'd be leaving soon, and along with him the sense of excitement and attraction that she hadn't felt in such a long time.

This small gift she'd received after all of the turmoil she'd been through would fade away as well.

'No, unfortunately not. Unless you know someone who has some money they're looking to give away,' she said with a half-smile.

An expression flitted over his face, a strange sharpness entering his eyes that she couldn't understand. She watched as he took a few breaths, wanting to know the thoughts she could see building in the way he looked at her.

'I actually do know someone like that who would be willing to be your new benefactor.'

The warmth drained out of her body, replaced by an unearthly cold as she processed his words, hoping against hope that they were true and she wasn't just imagining them because those were the words she'd wanted to hear. A new benefactor? Someone to replace what Daniel had stolen from them with his reckless libido?

'What...? Who?' It didn't matter that she wouldn't recognise the name. If he knew someone who could keep the doors of their sanctuary open, she didn't care if it came with strings attached.

'Me,' Rafael said, and heat swept through her once more, colliding with the chill in her bones and whipping up her insides into a merciless storm.

'You? But...you live in my guest room.'

'Ah, yes. Unfortunately, my money is tied up in some clerical red tape.' He looked away, a flash of discomfort and self-doubt in his eyes. 'My grandparents set up a trust for me, but they wanted their hard-earned money to benefit me and my siblings only once we were ready to start our own families.'

Maria furrowed her brow, her eyes narrowing as she looked at him. Who were his grandparents that they'd left him so much money? 'Clerical red tape?'

Rafael chuckled, a sound that stoked the already brewing storm in the pit of her stomach. 'My grandparents thought the best way to ensure all the Pedro grandchildren used their money how they intended was to put in a clause which only allowed us to access the money once we were married.'

Her heart leapt inside her chest, crushing against her ribcage. Her eyes darted to his left hand, scanning for a ring but finding nothing but an empty finger. If he wasn't married, how was he going to become their new benefactor?

The thought of Rafael getting married caused a strange dissonance in her mind, and she shook her head to get rid of the fleeting sensation.

'I imagine you're not married since you're telling me all of this.' The surge of hope she'd felt just a moment ago faded as quickly as it had appeared.

'No, I'm not married.' He paused for a moment, and the sudden intensity in his eyes made her breath catch in her throat.

Maria could hear nothing but her own heartbeat thundering through her ears as she realised what Rafael had just suggested. That couldn't be real. Was he seriously suggesting that *they* should get married? No, such a thing didn't happen in real life. This was the plot of a *novela*.

'I'm not sure I follow,' she forced herself to say, her

voice sounding distant. 'Because what I think you're saying makes no sense.'

'Maria,' he said, and took a step closer, 'I think the solution to your problem is to get married.'

CHAPTER TWO

As THE WORDS tumbled out of his mouth and into existence Rafael released the deep breath he had been holding. A sense of panic had gripped him when he'd realised what Maria was about to do. The charity was running out of money and if he wanted to keep his job, if he wanted to help his friend and remain near *her*, he needed to fix the problem.

But there was only one way he could fix it, and that involved marrying Maria, who he'd been quietly attracted to since he'd started working here. A move he wasn't sure would be a smart one, bearing in mind what was at stake. Knowing his family, they would come crawling out of the woodwork the moment they realised he was married and had access to the money—putting Maria and her entire family in the line of fire if he stuck around for too long. They had been trying for years to get their hands on his money and would stop at nothing to get it. If they had no problems paying a woman to pretend to fall in love with him, they would find some way to turn Maria against him—use his feelings for her to get what they wanted The thought stung, sowing doubt in his mind when he wanted to commit.

Wasn't that the best use for his money, even if it meant he needed to give up his place here? His fortune had cursed him his entire life, maybe this was the only way to lift the taint from it.

But such a suggestion was absurd. Could he even propose something like that to her? He knew her to be a good person, a friend—more than that in his dreams. Someone he could trust with such an absurd suggestion—even if she thought him ridiculous.

It was a leap of faith. The worst she could do was to say no.

'You can't be serious right now. We are not...' Maria said, breaking the charged silence between them.

'This would be out of necessity and nothing else. If I can submit a marriage licence to the bank, they will release the last block on it and the money will be mine—yours, if you want it.' He hesitated for a moment. Rafael knew she was in a vulnerable position and the last thing he wanted was to apply any pressure.

'This would only be temporary. A few weeks to sort out the trust and then we can file for divorce,' he added to reassure her when he caught her sceptical glance.

Maria took a step back, leaning her backside against the exam table, her arms crossed in front of her chest. A myriad thoughts and emotions rippled over her face, each one so fleeting that he wasn't sure what she was thinking. He wasn't really sure what he was thinking either.

Though this proposal was a snap decision born out of desperation, Rafael became more convinced as this moment went on. His sacrifice would be well worth it if it meant the sanctuary could stay open. Though he'd only been here for three months, the people of Santarém had almost immediately opened their arms, accepting him simply because they saw him as the restless soul he was—and offered him a home. Something he hadn't had for so many years.

Wasn't that what the money *should* be used for, even if it meant he had to leave? How could he stand by and watch Maria—and the entire village by extension—suffer such a loss when he had everything he needed to help? Everything but one thing…

'This is…' She stopped herself, scrubbing her hands over her face. 'I can't believe I'm considering this.'

Her voice sounded incredulous—a sentiment he could understand very well. After all, proposing marriage to his gorgeous boss was a first for him too. Maybe this hadn't been the most delicate way he could have put it. But she had been about to make a final decision about her sanctuary when she hadn't known that there was another way to help her keep the doors open.

'I get if you need some time to think,' he said to defuse the tension. 'I just want you to know that I'm serious about this. Both about giving you the money for your sanctuary and there being no strings attached to this arrangement. Nothing will change.'

There was no need to tell her how much he'd resisted marrying the women his parents had arranged for him to meet—or that the one woman he'd thought he would marry had left such deep scars that he'd vowed to never get emotionally attached to anyone again. Not while the curse of this trust persisted. Once people realised how much he was worth, their perception of him changed.

He hoped against hope that this wouldn't be the case here.

'How fast would you be able to get the money?' she asked after a while, and the question made his heart squeeze with hope.

'Once I submit the marriage licence to the lawyers, it should be a matter of weeks.'

Maria looked down at her feet, giving Rafael a view of the soft curve of her neck, her brown skin looking lush and soft even in the harsh light of the exam room. He had to bite back the impulse to reach out and touch her, trail his fingers along the sensual curves he saw underneath the uniform scrubs they all wore for work. An impulse he had to fight more often than he was ready to admit over the last couple of weeks. Her graceful sensuality had sneaked up on him until one day he'd found his gaze lingering longer and longer when it didn't need to.

The scent of freshly fallen rain and earth drifted towards him, igniting the need inside him he'd been fighting for so long. The impulse to step closer, to slide his hands into her thick hair as he pulled her face closer to his to inspect her dark pink lips with his eyes—and then with his mouth, to make sure they were just as soft as the visual examination suggested. To watch those brown eyes widen with surprise and pleasure as he explored her…

His throat constricted. Had this been a sound idea or had he just offered something he shouldn't have?

The air around them grew thicker with each passing second of silence, and Maria struggled to reconcile Rafael's suggestion with her own reaction to it. The word *no* had formed in her mind almost immediately, but her lips had refused to speak it. Of course she would not marry him. The very thought was ridiculous. So why did it make her heart beat so fast?

The looks, the fleeting moments they got to work together, and the warm trickle of sensation he caused to stir under her skin—those were not supposed to be real.

They were small indulgences she let herself enjoy, idle fantasies for a woman who was not available for more than that. Not when she'd found herself with an unexpected child and mounting financial troubles. His suggestion had given life to something that shouldn't have been more than a shadowy emotion dwelling in her chest, the longing inside her no more than a *what if* that she found refuge in when things got too hard.

Because a non-committal *what if* was the only thing she had space for in her life right now. Mirabel and the charity took so much of her time and passion, there was no room for anything else—especially not if it was Rafael-shaped. His mere presence in the room demanded so much of her, the air became hard to breathe until all she could think about was those full lips moving against hers.

And along with it all came a question she couldn't figure out.

'Why are you offering this? What's in it for you?' The question left her mouth sounding indelicate, making her cringe as the words filled the air between them. She didn't mean to accuse him of anything.

Rafael picked up on this as well, frowning slightly. 'I...'

He stopped, hesitating as he furrowed his brow. Was he thinking about what could be in it for him?

'You're my...friend, and I happen to have the solution to your problem. Of course I would offer it up,' he said after another moment of silence and shrugged. 'I'm asking something pretty big of you in return. Even if I don't benefit from it, I know it's a lot to ask.'

Maria nodded, her suspicion melting away under the concerned gaze Rafael shot her. The last man she had trusted with anything so personal had been her brother, and he had betrayed her on such a magnitude that she found it hard to trust anyone—even the man who had become her friend over the weeks he had been working here. Now soon to become more if she went through with this...

'How much are you expecting to get?' she asked with a slight hesitation. She wasn't sure if she wanted to know. The confidence with which he'd suggested this fake marriage to her made her believe the sum to be large.

Why was she even asking? It wasn't as if she was going to say yes. That was unthinkable. When she thought about her future husband, he was someone who she had a deep emotional connection with, someone to share her life—like her parents had. Though that person was nowhere in sight, and Maria worried that she had put off the search for him for too long. Something else always took precedence. Her studies, her job, leading the charity. Now looking after Mirabel...

Was this how it was supposed to happen for her? Convenience rather than true love?

Rafael smirked, a look of amusement to hide something underneath that dazzling smile of his. Embarrassment? 'My grandparents amassed quite some wealth during their careers. They gave a lot to their son—my father. But they also set up these trusts for their grandchildren.' He hesitated for a moment, those golden-brown eyes narrowing on her and sending an unexpected shiver down her spine that shook her all the way to her core. 'I'm expecting around seventy-five million *real*.'

The room went dead quiet, to the point where Maria could hear the animals rustling in their pens next door. Her mouth was dry, unable to comprehend such a large number in her head. 'Seventy-five million *real*?' she repeated, just to make sure her brain hadn't invented a number. With that amount of money, she'd never have to worry about any donations ever again. Was that why he had suggested getting married? Because he wanted to gain access to the money himself? Maria still wasn't sure she understood his motivation.

Why not find someone to marry for real? He had everything any woman would swoon over. The short hair just long enough to dig your fingers through it, an athletic build to melt against, and the most trusting eyes she'd seen in a long time. It was those dark looks he shot her whenever they met in the clinic or at home that made her shudder in secret.

He could find someone to care for, to love. Why go through the trouble of getting a fake wife when he could find a real one in a matter of weeks?

As she looked at him her eyes wandered over to the clock hanging in the exam room, and she pushed herself straight. 'Come, let's sit down at the table. Such a discussion warrants another cup of tea.' She also needed to be back at the house in case one of the children needed her.

The kitchen and living area were empty when she ushered Rafael in—save for her Great Dane, who didn't even raise his head before he went back to sleep. Maria busied her hands at the counter, putting on the kettle and preparing two cups of Earl Grey as her head still spun from all the information he'd given her. When she sat across from him, a steaming mug in front of each of them, she finally found the resolve to look at him again. Seeing him sit at her kitchen table had become so normal, their conversation casual and light as they drank their coffee together or when they were having dinner with Celine and the kids.

Too normal, really. Having these moments with Rafael was something she cherished. Would it all go away if they got fake married?

'Who were your grandparents that they had such a fortune?' That piece of information had been bugging her since he'd revealed how big his inheritance was. She tried to think of any famous Pedros she had heard of, but too many came to mind. How could she narrow it down? Were they vets too? Or was he the only one in his family?

'They invested in a production company that produced some popular *novelas*,' he said, sounding shorter than usual, and Maria bit her lip so as not to pry further. His grandparents had locked his inheritance behind getting married. Maybe their relationship had been complicated. If she knew anything, it was how draining complicated family relationships could be.

'How would this work? We just sign a paper and that's good enough? How do you imagine...us working?' The thought that there was an *us* type of situation was so strange Maria's heart squeezed inside her chest.

Rafael looked down at his tea, his fingers fiddling with the label of the tea bag in a rather uncharacteristic show of nerves. At work, he exuded an aura of confidence that only increased her struggle with her resolve not to steal another glance at him. The thought of being married to this man caused a multitude of opposing emotions to bloom in the pit of her stomach, making it hard to focus her thoughts on the moment.

This still wouldn't be real—if she actually went ahead with it. Even if they signed a paper, that didn't make them married. Just like Celine, whose husband had run out on her. They'd never signed the divorce papers, but that didn't mean her sister was married any more. Marriage required more than a signature on a piece of paper. Commitment, care...love. Those were the foundations of a marriage rooted in a mutual partnership. Without those things, their *marriage* would be just a piece of paper.

'I hadn't thought this far ahead. Up until the moment when I proposed this idea to you, I didn't realise this was what I was leaning towards.' He took a sip of his tea. 'When you spoke about your financial trouble, I wanted to help you. Being a part of Santarém's community has become important to me.'

There was something else as well. Maria could sense his hesitation, an unwillingness to put all of his cards on the table. Was this about his family again? There was clearly some tension, but he'd never spoken about his family or where he was from. This information hadn't mattered when Maria hired him. They still didn't matter since they would only be married on paper, but she wanted to know more anyway.

'We can go to Manaus, talk to my lawyer. I'm sure we can draft an agreement on what the conditions of this… marriage are to be. If we are both happy with it, we can go to the courthouse and sign the marriage licence.'

Maria searched his face as he spoke, looking for something, though she wasn't sure what that something was. Anything to raise a red flag, some kind of hint to tell her not to do this—because she was *so* close to doing this. This was the unexpected solution she had been praying for ever since Daniel left them.

But as she considered his proposal—in the most literal sense—Maria realised she would do a lot more to save her sanctuary. There were so many things she could imagine going wrong if she married the man she'd been flirting with for the last three months. The main one being that if she went ahead with this scheme, she would close the door for ever on any of the attraction becoming real. Money would exchange hands and that would alter whatever they had. It might even alter their easygoing friendship.

'Okay, if we're going to do this, we'll need to treat it like a business agreement and nothing else. I don't want either of us catching any feelings because we are pretend married and forced to act like that sometimes.' She paused, looking up from her mug as she acknowledged something neither of them had in the last few months. 'No more flirting with each other. That will only make things more complicated.'

There. Those were her terms. A part of her was certain she was making a big mistake, that two people couldn't just get married as part of a business deal. It just seemed to contradict everything she had believed about marriage growing up.

Except this wasn't a marriage. For all intents and purposes, this *was* a business deal. And she would do anything to keep her family's legacy alive, to keep helping the most vulnerable animals in their society when they depended on her for safety and care. Her own mother had sacrificed so much for this place; she couldn't let her brother be the end of that. Becoming a place of sanctuary for animals had become her life's work, her calling to it greater than anything else. The thought of giving up on it had robbed her of sleep, of her confidence and purpose. She couldn't let go of what brought her so much joy, what she had dedicated her life to. Especially not when there was a solution right at hand. No matter how strangely that opportunity had come into her life.

A fleeting look of surprise rippled over Rafael's face. Had he believed she would decline him?

* * *

Rafael didn't realise he'd been holding his breath. He let it loose, exhaling the full capacity of his lungs into the warm evening air. She'd said yes. The answer Rafael had been hoping for, despite his own trepidation.

There was no doubt in his mind that his family would get wind of this arrangement sooner or later. Their need for his money was far too great for them to just let him live his life. From the moment their media company had started to lose money, they had suggested he become an investor—brandishing their status as family like a weapon. They wanted to achieve the same level of fame that his grandparents had climbed to, and he'd learned in many painful lessons that nothing would stop them from trying. Not when that need had driven them to trick him into falling for one of their chosen candidates—breaking his trust in genuine love for ever.

What made him question his decision was the soft scent of subdued rain and earth drifting into his nose as he sat there watching Maria decide. It was a scent he wanted to get used to, one he yearned to smell in his bedroom as he drifted off to sleep—standing in direct opposition to the words she had just put out in the open. The fact that they had been dancing around each other for months without either of them making a move—their friendship the only thing they were brave enough to acknowledge.

Now, he needed to forget about the tantalising scent this woman left in her wake, testing his resolve ever since he'd taken up this position and moved into her house as part of his work assignment. This arrangement would not work if he let his attraction get the better of him.

'These seem like reasonable terms,' he said. 'And no more flirting.'

'So, what do we do next?' Maria stared down at her mug again, her wavy hair half obscuring her face and only adding to the almost irresistible mystery that was this woman.

'I'll call my lawyer in the morning to set everything up. I will let you know what documents he needs from you. Once we have an appointment at the courthouse we should take a trip to Manaus.' As he created their to-do list, he looked at her again, gauging her comfort level. He'd just dumped a lot of information on her, things he wasn't even sure about himself.

The agreement was more for Maria's benefit. He didn't need a piece of paper to hold him accountable for the things he had promised her, and he knew without question that she wouldn't abuse their faux marriage. Someone like Maria could never do that. Her integrity shone through every single action she took, something he admired about her. But he understood if she needed some sort of document to prove his intentions were just as pure.

Maria took her phone out of her pocket, swiping her finger over the display for a couple of moments. 'What about next Friday? Celine can cover the clinic that day. I'll just tell her we're both needed on a case in Manaus, so she'll watch the kids.'

Friday? That was a week from now. Rafael knew they were working on a tight deadline, but he hadn't expected it to be so soon. What had he expected? He wasn't sure, only that Friday felt close all of a sudden.

'I will check with my lawyer if we can get an appointment next Friday. Just…' He hesitated. 'Take some time to think it over.'

Maria nodded as she got to her feet, pushing the chair away. 'I'll check in on the ocelot tomorrow.'

'Thanks.' He smiled and his heart stuttered when her lips curved upwards in reciprocation, bringing a light to her face that was as breathtaking as she was. Their eyes lingered on each other for a second and he fought the urge to reach out, yearning to feel that kind smile under his fingers.

Why were these feelings emerging now, when they had more at stake than before? Or had his simmering feelings for her led him to make this preposterous proposition to begin with?

CHAPTER THREE

THEY WERE REALLY going to do this. Through some connections at city hall, Rafael's lawyer had managed to get them an appointment in a week's time. Had it only been seven days since they'd concocted this plan? Maria's heart pounded against her sternum, driving nervous energy through her body as she sat in the leather chair of this opulent office.

A part of her still wondered whether this was a good idea—a question she didn't have an answer for. Technically no—marrying the guy she had been attracted to since he'd stepped over the threshold of her animal sanctuary was a spectacularly bad idea. Marriage was such an intimate act, one she wanted to experience for real the way her parents and grandparents had. Had she waited too long, prioritised her career and passion over finding the right person to start her family with?

Maria had always thought she had plenty of time to find herself as the leader of the charity and then she'd be able to think about love. But struggle after struggle had forced her to put it off.

Now she'd found herself in a situation where a fake marriage was looming in front of her, once again stopping her from going for what she really wanted—something real. But—and that was the part that won every internal argument she had with herself—she didn't have any other choice. The money Rafael promised her would keep the sanctuary running for a few years at least, buying her enough time to find another donor. Looking at the paper the lawyer handed her, she realised how much money they were talking about.

'You'll donate this?' Maria's voice was no more than a whisper as she looked down at the paper again. This was so much more than her signature could ever be worth.

Ever since their hour on the plane together, Maria's senses hummed with awareness of the man next to her and the reason why she had insisted on no flirting drifted further from her mind. Why had she said that when those moments together were the only ones she looked forward to during her day?

'This is all already promised to your charity once the bank releases the funds. And I believe you find the rest of the terms acceptable?' No doubt amused by her shock, he smiled and paused. He must have grown up wealthy too, seeing the inherent ease with which he navigated their current situation. Maria felt the sweat on her palms as she looked at the paper again, while he seemed calm and collected.

The agreement stipulated that neither of them would seek any kind of marital asset division or alimony once they signed the divorce papers. Maria didn't need a paper to hold herself to that. If this wasn't a genuine marriage, she would want nothing that belonged to Rafael.

'How long will...this last? You said it wouldn't take more than weeks for the bank to release the funds.' She realised she didn't even know how long she should expect to be married to him.

'Bureaucracy can be slow. It can take up to six months

for city hall to issue a marriage certificate. But they usually arrive within thirty days,' the young lawyer, Sebastião, said to her.

Maria sent Rafael a questioning look. She knew there were a lot of things he wasn't telling her—like his underlying motivation. He said it was to help her—that he couldn't watch his friend struggle. But was that really all there was? Had her brother's betrayal shaken her confidence in the good intentions of people for ever, or was her hunch correct that Rafael had his own motives?

'Before you leave, I need you to know that I had my assistant change the hotel booking you requested from her to one room only,' Sebastião said with a pointed look at Rafael.

Rafael's eyebrows shot up, mimicking her own surprise at the lawyer's words. A sudden and visceral heat cascaded through her body, singeing the ends of her already frayed nerves. They had to share a hotel room? Her eyes shot over to Rafael and the nervousness that thought caused to bubble up within her must have been written on her face, for he looked back at the lawyer.

'Is that necessary? It's only one night, and you booked the plane tickets as well. There is no way they know I'm here.' Maria's ears pricked up at the last sentence as she glimpsed some of the personal history that informed his decision to marry her. Who were *they*? His family? An ex-partner?

The lawyer shrugged, as if expecting this protest from his client. 'You're underestimating them, Rafa. They may be watching you closer than you think.'

Rafael went still for a moment, his body and face unmoving. Only his eyes darkened with a dangerous glint that sent a shiver down her spine. Whoever these people were, they were not in good standing with Rafael and from the look in his eyes alone, she knew that she never wanted to be his enemy.

A strange sense of protectiveness came over her. What had these people done to him?

'All right,' Rafael said in a tired voice, and reached for a pen to sign their agreement. He passed the pen to Maria, who only noticed her hand shaking when she reached out to grab it. He must have noticed too, for he drew his hand back a little, a small line appearing between his brows.

'Maria, are you—?'

'I'm fine,' she said, and squared her shoulders.

For most of her adult life she'd run the animal shelter by herself, and when her brother ran away, abandoning his own child, she'd stepped up to take care of her as if she were her own. A little piece of paper would not defeat her. Not when that piece of paper promised everything she needed for a brighter future.

Everything except maybe one thing.

That was what the tiny voice in her head whispered as she took the pen and scrawled her signature onto the paper to seal the deal. The fantasy of Rafael that she'd been tempted to act on was now gone. Despite the hardships and the struggles of the last year, Maria still believed in love and wanted to find the person to complete her. She'd ignored her own dreams and desires over the years because the time had never seemed right. Kept ignoring them now as she entered into this fake arrangement...even though in the quietest of moments Rafael made her dream of more.

With a shake of her head, she pushed those thoughts away and gave the paper back to the lawyer. 'So, what's next?' she asked, clearing her throat of the last remnants of her unbidden Rafael fantasy.

'There is a car waiting for you to take you to the court-house. One of my clerks secured an appointment for you, so they will process you immediately.' The lawyer stood up from his chair and reached over his desk to shake Rafael's hand before turning to her and extending his hand again. Maria took it and plastered her most convincing smile on her face.

One more paper and her sanctuary would be safe.

The atmosphere in the courthouse was a lot different from what Rafael had prepared himself for. Though he wasn't sure what he *had* expected. Couples of varying ages sat in the waiting area, some dressed up for the occasion, some more casual, as if they had decided that today was the perfect day to make this long-term commitment to the person they loved. One thing they all had in common was the air around them, the aura of quiet celebration and...love.

It sent a shiver down Rafael's spine as he looked around and absorbed the energy of the surrounding people. By contrast, he and Maria must come across as downright miserable. Once he'd found himself in their camp, had been excited to spend the rest of his life with the woman he'd fallen in love with—only to find out she'd been pretending to love him for his money.

No other moment in his life had ever been so painful, teaching him a lesson he would never forget. As long as a relationship would unlock the money in his trust, he had to assume that none of the feelings were genuine. Rafael couldn't allow himself to trust anyone. The only reason Maria was different was because they were friends. Friends who might send each other heated looks, but friends nonetheless. Throughout his time in Santarém she had never pretended to be anything else.

'Feels like we're not representing the mood here,' Maria whispered, picking up on the same observation he had.

Her words had a calming effect on him. At least they could both admit that this situation was...weird.

'You're only missing out for a brief period. I'm sure you'll get to see that side of a wedding when this is all over,' he said, and hoped the smile on his face looked more genuine than it felt. There was something strange and upsetting about the thought of Maria with another man that raised the hair along his nape in defence. A flash of fury bloomed in his chest, one he shoved down and back into where it had sprung to life. She wasn't his, was never going to be either. No amount of rage would change that.

As soon as they presented themselves at the reception desk the court clerk waved them through to another room, passing more people waiting to sign their licences. Some couples had even brought a small contingent of their families to celebrate with them.

He pictured his family standing with him here today, and the smile on his lips died as quickly as it had appeared. Even if this were a genuine marriage, they would find some way to interfere. They would lie and deceive, turning his feelings for Maria against him until they got what they wanted. Or worse, they would somehow convince her that he was the problem.

That thought brought ice to his veins. The sooner he could give Maria the money and vanish again, the better.

Thirty days, the lawyer had advised him. Thirty days and then he'd be on his way again to find a place he might finally feel he belonged. He'd thought he'd found that place in Santarém. Working alongside Maria and Celine, getting to know the family and how they had been a part of the village for generations. Even though the close-knit community had seemed daunting, they'd accepted Rafael when they saw he genuinely wanted to belong. As if he were a stray in need of adoption.

The charity formed a strange but wonderful symbiosis with the rest of the village. Irina, the grocer, brought any food over that was about to spoil. Emanuel, who ran the café, brought them snacks whenever he saw the lights on late at night. They all worked together to make the dream of the Dias family come true, simply because they were one of them.

And Rafael had become one of them too, as he cared for their pets, treating their family members as if they were his own.

Not just the villagers, but Maria too had opened her home for him when he'd needed it. Though it was part of his working arrangement that she would provide him with a room, she also invited him to their family dinners each night. Or took him along on family outings to the weekly farmers' market or quiet walks along the river.

Rafael had never known he *wanted* to belong like that until it had happened.

It made leaving Santarém that much harder. But Sebastião was right. His family had set private investigators on him before, trying to unearth anything they could so they could force him back into the family fold and gain access to his funds. He'd have to stay under the radar until everything was done. Who knew what they would come up with if they learned he was finally married. He couldn't in good conscience bring this kind of energy into Maria's world when she had a daughter to protect— or rather a niece.

Rafael turned his gaze towards Maria as they followed the clerk down the corridor. He'd never asked about the circumstances that had led to her niece living with her. Could it have something to do with their financial problems as well? Did she have another sibling who'd passed away, leaving her to care for the child on her own?

The question burning on his lips died when they stopped in front of another desk.

'Dr Pedro and Dr Dias? Yes, I have you right here. Please follow my colleague. She will show you the room.' The receptionist waved her colleague over, handing her the envelope of forms the lawyer had given them with all the documents needed to get married.

She led them around the corner and through a door. A desk stood at the far end of the room, and several groups of chairs were arranged in neat lines. A couple sat in the very front row, surrounded by their friends who were chatting in quiet but animated voices.

'If you sit here at the back, the judge will get to you,' the woman said as she gave Rafael the envelope and left the room.

He glanced at the other couple once more before offering a chair to Maria and sitting down next to her. Her fingers were woven into each other and lay still in her lap. With a stiff spine, she looked straight ahead, her expression veiled and unreadable.

'Are you okay?' It wasn't the first time he'd asked that today, the need to check in with her a constant hum in his mind.

She nodded, her lips a thin line. 'Can I ask you a question?' she said after a prolonged silence, her voice low and melodic, seeping through his skin and igniting a strange heat in his chest.

'Anything,' he said with a nod, and startled himself when he realised he meant it. Because from the way her eyes drifted down to her hands, he could already tell what this was going to be about.

'Who are you so afraid could find us that your lawyer had to book everything for us?' She looked back up, her brown eyes narrow, bracing for whatever uncomfortable answer she had come up with.

Rafael hesitated, taking a deep breath to calm the intensity her lingering gaze had created. Not the question he'd expected, yet so much more personal than he was ready to admit to her. But Rafael couldn't deny that she deserved the truth—at least a part of it. Despite his best efforts, he *was* putting her near the line of fire.

'Mostly my parents. They have been trying to get me to marry a partner of their choice for some time,' he said, selecting each word with care. 'They made some regrettable decisions about their business. Instead of calling it quits, they pressured my siblings and I to invest in their business. Since my siblings are chasing the same fame my grandparents had, they jumped at the opportunity— and lost all of their money as well.'

Maria's features softened, a spark of understanding lighting up her eyes. 'You ran as far away from them as you could. I was wondering what brought you to Santarém. Whenever new people arrive it's usually because of personal circumstances.'

Rafael nodded and waited for the usual apprehension to flood his system whenever he spoke about his parents. But none manifested. A sense of calm remained, urging him to continue speaking.

'I knew if I stayed close to them they would eventually wear me down and get their say. Family is such an important thing—which makes escaping the grasps of a toxic one even harder.'

His heart squeezed tight when Maria nodded with a deep understanding that could only come from someone who had experienced something similar. The urge to reach out to her face and stroke the slight frown away thundered through him and he balled his hand into a fist to resist.

'Okay, who were your grandparents? Because when I heard the amount of money they had left you, I knew they must be famous. But there are so many famous Pedros, I wouldn't even know where to start.' Her lips curved up in a smile, as if she had been waiting for this detail.

That curiosity was what he needed. Even though he didn't enjoy talking about his famous grandparents, it was preferable to exposing how much he yearned to touch her in this moment.

'They were a pair of actors who made it big in different *novelas* in the sixties.' He paused for a moment, unable to stop a smirk from tugging at the corners of his lips. The next part sounded so unbelievable. 'They were best known for their roles when they played a very slow-burn romantic couple set in a...veterinary clinic.'

Maria's eyes widened and the blush blooming in her cheeks was exquisite. He had to ball his hand into a fist again to stop himself from reaching out to brush over her delicate skin.

'An actor and actress named Pedro...' she mumbled, seemingly to herself, and a second later her face lit up with recognition. 'Your grandparents were the couple in *Patas Para O Amor*?'

Rafael groaned. 'Please don't tell me you've watched that *novela*.'

'Are you kidding me? Celine and I used to watch it with our mother. She says the reason she went into veterinary medicine was because of that show. If it weren't for that, she would have never met my father.' Maria laughed, a sound so clear and full of genuine joy. His heart stuttered in his chest, making it hard to breathe for a moment.

'Didn't they end up bringing *Patas Para O Amor* to the US?' she asked, unaware of the heat she had caused to cascade through his body.

He nodded. 'That's where they made the fortune that my parents and siblings squandered away on their own attempts at fame.'

Maria lowered her eyes. 'Seems no one escapes complicated family drama,' she said, the smile fading away.

'You speak from experience?' His question must have touched something within her, for a hurt expression flitted over her face, showing him a wealth of pain before the walls around her came back up, leaving him on the outside—wondering.

The judge called their names and both of them stiffened, falling back into reality and remembering what they'd come here to do.

'You ready?' he asked, and Maria nodded.

'Let's go.'

The couple and their friends were still sitting in the front row, waiting their turn, when she and Rafael stepped up to the desk. Her heart slammed against her chest when he handed the envelope to the judge, who pulled out their documents to verify their identities and process their marriage licence.

'Are you with a party?' the judge asked, and Maria hesitated, looking at the man who was going to become her husband in the next few minutes.

'Ah…no,' he said, shaking his head. 'It's long overdue that we have our licence issued.'

And though Maria's heart was already working overtime, her pulse spiked when Rafael looked at her with a genuine smile on his lips as he took her hand and breathed a featherlight kiss onto her skin. Their connection created a spark, which sent a blast of heat from her arm down to her core.

This wasn't real, but rather another layer to their ruse to make their marriage look believable. His lawyer had warned them about any scrutiny they might face. For anyone outside of themselves, this marriage was supposed to look real.

So Maria did something dangerous—she stopped fighting the attraction rising between them. It would help her, she thought, to pretend they were an actual couple. Just for this day, until they were back at home and could go about their lives again.

She looked at him, her hand still close to his lips, and instead of fighting it she gave him the longing smile she had always wanted to.

The judge nodded, picked up her pen and signed the forms in front of her. She then picked up a hefty stamp, pressing it onto the open ink pad. With a slam that resonated in Maria's bones, she stamped the piece of paper.

Rafael released her hand and stepped forward when the judge turned the paper around for him to sign. She could feel the warmth of his body radiating towards her, fuelling her own heat. He placed the pen on the paper with no hesitation, signing his name on the indicated line. Then he stepped back, holding his hand out to her.

Maria took the pen and focused on the paper in front of her. A small tremble shook her hand as she put the tip down on the line and she hesitated, the weight of what she was about to do coming down on her shoulders. This was the price she had to pay to keep her sanctuary from financial ruin.

She swallowed the lump in her throat and signed her name with a flutter in her stomach. The pen came down on the table with a clang of finality. Done.

Maria was now married to Rafael.

They turned to look at each other, an unbidden current springing to life in her chest and arcing through the air between them. She shivered, biting her lower lip to stop her heart from racing and keeping her mind in the present. Nothing they were doing was real. It was all a ruse. The heat in her veins, the quiver in her stomach—they were the results of the circumstances and not true feelings.

Loud clapping jolted her out of the moment passing between them, and her head whipped around. The other party in the room cheered at them, clapping and hooting for the union they thought was as real as their own.

Maria's spine stiffened when someone from the group called out, 'Aren't you going to kiss your bride?'

Cheers erupted again, and Rafael glanced at her with a slight frown. The question in his eyes was easy to read. He wanted to know if he could kiss her.

That wasn't how she'd imagined their first kiss would go. In her fantasy there had been a lot more courting and genuine romance, not this subterfuge to keep up appearances since his family's eyes and ears could be everywhere.

Maria swallowed and gave the faintest of nods. His

features softened at her consent and everything around her slowed down as his hands wrapped around hers, pulling her closer to him. His scent enveloped her, the smell of lavender and something primal which eluded words. A tremble shuddered through her when she watched his hazel eyes narrow and his face come closer.

For a moment, Maria couldn't breathe as anticipation thickened the air. Then his lips brushed against hers, and the connection this touch created stoked the tiny flame she'd been carrying for Rafael into a roaring fire that pumped through her veins with every beat of her racing heart.

His hands kept her steady. She could barely hear the cheers from the group behind them, with the blood rushing through her ears, her pulse hammering against the base of her throat.

And as her lips moved against his—as the onslaught of desire consumed her—Rafael broke their connection. He took a step back to look at her, but his hands remained in place around hers. The ghost of a smile tugged at his mouth, and the look he gave her melted her insides.

They both jumped when the judge next to them slammed her stamp again onto the form they'd just signed before signing it and handing it back to them. Rafael let go of her hands, and that withdrawal was enough to plunge her back into reality.

'There you go,' the judge said as Rafael received the paper. 'You are now husband and wife. Your licence will be mailed to you in the next few weeks.'

This isn't real.

Maria repeated the mantra in her head as the heat from his kiss receded. Yet no matter how often she spoke those words in her mind, the memory of the fire licking in his eyes seared itself into her brain, almost wiping out every other thought about him. Was this just her imagination conjuring things that weren't there—or had Rafael lingered on her lips before he'd broken it off?

'Let's go.' His soft-spoken prompt ripped her out of her thoughts, and she looked at him. He'd taken her hand again and was now tugging her along as they left the building and entered the car already waiting for them. The car which would take them to the hotel they'd be staying at—sharing one room.

Maria swallowed again.

This wasn't real, no matter what she felt when Rafael touched her.

CHAPTER FOUR

THE PHANTOM OF the all too brief kiss they'd shared burned on his lips for the entire twenty-minute car ride to the hotel at the edge of Manaus. They stayed quiet, the air around them growing so tense each breath became a struggle to keep steady.

This feeling—the heated desire he bridled with every ounce of his strength—was not part of the plan. His attraction to her had been undeniable from the moment he'd started working at her clinic, where they'd become close enough to consider each other friends. The closeness they shared at work, the nightly dinners, the weekends at the farmers' market—he'd let himself believe that, because of those, she thought the same way about him. That the stolen glances and secret smiles spoke of a desire to make more of their friendship, but he knew better than to let himself indulge in that idle fantasy. Because he knew that his family would do anything they could to get him to surrender his part of the inheritance—including going after his wife.

Her reaction to his kiss was a clear indicator that his attraction towards her wasn't reciprocated. Why else would she tense up like that, seconds after his lips had brushed over hers?

Had he already ruined this entire scheme with one action? It hadn't even been his idea, though his heart had picked up speed when the group of strangers had shouted their suggestion at them. Kissing those full lips had been an unfulfilled fantasy for several weeks now.

Though in those daydreams he had never kissed her because they had entered into a fake marriage. That was a development he hadn't seen coming. Soon the money would be his—hers—and he would have to give up the one place that had become home to him.

'What are you going to do once we get to the end of this arrangement?' Maria asked into the quiet, as if she had picked up on the direction his thoughts were heading.

'I...' He hesitated, his mind forming words that his lips struggled to say. He wasn't going to tell her that he planned on leaving. How could he? Rafael didn't want to acknowledge that fact himself, let alone put the words out into the universe. 'I haven't thought about it much. To be honest with you, I never thought I would get access to the money because I ruled out marriage as an option early on.'

Her brown eyes flicked towards him in an expression that caused emotion to thunder through him in a confusing force of attraction and apprehension.

'You never wanted to get married?' she asked him after a beat of silence.

Was that disappointment lacing her words? A thickness coated his voice when he answered. 'No, I knew early into adulthood that marriage would not be fulfilling for me.'

'Why is that?' she asked, the same timbre in her voice giving him pause, constraining his chest as his heart squeezed tight.

Why didn't he want to get married? Because the concept of it had been weaponised against him from the moment he was old enough to understand how his grandparents had set up his trust. That had also been the moment when his parents started to push every single girl in his direction who would make what they deemed a good match—the only criteria being her family history and how they could gain from it. And even though he knew what they were capable of, he'd never thought they could be so heartless as to conspire with a woman to get him to fall for her so they could share the payout.

He hadn't believed Laura to be capable of that either, which showed that people would say anything if the sum of money was large enough.

But this trauma sat so deep in his bones, had so irrevocably shaped him as the person he was now, he couldn't let it go. He had lived such a solitary life, trust didn't come easy to him.

'I didn't grow up with a very stable role model of marriage. Neither my parents nor my siblings had what I would call successful marriages. They were far too concerned with what they could do with my grandparents' fortune to focus on their relationships. That obsession and dependency became their primary motivation for being together, even though they were—and still are—making each other miserable.'

He paused as an all too familiar bitterness rose in his throat, giving the words that followed the bite of ancient hurt. 'They claim to love each other, but that clearly wasn't a good enough foundation to save them from their own greed. So I decided to give up on the thought of marriage, of love. I would rather be alone than put anyone through the agony I see mirrored in my family every day.'

Rafael paused, the words tumbling out of his mouth before he could reconsider how much he wanted to share with her. It almost sounded like a warning.

Do not dare to fall in love with me.

'What about your siblings? You said they took their cue from your parents?' Her voice was soft now, a small frown creasing her brow as she absorbed the information.

'They did. My brother and sister are a few years older, so their turn came earlier than mine. But they had already bought in to the notion of fame my parents were yearning for and were eager to do their part. I don't know how I turned out different from them...'

Rafael's stomach lurched when a delicate hand appeared in his field of vision, her long fingers brushing against the top of his hand that was curled into a fist. Sympathy brightened her face, making him inhale sharply at the sight.

'I'm glad you didn't. Family is so important in our culture, it's hard to distance yourself from it, even if you know that's the best for you,' she said, her hand hovering over his as if she were thinking about wrapping her fingers around it.

A thought that brought a thrill to his chest. An inappropriate thrill that he needed to subdue before it turned into a spark.

'Don't feel bad. Because of my parents' fame-hungry attitude I grew up with a nanny, whose family owned a farm where she would often take me. I think without her, I wouldn't have become a vet.' Hiring someone else to raise him had been the only sane thing his parents had ever done for him. Camila had begun working for the family when their old nanny retired. By that time his siblings were already too infatuated with the image of fame and money.

Not Rafael. At ten the concept didn't interest him much, so when Camila started to take him to the farm his parents didn't object—his teenage siblings were old enough to look after themselves.

'A farm? I would have thought that would lead to a career similar to Celine's rather than family pets,' Maria said with a quirk of her lips.

'It was an option. Though I really bonded with the barn cats, to the point where they would follow me around the grounds all day.' A fond memory he hadn't thought of in such a long time, and one he was glad to share. The topics they had previously been talking about might leave the impression there was nothing redeemable about him either. What if she thought he was no different than his family, marrying her out of necessity and not love? He couldn't let that happen...

'Don't worry about us, though. Our arrangement here is different, and it's because of you and your charity that I wanted to do this. If it can buy you some time to find a new long-term donor, I'll gladly deal with some discomfort.'

Her hand stilled at his words, and the moment he said them Rafael regretted his poor choice of word. Had he just suggested that being near her was causing him discomfort? It was, but in an abstract and affection-starved way that he couldn't possibly explain to her without making it sound as if he had ulterior motives in marrying her.

How could he explain that his own attraction to her was the reason for any discomfort?

'I mean—' he started, the car coming to a halt interrupting him.

Before he had a chance to elaborate the meaning of his words further, the driver got out and opened Maria's door for her. She looked back at him and the disappointment in her eyes cut a lot deeper than he'd thought was possible.

* * *

They walked over to reception, where Maria could see a member of staff already waiting for them, clearly expecting them. Rafael remained right beside her as he handled the entire interaction with very few words. Clearly the lawyer had impressed on the hotel staff that they were to treat these two with the utmost discretion as they arrived in their car with tinted windows.

These were the lengths he'd go to for his safety—and hers by extension. What awful things had his family done to him for him to request something like this?

Though they had been spending a lot of time together as friends, Rafael didn't share a lot about his past—which she could understand. Though she regularly complained about Celine, or shared her struggles around raising Mirabel, she stayed away from the topic that hurt the most. Daniel. Of course the same would go for Rafael sharing his past only to a certain extent.

Today, though, she sensed they had taken the next step. Maria's traitorous heart had squeezed so tight when he'd spoken about his family, about his shattered belief in love—that he never wanted to get married. How uncomfortable it was to even be fake married to her.

The last part had stung a lot more than she cared to admit. Because this wasn't real. She didn't want this to be real because she *did* believe in love. Once the dust had settled, Maria hoped she could focus on that rather than her abandoned niece or the demise of her animal sanctuary.

Not that she had much experience on how to go about her search. Her most recent relationship had ended last year, when Daniel disappeared. Though she had enjoyed spending time with Maurice, there had been a distinct lack of a spark that had given her pause.

She believed there was someone out there for her to make her family complete, and that when she met that person there would be no doubt, the way there had been with Maurice. No, that missing piece was still out there, just waiting for her to discover it.

Rafael Pedro was not it. No missing piece of hers could carry such a pessimistic belief about love and marriage within his heart and remain compatible with her. What worried her about that was the sinking feeling in the pit of her stomach at this very realisation.

Her thoughts were interrupted when the woman at reception handed Rafael their key cards and pointed at the elevator.

He approached her, his hand coming to rest on the small of her back, where each finger left a searing indentation as they strode towards the elevator that would lead them to their room. Where they would share a bed.

The heat pooling below the skin of her back where his hand still lay exploded through her at that thought, settling in the pit of her stomach and streaking across her cheekbones.

Rafael stepped back when the elevator doors closed, pressing the button for their floor before giving her a tentative smile that only served to intensify the heat in her face.

'Don't worry about it. I can sleep on the floor,' he said into the silence.

Maria opened her mouth to reply when the elevator stopped and the doors slid open, admitting another person, who selected the eighth floor. Both fell silent, but she felt Rafael gravitate towards her while eyeing the stranger with a cool expression.

She remained quiet as they passed two more floors before they halted again, the six on the display lighting up as the doors opened to their floor.

Rafael ushered her out, his hand still firmly planted on her back, and as they stepped out he looked back, making eye contact with the person remaining in the elevator as the doors closed.

'You know them?' Maria asked, following his gaze.

'No, I don't think so. But we can never be too careful with my family,' he mumbled under his breath, as if he still expected the person inside the elevator to hear them and report back to the invisible phantom that was his family.

'What did they do to you?' she asked before she could think better of it.

Her brother, Daniel, had done unforgivable things, abandoned his daughter for the woman he had an affair with, yet even that pain didn't seem to compare with what he'd experienced with his family if that was his reaction to a stranger in an elevator.

Rafael didn't reply but walked with her to their designated room in silence, swiping the key card over the pad and letting them into the room where they'd be spending the night. Together.

Maria's brain went blank at that thought, her feet freezing before the threshold. Almost an hour had passed since they'd left the courthouse to come here, yet the moment she remembered what waited behind this door the memory of their kiss resurfaced. The warmth and softness of his lips had been intoxicating, even though the kiss had been no more than the gentlest of brushes. It raised the tiny hairs along her arms, a shiver trickling through her body that she tried, and failed, to suppress. The moment she realised how much she was enjoying the touch her body went rigid.

'You okay?' he asked when she didn't move.

'Um…yes,' she said, daring to take a step into the room.

Rafael went ahead, flicking on the light switch to illuminate the space. The cool blast of the air-con enveloped her as she stepped in, and she only noticed then the thickness of the humid heat surrounding them. It was a heat she was used to from living close to the Amazon and the rainforest. Though Manaus was a large city, it bordered on large parts of the rainforest, so much that they had seen several monkey troops in some side alleys as they'd driven to the hotel.

It was the cool air that drew her attention to the sweat on her skin, making her wonder if this was only from the heat or if Rafael had anything to do with it. It would be far better for her sanity if it was only the heat.

'Ah, this is perfect,' she heard Rafael say, and saw what he was referring to a moment later when she reached the end of the corridor that opened up into a spacious suite.

Rafael lay sprawled on a couch on the far side of the room, his arms tucked under his head and looking at her with a satisfied smile. 'I can take the couch.'

Maria barely heard the words he spoke over the thundering of her heart in her ears as her eyes wandered from his face down his body, taking in the picture of mouth-watering masculinity that presented itself in front of her. He'd worn a suit to the courthouse, playing along with the part of a lovesick man wanting to be married to the love of his life as soon as possible. It fit him way too well, the fabric accentuating the planes of his body and enhancing his handsome features to next-level gorgeous.

Her mouth dried, and she had to swallow hard to bring

clarity back into her thoughts. To her dismay, Rafael noticed her lingering stare, for his smile softened to something more delicate, more primal as his eyes narrowed on her before they fell onto her mouth for a second before coming back up to hold her stare.

The gentle heat the memory of their kiss had ignited flared up, radiating through her body in a sensual and highly inappropriate shudder that had her toes curling in her shoes. Despite knowing that this could never go anywhere, something inside her shifted when she saw her reaction reflected in his face.

He sensed something too.

The thought made her breath catch in her throat, and panic followed the mounting desire, quickly overtaking it, so Maria grabbed her bag and spun away from the image of Rafael to turn towards the bed. Putting her things on the white quilt, she took a few moments to breathe in and out while staring at the wall.

Maria cleared her throat, willing the thickness coating her vocal cords away. Behind her she could hear Rafael taking deep breaths as well. They grew quiet for some time before he said, 'My family believes that eventually fame will come to them. They just have to throw enough money at the problem. They have been circling around me since I left university, urging me to get married and help them. They arranged several matches with suitable women and went as far as sabotaging genuine relationships.'

The whisper of fabric filled the still air as he shifted, and Maria dared to turn around to face him again. She had not expected to get an answer to her earlier question.

Rafael was sitting upright now, slightly bent over with his face resting in his hands for a moment. When he looked back up, a hollowness had replaced the calm from moments ago. Whatever they had done to him still hurt so badly that it was plainly written on his face.

The instinct to comfort took over. Before she could think of how wise such closeness with Rafael could be, she kneeled before him and rested her hand on his knee. His towering height forced her to tilt her head upward to look at him, her breath once again stuttering when those warm hazel eyes focused on her.

'That's why you don't believe in marriage? Because it would make it too easy for them to get your money?' That didn't sound like a good reason to swear off happiness. Surely there were protections in place for such a case?

'No.' He breathed that word out, his chest deflating as he let out the air he'd sucked in, and the tension around his shoulders slowly dissolved.

Then he sat up so his elbows didn't rest on his knees any more. Slowly, as if time had stopped for a few heartbeats, he leaned forward as the lines around his eyes softened, giving way to a gentle smile. His left hand came up, his fingers curled so that his knuckles brushed along her cheek in a gesture so wrapped in affection that it trembled through Maria.

The air became charged, every breath harder to swallow as a million different signals fired in her brain, bringing a myriad sensations down on her that she had no capacity to process. Not when his cool fingers were touching her so gently.

Then everything inside her ebbed away when his head followed his hand and brushed a tender kiss on her cheek.

'It's sweet how much you care, Maria. Thank you.'

He couldn't tell her, even though the words were right there on the tip of his tongue, just waiting to finally be released into the world. To connect with someone over what had happened to him, how it had changed him as a person. But when he tried to put the hurt into words his chest seized, forcing any air in his lungs to remain inside and giving him no breath to speak.

Rafael just couldn't. It would be inviting Maria into a place inside him that no one had ever seen before—and no one ever would.

That required trust, and it was that kind of trust that he'd learned to withhold, thanks to the damage his family had done to him. If he hadn't trusted Laura, his ex-fiancée and his parents' undercover match, she wouldn't have slipped past his defences so easily, almost robbing him of everything he'd worked so hard to achieve. Her whispers had made him reconsider his family's stance, had made him doubt his own sanity around their toxicity. She had wanted him to make peace with them, so when they got married they could become a real family—a value so important in the Latin community.

And a value that she herself had failed to embody when he'd caught her conspiring with his parents, hearing her promise them that she had 'almost turned him around' the day after he had proposed. His heart had broken into a thousand pieces then and there, the tiny fragments scattering in the wind of this betrayal so he could never be so foolish to trust anyone with it ever again.

That included Maria Dias, no matter how much he yearned to place a second kiss on her full, dark lips as a soft peach tone dusted her cheekbones in response to the kiss on her cheek.

Something Rafael knew he shouldn't have done, but he couldn't help himself when he noticed the genuine worry in her eyes. She wasn't asking to prise information out of him. No, she cared about him like a friend would.

He sat up straight as he realised that he was enjoying her blush a lot more than he should, a lot more than would be appropriate for two people who were *just* friends—and he needed to remind himself that their relationship was just that. A friendship and nothing else. Their ruse had removed whatever other possibilities there might have been if he had found the courage to voice his feelings.

'How about we find somewhere to eat? It's been a long day for both of us. Some food will do us good.' Eating was far from Rafael's mind, but it might help them to calm down. Food had always been something they'd bonded over, whether it was a quick dinner in the kitchen after a long day of work, or during the Sunday farmers' market in the town square, where they tried every new food truck that came to the village.

Though whenever they did that they were never alone in a dimly lit room with soft music setting the mood for something entirely different than a friendly dinner.

Okay, maybe an early dinner was a *terrible* idea.

'I...' Maria started, getting to her feet. He could see the thoughts racing behind her eyes, a sight he didn't get to witness very often. It was her gift for making decisions on the fly that made her such an excellent vet in emergencies, her hand acting the moment she identified a problem.

Her delicate and capable hands. How would they feel running up and down his bare back, clawing into his shoulders as he...?

'Sure, that sounds like a...good idea.'

Rafael breathed out a thankful sigh as she interrupted his lewd train of thought, for his heart began pumping blood in all the wrong places.

'Good,' he said, and got to his feet as well, clearing his throat to chase away the phantoms of his fantasies. 'Let me get into something more comfortable, and we'll go see what's in the area.'

Maria nodded, her expression veiled, and he hoped it was because she was processing her own thoughts rather than seeing the blatant desire written in his eyes as he looked at her.

He locked the bathroom door behind him and pulled at his tie, tossing it at the side of the sink as he undid the first two buttons of his shirt. Then he turned on the tap and splashed cold water on his face to cool himself down—both physically and mentally.

Unbuttoning the shirt, he threw it off with a shrug and grabbed a plain dark blue shirt and some black shorts from his duffel bag, into which he stuffed his tie, shirt and the trousers, before looking back into the mirror and ruffling a hand through his dark brown hair, its unruly waves hard to tame.

His heart still raced from the memory of his kiss on her cheek, a friendly and innocent gesture if it hadn't cost him so much strength not to claim her mouth with his in a sensual re-enactment of their earlier kiss.

Rafael needed to be careful. The walls he'd built to hide away the pain and damage dwelling within him were there because he needed them—for his own sake as well as for anyone who tried to scale the walls.

He couldn't let that happen. Even though he'd caught himself lowering them just to feel her closeness for one moment. This was the one act of attraction he permitted himself to indulge in, and now that the moment had gone he forced himself to go back inside his fortress, where he planned on spending the rest of his life in solitude.

CHAPTER FIVE

THE DAY MARIA got married had turned out a lot stranger than she had anticipated when she had started dreaming about it as a young teen.

Really, the only thing that matched her expectations was the low hum of awareness vibrating through her body as she walked beside her husband, an arm's width of space between them that was narrowing every now and then, getting them close enough that their arms brushed against one another. Each minuscule touch sent bolts of lightning skittering down her nerves, making it hard to focus on the conversation they were having.

They'd had an early dinner at a small restaurant a short walk from the hotel, their conversation staying away from the heavier topics they'd spoken about in their room. Maria now had a better understanding as to what kind of people his family were, and it made her think that they had a lot in common in that area. Even if the hurt had a different cause, the result remained the same.

'Have you ever been here?' he asked as they walked down the street.

Instead of walking back the way they came, Rafael had suggested a more scenic route that wound itself closer to the edge of the forest. Without the hectic traffic of the main street, they could hear the insects chirping and see fireflies coming to life as the sun dropped beneath the horizon, casting a soft purple glow onto the city and the adjacent trees.

'Yes, every now and then I come down here for a case or the occasional workshop with other vets.' Due to its proximity to the rainforest, Manaus was the perfect base for the federal institute for veterinary medicine. What Maria did on a smaller scale—rescuing injured wild animals and rehabilitating them back into the wild—happened here in much larger numbers.

'You come all the way here to consult on cases?' Rafael asked, his gaze still trailing the edge of the forest, a fascinated expression on his face.

'Rarely, but yes. I studied here, as did Celine, so we have a lot of contacts here that we've kept in touch with over the years. My sister is somewhat of a protégée in the vet circles here, so even though I don't have nearly as many accolades as her, they still come with the occasional questions when it comes to rare reptiles they're dealing with.' Unfortunately for reptiles, they were rarely the favourite pets her fellow vets wanted to deal with, even though their healthcare needed specialised attention and compassion. Though dogs, cats and rabbits tugged on her heartstrings whenever they came in, it was the snakes and lizards that needed her help the most.

Even the most harmless of snakes would strike terror in someone unfamiliar with them, so a lot of the snakes brought into her clinic were injured by fearful humans who didn't know any better—or didn't care to learn.

'I thought Celine was a bit…young, but I didn't want to assume anything from just looking at her,' Rafael said.

'She is incredibly smart and, coupled with the stubbornness of an old mule, there isn't a single thing she couldn't achieve if she sets her mind to it.' Maria smiled, a familiar warmth rising in her chest as she thought about her baby sister. 'Celine was so gifted growing up, she graduated high school early and started university while I was still there.' Something that had fused those two sisters together, forging an unbreakable bond that lasted to this day. Whatever life threw at them, Maria knew they would deal with it together. Like the crisis they were dealing with right now.

'They had never seen such a young student at the school—she was only seventeen. I was in the final year of my doctorate when she joined,' she continued, smiling at the memory of their time together. 'All of us thought she would go into research or become the state veterinarian overseeing the institute here in Manaus. But instead, she chose to stay in our little village and run our parents' charity with me and our brother, Daniel.'

Rafael tore his gaze from the treeline to look at her, his expression one of surprise.

'But if Celine is that young, she must have had Nina when she was in her early twenties?'

Maria nodded, remembering the day she'd found out about Celine's pregnancy—along with the less desirable news that her husband, Darius, had left without any trace or word. Though Nina was her niece, she felt like a second mother to the little girl, filling in whenever Celine was busy and making sure she had everything she needed.

'It was quite the shock for both of us, but we pulled through. Celine didn't have anyone else to rely on and so we decided to raise her together. When Mirabel came along, I had at least *some* skills in motherhood to be more comfortable.' Her words skated over the hardships they'd faced, but those memories of her and her sister were fond ones. They had struggled, yes, but knowing both Nina and Mirabel, having those two girls in her life was worth any struggle ten times over.

'How did Mirabel come to live with you? I suspected you must have another sibling, but I didn't know you had a brother,' Rafael said in a casual tone, not knowing the wound he was prodding at. Even though they had grown close over the last three months, she had stayed away from anything relating to Daniel.

The smile faded at the memory of her brother, the taste in her mouth turning to ash. How could he have done that to her, after she had paused so much of her life to keep the family legacy going? He'd left because he'd fallen in love, not realising that Maria too had that yearning—and had chosen to focus on her family first.

'Because oftentimes I pretend like I don't,' Maria said, surprised by the sharpness in her voice. 'He wasn't a vet like Celine and me. He went to school for business to help us run the charity from that angle, maybe even grow it beyond what we were doing back then.'

She paused, a wry smile pulling at her lips. 'He was the one who initially wanted to introduce a general vet practice to increase our funds, but I refused because I didn't want to bring an outsider into our charity. Sometimes I wonder what he would think that his actions forced me to implement an idea we fought about so often.'

'Where is he now?'

Wasn't that the question? Maria hesitated, her tongue darting over her lips and wetting them. Where had the superficial conversation gone? No one knew the circumstances of Daniel's disappearance, and Maria had never wanted to tell anyone—the fear of being judged scaring her away from any such conversation.

But Rafael somehow made it easy. The non-committal banter as well as the heartfelt conversation—they both seemed to go so much easier with him.

'He ran away with the woman he was having an affair with. We had a wealthy donor who had picked our charity as his focus when we saved his daughter. She had suffered a snake bite while they were hiking nearby. Given my work, I always have the antidote for most local snakes around, so we were able to help her when they rushed into town to call for help.

'Daniel got too close to his wife and they…fell in love. So he left with her, and with him went the donation we depended on. Mirabel is his daughter. He left her too, when he ran.'

Just saying these words out loud was surreal, the story sounding made up.

She glanced at Rafael, whose thoughtful expression had given way to something much stonier. Then he asked, 'He left his daughter behind with not a second thought as to what that would do to her—and you?'

The intensity in his voice took her by surprise, his eyes darkening, but not with the attraction she swore she had seen on his face when he had kissed her cheek. No, this was on the other side of the primal spectrum, her hurt somehow triggering something within him.

Or was she reading too much into the situation? Reading too much into that kiss as well?

'I—'

A soft whining interrupted her, a noise Maria had heard so often it triggered a response without hesitation.

She stopped dead in her tracks, her finger raised to her lips as she strained her ears to hear the direction the noise had come from. Rafael raised his eyebrows in a silent question, but his eyes went wide when the noise sounded again, pulling them towards the path on their right, leading to a narrow gap between houses.

There, in the middle of the alley, stood a small monkey, its open mouth producing the same whining noise they had just heard.

'Is this a...?'

'A tamarin monkey,' Maria finished, taking a hesitant step forward and crouching down to look at the squirrel-sized monkey. Its white fur curled like a moustache around its mouth, giving it a sentient air as it blinked with intelligent eyes.

'They stay in the city?' Rafael asked, to which she nodded.

'They have to. With all the urban development happening in recent years, the city cut more and more into the monkeys' territories. They could have fled inland, but they soon realised that the city was a perfect hunting ground for food—what with all the humans throwing things away.'

'This one seems to be behaving oddly.'

'It is...'

Maria got back up and took another step towards the monkey. It stilled as it beheld the two humans, head slightly cocked. Then it turned around, running a few paces down the road before it stopped again, looking at them with another low cry.

Maria and Rafael exchanged questioning glances. 'I think it's asking us to follow it,' he said, scepticism lacing every word.

Scepticism that Maria didn't quite share. She'd worked with enough monkeys to understand their inherent intelligence, their adaptability to changing circumstances something to marvel at. The tamarin monkeys were a perfect example of that. It had taken them only a few years to adapt to urban life within the city.

Together they stepped forward and when they got close enough to the monkey it turned around again, leading them down the street until they spotted another monkey lying on the floor.

Maria's vet instincts kicked in immediately, and so must have Rafael's for she felt him tense up next to her and they crossed the remaining distance at a sprint. Two smaller monkeys sat close to the one lying prone on the floor—likely their parent. Its eyes were open, but its breath shallow by the look of its chest, only rising with agonising slowness.

'What happened?' Maria asked no one in particular as she knelt down, brushing away the remains of a half-eaten sandwich and some other food waste that the other adult monkey had collected—no doubt in an endeavour to help its mate.

She patted down her trousers, searching for her phone, when a light above her shoulder clicked on. Turning her head, she watched as Rafael knelt beside her with his phone in his hand, shining down on the family of tamarin monkeys so they could assess the extent of the injury.

With the light shining, it took Maria all but one glance to see what had happened to the monkey. Its leg lay stretched out at an unnatural angle, old blood crusting its fur. Somehow it had got its leg stuck in something and had ripped the skin open when trying to escape, likely breaking a bone. In the rainforest such a misstep would have meant its demise, but with their new urban lifestyle the monkeys faced a far more painful death removed from any circle of life.

Not if they could help it. Maria shot Rafael a sideways glance. 'I have an animal first aid kit in my bag at the hotel. Can you run and get it while I assess the situation? We need to get all these monkeys to a clinic.'

Rafael nodded, handing her his phone, which she propped up against the wall so she could approach the injured animals with caution. She didn't have any protective gear on her, no long sleeves or thick gloves to ward off any bites that an injured and frightened monkey could resort to.

'You did good in alerting us,' she said to the monkey that had led them here. It was waiting a few steps further along, eyeing her. 'I can help you.'

She leaned forward with deliberate slowness, her hands stretched in front of her and open so they could all see her palms and understand she meant no harm. When she finally got closer, she reached out her hand and leaned over the injured tamarin monkey, careful not to touch it until she was done with her visual examination.

'Are you their mother?' Maria asked in a soothing tone that she had learned put frightened animals at ease. From looking at her belly and her teats, she could see that the mother monkey was still breastfeeding her young.

They must not have eaten since their mother had collapsed. Their stress levels must be through the roof right now, but even then, the other monkey had realised that they needed intervention from a higher power. Very curious how the urbanisation worked for them, she thought to herself.

'I think you got your leg caught somewhere and when you strained to break free, you damaged a bone and tore your skin open.' She liked to explain the procedure to the animal as she was tending to them. While she knew they didn't understand anything she said, it helped them to hear someone speak to them.

'Once Rafael gets back, we will see if we can figure out your break and splint it to transport you to the clinic where I used to study.' She lifted her head to look at the young monkeys and the father. 'You can all come too. Once Mum is better, you'll be released back into the forest.'

Hurried footsteps echoed behind her, prompting her to release a sigh of relief as, a few moments later, Rafael came to a halt next to her, handing her the first aid kit. Years of working on the road had built the habit to bring the very basic equipment she needed with her, no matter where she went.

Rafael's eyebrows shot up when he put the bag down and watched her unzip it. She'd called it a kit, but he thought it was more akin to a miniature veterinarian clinic than a simple first aid kit as he saw the contents. Stethoscope, gloves, gauze, thermometer, and even a variety of oral medication and ointments were in the bag, giving them everything they needed to help this animal in need until they could get them to a safe place. The clinic, she had said, but what exactly that place was Rafael wasn't sure. She didn't mean the federal institute for veterinary medicine, did she?

Maria had said that she was familiar with some people there, but could they just walk into a government agency like that?

Wherever they would end up going, he was glad she was here to lend her expertise. Each veterinarian learned about a breadth of animals, but never as much as about the ones they chose to specialise in. For Rafael that had been dogs, cats and small animals typically found to be people's pets. While he knew enough about animals in general to help with simple ailments, anything beyond surface level needed an expert in more exotic animal care.

An expert like Maria Dias.

He had to admit that he'd only looked her up after he'd accepted the job at her charity just because he'd wanted to learn more about what it did and what he would be a part of. He wasn't prepared for the praise and accolades from different animal rescue organisations that her charity had worked with.

A couple of hours ago she had called her sister Celine a protégée, completely downplaying her own effort when it came to rescuing and rehabilitating the wildlife of the rainforest which fell victim to constructions and deforestation.

It was that compassion and care that went beyond the call of duty that had drawn him to her after a few days of working with her. While Rafael cared for animals just as much as she did, the thought that he was treating someone's family member kept him humble and hardworking, wanting to make sure that they got the very best of care.

Maria, on the other hand, became the family member of the animals that wound up in her care, because there was no one else to care for them. Just like she was demonstrating right now as she pulled the latex gloves over her hands and handed him his own pair to put on.

He obliged, waiting on the sidelines for any instructions she might give. In this situation he was no more than her assistant, helping her with whatever she needed to get that monkey back to full health.

'The injured monkey looks to be female, gave birth probably two months ago judging by the size of her babies.' Rafael nodded, even though he could tell she was mostly talking to herself. A habit they shared, as he liked to record his examinations so he could play them back later to take patient notes.

'What are our next steps?' he asked when Maria remained quiet.

'I'll try to touch her and see from there,' she said, and reached out a careful hand.

The young monkeys looked at her with wide eyes, one of them baring its teeth as she got closer, but neither them nor the adult monkey a few paces behind them moved. They all watched as she laid a tentative hand on the female monkey, gently stroking her with a cooing noise.

'Okay, we are good to go to the next step. Let's get her on some painkillers before we inspect her leg. There will still be discomfort, but at least we can lessen it somewhat. Can you see a bottle labelled ketoprofen in the bag?'

Rafael picked up several bottles, reading their labels, before he found the medication she mentioned. He glanced at the tiny monkey, the adult one not much larger than a squirrel, and picked the smallest syringe available.

'How much?' he asked as he poked the thin needle through the cork of the bottle to pull some of the solution out.

Maria took a second to look at the monkey, tilting her head left and right as if she was trying to get a good measure of the animal before she said, 'I don't think she weighs more than a kilo, so let's go with two millilitres, and remember to note that when we bring her in.'

He nodded, then drew the small amount of liquid into the syringe and handed it to Maria. She took it from him, pausing a moment before taking some of the monkey's skin between her fingers and injecting the medication subcutaneously and giving it a few moments before she handed the syringe back to him.

Rafael dug around the kit and found some bags marked for biohazardous waste and dropped the syringe in there before clamping it shut. Then he took out a small spray bottle that he assumed was either filled with water or saline solution, and a medical wipe, handing her both just as she opened her mouth to say something.

She closed her lips and the smile that appeared on them knocked the air out of his lungs, not because of her feminine sensuality that lay underneath every one of her moves, but the sheer purity of the moment as they worked together to help an injured animal. Even though they worked in the same spaces, their paths rarely crossed. Now they had finally got to share such a moment shifted something inside him, changing something within him he wasn't sure he wanted changed.

It went beyond the professional admiration he had for her, and tapped into the hesitant flirting they had indulged in over the three months he'd been working for her charity, always in the secure knowledge that the words, the glances and the smiles would never go anywhere beyond what they were. They were only ever supposed to be friends.

But this… Seeing her compassion and skill in action was an experience he'd never thought would impact him as much as it did right now. He wanted more of it in his life, more of *her*.

All those thoughts flashed through his mind in a matter of seconds as their eyes locked, her gloved fingers grazing his when she took the items from him. Then she tore her gaze away from him, leaving him with sudden vertigo as his consciousness crashed back into reality. What had just happened?

The monkey whines were barely audible as Maria sprayed the solution in the bottle onto the mangled leg and carefully wiped it clean of the crusted blood that covered the fur. He handed her another wipe when the one in her hand became caked in blood and this time she accepted it without looking at him, her full attention on their patient in front of them.

'You're doing so great, mama monkey. I can see you have some cuts on your upper thigh that are looking a bit infected. I'm going to see if I can figure out where else you hurt your leg,' she said to the animal, then she gently lifted the leg to slide one of her hands underneath it, probing the flesh with gentle fingers.

She squeezed her eyes shut as her hands worked up and down the leg, only ever pressing as much as she needed to understand what lay beneath the skin, a skill Rafael admired in her. Under normal circumstances they would get an X-ray of the injured area to look at it on a film and take any of the guesswork out of it.

Though he had never really thought about it until this moment, he understood now that this was a luxury she oftentimes didn't have if she was out in the rainforest responding to a call the locals had put in to alert her of an injured animal requiring help. At least on a first pass she needed to figure out what was wrong so she could stabilise her patients and get them to the clinic.

'I think she broke her tibia,' she said when she opened her eyes again. 'She probably needs a splint to keep from moving, but I can't do that here without a way to see what the break looks like. If I set it now the bones might not line up enough to promote a clean heal.'

Rafael nodded. 'So we need to bring her to the clinic. Any idea how we can transport all of them?'

Though Maria travelled around with a small veterinary surgery in her pocket, he knew that she didn't have a carrier she could put the monkeys in. She sighed as she looked around, no doubt thinking the same thing.

'Let me call the clinic and see if they can pick us up,' she said, letting go of the monkey's leg but keeping her left hand on its stomach in a reassuring pat as she peeled the glove off her right hand and took her phone out of her back pocket.

'Come on, pick up your phone,' she whispered after several rings, and Rafael felt the relief he saw washing over her face in his own body when the call finally connected.

Rafael lay on the couch, the room veiled in darkness, and listened to the steady stream of the shower sounding down the hall. His chest tightened at the thought of Maria standing under the water, dark brown skin glistening as tiny drops pearled down her delicate throat and collarbone and then...

He shook his head, banishing the unwanted images into a place inside him where he could lock them up and forget about them. Because that was what he needed to do in this situation. Forget about the alluring femininity and grace that had showed in every one of her movements as she'd examined the helpless tamarin monkey they'd found in the alley.

After calling her friend at the federal institute, a car had come to pick up the monkey and its family in a carrier, and the vet had assured Maria that all would be taken care of. She'd hovered for a second back then, making

Rafael think that she might be invested enough to jump into the car with the other vet to see to the treatment of the monkey herself. But then she'd stepped back, letting them take the family of four away, and they'd walked back to the hotel in silence.

Rafael's stomach still roiled from the information she'd shared with him, letting him see the depth of her hurt, and his own wounds had responded in a way he hadn't anticipated, hadn't wanted them to either. What had happened with his family, with Laura, didn't concern anyone but himself. Everything would stay locked behind the thick walls he'd built.

Walls Maria seemed to dance around as if they weren't tall and imposing.

It was the compassion he'd witnessed within her tonight that had cracked open those ancient bricks hiding away his fear, daring to shine some light into the fissures—a light coming from her and the depth of care she'd given those monkeys.

It made him proud to work for her, work with the charity that facilitated such necessary acts every single day. But it was also seeing her live by the values she preached at her donors. She wasn't just a pretty face—and dear God, what a stunningly pretty face that was. No, she also cared so deeply that it put everyone else to shame in comparison.

That was a good reason to give her his money, though he still carried some hesitation in his chest. Throughout the day he'd watched his back, looking every stranger they encountered over twice while leaning into their fake romance as much as possible. If his family was sniffing around—and he had no doubt that was happening—they would go to great lengths to invalidate his marriage if they even as much as suspected that it wasn't genuine. It was the one risk that could blow up this whole plan. If they found out they weren't married the way his grandparents had meant for him to be married, they could hold up the money in a drawn-out legal battle. The charity couldn't afford that if it wanted to stay open. They needed access to his trust as soon as possible.

But what was he supposed to do? He had no idea what married life would look like for them once they were back in Santarém. They already lived together since his contract included her guest room free of charge. They had their daily routines, like having coffee together while talking about the previous day's cases, or dinner with Celine and the girls.

Would any of that remain, now that they had altered their relationship irrevocably? If he was honest with himself, Rafael hadn't really thought beyond this point when he'd come up with the ruse.

Or the fact that the attraction he sensed zipping between them when he looked at her a fraction too long was genuine. No, he'd thought this was no more than a fleeting infatuation for a man who had long since given up on love and any physical intimacy with it.

The trickling of the water stopped, snapping him out of his contemplations and catapulting him back into the room. He listened to her shuffling footsteps and, a moment later, the door opened. The bathroom light shining from the back obscured everything but Maria's silhouette, a shadow of curves and sensuality that summoned a rush of blood to his groin. Then the light went off, and his eyes needed a moment to adjust to the complete darkness until he could see in the gentle moonlight that filtered through the slats of the blinds.

Maria must have seen his open eyes for she smiled at him before she sat on the bed, her eyes darting between him and some invisible point on the wall only she could see.

In the dim light of the moon she looked absolutely striking, her dark skin deepening and highlighting what he knew to be velvety sweet to the touch. He swallowed the lump appearing in his throat, his thoughts turning to the unbridled desire he'd been staving off for months now.

It had been building throughout their friendship, so subtly that he didn't even realise how much he'd grown attached to her emotionally—on a human level. Though he'd been attracted to other women, the desire never ran so deep, the urge to conquer so all-consuming that he could think of little else in her presence. It was the kind of passion that came on the back of a more important emotional connection.

And it struck fear in his heart.

'Did I wake you?' Maria said, her voice just above a whisper as if she was afraid to wake him, when sleep was the furthest from his mind. How could he sleep with this fire of desire burning in the pit of his stomach? With the fear that came along with it that he had slipped too deep into this deception already?

'No, I was still awake,' he simply said, propping his head up on the couch so he could get a better look at her, and immediately regretting it when the heat contained in his belly spread like a wildfire to every remote corner of his body.

She wore an oversized shirt with a faded print he couldn't make out from his position, and a pair of linen shorts that hid just enough of her curves that his mind went wild imagining what lay underneath the tantalising strip of cloth. Even in scrubs Rafael hadn't been able to keep his eyes off her, his gaze following her around whenever he thought she wasn't watching—sometimes getting caught with a smile and wink.

There was no wink now as his eyes roamed over her, following the curve of her long legs that vanished under the thin covering, before going back up her body. Her chest rose and fell in an uneven pattern, her breasts pushing against the fabric of her shirt, and between the flecks of print on the shirt he saw the tips of her nipples straining against it.

His eyes darted to her face as heat exploded through his body again, bringing his blood to an impossible boil. From the wide-eyed expression on her face, he could glimpse that her body's reaction was as involuntary as his. Neither of them *wanted* to be in the situation they currently found themselves.

'Are you sure you'll be okay on the couch? It looks a bit short,' she said with a gentle clearing of her throat.

'I'll be fine. It's only a couple of hours and then we'll be back in Santarém.'

Maria hesitated for a moment, then she said, 'I don't mind if you want to be more comfortable.'

Rafael blinked slowly. He needed a few seconds to process what she had just said, because it certainly couldn't be what his lewd brain was telling him it was. No, this was his lust reading into a perfectly innocent statement.

This was not an invitation to anything other than a restful night.

Rafael shook his head, knowing his voice might betray his desire. Instead, he opted to change the subject.

'That was some quick thinking today. I don't think the mother or her babies would have made it without your intervention,' he said, recalling a part of their day that was safe to talk about.

Maria smiled again, a lot brighter than a moment ago, and her white teeth showed in stark contrast to the darkness swallowing her as the night progressed. Rafael shifted around for a moment, both to escape the heat her gaze was searing through him with what could only be described as an innocent smile, and to look through the blinds up into the sky.

The moon had dipped below the tree line of the rainforest, whose ancient branches reached high up, almost enveloping them in a canopy of green. Though Manaus was built to be a gateway into the Amazon and its beauty, the glow of the city still polluted the sky, dimming out the light of the stars. Though he'd lived in Brazil his entire life, he'd only once been to a place remote enough to see the stars in their full glory.

'What was it like growing up with famous grandparents?' Maria asked into the quiet, drawing his attention back to her.

'What?' he asked in return, the question dropping deep into the memories of his subconscious and only slowly resurfacing.

'You said they were part of *Patas Para O Amor*, right? There's hardly a *novela* that is more popular than that one, especially in vet circles. Did that impact your decision to become a vet as well?'

Rafael blinked a few times, trying to untangle the painful emotions from the few happy ones he knew lay within him. Something outside of the trauma his parents had inflicted—the trauma his grandparents' money had contributed to—that he could share with her. Because he *wanted* to share something of his. Something that wasn't all doom and gloom, but something light. Something she could appreciate about him, and yes, maybe even find attractive. Though why he wanted to appeal to her, he didn't know. Other than that hunger within him that wanted—*needed*—to be close to her in any way he could.

'I think they showed me the possibility, yes. By the time my nanny brought me to the farm on a daily basis I knew the concept of a vet. Though by the time I was old enough to make this decision, they had already passed away. I give them a bit of credit, but most of it goes to Camila and her family's animals.'

He paused before he continued. 'The show had stopped before I was even born, but the memory of their achievements were very prominent in our house and they spoke a lot about how *Patas Para O Amor* helped the family become what it was. So maybe in a way they inspired me?' He shrugged, the memories pouring from his lips as if they had just been waiting for Maria to arrive so he could finally share what had been buried inside him for years.

'I always had an affinity for animals,' he said with a chuckle that vibrated through Maria's body all the way down to her bones. 'The person everyone thought was my best friend in high school only hung out with me because his parents had got a dog for him, and he was tired of taking care of it. So I became the dog's caretaker and took him with me when I left for university.'

Maria smiled at that. Even back then he had volunteered his own time to help an animal who needed him. It was a trait she'd noticed in him when he'd started working at her clinic. Many times she'd found him there late at night because a panicked owner had swung by at an ungodly hour. More often than not the owners were making a big deal out of nothing, but Rafael always took their fear at face value. He understood that these were family members and that sometimes people didn't think rationally when it came to their loved ones.

'You didn't have your own pets?' she asked, surprised at that. In *Patas Para O Amor* they'd worked with a lot of show animals, so she had been certain their own home would be full of animals as well.

But Rafael shook his head. 'Outside of the horde of barn cats that considered me their king? No, sadly not. Maybe that's why my parents thought I couldn't be serious about my plans to become a vet.'

His voice was strained, and Maria sat up just a bit straighter at that. 'They didn't approve?'

A strange concept in her mind. Even though she frowned upon it, she knew that society didn't place a high value on vets, thinking that they *only* worked with animals. None of them considered how much harder it was to treat the medical condition of a living being that couldn't articulate where it hurt. *They* had to be the ones so tuned in to the animals' wellbeing that they could sense and understand their various ailments.

Rafael shook his head, his lips pressed into a thin line that she yearned to soothe away with her fingers. His help with the injured monkey had been so invaluable today, and he hadn't even hesitated for a second, knowing exactly why she needed to help—and giving her the space to do so. In a professional capacity she had dealt with many vets, talented people who sometimes couldn't step away when someone with more expertise took charge of a situation.

He'd been nothing like that, yielding to her requests as she'd sent him off to fetch her first aid kit so they could patch up the monkey well enough for transport to the clinic to arrive.

This evening would be one she'd remember for a long time after they parted ways. That thought caused another twinge in her chest, making her swallow hard as things within her surfaced that she didn't want to, didn't have the space inside her to process.

She absolutely could not be this attracted to Rafael. It was bordering on self-destructive insanity that her hands twitched with the need to smooth away the worry lines appearing around his eyes and the corners of his mouth. Longing gripped her, radiating tantalising warmth through her body, and Maria had to admit that she had lost control over her mounting desire for this man.

'No, they didn't approve. The one thing my parents always wanted, above anything else, was the fame and acknowledgement that my grandparents got for their work in the field of television. With the fortune his parents gave my father upon marrying my mother they founded a media company so they could recreate *Patas Para O Amor*, hoping that the family name would carry them along. It did, and that was their demise when it came to turning promises into action.' Rafael sighed and his head rolled backwards against his cushion so he was staring up at the ceiling.

Maria remembered the reboot of her beloved *novela* and how she'd watched two episodes before turning it off for ever. It just didn't have that magical feeling of the original, but she'd always thought it was her not being able to appreciate the reboot for what it was through her thick nostalgia goggles. Rafael seemed to suggest the production really was inferior.

'They ran out of money quickly, which is when they

turned to my siblings and me to see if we wanted to *invest* in their company. Both my brother and sister had been raised as fame-hungry socialites, so they jumped at that opportunity, and they too put all their trust money into my parents' company at the chance of being a part of the show.'

Maria frowned, the quiet pain in his voice like a knife cutting through her. 'You don't have a relationship with your siblings either?'

He'd alluded to this when they'd spoken earlier, his discomfort around his family clear even as they'd planned this ruse back in her clinic.

He shook his head. 'They chose to accept the arranged matches from our parents—the children of other executives in the entertainment industry. I might have been able to set my differences with them aside if they weren't just as bad as my parents when it came to my trust.'

'They were also pressuring you into things you didn't want?' she asked, a shiver shaking her.

She was so close to her own sister, their lives so intertwined that she couldn't imagine not being a part of her life—or be so different from her that she couldn't.

'Pretty much. They would do whatever they were commanded to do by our parents. I thought I could trust them at one point, until…'

His voice trailed off and Maria strained to hear the rest of the sentence, but he didn't reveal anything else.

Not that he needed to. Today Maria had learned a lot more about his family and was appalled at their behaviour. They would put their children, people they'd promised to protect, through financial ruin, just at a chance of fame and riches? It sounded absurd, especially since it sounded as if they were already very well-off with the money from their trusts. Why risk it all for something so vapid and insubstantial?

'And now you are the only remaining Pedro child to hold out?' she asked, and he gave her a slow nod, his eyes still searching something invisible on the ceiling.

'They almost got me too. For years they tried to match me with people they thought would bring an advantageous family connection. Daughters of other media moguls or wealthy personalities in Brazil. When I turned them all down, they eventually stopped. And then Laura appeared out of nowhere, as if sent by some higher power, and I...' His voice trailed off again, and it was only then that Maria noticed she had been holding her breath in anticipation of his confession. Even in the dim moonlight she could see the pain etched into every feature of his handsome face that normally shone with compassion and kindness. It seemed so wrong to only see hurt and bitterness reflected in it now.

Was that what he'd wanted to say a few moments ago? Had his siblings been involved with this Laura as well?

He cleared his throat, and the thickness in his voice was apparent. Whatever had happened with this woman had changed him for ever in some way. Was that why he didn't believe in love any more? Because his attempts had failed?

Maria almost prompted him to finish his sentence but closed her lips again when he shook his head. She'd never seen him so torn up and it took a considerable amount of her willpower to keep sitting where she was when everything within her wanted to get close to him and hug him tight, kiss the pain away. Let him kiss her pain away too...

'We should sleep. The flight leaves early tomorrow, and

we'll have to be on our best behaviour.' These was an undertone to his words that Maria struggled to understand.

What did he mean by that? That he sensed what was
going on between them and was reminding her that it was
all off-limits? Did that mean he felt it too, the attraction
brewing between them since they'd started working together?

Her mind ran in circles around this one sentence, ana-
lysing the myriad meanings his words could have, and
drawing up short on all of them.

So she just nodded, sinking down into her pillows when
his strained voice sounded once again. *'Boa noite.'*

CHAPTER SIX

MARIA WOKE UP to the scent of food wafting up her nose. She squeezed her eyes shut, turning around in her bed, trying to find her way back to sleep. But the smell of burnt toast had her open one eye to look at the alarm clock on her nightstand. Barely past eight and Celine was already destroying their kitchen? Since when did her sister bother to cook anyway? Most of the time this woman lived off nothing but black coffee and the occasional piece of fruit.

With a groan Maria forced herself out of bed, the motivation that her sister might burn their house down if left unattended in the kitchen enough to wake her up. Celine must have just arrived home. Her specialty as a livestock vet meant she serviced a lot of farms in the surrounding area, oftentimes needing to attend them for the calf and foal season to supervise the trickier births. Those couldn't be scheduled so that meant her sister had to attend whenever they happened—even when it was the middle of the night.

She hesitated in front of her dresser and looked down on herself. Should she get dressed before leaving her room? That question had never entered her mind before she and Rafael had entered into their ruse. What was now different that she didn't want him to see her like that?

Maria's pulse stumbled as it accelerated, and she forced

herself to open her door and step outside. Relief mingled with something else far deeper and more primal within her as her eyes fell on Rafael's closed door. He wasn't up yet. Good. She needed a moment alone with her sister to talk about what had happened in the last week.

She stepped out of her room and glanced through the door next to hers into her nieces' room. Nina's bed was empty, no doubt *helping* her mother prepare breakfast downstairs, but Mirabel sat at her desk, headphones on as she quietly drew on a piece of paper.

'Bom dia, amor,' Maria said loud enough so her niece would hear her through the headphones.

She looked up from her artwork and pushed the headphones off her ears. *'Bom dia, Tia,'* she said with a small smile that made an ache bloom in her chest.

After all that had happened to her, she seemed so calm when Maria knew that her father abandoning her must still hurt, even after so much time. Maria and Celine had tried to get in touch with their brother, urging him to come back, not for them but for his daughter, promising that they would forget what had happened and that it wasn't about the money. But Daniel had never replied, never even asked about his child and how she was doing. It was that callousness that turned the blood in her veins into raging lava. How could he have done that to his little girl, all for a woman he'd met a couple of times? The *love of his life* as he had put it in that pathetic excuse of a goodbye note for her and Celine.

'Your *tia* is making food for us. Are you coming downstairs?'

Mirabel made a face that reflected the feelings Maria herself had about Celine's cooking. 'I had cereal when

I woke up,' she said, her nose crinkling as the smell of burning food intensified around them.

'Solid choice. Maybe it's not too late for me to do that as well.' Her niece chuckled, transforming the thunderous rage in her chest into a warm sensation of unconditional love for the child who had become her daughter in everything but name. 'Okay, let me help your aunt before she renders us all homeless because of an uncontrolled kitchen fire.'

Mirabel put her headphones back on, and Maria hurried downstairs, inspecting the scene as she rounded the corner into the kitchen.

Celine stood half turned from the stove, scraping way too hard at a substance in the pan that resembled scrambled eggs but didn't quite have the right colour or texture to be considered that. The pieces of bread sticking out of the toaster were almost black. The expression on her younger sister's face was one of pure concentration as she squinted at her phone propped up against the wall on the kitchen counter. Was she reading a recipe for scrambled eggs?

The entire scene was so bizarre, Maria couldn't stop her laughter from erupting, prompting Celine to whirl around to look at her in surprise.

'What do you think you're doing, *bebê*?' she asked, propping her hands on her hips as she beheld the utter chaos that reigned in her kitchen. 'You know you can't cook.'

'I can perform surgery on a newborn rabbit, I should be able to make scrambled eggs,' Celine replied, though the glance at the pan in her hand didn't convey any of her false bravado. 'Anyway, this isn't for you. This is for...Alexander.'

At the mention of his name, the Great Dane raised his head in question, bumping against the dangling feet of her other niece, Nina, who sat on a comfy armchair with a tablet in her hand, watching something flashing on the screen.

'I promise you even he won't eat that.' Maria stepped closer and snapped her fingers, summoning the large dog to her side before snatching the pan out of her sister's hands and presenting it to him. Alexander looked inside the pan, sniffing at its contents and then raising his snout at her with another questioning look.

'See? He doesn't even interpret it as real food,' she said with a laugh, Celine's expression turning thunderous.

'I'm never going to do *anything* nice for you ever again,' she hissed, before leaving the house to throw the failed attempt at breakfast into the compost bin around the back of the house.

Meanwhile, Maria poured herself a coffee from the already steaming pot. Her sister was so dependent on her caffeine that she knew she could trust her ability to make coffee without hesitation. Then she followed Mirabel's suggestion and poured herself a bowl of cereal just as Celine returned, sitting down on the chair across from her with a still sour expression that made her chuckle.

'Okay, how about I acknowledge that you tried to make breakfast for me, and I'll appreciate the gesture and spirit behind it without actually having consumed any of it.' She sipped on her coffee, its sweet taste chasing away the final remnants of sleep clinging to her. 'And in return you'll tell me why you chose to endanger the kids and me with your cooking.'

Celine scowled, taking a deep drink from her own mug. 'I need a reason to do something nice for my family? I haven't seen you in a while, with all the work going on in the farms. We need to talk.'

There was an undertone in her voice that wasn't lost on Maria. They *had* a lot to talk about, because the last time they'd spoken was the night they'd discussed the demise of their charity at the hands of their brother. She'd told her sister that she needed to fire Rafael and make some arrangements to forward animals in need to a clinic a few hundred kilometres south. That had been almost two weeks ago. *A lot* had changed since then.

'Okay...' Maria nodded, taking a deep breath as she considered where to even start. She and Rafael had come back from Manaus the day after they'd signed their marriage licence. On their way to the airport his lawyer had called, informing him that he'd submitted the papers to the bank, but that it would take at least a month for the funds to be released. A whole month where they needed to pretend they were a married couple on the off-chance that someone came sniffing around them to expose their marriage for the fraud that it was.

Both working and living together had changed since they'd returned back home, their interactions fuelled by the persistent undercurrent of mutual attraction. Somewhere in all of this, she had reached the understanding that the electric charge between them was *very* real and not a figment of her affection-starved imagination.

But their agreement was so simple it almost became complicated again. Their one rule was to make it believable, and Maria knew, from everything he had told her about his family, that everyone around them needed to believe that they were a genuine couple. That meant telling the whole village that they were married, acting like they were in love in front of everyone...

How could she do that to her friends? The people in Santarém were almost a part of her family. They would be so hurt if they found out that Maria had lied to them. Or would they ultimately understand that she had done it to save her sanctuary?

How would the villagers treat Rafael when they found out? He'd been nothing but gentle and kind to her throughout this entire process.

The night in the hotel flashed in her memory whenever she had an unguarded moment, rocking through her with an intensity that was ridiculous. *Nothing* had happened. The flash of a moment where he'd looked her up and down, his thoughts matching the rapid beating of her heart as they'd both admitted to something non-verbally. That their forced kiss had affected him as much as her, and that she wasn't alone in her yearning to repeat it— without the audience this time.

'You probably noticed that Rafael is still here.' She didn't know where exactly to start her story, but this piece of information was as good as any.

Even though they'd agreed that they wouldn't tell anyone that their marriage was fake, Maria had no intention of withholding that information from her sister. She couldn't. The charity was *theirs*. They had each put so much work and passion into it, she needed to know how she was saving it.

'That's one of the things I was wondering about.' Celine paused, smirking. 'Is it because you like him that you couldn't do it? Do I have to be the bad guy?'

Maria flushed, giving her sister exactly the reaction she wanted. 'No, that's not it.' How was she supposed to tell her that she'd got fake married? It was such a strange concept that she could barely articulate it.

'That evening we had an emergency admission, and after we took care of it I spoke to him about our problems. That we had to shut down the charity because we couldn't find enough donations to keep things going, even with the extra cash from the vet services.' She paused, the memory of that evening so fuzzy compared to the vivid details of what had happened since then when they'd travelled to Manaus.

'When he heard that we might close because of financial trouble, he offered to donate some money to buy us more time to look for a permanent donor.' Maria let out a breath when she noticed her voice quietening. So far so good. She could get through the rest of it as well.

Celine raised her eyebrows. 'He has enough money to bankroll us until we can find someone else? Why is he here in Santarém when he has so much money?'

'You remember *Patas Para O Amor*?' she asked, already knowing the answer.

'Of course, how could I not remember?' Celine blinked, clearly trying to make a connection between what she had just heard and that seemingly unrelated question.

'The lead couple from the original were a couple in real life, I don't know if you remember that. Anyway, turns out Rafael is related to them, and owns quite a fortune thanks to the success of his grandparents.'

She stopped, watching Celine carefully as she said each word. Her sister's eyes went wide at that nugget of information, almost making Maria laugh at the absurdity that was about to come out of her mouth next. If she was shocked right now, she would faint when she heard what she was about to share.

'So again, what on earth is he doing here if he is rich?' Celine asked, giving voice to the question that had led her down the road of marriage almost two weeks ago. Two strange weeks where the air around her and Rafael had been changed for ever, the easygoing nature of their friendship replaced with some hot and intense simmering that neither of them wanted to act on for various reasons.

For Maria it was simple enough that she *knew* they weren't compatible, knew that they wanted different things from this life and that they might have attraction and chemistry, but that meant little if their life goals didn't align.

'Well...' A lump appeared in her throat and she grabbed her coffee to mask it, taking a sip of the already cooling liquid.

Celine raised a questioning eyebrow, seeing the gesture for what it was—a strange attempt to stall at what was coming next.

'Turns out his grandparents were rather traditional people so, instead of giving their children and grandchildren money, they set up a trust for each of them so that they could only get the money when certain...conditions were met.'

She took another sip as her sister's eyes narrowed on her. Understanding dawned on her face, though Maria knew there was no way she could have correctly guessed what those conditions were. Or maybe she'd just realised that whatever conditions there were, Maria was the one who could meet them for Rafael and knew they had entered some sort of deal.

'What did you do, M?' she asked straight away, and any hope Maria might have had of pulling out of the conversation was gone.

She swallowed again, willing her voice to remain

steady as she confessed to the scheme she and Rafael had hatched.

'His grandparents wanted the money to go towards keeping the Pedro family name going and whatnot. To ensure that was how the money was used, they put a clause in the trust that required Rafael to be married before he could access any of the funds they left him.'

Maria paused, letting that information float between them and giving her sister some space to process this. Celine remained quiet, looking straight at her with unblinking eyes. Where there had been an expression of scepticism on her face was now a mask of emptiness, not letting her catch a glimpse of whatever her sister was thinking. Though she wanted to interject and potentially overexplain, Maria remained quiet, giving Celine the time she needed to process. Even though she had not directly said it, she had dropped a big bombshell with this information.

Finally, Celine looked down at her mug, clearing her throat. 'Excuse me, I think I still don't understand then. Because it sounds to me as if you are telling me that you *married* him to get the money, which I know you can't have done.'

'Okay, hear me out—'

'Maria, are you serious right now?'

'It was the only way to save our business, Cee!' Maria cringed at her raised voice, and both women looked to the side to check on Nina, who was still staring ahead at her tablet without a care in the world.

It happened every now and then that the sisters had a disagreement, but whenever that happened, they tried to have it out where the children—and, more recently, also Rafael—couldn't hear them. Since neither of the children's fathers were in the picture any more, they'd assumed the role of both parents in their children's lives, and as such they always strived to appear as a team to them.

Celine had got pregnant on her wedding night, when she'd married her then boyfriend in an impulse elopement that Maria hadn't known about—only for her husband to vanish off the face of the earth a few days later without even a note as to what had happened. They'd eventually found out that he had left Brazil to return to his home country of Peru, though any attempts at contacting him had gone unanswered. Which meant that he didn't even know about his four-year-old daughter.

It was also the reason Maria knew her sister would be very sensitive to her getting married without saying a word about it. Even though it had happened almost five years ago, the wound remained at surface level, making Celine skittish to the concept of marriage, no matter the intention.

She lowered her voice before she continued. 'I know you have strong feelings about people getting married, but this is purely for convenience. I made that choice to save us. With the money he's offering us, we can keep our heads above water for a few more *years* before we need to look someplace else. Think of that before you judge.'

Celine's jaw tightened, a muscle in her face feathering with the comment she undoubtedly swallowed so as not to throw it in her face. Restraint that Maria was grateful for. Though Celine was the child protégée, the eight years they had between them in age showed in situations like this, reminding Maria just how young her sister actually was and how her gifts had forced her to grow up far faster than any child should.

She glanced over at her niece, hoping that she could

grow up at her own pace with the support of her mother and her aunt.

'You have feelings for this man, Maria,' Celine finally said, at which she instinctively scoffed.

'Feelings? Don't be absurd. This has never been more than a very innocent flirtation between two friends working together—taking the edge off the sometimes grim work we have to do.' Her chest tightened, and she prayed that it wasn't visible on her face. It was a small lie, one to comfort herself as well as Celine.

She didn't have *feelings* for Rafael, not the way her sister believed she had. Yes, she was attracted to him, and yes, the kiss they'd shared popped into her memory at the most inconvenient times, cascading sparks through her body that she willed away whenever they appeared. But this was all temporary. It would go away, she knew that, because there simply wasn't an alternative.

He didn't *want* what she wanted—and she didn't want him because of that.

'Oh, okay… If you believe that then I guess Darius and I will be ready for our couple's vacation once you come around.' Her sister's sarcasm bit, and Maria reminded herself that she was speaking from a place of hurt that came from the exposed wound of her estranged husband—Darius.

She needed to be patient as she introduced her to this temporary new reality.

'This is controversial, I get it. But I need you to support me regardless of your feelings. I made the choice, so we can only move forward from this point.' There were still a few open questions to discuss before they could move on from this.

From the scowl on Celine's face she could tell her sister

was processing the information with sceptical reluctance as she asked, 'So how does this all work?'

Maria huffed a laugh at her directness. It was always straight to the point with her. 'We have to sell this marriage as real or his family could contest the trust and he wouldn't get the money.'

'What does that mean?' Celine asked, giving voice to the difficult question Maria had been rolling around in her mind ever since they'd got back from Manaus.

'I don't know... I'm not telling anyone that we're married. Otherwise, I'd also have to explain getting divorced so soon after. But outside of this house we'll have to pretend to...be dating?' Her voice rose to a questioning pitch, as she herself wasn't sure this was a sound idea. Only problem was—there wasn't an alternative. They *had* to at least show some level of affection whenever they went outside.

'Why do you need to pretend?'

'Because...' Maria paused and downed the remaining coffee from her mug. 'His family is trouble. I don't want to say much else because it's not my place. He's dealing with some messed-up stuff there, and that's a large part of why he chose to live here in the middle of nowhere.'

Though the sisters normally shared everything, it didn't seem right to share his story when it had taken him so much effort to confide in her alone.

Celine shook her head, crossing her arms. 'Maria, I don't know about this.'

'Remember when we found out you were pregnant? I needed some space to process my feelings, but I did that while we attended birthing classes together, read all the parenting books the library had to offer and turned our study into a nursery.' She paused when her sister's eyes narrowed. She knew where she was going with this. 'I need you to be like this now, okay? Process whatever you need to process about my fake marriage. But while you do that, I need you to support me.'

Celine took a deep breath, and Maria could almost feel the resistance to this idea. She was stubborn, all right. Most of the time that energy could be harnessed for great success, but the flipside was situations like this where she needed her to go along with something.

'What are you going to tell the kids?'

Another question Maria had been agonising over, and the obvious answer would get her another look from her sister. 'Honestly? I think we can just let them believe Rafael and I are dating. Nina is too young to understand the concept, and Mirabel... I'll explain to her that things didn't work out between Rafael and me when the time comes.'

A frown appeared on Celine's face. 'I don't like this,' she mumbled.

A buzz of the intercom at the wall interrupted the conversation, and Maria got up with a sigh of relief to check the little screen on it. Before she pressed the button, she looked at her sister over her shoulder. 'You don't have to like this. I just need you to play along until *our* charity is safe.'

She turned back around to press the button on the little screen.

'Yes, hello, how can I help?' she asked through the intercom as she studied the fair-haired man standing in front of the clinic's door. Her eyes narrowed on the pet carrier she spotted at his side. His face wasn't a familiar one.

'I'm looking to schedule an appointment with Dr Pedro.

Is he here?' the man asked, looking up at the building as if he was trying to spot her.

Maria's eyes darted to her sister, who glared at her in return. His name was the last one she wanted to hear from anyone right now.

'I'll be out in a moment,' she said into the intercom, then turned to go upstairs to put on something slightly less revealing than her PJs, pausing at his door.

Should she tell him someone was looking for him? She didn't recognise the person standing outside, and that was unusual in this small community. Maria shook her head, then stepped into her own room to get dressed.

She would handle the situation herself. If it was someone asking strange questions, she would be able to play the part of his doting wife. And if someone needed medical attention for their animal she could deal with that as well.

If the person turned out to be suspicious, she would tell him. If not, he didn't need to know. The last thing she wanted was to worry him unnecessarily.

Though it was Saturday, and technically his day off, Rafael found his way into the clinic in the late afternoon. A glance outside the window told him that Celine was out working, though when he came downstairs he only found Mirabel and Nina in the living room, with no trace of Maria. They informed him that she was in the clinic.

Restlessness sat deep in his bones and the one thing he knew to do was to dive into work headfirst to forget the warm tendrils of desire rising within him the more time he spent with Maria. A desire he didn't dare to utter, even in his thoughts, for the fear that he might ruin their friendship.

Because he knew he *didn't* want her to be more than his friend, not really. This feeling in his chest was nothing but an overreaction of his brain because their relationship had changed. Outside of the kiss they'd shared, nothing had happened that would change their feelings for each other, and even that kiss had been as fake as their marriage was. It had happened as a cover, in case his family had their spies inside the courthouse already. An unlikely scenario, but Rafael wasn't taking any risks when it came to his deranged family and their obsession with his money. Not after what they'd done with Laura.

A part of him was suspicious that his family hadn't made a move yet, hadn't even tried to contact him. What were they waiting for? It had been two weeks since they'd returned from their *elopement*, and his phone had stayed quiet. He'd expected them to try to get in touch with Maria, attempt to convince her that she didn't know him at all—that they were the victims in all of this, and Rafael was standing in the way of their dreams, that he had so much while needing so little. They knew he would never listen to them, so the only way they could get to him was to turn the people he cared about against him.

Just like they had done before with Laura.

Had they given up? That was too good to be true.

The door was unlocked when he pushed it open and he couldn't stop the smile from spreading over his lips. He'd worked in a lot of different clinics over the years, but none of them had been like this one. The intrinsic trust and affection people shared with each other in this town was so deep and warm. Rafael hadn't realised he'd wanted something like that his entire life. Someone like Maria, but also a place like Santarém where people were checking in on each other to make sure they had everything they needed—not because they were envious of their neighbours.

The thought of leaving it all behind broke his heart in two and only because he was giving it all up for the greater good kept him from hurting beyond repair. What he was doing—it was what the people of this village would do for each other without hesitation.

His ears pricked up when a soft rustling came from the area where they kept the animals for observation or post-op care. The thought of seeing Maria was as tempting as it was daunting. Since they'd come back, the energy between them had changed. They didn't run into each other as much, their morning coffee breaks invaded by this undercurrent of desire that threw both of them off.

There was no denying what was happening between them, or what they wanted to do about it. Nothing. Because they understood that they didn't have a future together. Because he cared for Maria, because she was his friend, he couldn't let her hang on to him for too long. He knew she wanted more from a relationship—true love. He wanted her to have that, and it hurt more than he was prepared to admit that he wasn't, and couldn't be, that person for her.

'Hey, Ma—' The words got stuck in his throat as she jumped out of her chair, clutching the baby ocelot to her chest while pointing the feeding bottle at him.

She relaxed when she realised it was him. 'Oh, my goodness, you scared me. What are you doing here?'

'What are *you* doing here?' he asked her instead.

'Me? Rafael, this is *my* clinic.'

He laughed at that, pulling up a chair from the other side of the room and sitting next to her.

'You could have asked me to take care of the ocelot

if you want to hang out with the kids.' Even though he knew that this building and helping these animals was her entire life—and the reason she had agreed to marry him—he wasn't someone who just left after he'd seen his last patient, letting her deal with all the administrative stuff of the clinic herself.

Judging by the sparkle in her eyes, she recognised the efforts he'd put into this place as well, a grateful smile curling her lips.

'They know to come over here if they need any help. Plus, I didn't want to bother you on the weekend.'

'When your vet clinic is ten metres from your home, "weekend" becomes a very loose term,' Rafael replied, and the laugh he earned for it was so rich and vibrant that it made the hair on his arms stand on edge.

'Okay, but what are you doing here right now?' She looked around at the animals, searching for the one patient he might have come here to check on.

'I just needed to stretch my legs for a bit and so I thought I'd check in on some of our patients,' he said, leaving out the part where he was hoping to find her here.

'Lia here is doing a lot better. I think we can fly her to the institute soon.' She smiled at the little ocelot as she fed it.

'Ah, did you finally settle on a name for her?' he asked with a chuckle as he watched her press her mouth against the nozzle of the bottle.

'Mirabel did. I took her to see her a few days ago and she said she looked like a Lia.' Maria shrugged. 'I agree. It just seems right.'

'Do you have to take her to Manaus?' he asked, reaching out across the space between them to run his hand along the ocelot's back.

Maria shook her head. 'I know a shipping agency that has experience with exotic animals, so I don't have to take her. But she must go to the institute. With her being so young I don't think she could survive on her own just yet, and we don't have a way of tracking down her mother or anything. I'm not sure she'll ever be able to live in the wild now, but the institute is her best chance at that. They have some ocelots there that they're currently rehabilitating. If one of them adopts her as their own, we might stand a chance of getting her back out there.' Maria looked down and the gentleness radiating from her smile was so bright and pure that his breath caught in his throat.

It was moments like this that made it so hard to remember why he didn't want her in his life as his wife for the rest of eternity. In his mind he knew it wasn't about her, that it didn't matter who she was or how much time he actually wanted to spend with her. How he noticed every moment that he wasn't here, in her presence. That he wanted to learn from her, absorb her knowledge and her talent. Be blessed by her kindness.

But there was no way this could ever become a reality. He was too broken, his family too toxic to put anyone through it when he knew exactly how this would end. They hadn't shied away from infiltrating his life—his *heart*—to get what they wanted. They would not stop at genuine love either. No, they would somehow find a way into his inner sanctum and rob him of whatever little joy he'd been able to amass while they weren't looking.

If they ever found out that Rafael might harbour genuine feelings for Maria, they would use that as a weapon against him. Over the years in the entertainment industry, they had honed the craft of manipulating people—him included. He could not let them come here and ruin the goodness of Maria, of the people here in Santarém that he'd become so close to. Just by being related to them, he himself became tainted. He had already risked too much by getting attached the way he had.

As soon as matters were settled, he needed to leave.

'Let's hope for the best for the little one,' he said when he still felt her eyes on him, waiting for an answer.

'I want to shoot a small video with her before we send her off. They are organising a charity event to drum up funding for their newest project, and my colleague managed to get a slot for me in the presentation. Lia is the perfect subject to showcase what the charity is all about. Hopefully, she will catch the attention of a wealthy donor to help us out in the future.'

The prospect of Maria finding a new benefactor for her charity so soon struck unexpected fear in his heart, for he hadn't yet fully processed what would happen once their ruse was done.

He would have to leave, or he'd risk his family accosting her for the money they might think she possessed—or, worse yet, turn her against him. Even though the thought of leaving Maria and Santarém behind seared through his chest in a painful stab that forced all the air out of his lungs.

'I'm rooting for you,' was all he managed to press out, hoping that she didn't sense the inner turmoil their brief conversation had stirred up.

Maria remained quiet for a moment, looking down at Lia the ocelot, who wasn't showing any interest in her food any more. She got up in a fluid motion that had him run his eyes over her in an instinct to imprint everything about her into his memory, wanting to remember these precious few weeks he had spent here, enjoying his job and his place in life for the first time in years.

Who wouldn't with a person like that?

He followed her with his gaze as she put the ocelot back in its enclosure. Unlike during the week, she wasn't wearing scrubs right now but rather her casual clothes— if that wrap dress clinging to her curves could even be called casual. Even though the dress flowed at the back and around her arms, it sat tightly around her waist and chest, accentuating the beauty of her full Latina figure, and desire thundered through him with such a force that it knocked the wind out of him.

God, she was beautiful. How could he be *fake* married to this person? How was it even possible that there wasn't an entire line of men waiting to court her?

The heat pooling in her belly ever since Rafael and she had started talking spread through her body in a star shape after she put down Lia and turned around, finding the man's eyes trained on her. The hazel colour of his eyes had darkened, his pupils dilated, giving voice and shape to the desire that uncoiled from the depths of her being. She breathed out with a slight tremble, the fabric of her dress rustling as she walked back to her seat, her skin alight with tiny fires that had erupted just below the surface.

Why was he looking at her like that—like the attraction between them was more than just an idle fantasy she liked to indulge herself in when her days got quiet? Because that was all there was to it, all there would ever be to this faux marriage. And the twinge this caused inside her chest could not be one of regret, because that would mean he meant something more to her than just a friend would—that just couldn't happen. Not with how definitive his answer had been around having a real marriage. Not with Mirabel living with her, who needed stability more than anything else. Her own needs hardly mattered when she weighed it against what her family needed.

And her family needed the doors to this clinic to stay open, to continue the legacy so many had given so much of themselves to.

'Anyway,' she said as she sat back down, her voice a lot lower than she had intended it to be. 'The reason I bring it up is that I would love for you to be a part of the video. You were the one who treated Lia, and I thought…maybe if they see us as a…family they will be more inclined to donate. I already asked Celine to take some shots of the market tomorrow, so we can sprinkle those in there along with Lia's story. It would be good if we can be seen there as well…together.'

The lump in her throat got thicker as she spoke, with Rafael's eyes still lingering, his arresting face schooled in an expression that made her knees weak. She watched as the same thoughts she'd had earlier rippled in different expressions over his face. Appearing together in public would put their ruse on display for everyone in the village to see. They'd have to convince everyone that they were a couple in love. Even if they weren't considered affectionate people, they wouldn't be able to keep their distance.

And, even though she didn't want to admit it, the yearning for his closeness had driven her to extend this invitation more than anything else. Even if it was just once, Maria wanted to live the fantasy haunting her in her sleep.

'You want to spend tomorrow morning the way we usually do, but with a camera? Appear at tomorrow's market as a couple?' he asked, and if she had found her voice low, his was several octaves deeper, and ringing through her blood.

She swallowed visibly but nodded.

'If you want to capitalise on us being what looks like a family in the video, and this video will be shared with a wider audience, I hope you realise that we *will* have to ensure people believe we're a real couple. Depending on the audience the institute invite, some of my family's friends could be there. Chances are they will see this video. We can't give them any reason to doubt us if they see it, or they could contest the trust and draw everything out. I'm willing to risk it for you, but I need you to be aware of what you are asking me to do.'

A shiver clawed its way down her spine and she had to fight the urge to shake, even though she was pretty sure that he'd noticed anyway. Maria had thought of that, and the reward must outweigh the risk. The attraction between them was genuine, after all, their close friendship helping to show that they cared for one another. They would behave like a couple in front of the entire village, and hope that what they felt for one another was enough to pass scrutiny.

The thought of walking around town holding Rafael's hand sent a thrill of excitement through her that she fought back down into her subconscious. When had the desire between them escalated? A few weeks back, this had been no more than some smiles exchanged across the exam room, and now she was dreaming about the lips that had kissed her so gently. Imagining what they'd feel like on other parts of her body...

'Yes, I'm aware of that,' she said with another swallow, her heart slamming against her ribcage in an erratic dance.

Rafael leaned forward, the dark brown hair swaying over his brow as he braced his forearms on his thighs and looked at her—his gaze striking, stripping her bare without even touching her.

He got off the chair, the muscles under his shirt rippling with power and the promise of something primal that made her mouth go dry. Her breath trembled when he took a step towards her and her pulse ratcheted up with each subsequent step that brought him closer to her, until she needed to lean back to look up to him.

'Here's the thing, Maria,' he said, every note in his voice seeping in through the pores in her skin and sinking down into her body, every vibration of his rich baritone settling in a fiery pinch right behind her navel. His head dipped lower, his breath grazing her already heated cheeks.

'If we show ourselves out and about here in Santarém, we must pretend to be a real couple whenever there are people around us. This wasn't a problem when we went to Manaus to get married, because we were mostly alone. This will not be the same, even at a small market like ours. People *will* talk, and you know gossip can spread over several towns.'

Maria took a deep breath, not backing down from the intensity of his stare. 'I'm aware of that too.'

He leaned further in, his face going past hers and down to her ear, where he whispered, 'I don't know if I can stop pretending once we're behind closed doors again. It's already so difficult not to touch you.'

His voice was almost a growl as she turned her head to look at him again, seeing the fire raging within her stomach reflected in his eyes, the desire she'd convinced herself had been a figment of her imagination blazing in them—along with a promise of pleasure that had her curling her toes in her shoes.

'I might not want you to stop pretending.'

Rafael's mouth twitched, the corners of his lips quirking as if he couldn't believe she had just said that. Hell, she couldn't believe she had just said that either. Not once in her life had she been so brazen, no man ever catching enough of her attention to be worth stopping for him. Other things had always taken precedent—her studies, her career, her family.

And even this thing between them had only happened because she was trying to save her family's legacy, no matter the cost. But, in the process, this had also turned into something for her. A tentative permission to forget about caution, to give in to that tiny spark that glowed with delight inside her chest every time Rafael looked at her.

Even if this wasn't real, what if they pretended just for a few hours that it was? What was the worst that could happen? They both knew where this would end, knew where they'd get off the ride. So maybe she could let herself sink just a bit deeper into this thing with Rafael.

Rafael's hand came up to her face, but stopped just shy of touching her, leaving a phantom of his touch on her skin that exploded a yearning for more through her body. 'Maria, I don't know if this is a good idea. What if—'

The rest of his sentence got cut off when Maria stood up, diminishing the space between them to virtually nothing, and then snaked an arm around his neck to pull him closer, sliding her lips over his in a kiss that she'd been longing for since his mouth brushed so gently over her cheek in Manaus two weeks ago.

Fourteen days of pent-up desire and sexually charged

energy that culminated in this one kiss she pressed on his lips.

Rafael tensed for a moment as her hand came to a rest on his broad chest, and she thought he would pull away, that she had somehow managed to misread the signs of mutual attraction arcing between them since the day he'd started at her clinic.

But then he relaxed, his arms coming around her waist and his hands roaming up her back to press her closer to him in a crushing hug that confirmed what she hardly dared to believe to be true—that he was feeling this too and, more importantly, that he *wanted* this as well.

The kiss was almost the polar opposite of the kiss in the courthouse. Where their first kiss had been tentative and shy, a mere whisper of the attraction between them, nothing more than a piece of performative art as they began their journey as a fake couple, this one was all tongue and teeth and weeks of repressed desire bubbling to the surface in an explosion of passion that had them both catching their breath.

Maria moaned against his lips when he slid his hands through her hair, pulling her head back to deepen the kiss. Her fingers roamed over his back, searching for anything to hold on to as her mind was set adrift with the onslaught of sensation, each part of her body reacting to everything that was Rafael.

Everything she'd wanted to have for the last three and a half months. How could she have ever doubted that she was making this up in her head? That being around him would ever be enough without possessing a piece of him that was only hers?

She gasped when his mouth left hers, the brief emptiness she felt there soon replaced with the kisses he lavished on her skin, making his way down to her neck and licking along the column of her throat in a primal, possessive move that had her knees trembling.

The sound of the animals around them drifted to the back of her mind, leaving every one of her senses focused on Rafael and the fire that his touch left in its wake, each part of her body pliant and ready to submit to the desire that had finally escaped its tight cage.

Kissing Maria was better than he remembered—and so much better than he'd ever thought it could be. Though the kiss at the courthouse had everything to do with why he was here now, kissing her like the essence of life lay on her lips and he was all but one breath away from fading away, he'd sworn it was only for performance. That this would never happen again—could not happen again.

Because giving in to his desire for her was selfish. It was what he wanted with every fibre of his being, but from speaking to her he knew that this was not what she wanted. No, she wanted the fairy tale romance, a man who would bring joy and sunshine into her life—not one who was plagued with darkness the way he was.

He was being *so* selfish.

The thought barely managed to surface in his consciousness as his lips trailed down her neck, his nose nestling below her collar and breathing in her scent. She smelled divine, like the rainforest, sweet and earthy.

The strangled gasps dropping from her lips as his hand slipped up her thighs to caress her butt made Rafael hard, the ache originating from his chest extending through the rest of his body. He wanted to have her so badly, wanted to be the kind of person she needed in her life.

'Stop,' Maria said, and every muscle in his body went rigid at that command.

He withdrew from her a moment later, the clouds of passion filling his mind receding as he leaned back, chest still heaving from what had just happened. Maria was in a similar state, her breath leaving her nose in strained huffs that spoke of the desire he felt mirrored in his own body.

She looked straight at him, her eyes dark and filled with longing, bringing the already heated blood in his body to a near boil.

'Are we doing this tomorrow?' she asked, and Rafael had to take several breaths as his mind tried to catch up.

'What?'

'I need to know if you want to come with me. Be a part of the video,' Maria said, seemingly picking up their conversation where they'd left it before control had fully slipped Rafael's grasp and he'd given in to the need that had been bubbling in him since he'd arrived here.

'I… Did I just zone out for a moment and the last ten minutes didn't happen?' He looked down at her face, his eyes catching on her full dark lips, still swollen from their no-holds-barred kiss.

Maria seemed to notice his eyes drifting downward for her hand came up to her mouth, as if she also needed to confirm the phantom of his kiss still lingering there.

'I have two nieces, a sister and a fake husband who live with me. So I'm not exactly…available to do as I please right now,' she said in a low tone, each word chosen with such deliberation as if she was rethinking them as she spoke. 'But tomorrow the kids are at sleepovers and Celine is working. So… I will have the house to myself. *Ourselves.*'

Rafael paused, his brain still wholly focused on her full

lips and the blood pooling in his lower body that it took him a moment to catch up. 'Oh… Oh.'

Maria had thought enough about him to devise this plan when an opportunity arose—both professionally, with the idea of the video, and arranging for them to be alone.

That thought should have struck terror in his heart, because it sounded like so much more commitment than he could give. She had made a plan with him. Plans. Those were for available people, not him, who had to look over his shoulder every waking hour of the day, who had moved into the heart of the rainforest to be as far away from his family and their drama as he possibly could.

Here, he had found his community and a woman who completely took his breath away, and she was now offering something he'd been dreaming about since his lips had first touched hers. The culmination of all their secret looks, sly touches and the ruse they had devised to save her business from ruin.

Rafael knew the wise thing to do here would be to decline, keep his distance and leave as soon as he transferred the money over to her. A smart man would do exactly that. Hell, he should probably already be interviewing for new positions, not lusting over a woman he knew he couldn't have.

Yet everything about her just made him want to yield. Yield to her talent, her compassion, to her stunning beauty.

'Nothing about our situation has changed, Maria,' he forced himself to say, his voice betraying the huskiness their kiss had stirred inside him.

He watched her carefully, looking for any sign that she, too, had grown too attached. Did this invitation mean she wanted more from him, felt a similar yearning in her own chest? But her expression didn't alter, the only sign of nervousness her hands as she intertwined her fingers.

'I don't mean to change our relationship or the terms of our agreement. You have shown incredible generosity towards me and the animals we care for. Far more than I could ask for,' she said with a steady voice that didn't quite reflect what they had just done. 'This...invitation is something that exists outside of that. Something that has nothing to do with our deal and won't interfere with our plans.'

She dropped her eyes to her hands for a moment, then raised them again, the intense fire of passion in them inflaming his own need to be with this woman. He couldn't stop himself from leaning in, his head tilting back down towards her until their noses rubbed against each other. Then his lips brushed over hers in a tentative kiss, more exploring than passionate, as if to gauge her reaction.

Did she guess he planned to leave once the money arrived? Was that why she'd suggested what sounded like casual sex to act out what both had fantasised about for the last few months?

And he was leaving, so what was the harm?

'As long as we're clear that this isn't going to become anything more,' he said, and pulled her into another kiss, his tongue darting over her closed lips as if to underline his words.

'Crystal-clear,' she mumbled against his lips, and that was enough for Rafael to let go of his restraint once more.

His hand slipped along her spine and down to the small of her back, pressing her closer to him as his mouth claimed hers once more, putting all the desire and unfulfilled longing into this one kiss in the hope that it would serve to take the edge off…whatever this was that he felt for her. This unrelenting need to just *be* around her.

When Maria separated their lips with another huff that spoke of the fire burning within her—burning for *him*—he fully let go of her and stood up to bring some distance between them. If he let himself sink back into that kiss, he knew he wouldn't stop until they were both spent right here on the floor of her beloved clinic. Not the place he'd imagined when he'd thought about sleeping with her.

And he'd thought about that far more than he cared to admit.

'So tomorrow at the usual time?' he asked, his voice dropping by an octave.

'Yes,' she said, and he noted with a strange male satisfaction that this time her voice did waver, as if their kiss had left her rattled.

It certainly had left him catching his breath.

'I'd better go before I…' He left the sentence hanging in the air when the words eluded him. Before he dragged her down on the floor and made her scream with pleasure?

Even though they had agreed to do just that, it felt strange to say it so openly when most of their attraction had been conveyed non-verbally until now. Something he realised now that he had quite enjoyed, not wanting to spoil those moments with unnecessary words.

'I'll see you tomorrow,' she said with a smile that almost made him turn back to make good on the fantasy of having her right now, and he forced himself, with the last shreds of his willpower, to leave, having done none of the administrative work he'd planned on doing when he'd come here.

CHAPTER SEVEN

THE AIR BETWEEN Maria and Rafael was so thick she could almost grasp it with her bare hands. She wanted to blame it on the humidity of another midmorning in the rainforest rather than what lay between them. She had spent a restless night. Memories of their intense kiss had chased away worries about what to expect from today—what would happen tonight.

Celine had dragged her out of bed early so she could record a video of her feeding Lia. The way she had focused on her had Maria worried, but her sister guaranteed that it would be an eye-catching clip that would help them find a new donor.

Showing Maria and Rafael as a family had been her idea as well, which had surprised Maria. She'd come around to the idea of her fake marriage a lot faster than expected if she was already scheming on how to make the best out of this situation. Though she could see the value in it all—and at this point she was willing to try *anything* to find a new donor—the thought of being so openly affectionate with Rafael sent nervous flutters through her entire system.

What if they weren't convincing? Were they risking too much just to get some video footage of them holding hands while strolling through the town square?

Her stomach flipped over when Rafael reached out and placed his arm around her waist to pull her closer as they walked down the road to their destination. She looked up at him and saw none of the nervous energy fizzing within her reflected in his face. He'd slipped into the role of her husband without much effort—or was he just really good at hiding it?

'You look beautiful today,' he said with a smile that was so genuine that her breath caught in her throat.

Had anyone looked at her like that—ever? There was a nagging suspicion that she liked Rafael simply because he gave her the attention she had always rejected because she was waiting for *the one*—the person she wanted to make her family with. It was a thought so dear and intrinsic to her as a person that she had rejected casual dating or one-night stands, as she believed they would cheapen the connection she sought.

As the official head of their family charity she'd soon realised that she had to put everything she was and had into this to be successful. Her dream of finding the person to spend the rest of her life with would have to wait—or they would have to understand that helping these animals would be a big part of their shared lives.

Something Rafael definitely understood.

The thought scared her to her core, so she looked at him to distract herself. 'Thank you,' she replied with a small smile and leaned into his touch, wrapping her arm around him as well.

Hunger blazed in his dark eyes that tracked her every move as she swallowed, the same need setting her blood alight. Anticipation mingled with an unnamed fear of what they had promised each other for tonight.

They would play the part of the newlywed couple for

the entire village to see. A risk that they had to take if they wanted to get the most attention in what little time the institute had been able to give her. With such a large audience of wealthy benefactors attending their event, she absolutely needed to go above and beyond to catch people's attention.

If that meant pretending in front of everyone that they were in love, then so be it. It was an act that came to her easier and easier as time passed, as if she was absorbing the role into her flesh and simply living it. Though she knew that wasn't an option—Rafael had said so on more than one occasion.

And while the unbridled desire she saw written in his eyes made her wet in anticipation, it also caused her heart to beat faster for him. How was she supposed to stop that when the fate of her charity was tied to this man and her pretending to be in love with him?

The mumbling of a gathered crowd drifted towards their ears and when they rounded the corner they saw a small collection of people milling around the town square.

'You ready for this?' he asked as he turned to her.

Maria nodded, parting her lips to reply, but before she could do so Rafael stopped and leaned down. His hand slipped onto her cheek, pulling her up towards him as he brushed a short but indulgent kiss onto her lips that made the words die in her throat.

'You okay?' he asked as they approached the crowd.

She looked up to him, wondering if she could sense a different kind of tension rippling through her body. One that had nothing to do with sex, but something much more primal, much deeper. The kernel of a truth she would fight until the bitter end, because letting it take root meant she would be doomed.

'Yeah…' she breathed, then looked to the front as they stepped into the milling crowd.

Like every Sunday, different vendors—both local and from the surrounding villages—had gathered on Santarém's spacious town square to set up their stalls. Several vendors were showing off their fresh produce, homemade cosmetics, cakes, honey, and Maria spotted a new person who was selling her crochet blankets and other accessories.

On the other side of the vendors were food trucks with people already queueing to get their early lunch served.

And, weaving in and out of the crowd, Maria spotted her sister, phone held out in front of her as she captured the entire scene. She paused in her tracks when she panned over to them, and Maria was suddenly hyperaware of every single point where her body touched his.

Celine narrowed her eyes at them, then continued on her way.

'Well…she certainly can't wait to find a new donor for us,' she mumbled, astonished at her sister's eagerness.

Rafael chuckled, and she was glad he wasn't taking Celine's behaviour as an insult. 'I don't see her here often. Or at all, really. Did you come here by yourself before I came along?'

Maria nodded. 'My parents used to bring us here every Sunday before they retired and moved to Switzerland. Celine stopped going shortly after. I always assumed it was because she was only doing it for them.'

'Why did your parents move so far away? Isn't Switzerland really cold most of the year?' He shuddered, drawing a laugh from her with his theatrics.

'It's a strange story, to be honest,' she said, turning around enough for his hand to slip off her waist. She reached out to grab his hand, then pointed at one of the coffee carts. 'Even though my mother loves all sorts of animals, she loves rabbits the most. So much that she developed a reputation as a rabbit specialist throughout the country and people would bring their bunnies here for really complicated cases. Unfortunately, she was also *very* allergic to rabbits.

'But she didn't let herself be deterred by that, to the point where she had stressed her lungs so much with the exposure to them that she was left with respiratory problems. They always wanted to go and see Switzerland—it just seems like the polar opposite of what they had here. But when they realised how good the mountain air and low humidity was for her lungs, they decided to retire there.'

She paused when they got to the front of the queue to order their drinks.

Emanuel, the proprietor of the local café, started their order and heat rose to Maria's cheeks when he did a double take, his gaze dipping down to where their hands were intertwined.

'*Deus*, are you telling me that you two are finally...? Did you see Tina already? She is going to be over the moon to hear this,' the bearded man said, and Maria had to swallow the denial bubbling up in her throat.

She shot a sideways glance at Rafael, but if he was as panicked as her about the first comment about their fake relationship he didn't let it show. Instead, he smiled, raising her hand to his mouth and placing a gentle kiss on it.

'I knew the moment I arrived here,' he said with a smile so genuine that it took her breath away.

'People have been rooting for you two, you know that?' Emanuel said as he ground the coffee beans for their order. Years of experience meant that he didn't even have to look at his hands to know what he was doing.

'They have?' Maria's eyes went wide as the man nodded with eager excitement.

The *whole town* knew about her feelings for Rafael, and they were rooting for her? Had she really been that obvious? Sweat began coating her hand as the nervous energy around their outing today burst free from its restraints.

Rafael wrapped his hand around hers a bit tighter, shooting her a soft smile that mixed with the unease rising within her, plunging her insides into even more chaos.

'How is Rex? Did he recover from his food poisoning?' he asked to change the topic.

Rex was the dog they had treated some weeks ago when he ate some chocolate he wasn't supposed to. The man nodded with a grateful smile, the love for his pet obvious for everyone to see.

'He is much better, and now we have a new lock on the pantry so he won't be able to sneak in there,' he said, and handed over their coffee order to them. 'Seriously, please go find my wife and say hi. She's probably going to ask for a deposit for a wedding cake the moment she sees you.'

Maria swallowed as the words sunk in. They were acting like a couple, but the fact that they were actually married remained a secret. How would the people in the village react once they found out?

The nervous flutter in her stomach almost made her spill her coffee, her hand gripping Rafael's for support. He glanced at her, his expression one of calm and coolness and completely unlike the turmoil she was experiencing. Where were the nerves of steel she had honed through so many emergency situations when she desperately needed them?

She didn't have any time to further contemplate, for when they turned around to leave the coffee cart a trio of old ladies stood in front of them like a panel of judges—which was quite the apt description for them as they often served as Maria's judges whenever they put on a silly animal show for the village pets.

'Bom dia, senhoras,' Rafael greeted them with a smile so dazzling, all the women—Maria included—swooned at the sight.

'Well, if it isn't Santarém's most eligible bachelorette and her new squeeze,' Angélica, the leader of the troop of old ladies, said with a smile on her face.

Maria blushed, visible enough it seemed, for the ladies giggled while shooting each other knowing glances. How fast had this news spread? Emanuel couldn't have worked that fast, they'd left his stand but a minute ago.

'We're—' she began, but was interrupted by Lucinda waving a hand at her.

'Oh, you don't have to say anything, querida. We've known this was going to happen for quite some time. We're happy for you, right, ladies?' She looked around to her companions, who nodded eagerly.

'I mean... I might have been entertaining the thought myself for a while there. My dear José always said I should find love again. But I don't think he meant that to be while he was still alive,' Elisabete, the last one in the trio, quipped, and the other two laughed with her.

'If I run afoul of José, who will take care of my dry cleaning?' Rafael replied with an indulgent smile, at which Elisabete blushed.

Then he turned his gaze towards Maria, his hand releasing hers to snake around her waist and pulling her closer into his side.

'As it turns out, I found what I wanted right at home,' he said, and heat exploded through her entire body when he leaned in to feather a light kiss onto her temple.

The three *senhoras* sighed, giving him the reaction he'd undoubtedly wanted. Maria wasn't sure, for her brain had temporarily stalled as she processed what he'd said. He'd found what he wanted right here? Was he serious about that? No, he couldn't be. Falling in love was not a part of their agreement and whatever he said today wasn't real either. They were playing a role, and Rafael was simply better at it.

A thought that gave her pause. Either he was really good at pretending or she was terrible at seeing his behaviour for what it was—an act. Neither option boded well for her when she had invited Rafael to her place tonight because of what he'd said at the clinic yesterday— how hard it was for him *not* to touch her. Was that true or just part of the act?

They spent the next hour walking around the farmers' market the way they usually did, with only one key difference. Now people kept approaching them to express their happiness that they had finally become a couple— something Maria had been unprepared for. That meant that *everyone* had noticed her feelings for him develop. Everyone but her, apparently.

Rafael, meanwhile, gossiped and laughed with everyone who approached them, none of her own nervous energy showing in his interactions. It was the first time she noticed how seamlessly he'd integrated into the community of her tiny village. Everyone was just so…happy to see them together.

When they finally got to sit down with two plates from a new food truck claiming to sell authentic gyro wraps, Maria was too exhausted to dwell on what had just happened—how readily everyone had accepted their romance as genuine. This was something she needed to think about later, when she wasn't starving.

Celine sat two tables away with Nina and Mirabel, in an attempt to give them the privacy a newly formed couple might want from their first date in town. Maria's heart softened as she watched her two nieces share a slice of cake from Tina's stand while talking to each other animatedly enough that their voices drifted over to them.

'It's the first time I've seen Mirabel here at the market,' Rafael said when he noticed her gaze drift towards her family.

The smile that had just been pulling on her lips faded. 'She used to come here with her father. When he left, she didn't show any interest in joining us and I didn't want to force it on her...' she said, her voice trailing off at the thought of her brother.

Rafael's eyes narrowed, his expression turning thunderous at her words. 'He never asks about her? No calls or texts?'

She shook her head. 'No, he's not been in touch since he left. We tried to contact him, wanted to arrange a truce, if only he would come back to see his daughter and be a part of her life again. Surely whatever this woman could offer him wasn't enough to abandon his child like that.'

Maria's hands curled into fists as she went on. 'I still can't believe my brother could do such a thing. I don't know what I would have done without Celine's help. We went through her pregnancy together, and I was the one who played the second parent role for Nina. So raising a child together isn't anything new for us...but, even then, we didn't know how we should...explain to Mirabel what happened. I mean, how do you explain that to a twelve-year-old?'

Her breath shook as she inhaled and a moment later Rafael's hand was wrapped around hers, leaving a sensation so warm and right she didn't want to imagine life without it. In moments like these she sought the comfort of a man's support, to help her through life just by standing by her side.

A dream that had lain dormant in her chest until Rafael had arrived in her life, sweeping her off her feet. Only what they had wasn't real either, no matter how she felt.

'What did your parents think about that? Did they ever come back to talk to him?'

Maria dropped her gaze down to her food, pulling at the soft pita bread without any intention of eating it. 'No,' she finally said as she looked back up. 'Celine and I debated whether to tell them, but in the end we didn't say a word about anything. They would upend their lives and come back here immediately. Neither of us want that for them, especially with how much our mother struggles with her asthma.'

'Mirabel's lucky to have you, you know that?' he said as he got up, circled around the table and sat down on the same bench as her so he could pull her into his arms.

'I'm not so sure about it,' she replied, letting insecurities she'd never shared with anyone bubble to the surface for him to see. 'I wasn't able to attract a new sponsor in time to keep the doors open.'

A gentle chuckle shook his chest, vibrating through Maria's bones as she remained pressed against him.

'But you did, just not in the traditional way you'd hoped to. You took on the burden to marry me and go along with my ruse to buy your charity more time. Not many people would be able to give so much of themselves to save their legacy.'

'Being married to you can hardly be called a burden.'

The words left her mouth before she could think better of them, flowing over her lips and into existence, sharing a piece of her that she had not intended to show him. Rafael stiffened under her hands, his muscles tensing in a foreboding way that struck dread in her heart.

Why had she said that? When she'd been the one to tell him that she would keep things separate, that their deal remained the same?

'What I mean—' she began to explain, but was interrupted by a familiar voice calling Rafael's name.

'Rafael, quickly!' Tina, Emanuel's wife and the baker of the village, urged when she came to a stop next to their table, her cheeks red and her chest heaving from exertion.

'What happened?' he asked as he and Maria jumped to their feet, a wary glance passing between them.

'I asked my daughter to bring some of the cardboard into the waste-disposal area. She asked me to come back with her when she heard a sound and we found something abandoned in a box.'

Her expression was distraught, telling Maria everything she needed to know. If Tina was this concerned about the contents of a cardboard box, it could only be an abandoned animal.

The day had been the sweetest agony Rafael had ever put himself through. Being so close to Maria was intoxicating, every fibre of him that had been screaming for him to touch her as if she was his to touch finally satisfied as they'd walked around the town square.

Their outing had taken a sharp turn when they found a

mother cat and her entire litter abandoned in a cardboard box among some other garbage. They'd rushed back to the clinic with their patients, and he was now examining the tortoiseshell cat with a soft and cautious grip.

'Who does something like that? Throwing away a cat and her babies as if they were no more than trash,' Maria said beside him.

When they'd tried to separate the kittens from their mother so they could give them a health check they had quickly realised that the cat was too nervous to be separated just yet. To avoid putting more stress on her, Maria had taken a step back and was observing and giving Rafael the space he needed to gain the cat's trust.

He sat down on a stool he'd pushed all the way to the exam table, remaining close enough to the cat for her to pick up his scent, but far enough so she wouldn't feel threatened.

'We don't know that someone dropped her off. This might be a stray that got comfortable in this box. From looking at her, she might have been there a day or two. She doesn't look malnourished, but she gave birth on her own without any supervision.' He glanced at the remnants of the cardboard box lying on the floor. 'They might have put her in there before she gave birth. Would explain the exhaustion I'm seeing in her.'

Her tortoiseshell pattern was a mixture of cream, dark brown and a blueish black splashed on her entire body in a chaotic pattern that was unique to this cat. His heart squeezed, both at the injustice of just being left in a cardboard box next to some rubbish, and also...

'She reminds me of my nanny's barn cat. It's the same cream colour, though the pattern was much different. I wonder if this one here is just as clingy as Donna. The moment I got on the farm, she wouldn't leave my side—would even try to climb into the car with me when it was time to leave.' He chuckled at the memory he'd long since forgotten. Even though his parents had been too busy chasing a dream that would never come true, his childhood had been more than that. He'd at least had Camila to look out for him, teach him about the farm animals and what his life could be if he applied himself.

'Does she have a chip?' Maria asked from behind him.

'I don't know.' He pushed the chair back and opened a drawer behind him, retrieving the scanner they used to scan the microchips some owners used for their pets. They contained important information about how to contact them in case their pet got lost.

He swiped the scanner over the cat to try to locate a chip, but the scanner didn't react—nor did the computer that would automatically search the country-wide database for a match.

'Doesn't look like it,' he said, putting the scanner down.

'Well…we can put her pictures up on our social media pages, but if no one claims her we can keep her and the babies until they are old enough to find new homes. Alexander won't mind.'

Rafael whirled around in his chair to look at her, his eyebrows raised. 'You would let me keep this cat in your house?'

The smile that spread over her face as he asked the question was so genuine and pure it took any remaining breath out of his lungs. He hadn't said much about the fond memories of his past, not much of the bitter ones either. Because opening up to her meant guiding her to a place he'd never shown anyone else in his life. But it seemed he didn't even have to open himself to her. Maria understood him intuitively, without any friction or tension. She knew when to stay close, when to let go and when to just be there.

How had he let this go so far? She was not meant to be this person for him who made his heart beat so much faster.

'Of course. This arrangement between us might be fake, but you're still my friend. You say you want to keep her, let's do it,' Maria replied.

And, just like that, his heart tumbled out of rhythm, leaving him with a cold sensation spreading through his chest. This was a gesture of friendship—what else could it have been? Despite acknowledging that friendship was all that had ever been discussed between them himself, he couldn't ignore the icy grip of disappointment.

'Let's see if we can find out more about her,' he said to turn the conversation in a different direction.

When he moved his hand to touch the cat once more she twisted her head to look at him with bared teeth. Her ears were pressed flat to her head and a low hiss filled the air, making him take a step back to assess.

'She is too nervous for me to handle her. I don't know how long she's been in this box. She might be overstimulated and stressed.' He paused with a frown. 'I'd have to sedate her if we want to proceed.'

'Should I prepare some acepromazine?' Maria asked, getting to her feet.

Rafael looked the cat over once more, then shook his head. 'Without knowing anything else about her, acepromazine might already be too risky... Best to observe her for a few hours and then make a decision. Let's move her into a pen.'

Maria nodded, then opened a cupboard behind her and retrieved a bowl and a package of dried cat food.

'She must be hungry,' Maria said as she handed him the items.

Rafael poured the food into the bowl, then set it down in front of the cat. She sniffed at it for several moments, then with a shy and tentative bite took the offered food and chewed loudly on it before swallowing it.

'I'll go set up the pen,' Maria said, and left the exam room while Rafael stayed with the abandoned cat, observing her as she ate more of the food. When her ears popped back up and she no longer hissed when his hand came close to her, he felt confident enough to move her to the pen for observation.

Rafael was sitting in the back, watching the cat, when Maria stepped back in after checking in on some other patients that were staying with them. Instead of taking the seat next to him, she stood behind him so her stomach was touching his back and, in a far too intimate instinct, laid her hand on his shoulder. She breathed in his scent, the aroma of lavender calming her beating heart as she allowed herself this show of affection.

'How is she doing?' she asked as she watched him work.

'She's behaving fine. I don't see anything unusual. I think once she's had some time to recover we can give her an exam,' he said more to himself than to her as he cocked his head to one side.

Maria shifted her hand to lay more on his back as he bent down to look into the pen, and a moment later the door swung open. Celine stepped in, dressed in scrubs and the bag with all her equipment swung over her shoulder.

Her eyes rounded when she saw them, then narrowed in an expression Maria knew meant nothing good. They would have to talk about this once they had a moment to themselves.

'I caught you finding the cats on camera. Let me take some footage of her resting so that I can include the happy ending as well. Pretend like you are examining her.' She didn't wait for them to say anything, but rather dropped her bag on the floor and whipped out her phone. Celine hovered over the cat and the kittens for a few seconds, then she panned upwards and urged Rafael to continue with his observation with an impatient hand gesture.

Rafael furrowed his brow and glanced back at Maria, who had lifted her hand off his back but was still standing close enough to him to feel his heat radiating into her. She gave a small shrug.

'The kittens are eating well and she's no longer reacting negatively to my presence. Good sign. Means she is getting more comfortable,' he said, and shot a pointed look at Celine.

'I got all I needed, thank you. I'll cut it all together into a montage and upload it to the website and our social pages.' She paused for a moment, her eyes darting to the place where Maria and Rafael touched, before coming back up to look at her sister. 'You two be careful.'

She left and only those words remained hanging between them.

They stayed there for a while, watching the cat and her kittens settle in. When Rafael eventually turned to her his expression was veiled, but she sensed tension snap into place between them.

'Celine was right, you know. We need to be more careful, or next time it might not be your sister who walks in on us. What if we had said something about our arrangement?' His gaze was dark when he looked at her, genuine concern etched into his features.

'You think they would break into my clinic to talk you into giving them money?' Maria asked, scepticism lacing her voice.

'You don't know the things these people have done in order to get me to hand over my money to them,' he ground out between clenched teeth, sending a clear signal for her to tread lightly.

But his tone didn't stop Maria. They had shared enough closeness, enough passion and affection that she was done letting him shut her out. She raised her chin and squared her shoulders as she said, 'Then tell me.'

He opened his mouth but no words came out. Then Rafael reached around her waist, tucking her closer into a blissful embrace.

Maria's heart slammed against her sternum in an attempt to escape her body when Rafael pulled her into a hug that melted all the anxiety this day had summoned in her. All except one—and she was so certain that he wouldn't tell her about what had happened to him that she let her mind drift to what was waiting for her once they'd wrapped up here. Celine had left, taking the kids to their friends' house. It would be just them and...

Maybe this wasn't a good idea, after all. Though they had agreed that their desire for each other—and the decision to take their attraction to the final step—existed outside of their agreement, something inside her balked at the idea that he withheld so much of himself when she'd exposed so much more of herself than she had intended to.

Or was this the reason why she should be comfortable sleeping with him? Because, unlike her, he had not developed a deeper bond and didn't want to change their friendship. Otherwise, he'd have said something by now, no? Maybe he was saving them a lot of heartache down the line by keeping her at arm's length.

'I used to be engaged to a woman named Laura,' Rafael said, and she held her breath, not daring to say anything as he surprised her by replying.

'We were set up by a mutual friend, and I didn't think anything of it. At this point my parents had already tried to get me to marry the daughter of the CEO of another media company so they could benefit from this connection. Their hope was to combine resources so they could take advantage of his success.' He stopped, his chin coming to rest on top of her head, his heat sinking through the soft fabric of her dress and into her skin.

'I refused, like I refused many other matches they thrust my way, until they finally stopped bothering me. Though I should have known better, I thought I had refused them enough for them to give up. And then I met Laura, and it seemed to me that a lot of things in life suddenly made sense.'

Pain bloomed inside her chest as his voice revealed a hurt edge, mingled with regret. As if he lamented how things had ended between them. But how *had* it ended?

Maria didn't dare to ask, on the off-chance that it made him retreat again when he was finally sharing with her. So she let her hands roam over his back instead, each stroke calming and urging him to shed the defences she sensed around him.

'I fell for her in a matter of weeks—each time I met her bringing me closer to the conclusion that I had met my soulmate. The love of my life. For the first time, I thought maybe I could have this magical thing too. And so I asked her to marry me when we had our six-month anniversary. I had met the one person I was meant to spend the rest of my life with, so why wait, right?'

The hurt lacing his voice turned to bitterness, and Maria clung to him even harder, as if her touch could soothe the edge of those unwanted feelings resurfacing as he recalled those memories.

'One evening I dropped by my parents' house. Her car was in the driveway, which was strange because she knew how strained my relationship with them was. Still, back then I gave her the benefit of the doubt, thought she might have been there to mend fences. She had been urging me to bury the hatchet and, again, I didn't question it. Of course, she just wanted us all to be one happy family, the way we are taught to value family.'

He paused to let out a huff of contention. 'I got as far as the door before I heard Laura and my mother's raised voices filter through the open window.'

A small gasp escaped Maria's lips when his grip around her tightened, his head above her moving. A moment later his soft breath grazed the crown of her head as his hands swept up and down her arms. The closeness they shared wrapped them in their own little bubble, tuning out the noise of the animals around them.

Rafael continued. 'My mother was asking Laura to convince me to move up the date of the wedding since they needed money right now. The idiot that I was, I still believed that my mother had lured her there under some false pretence, to pressure her in a way she knew she couldn't pressure me.

'But then Laura said it had taken her so much effort getting me to this point in the first place, she wasn't going to risk all of their payout just because my parents were getting impatient. "A few more months and then it's ours, and you'll get what you hired me to do." That was what she said.'

Maria's eyes went wide, her hand darting to her mouth, where she pressed it against her lips as the puzzle pieces regarding Rafael's stalwart defences fell into place. She couldn't help but raise her head to stare at him, her mind reeling from such a cruel betrayal.

'She…pretended to be in love with you for the money?' she finally asked when he remained quiet, his expression hewn out of stone.

'Since they hadn't been able to convince me to marry their choice of woman, they decided to sneak someone into my life instead. That was the moment I learned that I would never have love and marriage the way other people did, because the trust money would always ruin it. My parents, my siblings—their decisions were guided by profit, by what would help them succeed in this business they knew nothing about, so they could chase my grandparents' fame. And that was also the kind of people they attracted into their lives.' He shook his head, a rough, humourless laugh dropping from his lips that almost made her flinch in his arms.

'While my grandparents had the best intentions for us, they ended up cursing everyone with that clause in the trust fund. My siblings with unhappy marriages, and me to an eternity alone. Because of them, I will never know if someone is with me for myself or for the money they know I have waiting for me.'

'That can't be true. I—' She stopped herself from finishing that sentence when she realised where it was heading. Maria's interest in him, the connection that had formed way before they'd come up with their marriage ruse, had not been based on money but on genuine affection—on their friendship.

But how could she say that when she'd married him for the money as well? Was she any better than Laura, entering a fake marriage with him so she could save her own business?

Rafael shook his head, reading the thoughts reflected on her face. 'I entered this arrangement with my eyes wide open. Love was never part of the equation here, and we will separate with our dignity and hearts intact.'

Maria swallowed as doubt crept into her, its cold tendrils reaching across her body and settling in the pit of her stomach in an icy pool of blackness. Would her heart survive this, when it was already breaking for him?

She forced herself to nod, not feeling the confidence that gesture conveyed, and, by the look of scepticism on Rafael's face, he might not really believe her either.

'Thank you for listening to me. I've never told anyone this story,' he said, then he grabbed her hand and pressed it over his mouth, pressing a gentle kiss onto her palm.

A gesture that told her everything his words couldn't. That he wasn't scared she would break his heart like Laura had because, even though he liked and desired her, he would never love her. Would never let himself get so close to someone again because of what had happened to him.

And even though Maria knew that this should be a relief—because she didn't want to be with someone who didn't want the same out of life as her—a traitorous part of her heart broke off, shattering into tiny pieces as the far-fetched possibilities she had envisioned with Rafael scattered into the wind, along with the hope that maybe their connection was real, was more than just physical attraction.

Leaving her with a sense of sadness that she'd need to process once their divorce was through in a couple of months. But, until then, she would let herself have this one small piece of Rafael that he'd offered her and be glad of it, even if it wasn't what she truly wanted from him.

She could have tonight, at least.

So she swallowed the welling sensation of deep loss, locking it away inside her, and focused instead on what she knew he wanted of her—some physical closeness that existed outside and was removed from their fake marriage arrangement and her increasingly complicated feelings for this man.

'I think Mama and her babies are settled in. Do you want to get out of here?' she asked, and the dark gleam in his eyes as she said those words almost managed to push the doubts and longing for more away as he smiled at her, his face all male seduction and intensity.

'Let's.'

CHAPTER EIGHT

RAFAEL WAS IN deep trouble. He'd suspected that from the first moment he'd walked into Maria's clinic and been unable to take his eyes off her. And over the months they'd interacted with each other the innocent friendship that had clicked into place when they'd met had evolved into something more tangible, more real, that infused his blood with new life. But he knew that he'd made a mistake, let things grow too far, get too comfortable, when his lips brushed over hers in a gesture that could barely be described as a kiss.

The idea to get fake married had been necessary even though he'd known it would be a struggle for him to keep detached. He'd had no chance of doing that when he was already so invested in the fate of this town, who had given him a home when he'd needed one. When his own family had pushed him away with their actions...

He had long since made peace with the fact that he would never have access to his fortune and that he'd gladly trade it to have a life away from the toxicity that was his family. And then Maria had confessed to being in trouble, and he'd *needed* to help her, knowing he would regret not doing so more than the sacrifice he knew waited at the end of this arrangement for him—he needed to leave. Despite that, there'd been no way he could stand by when he'd held the solution.

Because he wanted her—so bad that it was hard to breathe, impossible to think straight, to…remember why they could never be together.

The tension between them finally snapped when they walked upstairs to the door Rafael had been staring at with hidden longing ever since he'd moved into her house. She stepped over the threshold of her room—right where he needed her to be, to give in to this fantasy he'd been nurturing in his heart for so long.

'So Raf—'

The moment the door closed behind them, Rafael turned around and grabbed her by the waist, hauling this woman into his arms, his mouth crashing down on hers. Urgency unlike any he'd ever felt before gripped him, his hands roaming over her body as the need to explore every inch erupted in him.

Maria went soft and pliant in his arms, leaning into the touch with a soft moan that rippled through him in a tidal wave of heat and ice, creating a storm in his chest that threatened to break loose and take him with it.

He wanted to pause, to go slow and savour every moment of this one night they had. Because one night was all they were going to get. One night to live like this thing between them was real. But the primal part of his brain had taken control of his body, urging him to let go of his final hesitation when the woman he cherished and longed for lay in his arms.

A deep peach colour dusted her high cheekbones as he pulled away from Maria to look at her. Her lips were parted in a soft sigh, her eyes ablaze with the same intensity rocking through his own body. His hand came to rest on her cheek, his thumb brushing over her heated skin.

'Sorry, I interrupted you. That was impolite,' he said, his voice all thunder and gravel with barely restrained need.

'I...' Maria blinked twice before a tentative smile spread across her lips. 'I don't think I remember what I wanted to say. This is better than talking anyway.'

Then she leaned forward, lush mouth pressing onto his as she gave him silent permission to continue, her eagerness such a turn-on that his blood rushed to the lower half of his body and he gave a muffled groan. His hand slipped into her hair, cradling the back of her head as he pulled her deeper into their kiss, his tongue sweeping over her lips and begging for entry.

Maria sighed into his mouth, a sound filled with longing and pleasure that set his entire skin ablaze. Then she opened her mouth to his tongue, and what he'd thought to be everything his body had to offer intensified again, bringing him to a higher plane of existence as she met his every stroke with the same urgency and need.

'*Deus*, Rafael...' she whispered when they broke apart, her chest heaving as she caught her breath.

He kissed her again, gentler this time, a mere brush on her passion-swollen lips, before he moved down to nuzzle her neck. The scent of earth and flowers filled his nose, sending a renewed wave of pleasure through his system as he breathed in again. He wanted to remember this scent for the rest of his life. It was the fragrance that drifted through the clinic whenever he arrived in the morning, mixing with the quiet longing that he had nurtured in his chest despite knowing better.

If this should be the one night they had with one another, he would make it count.

The world around Maria faded away as her senses homed in on Rafael and where their bodies touched. There was no bedroom around them, the soft carpet only a faint sensation as her toes curled into it. There was only him and the touch she'd hungered for since she had first admitted her attraction towards the new vet all these months ago.

Now his fingers were tracing down her side and with it soft trembles that left her mouth in shaky sighs. How was she going to survive this exquisite torture, where every touch, every breath grazing her skin hurt in the most pleasurable way?

His teeth scraped over the sensitive skin of her neck, his hands slipping lower and lower until they rested on her butt. The fabric of her summer dress rustled, the only sound in the room outside of her soft moans as Rafael explored her body at his leisure, seemingly in no hurry to get the clothes blocking them out of their way.

Rafael's hands slipped back up, trailing to the front of her body, where his fingertips grazed over her breasts as his mouth dipped further down to kiss her collarbone.

'Tell me what you want, *amor*,' he whispered against her skin as his hands moved further, settling right next to her zip.

He chuckled against her neck when she arched her back, pushing against him with her hips. 'You,' she replied, feeling his considerable length straining against her.

Deus, were they really going to do this? Unbridled need mingled with a low simmering panic at the prospect of sleeping with Rafael, letting him see her as hardly anyone had ever seen her. It had been years since her last time, so long that every touch had her sensitive and yearning for more.

But, instead of continuing downward, Rafael brought his face back up to hers, his nose gently stroking the side of her own. 'I want to know what you like, Maria,' he said before he kissed her again, her knees shaking from the unending gentleness of his kiss.

What she liked? That question had never factored into any intimate moment she'd had so far—which wasn't a lot to begin with. Had no one ever asked her this question before? She'd not been with a man in two years, and before that her relationships had been few and far between.

The fire in her dampened, making way for insecure confusion as her eyes slowly drifted back into focus. The extent of her inexperience had never bothered her...until now.

'I...don't know what I like,' she finally admitted, and had to swallow the sigh of relief building in her throat when Rafael only smiled at her, before coming back in to steal another kiss off her lips.

'Let's try a few things and see if you like them. But you have to tell me what works for you and what doesn't.' His voice was deep, filled with gravel and promise that by the end of this night she would *definitely* know what she liked.

That tone alone sent a shockwave through her that settled in an agonisingly needy pinch right in her core. A shudder trickled down her spine, shaking her every limb. Rafael must have felt it as well. His smile turned pure male when his fingers finally grabbed her zip and pulled it down, exposing the skin of her back to the cool room.

Another shiver shook her when he peeled the dress forward as she took out her arms. Another tug and the dress glided down her body, pooling around her legs like a flowery puddle of water. Rafael took a small step back, enough for him to see her without having to let go of her hips. The hiss he let out as his eyes roamed over her bare breasts and the small black lace triangle that covered her sent a hot spear of pleasure through her.

The reverence in his expression was something she had never seen before, cascading goosebumps all over her skin as his hands slid back up, gently caressing her ribs before they palmed each of her breasts with a gentle squeeze that shot fireworks into the pit of her stomach.

'Good thing I didn't know how exposed you were underneath that dress or I wouldn't have been able to play the dutiful husband for you all day,' he said with a grin that caused her breath to hitch as images of him dragging her into the clinic's broom cupboard to bend her over flashed through her brain, making her dig her toes into the plush carpet.

'You are just...*perfeita*,' he murmured.

Maria opened her lips to say something, but only a strangled moan came out when Rafael brushed his thumb over her erect nipple.

His breathing became just as laboured as hers when he did it again, watching another moan build in her throat as her eyes squeezed shut and her body twitched under his touch. Heat rose to her cheeks, her hands digging into his shirt as if that would help her to hang onto reality as the room around her grew even dimmer.

She thought she was getting used to his touch, her skin less sensitive, until he dropped his head even lower and took one of her dark brown, taut nipples into his mouth. The universe around Maria shattered into a million pieces which all drifted away into nothingness. There was only her body and his, each touch so intentional and aimed to please her.

It wasn't like anything she'd ever experienced.

'Is this good for you?' he asked as he pressed his lips against the skin between her breasts, each word forming a kiss on its own.

'Yes...' she replied, barely able to get the affirmation out as his lips wandered over the swell of her breasts to the other nipple, repeating the delicious process with cruel slowness that left her shaky on her feet.

Maria's hands were still grasping at his shirt, pulling him closer despite the lack of space left between them. With each lick of his tongue her mind had drifted further away, the overthinking and worry about their future or what this meant for their arrangement floating away. Her lack of experience was only a small noise in the symphony that was Rafael's touch.

Her body took over as the worry vanished into nothingness, and her hands found the buttons on his shirt. Eyes still closed from the pleasure rippling through her, she felt down his chest, her fingers almost frantic in their quest to get rid of the fabric impeding her senses.

His lips vibrated as he chuckled again, teeth still scraping over her nipple as he rolled his tongue over it and sent a lightning bolt of tension and pleasure right to her core. The emptiness that followed when he let go of her was almost too much, and Maria instinctively pushed her chest out as if to reach for him.

'You want this gone?' Rafael grabbed both of her hands that were unbuttoning his shirt with a haste and greed that made his erection twitch in his pants.

Though he strained for release and wanted nothing

more than to entangle himself in the bedsheets with her, he forced himself to take it slow. Though she hadn't said anything explicit, the way she touched him spoke of something so special and innocent he wanted to ensure that their night together would be exactly what *she* wanted and nothing else. That she couldn't tell him what she liked was an indication of how selfish her lovers in the past must have been.

A thought he pushed away as his temper surged at that. How could anyone look at this woman without giving in to the urge to worship her for however long she pleased? If she was willing, he would do exactly that, no matter how much he himself ached.

Her eyes were ablaze with a want that made him swallow hard as his breath came out in ragged bursts. 'I want all of it gone,' she said, confidence ringing in her voice for the first time since they'd started making out.

He shot her a grin, lowering his head as if to sketch a bow. 'Tonight, your wishes are my command, *amor*,' he said in a low rumble before he loosened the remaining buttons and shrugged the shirt off.

Then his hand went onto his waistband, but Maria's hands clasped around his wrists before he could do anything.

'Let me,' she said, causing another twitch of his manhood as he anticipated her touch with an unbridled eagerness that almost made him burst on the spot.

Taking a deep breath, he nodded and watched with narrowed eyes as she unbuttoned his trousers, revealing his erection straining against the fabric of his underwear. The last barrier that stood between them.

She stared for a moment, her lower lip vanishing between her teeth as she looked at him, his desire for her on display for her to judge. Of course he reacted instantly to her touch when he'd longed for her from a distance for so long—spending long nights in solitude with nothing but his thoughts and her lingering scent to keep him entertained.

Rafael had been lost from the start, enthralled by her dedication and love towards her animals and the lives she saved every day. Who could resist such a powerful and sensual woman?

His thoughts scattered when she reached out with two fingers, tracing the outline of his length against the dark fabric of his briefs, smiling when she got a longing twitch as a response to her touch, begging her for more of her, more of everything.

'*Deus*, Maria...' he gritted out, and the appreciative laugh he received in return nestled its way into his chest and settled there, soft and warm. 'I've wanted this for so long.'

She looked at him, her eyelids heavy with the desire zipping between them. Her palm grazed over him again as she brought it upwards, then she grabbed his hand and guided it towards her front, where the tantalising lacy thong still covered her. With a smile lighting up her face, she pressed his hand against herself as she whispered, 'Me too.'

Rafael swore under his breath as dampness clung to his fingers that had soaked through the fabric. He'd known she wanted him, otherwise she wouldn't have invited him to her room. Yet somehow the confirmation of it, feeling her eagerness for him loosened all the restraints he had imposed on himself.

Slowness suddenly seemed like an unnecessary torture he'd agreed to put himself through. He needed to hear her pleasure. Now, or he might explode from all the sensation rioting in his body.

As he captured her mouth once more, he worked the fingers she had just placed on the apex of her thighs in a slow circle through the almost sheer fabric. Maria's reaction was instantaneous. Her hips bucked forward as his passionate kiss swallowed the drawn-out moan escaping her throat. Her head lolled backwards as he continued, her breaths increasing as her lips parted.

Rafael watched her with intent, took note of every facial expression, every twitch of her mouth as he pushed her thong down and slipped his fingers through her folds.

'Is this what you want?' he whispered close to her ear, relishing the soft mewls that were increasing in volume with each stroke of his fingers.

'Yes, this is *exactly* what I want,' she huffed out between moans, her hands clawing at his back as if they were searching for anything to hang on to as he pleasured her. 'I'm so…close.'

The last word came out mingled with a sound of such guttural pleasure that his eyes fluttered shut as he reined in his own release barrelling towards him.

He hissed when he slipped a finger into her wet heat, the sensation so tight and perfect as she moved her hips against him.

'Do it for me, Maria,' he said against the shell of her ear, kissing her just below and down her neck as he increased the pressure of his fingers.

A blinding white light flooded Maria's senses as her mind got lost in the currents of her own pleasure, the warmth of her climax spreading through her as her muscles clenched and released.

It took her a few breaths to realise that the scream that had echoed through the room was her own. Her hand flew to her mouth as the realisation struck.

'Oh, my God,' she whispered behind her hand, shaking her head.

Her eyes widened as she met his gaze, pure and primal masculinity written in his eyes. The gleam of a predator that was studying his prey. The intensity sent renewed shivers through her body, disturbing the balance of already unsteady feet.

Her inner voice had long since quieted, letting her body do what it knew to do through instinct alone as she gave herself to Rafael and discarded the last vestiges of modesty to be with him. And now she really *needed* to be with him, for the fire burning inside her had not been extinguished but merely tempered by the aftershock of her orgasm. The way his dark gaze roamed over her reignited her core again, her body pliant and ready for his touch.

Without overthinking it, she slipped her fingers under the elastic of his briefs and tugged at them, bringing them to his ankles in one move. A sound loosened from his throat that sounded like a growl escaping from deep within him. She stripped off her own underwear and gave in to what her legs had been begging for several minutes now—she let herself fall backwards and onto the bed, arms propped up so she could look at him with passion-glazed eyes.

'I want you,' she said, her eyes pointedly dropping to his erection, 'to do what you just did with your fingers.'

That was what he'd asked for, wasn't it—for her to tell him what she wanted? The idea had shocked her a few minutes ago, bringing forth a shyness she didn't know she possessed in the first place. Confidence was her default when she dealt with animals, nervous owners and anyone else bringing animals into her care. Maria had worked hard to become an authority in her field, to command legitimacy when it came to the effects of deforestation on the local wildlife.

Speaking to people was something she did every day, yet she froze when Rafael asked her what she wanted, unable to voice what was in her head. It was simple.

I want you.

The words echoed in her mind unspoken, knowing that she couldn't have that, couldn't have him be hers alone. Even voicing that desire would be a betrayal of their agreement. So, instead, she had to remember this night and everything it meant to her.

Rafael grinned at her request, then bent down to scoop up his trousers from the floor. His hand slipped into the pocket, and he held a small rectangular packet between his fingers when it reappeared.

An involuntary laugh left her lips when she recognised what it was. 'You were carrying a condom with you all day?'

He shrugged, ripping it open and rolling it down his shaft. When he turned back towards her intent gleamed in his eyes and Maria shuddered with anticipation.

'When I saw you in that sexy summer dress, I wasn't sure how fast we would get to the main event,' he said, then approached the bed and crawled over her, his body covering hers. 'You have been very hard to resist, as I'm sure you can tell.'

Maria gasped when his length came to rest between her thighs, excitement clenching her core.

'Kiss me,' she whispered back at him as she wrapped

her legs around his waist, shifting him to where he needed to be.

Rafael brought their faces together. 'I can't tell you how much it turns me on when you tell me what you want.'

She didn't get a chance to reply, for Rafael closed the tiny gap between them and laid his mouth over hers just as he angled his hips towards her to push into her. Her moan was swallowed by the dance of their tongues moving against each other as he thrust in and out in a steady rhythm that spelled comfort and safety.

Understanding. That was what Rafael had brought into her life from the very beginning. A deep sense of understanding for her work, her passion, the predicament she had found herself in. He shared her ideals, loved working with animals just as much as she did, and throughout their fake marriage he'd not once made her feel like she was less to agree to such a deal in the first place.

Her hands clawed against his back, digging into the strong muscles there that bunched and released as Rafael kept their tempo, each thrust bringing her higher, to a place that was filled with pleasure and his scent that she couldn't get enough of.

'I'm almost there again. Please, Rafa—' she started, the rest of her words disappearing as her body trembled, bringing her closer to the edge again.

Rafael's elbows came down on each side of her face as he thrust deeper, his forehead touching hers, a primal grunt filling his throat as he forced a breath out of his chest.

'This is so much more than I thought it would be,' he whispered against her skin, just as the borders between pleasure and pain blurred for the second time today.

Maria's head fell back, her mouth open with another

moan of pleasure as her muscles squeezed tight before releasing her into a blissful state of nothingness.

His words barely registered as he, too, let out a groan, his fists bunching into the sheet as they came together, leaving him trembling on his elbows until he gave in and collapsed on top of her.

Maria smiled through the bliss, her fingers running through his short hair and down his spine, picking up beads of sweat as they trailed over his back. This moment was perfection—but it led her to a realisation that she wasn't ready for, yet could no longer ignore as she had done over the last couple of weeks.

Rafael was who she wanted to be with, and as he looked at her with those passion-glazed eyes, seeing the respect and affection lying underneath, Maria felt her heart crack as she realised that she wouldn't be able to lose him—not without her heart fully breaking apart.

CHAPTER NINE

THE NIGHT AFTER they had played a married couple for
the entire village, and the subsequent week, had been an
out-of-body experience for Rafael in more ways than one.
Though they had agreed that their night together would
exist outside of anything else they had going on, neither
of them were able to keep away from the other.

Hot kisses were stolen between patients, each one filled
with a sense of urgency and longing that gave Rafael
pause. He knew where this was coming from—the deadline was approaching its end.

After their first night together, Rafael's lawyer had
informed them that the final paperwork was being processed by the bank and that they'd be able to release his
funds in two weeks. Though neither was willing to spell
it out, they treated each kiss as if it were the last. Because
their breakup was inevitable—and the devastation this
thought summoned in him was one of genuine heartbreak.

Despite dismissing the risk of this happening as minuscule, Rafael had fallen for this amazing woman who
had agreed to be his wife to save her family legacy. The
people in his life had always been in pursuit of their own
agenda, serving only themselves and their goals to the
point where he'd believed all humans to be like that.

Until Maria had come into his life, and he'd suddenly

understood what had been missing all those years filled with emptiness—her. And even though he recognised the kernel of light growing within his chest as genuine affection and love, he had to leave. He *had to,* because his family would never let him have this happiness. No, he was tainted by association alone, and because she and this place had become so important to him he needed to go. The curse his grandparents had created with their trust bound him to his family, not letting him lead a normal life. His bags were already packed with whatever he had left in his room, ready to leave this town—and the promises it held—behind, to vanish into obscurity.

It surprised him that his family hadn't made a move yet, that they hadn't heard about his marriage. Maybe they had believed Rafael when he had told them he would never get married, so they'd stopped keeping an eye on him. Though if they didn't pay attention now, they would when they heard that he had access to the money in his trust. He needed to be gone from here before they found out or they might find Maria—might learn how much she meant to him and use that against him.

As if his thoughts had summoned her, Maria opened the door to his small office, a wary expression on her face. His back stiffened at the alert in her eyes, and he whirled around in his chair.

'What happened, *amor*?' he asked, the endearment slipping out before he could help himself. Love. That was not what he should call her—ever.

'Celine sent me a picture of a headline in a magazine. She's on her way back here, but…'

Rafael's blood ran cold at her words. He got to his feet, his hand wrapping around her arm and pulling Maria closer. 'This must be my family's doing. I was wondering when they would get involved in our deal and try to give themselves a pay day from my money.'

He swore under his breath when he looked at a picture of them kissing, plastered on the front page of a minor tabloid in Brazil—a small blessing. Clearly the major publications weren't interested in the grandchild of former *novela* stars.

'Pedro Media's disgraced son seen with rural vet,' he read out loud, then sighed at his own description.

Disgraced son? That must have been his parents' idea, planting the rumours that he had run away and turned his back on the family business, when it had been their toxic behaviour that had forced him to make that decision. Family was everything in their culture and that they had told people he had gone without so much as a word or care brought a wave of nausea that rippled through his body. What if someone in Santarém read this and believed them over him?

'How did they get this picture?' Maria wondered.

He looked at her through narrowed eyes, taking in her expression. She sounded more curious than outraged. How could she not have an instant and visceral reaction to such a betrayal of their privacy?

Rafael looked at the picture, frowning. It showed them locked in an embrace here in the clinic. His family had sent people to check on him after all. He just hadn't seen them. Clicking on the photo, he found who the photo had originally belonged to before they'd licensed it to the publication. Then he showed Maria his screen with a picture of the photographer on it.

Her eyes widened in recognition.

'You've seen him around the property?' he asked, his voice sharp.

Maria nodded. 'He rang the doorbell some weeks back and asked to speak to you. You were still sleeping, so I went to see him. He…had a cat with him, so I didn't think anything of it when he asked for you. I didn't say anything because…he was just another patient.'

Colour drained out of her face. 'This man was stalking around my property with a camera and a cat as a *prop*? Where did he even get it from?'

Rafael stepped closer to her, his arm coming around her waist as if his embrace could protect her from the media circus his family was trying to inflict on them. This would be only the first step in many to wear them down, and he knew exactly what they wanted in return.

'I'm sorry you've had to find out first-hand how unhinged my family are. They will not stop until they have my money.' He paused, a lump appearing in his throat that he had to swallow before he could continue. 'It will only be a week or so until the transfer is through. Then I can make my donation and be on my way.'

'Wait… You're—'

The door swinging open interrupted Maria, and his arm tightened around her instinctively, hauling her closer to him. They both relaxed when Celine stared back at them. Her eyes darted down to where his hand clung to Maria's hip, then she shook her head.

Whatever communication had passed between them about his relationship with Maria must have been silent, for after a shake of her head Celine nodded towards the computer Rafael had been working on moments ago.

'Did you look at it?'

'Yes,' he said.

At the same time Maria breathed, 'No.'

They turned their heads towards each other. Rafael was

the first one to speak. 'You didn't come here to show me the tabloid picture?'

'I did, though not because of the reasons you think I did,' Celine replied, then brought her phone back up to show him the article associated with the picture.

'The video I made last week for you to send to donors? I included the footage of us finding the abandoned cat. For reasons beyond me, this tabloid thought it was a good idea to embed the video in the article,' she continued as she sat at the desk to bring up the website of the animal charity.

'Wait, so they went to our social pages to include a video that's an ad for our organisation?' Maria asked, furrowing her brow.

'Yeah, no idea who came up with this. But…it worked out great for us.'

Rafael looked at Maria, who stared at the article on her phone in bewilderment. As she scrolled down, the video appeared. Lia immediately caught the attention of any viewer, and after the first two seconds Celine's voice started to narrate the benefits their charity brought to the community.

'I don't understand how this is good for us, Cee.'

Maria stepped closer to her sister to look over her shoulder as Celine explained. 'After Daniel left, we realised we wouldn't be able to keep ourselves afloat with the current donations, so we put a cry for help on the front page so anyone visiting it would know to donate. We put up a counter so people could see what impact their donations were making, however small.'

Rafael shot her a questioning look. 'You think enough people read this to have an impact on donations?'

Both sisters shook their heads. Then Celine said, 'No,

but because they included our video, a famous animal rights activist saw our compilation and highlighted it on her own social media pages. She has over a million followers and chose to highlight our charity after watching our video and hearing our call for donations. That video—along with our own—got shared like crazy in the last week. It went absolutely viral.'

She stopped, looking at Maria. Both of their expressions were incredulous. The donation target on their website was set to five hundred thousand. A number next to it was blinking in a grass-green colour, and Rafael immediately understood why both were suddenly lost for words. The figure read three million.

'*Meu deus...*' Maria whispered, first looking at Celine and then at him. 'Can someone tell me that this is really happening?'

His heart squeezed tight at the unreserved happiness in her gaze as she smiled at him. 'This just bought us so much time,' she said, then jumped off her chair in a sudden move to hurl herself against Rafael.

Her hair obscured his face as he wrapped his arms around her midsection, drawn towards her for what he knew to be one of the last times. Though the relief in her voice touched something deep inside him that he didn't dare to examine closely for the fear that it would make him reckless, his chest tightened as the plans he had been stewing over for the last several days were set into motion.

'Listen, Maria…' he started, but got cut off by Celine.

'How many of them do you think are monthly donors?' she asked as she took a seat in front of the computer.

Maria twisted in his arms to look at her sister. 'We can check the registration forms.'

She moved out of his grasp but then briefly turned around again. 'What were you going to say?'

Rafael shook his head, not wanting to spoil the moment with news he knew would hang like a dark cloud between them. 'Nothing important. I'll talk to you in the evening.' He paused, then said to both sisters, 'Congratulations. I'm glad you get to fight for the animals that need you yet another day.'

Maria beamed at him, a look so filled with affection and warmth that he had to immediately turn away and leave the room. She could not look at him like that. Not when he was about to let her know that he would be gone tomorrow.

Sooner or later his family would find a way to ruin this relationship, to turn her against him. Or worse, they had their fingers in it all along. The way they had with Laura. Rafael wanted to preserve his memory of this place—and her memory of him—so even though the decision to leave had caused a constant pain in his chest, the choice remained the same.

Better leave now and preserve what they had built with his legacy than wait for his family to lie and manipulate their way into Santarém, into Maria's family, making him out to be the person who'd destroyed their family.

The day had gone by in a flash after the explosive news of the morning, with both Maria and her sister reeling at what had happened to them. Whenever she had thought of a new sponsor, she had always sought out people with big money. Never had the thought of approaching strangers on the internet crossed her mind—though now it seemed like that was what she should have done in the first place. That a clickbait article about his family's media company should be the thing that saved her family's legacy from complete ruin was too much for Maria.

Most of the donations were one-off gifts from sympathetic people who had seen the viral video of Rafael finding the cats in the box, but there were enough monthly donors to keep them operational. More would be better, but now that this had been revealed as an option Maria could spend more time finding the kind-hearted people who cared about animals just as much as she did rather than going after rich people who had too much money and not enough things to do with it.

It also meant that she didn't need Rafael's money any more. With the reason for their fake marriage gone, did they need to stay together?

It was that part that poured icy water through her veins, filling her with a sense of dread. Because this was always supposed to end. From the very beginning their fake relationship had an expiry date that they had agreed on. Was it disingenuous of Maria to want to change that? To give in to the real feelings this faux marriage had conjured up within her?

After the weeks they'd spent together, Maria had to admit to herself that she was in love with Rafael. Had been heading in that direction even before they had made this deal, when they were still trying to be friends.

Maria's head sank into her hands as she thought of the choice ahead of her, her chest squeezing so tight it became hard to breathe. A desire manifested within her, one so wild and outrageous that she couldn't believe it was even living inside her mind.

She wanted to ask Rafael to stay married. For real.

They'd skipped a few steps of the more traditional relationship, but something about that felt right, like it was meant to be. Had they not shown up for each other through this brief relationship—the way a husband and wife would?

The only thing that gave her pause around this entire idea was a simple but important matter—did he feel the same way for her? And after much deliberation and examining the situation from every possible angle Maria came to one conclusion. She needed to tell him how she felt.

Even if sweat appeared on her palms if she just thought of saying those words to Rafael. Though they were true, and her intention was only to let him know her feelings for him, a part of her balked at the thought of betrayal. Daniel had gone back on their implicit agreement as a family. He had put his own needs ahead of everyone else's and almost ruined their legacy by doing so. Was she not doing the same by going back on their agreement that this was a fake relationship and nothing more? Was it wrong to *want* more?

The door behind her opened, and as Rafael walked in with a veiled expression Maria knew the choice had just been taken out of her hands. She needed to tell him, or she would never forgive herself.

He smiled, though something lay beneath it, a reluctance that sent a cold shiver tingling down her spine. There was something amiss. Did he guess what she was about to tell him and that was where the faint displeasure she could see in his face came from?

'What's wrong?' she asked before she could stop herself, wanting to know the answer despite the premonition pooling in her stomach that it wouldn't end well for her—*them*.

'I wanted to apologise for the media circus my family put you through, but it's feeling like this did way more good than it did harm,' he said as he walked over towards her.

He didn't take the empty chair next to her but rather elected to stand, his hip leaning against the desk as he crossed his arms in front of his delectable chest.

'What *were* they trying to achieve?' Maria asked.

The question had been at the back of her mind. She'd read the article and scoffed at a couple of passages where the tabloid tried to claim that Rafael was the disgraced son kicked out of the family after wronging them, and that he was now trying to get his hooks into someone else—her, of all people. They clearly hadn't done their research on her or they would have known that she was as broke as they got. No one ran a charity because they wanted to become rich.

Rafael's expression turned dark as he shook his head. 'This was them sending a message to me.'

'A message?' Maria furrowed her brow, her rise in tone prompting him to elaborate.

'They wanted me to know that they know we are married. It wasn't clumsy or an accident that the person who took these photographs rang the doorbell to ask for me. They wanted me to know that they were watching us,' he said, and the darkness in his eyes was different from anything she had seen in him since he'd arrived in her life—completely upending it.

'I don't understand how planting an ostensibly fake story in a small tabloid helps them get closer to your money,' she said as she tried to piece the information together.

Rafael huffed a humourless laugh. 'These are mind games, Maria. They want us to know that they're watching and waiting—for us to show a weakness. They know the only way I will give them anything is if they can use the people I care about—use them against me.'

Maria frowned, worried about how his reaction was the polar opposite to hers. 'This turned out well for us in the end though, Rafael. Thanks to them, we reached the people we didn't even know mattered.' The obscure intentions of his family were scary, but Maria didn't want to forget about the silver lining to this story. 'Whatever else they have to throw at us, we can take it. Together.'

Rafael's eyes widened when the last sentence slipped through her lips unbidden. Though she hadn't decided on how she planned on initiating this conversation, this starting point seemed as good as any. Because if she didn't say it now, Maria knew that she would never find the courage to say it at all.

'I... I want us to...try,' she began, biting her lower lip when the first words came out in a broken voice. How come she couldn't tap into the confidence she usually felt when it came to talking about her feelings for this man? Especially when she had already shared so much of herself with him. Only one thing remained for her to share with him—that she was his, and that she wanted him to be hers.

'Maria...' Rafael said, but she shook her head as she got to her feet to be on the same level with him.

'I know I'm about to change the agreement that we had, and I hope you know I'm not doing it lightly. But I need you to know that I'm willing to try being in this relationship for real. Not because at the end of it there is a big donation, but because of you. Because I'm in love with you.'

The sound of her shaky breath was the only sound in the room as they kept staring at each other. Maria grew more and more nervous as the silence went on, her heart squeezing so tight she knew any more pressure would break it. It—along with so much more—now lay in his hands, to do with as he pleased.

He sighed, and when he did it seemed to cut the ground from under her feet, making her stagger back.

'Oh, my God…' she whispered, her wide eyes scanning his pained expression. 'I can't believe I was wrong about this. You…don't love me.'

Rafael stiffened at those words, his hand reaching for her, but she took a step back, evading his grasp. 'No, Maria, that's not—'

'I'm such a fool. I thought there was something between us, something that existed before we even entered into this agreement. This is all my own fault for letting it get so far.' Maria shook her head, biting her lower lip to force the sting in her eyes away. She would *not* let him see her cry.

'Love has nothing to do with this.' He raised his hand, indicating the space between them. 'Don't you see what my family has done the moment they figured out that you mean something to me? They are relentless when it comes to pursuing what they believe to be theirs.'

'So they alerted the tabloids about some non-story. That served us quite well.' Maria took another step backwards, bracing her hands on the table behind her. Her mind was racing, looking for ways out of this conversation she had let herself have with him. How was it possible that he didn't feel the same way? Was everything that happened between them really no more than a figment of her imagination? The night they'd spent together simply to satisfy a physical need that had been building for both of them?

'I told you, that is only the beginning. They won't stop at that and will find ways to insinuate themselves into…'

His voice trailed off, and Maria realised it was because he didn't know how to end the sentence. He didn't know what they were, hadn't bothered to think about it.

'You know exactly what I went through with my brother. I can handle myself,' she replied, unsure of what she hoped to achieve. Was she trying to convince him that what they had was worth fighting for?

'But *I* cannot go through the heartbreak again. I can't be the person to bring such chaos into your life. No, I won't. They *will* find a way to get to you as long as we are close,' Rafael said, his face a mask of the ancient pain he'd shared with her in the past few weeks they had spent together.

A tremor took hold of her hands as she dug them into the wooden desk behind her. It took her several breaths to put his words into context and a few more to understand what he was saying.

'Are…you leaving? After everything? Regardless of this marriage, you never said you'd be leaving… Rafael…'

The muscles along his jaw tightened, his hazel eyes that were normally filled with so much kindness and affection suddenly cold as stone.

'That's why I said from the very beginning this can never be more than the deal that we agreed on. I don't *want* to leave, but that was always my plan. I can't stay here, not now that my family knows you mean something to me.'

'What…?' The word came out in a hushed whisper as the scene before her unfolded, none of it making any sense. Because this man in front of her with the ironclad defences surrounding him was not the man she had spent the last four weeks with. He wasn't who she'd fallen in love with.

'So you made the decision to leave all on your own to… protect me, without even asking me first? Why? Because you don't trust me?'

Rafael sighed again, his gaze dropping to the floor. His hands, tightly curled fists at his sides, relaxed before he raised them to his face to scrub over it.

'It's not you, Maria. I don't trust *them*, not after everything that's happened.' He stopped to look at her, and the look of profound sorrow shining in his eyes burst her heart into a thousand tiny pieces.

With a frown he continued. 'I came here to tell you that I'm leaving tonight, and I know eventually you'll understand why I had to do that.'

'Understand?' She crossed her arms in front of her, her jaw clenched so tight the muscle throbbed with pain. 'All this time I thought we were in this together…that you might not love me but at the very least care about me.'

'I do this *because* I care for you, so much more than I could have ever anticipated. They might sniff around here for a while, but once they notice I'm gone they will hopefully leave you alone, since you're not the one controlling the bank account.' He reached down, picking up the backpack and slinging it over his shoulder. 'I really wish it didn't have to end like this.'

Maria swallowed hard, then raised her chin when he made to touch her. 'It doesn't have to, Rafael. If you don't feel the same way for me, just say it and we'll go back to what we agreed on. But I don't need you to decide for me what I'm capable of handling. I thought you knew me better than that.'

His hand stilled in mid-air, as if her words had struck him in a place only he could feel. Something in his eyes softened, showing the wealth of pain he tried to hide despite his masked expression. Then he turned around and left through the door—as if he had never entered her life and completely reshaped it.

CHAPTER TEN

'YOU'RE SURE ABOUT THIS, *amigo*?' Sebastião asked, looking at him over steepled fingers.

'Yes, I'm sure. It's what we agreed on, so let's get the ball rolling.'

Rafael sat in the all too familiar office of his lawyer in Manaus, trying to tie up the remaining loose ends of his marriage to Maria. *Trying* because every time he thought about ending this wonderful and amazing thing that had grown between them his heart pounded against his chest as if it was determined to escape, his hands getting sweaty, and it became harder to breathe. He'd told Sebastião about that as they'd sat down, needing to get this off his chest.

Sebastião had suggested that he was having a panic attack, though Rafael wasn't ready to admit what that meant regarding his feelings for Maria. She had said what he had been too afraid to admit—facing him with bravery and resolve when he could do no more than walk away. What kind of man wouldn't fall in love with her?

Though being in love with her didn't change that they were doomed to fail. The damage done to him was too severe to be repaired, not even by the loving touch of the most amazing woman he'd ever met.

'Walk me through what happened again? The divorce seems a bit…abrupt,' Sebastião said, and Rafael sighed.

'She told me she loved me and that she wanted to have a relationship with me without the pretence. She wanted us to try to be together.' A searing pain buried itself between his ribs as he recounted the devastating moment, the memories still clinging to him whenever he let his mind wander for too long.

'And why did you say no to that? It sounds like this is what you wanted.' Sebastião cocked his head, eliciting another sigh from Rafael.

'It's not as simple as you make it out to be. My feelings aside, it was never supposed to be real. She needed the money for her charity, and I…' His voice trailed off just as a smirk appeared on the lawyer's face.

Because Rafael didn't know how to complete the sentence. He'd wanted to help his friend, but even that excuse didn't hold up to closer inspection. She and the village had been so warm and welcoming, letting him join the community without a single question, so when the moment to repay her had arisen he couldn't say no—even though he knew it meant the end of his time in Santarém.

'You wanted to help the woman you love,' Sebastião said, finishing the sentence for him and verbalising his thoughts.

'I *can't* love her, Seb. They will find a way to ruin it,' Rafael gritted out between clenched teeth.

'What makes you so sure of that?'

'When I started dating Laura—'

'Let me stop you right there. Laura was an opportunistic socialite who would do anything for exposure and fame. She would fit perfectly with the rest of your family. And you were so much younger back then. So I think you can finally stop beating yourself up for trusting her. If you don't find it in you to forgive yourself, you won't ever get to move on—not truly.'

The jovial twinkle in Sebastião's eyes vanished, replaced by a serious expression as he spoke to Rafael on a level that hardly anyone had spoken to him before. There was a truth in this situation that made him perk up and pay attention to himself the way he hadn't done before.

Forgive himself? Was that the demon that had been plaguing him since the painful incident with Laura and their broken engagement?

He swallowed when a lump appeared in his throat. 'I...just want to keep her safe,' he said, but the words felt wrong on his tongue.

His lawyer must have heard it too, for he shook his head. 'From what you've told me, Maria went through her own share of trouble and managed to remain standing by her own merits. She doesn't need you to deny your feelings to protect her.'

Rafael balled his hands into fists, bunching up the fabric of his trousers. 'Okay, *I'm* the one who is scared. Is that what you wanted to hear? I'm too broken to let anyone near me because the thought of this turning out the same way...'

'You are letting *one* experience ruin the rest of your life. Which brings me back to my point—when are you going to forgive yourself? Because someone like Maria won't be waiting around for you to get your life together.'

Rafael scoffed. 'You say it as if it is the easiest thing in the world.'

'It's not as hard as you pretend it is. What would happen right now if you went back to her, admitted your feelings and lived as if you were truly married?'

Rafael paused, letting the image take root inside of him. What would happen if he went back to confess his love for her? They would run the charity together, become the family both yearned to have. The money he had been cursed with would go to the noblest purpose he could think of, and he would support his wife as she advocated for the most vulnerable creatures in the rainforest.

And his family? They would be circling like sharks, wanting their bite out of his little slice of paradise that he had built for himself and her. They would try, but Maria was the best person he knew without a shadow of a doubt. When she'd learned she didn't need money from big donors she had been so relieved, glad that she could save the animals with the help of ordinary people.

This woman had said she loved him. Him, who was so wholly unworthy of her affection that he had pushed her away instead of accepting this blessing life had bestowed on him. He had let a mistake he'd made get in the way of what could have been the rest of his life.

'It would be so good,' he whispered after a few moments of silence, prompting Sebastião to smile at him.

Rafael blinked several times, clearing away the remnants of his daydream as realisation thundered through him. How could he be so arrogant to pretend he knew what was best for Maria when his own fear of loss was driving his decision-making process? There was no way someone like her would ever be influenced but, instead of showing up as bravely as she had, Rafael had let his fear take over and he'd pushed her away.

And with it a life he desperately wanted to live.

He surged from his chair. 'I have to go back,' he said as he looked at his lawyer.

'There we go, you got there.' Sebastião paused to push

away from his desk, accessing a drawer. He retrieved a paper folder and put it in front of him.

'The bank has released the funds. They are currently still in the trust's account, so I would advise you to move it to a new bank soon. You still want me to make the donation to Maria's charity?'

The money hadn't even entered his mind. Rafael paused for a moment, then he said, 'Donate the entire sum.'

Sebastião looked at him with raised eyebrows. 'You want me to donate all of your wealth?'

'Yes, donate it all to her charity, and let my family know that what they are looking for is gone for ever. I'm not keeping any of it, I don't need it. Maria does, and so do her animals, so let the people who really need it have all of it.'

Sebastião didn't argue, something Rafael was grateful for as he grabbed his phone out of his pocket, looking at available flights as he prayed that his foolishness hadn't cost him the best thing to ever happen to him.

He stopped when an idea popped into his head. 'Give me two hours to buy something, then send whatever is left over.'

'Is Tia okay?' Mirabel's voice was no more than a whisper, yet it carried far enough for Maria to hear.

'She will be okay, yes,' Celine replied, a lot more audibly, and Maria almost smiled at that. It was very much like Celine to use this moment as a teaching opportunity, showing their niece that she could talk to them about their feelings and that people were sometimes sad.

Though from where Maria was standing, she wasn't sure if she could confidently say that she would be okay ever again. There was a gaping hole in her chest, her heart shattered into pieces and her life so much emptier. Rafael had made good on his promise and left without looking back, and the clinic hadn't been the same since. Not because of the patients or the revenue from having regular vet appointments—she and Celine had been splitting time doing clinic hours until they could find a new vet. No, something fundamental was missing from her life and that was him.

'Mirabel, could you go to your room while I talk to your aunt, please?' she said, and a moment later Celine appeared in the kitchen and sat down on the chair next to her.

'Bad one today?' she asked, and Maria nodded.

'How did you survive when Darius left you like that?'

Her sister had been married for a lot longer than Maria herself, though she'd spent those years estranged from her husband after he'd fled the country—never to be seen again. It had devastated Celine, especially when she'd found out that she was pregnant with Nina. That they would now share the pain of this experience was so surreal to Maria.

'I didn't have a choice,' Celine replied, and nodded towards the sofa where her daughter was fast asleep, wrapped in a cosy blanket.

'I guess that still holds true. There won't be any less work just because my heart is broken.' Maria tried to smile at her sister, but she raised an eyebrow in question, clearly not convinced.

'Or you could muster up some more strength within you and fight for him.'

'Not this again,' Maria sighed, her eyes dropping down to the glass of wine she held onto a little too tightly. 'He said he didn't love me, so that's the end of it. I can't make someone love me.'

'And I'll tell you again that this is not true. I bet he didn't say that he doesn't love you. I'm sure he said a lot of hurtful things, but that wasn't one of them.' Celine crossed her arms in front of her chest. 'He doesn't strike me as a liar.'

'He's not,' Maria replied, bristling at the idea that someone would call him a liar.

Even though he had been gone for days, the urge to come to his defence was still a reflex that she didn't quite have under control.

It didn't really matter what words he had said, his actions told her all she needed to know about his desire to be with her. He had left, had *planned* on leaving since the moment they'd entered into their fake marriage agreement—something that had become clear to her over the last few days as she'd replayed that scene over and over. He'd always known his family would do something eventually, and that would be the moment he left.

Except Maria was willing to fight for him, defend him against whatever they had planned for him. If she knew anything it was how to deal with a complicated family.

Did Celine have a point and she might have given up too soon? Because if Maria was honest with herself, she had been petrified to say anything to Rafael as he'd left, trying to find excuses that would make it okay not to share her feelings with him.

'Stop it, Cee!' Maria groaned, burying her face in her hands.

Her sister looked at her with a stark line between her brows. 'I didn't say anything.'

'Yeah, but all your arguing is getting in my brain. I *can't* go back to him.'

'Why not?'

Such a simple question that branched out into a hundred different paths. Why did she not stand up and fight when that was what she did best? Because it was hard? Or because there might be rejection waiting at the end of the path?

No, the truth of what rooted her to the spot and made her unable to move lay much darker and far deeper than whatever superficial excuse she could come up with—the fear that he didn't really love her, and that she had invented this affection between them. That she was incapable of understanding when someone was sincere—be it Rafael or her brother. Could she trust her own feelings?

And if she never asked then no one could prove it fake.

'Because...he doesn't love me. Regardless of what he may or may not have said, I know it's true.' The words turned bitter in her mouth, lying on her tongue like thick ash. She knew that wasn't the whole truth, or at least not as clear cut as she wanted Celine to believe. But she'd had enough of this discussion. Rafael was gone and there was nothing left but to move on from the idea of their marriage turning into something real.

Her sister opened her mouth to reply but stopped herself when her phone buzzed on the table. She picked it up, pressing on the screen for a few moments with a confused look spreading over her features.

'What?' Maria asked, leaning over to see her screen, but Celine pulled away at the last second.

She then smiled, a small but wicked grin that Maria knew all too well from their childhood. It was the smirk she had every time she had been right about something.

Though they were eight years apart, her sister had absorbed knowledge like a sponge, understanding the subjects that Maria was studying long before Celine herself would learn them in school.

That look never meant well for Maria's pride.

'I'm pretty sure he does love you,' she said, that smile growing wider as she glanced down at her phone again.

'What? Who is messaging you?' Maria demanded and scowled at her sister when she finally turned the screen around so she could see it.

They were looking at the donation goal on their website again. After the viral video of Rafael rescuing the cats from the skip they had updated the goal to aim higher, though she could see that it had already been surpassed again by one big donation of...

'Seventy-four million *real*?' she breathed, the blood rushing to her face as she tried to imagine that large a sum. Who would donate such a fortune...? 'Oh, no...'

Realisation shot through her like a bolt of lightning, kicking her pulse and brain into overdrive. She stared at Celine in complete bewilderment as no coherent thoughts crystallised in her mind. 'This is almost *all* his money. He told me that's how much was in his trust.'

'So tell me one more time that this man doesn't love you.' Her sister crossed her arms. 'A gesture of love can't get any bigger than that.'

Maria stared at the screen. With such funds they could invest in better technology, expand their operations, maybe even hire some more people to help. Why had he done so much more than they had agreed on?

Was that his way of telling her how she felt?

Maria's heart beat against her sternum erratically, pumping hot blood through her veins that made it hard to think. If it was possible that he loved her the way she loved him, then there was a chance for them. If a piece of his heart belonged to her, she could fight for it.

'I have to—' She stopped when Celine threw her car keys at her, already aware of what her sister was saying.

'Get out of here and get him back.'

Slipping into her shoes, Maria reached for the door handle when the video intercom rang. 'You have got to be kidding me...'

She brought up the feed and paused when a familiar face looked back at her. Her breath caught as she hurled the door open and sprinted to the front of the clinic, right into Rafael's outstretched arms.

She felt the vibrations of his voice as he mumbled something into the thick curtain of her hair, his words getting lost in the beating of her own heart in her ears. Maria pressed herself against him, her arms slung around his midsection as if to anchor him to this spot in front of her clinic—right where he belonged.

'What did you do?' she said when she leaned back for a moment to look at him.

'I came to try. For real,' he said, mirroring the words she'd said to him last week. 'I let my fear get the better of me, I'm sorry for that. The thought of my family bringing their toxicity into our little sliver of paradise scared me to the core, and I didn't know what to do about it. So I found an excuse to keep up my habit of distrust and I ran.'

His expression was grim, his eyes shining with the sincerity that was woven through his apology. Maria shook her head, not needing to hear anything more.

He's back. That was the predominant thought echoing through her head, elevating her heart to new heights as it slowly knit back together.

'I should have fought more. I was scared of going back on my word and changing our deal when I was the one who caught feelings for—'

Rafael silenced her with a gentle brush of his lips against hers, the kiss vibrating all the way to her bones and drawing out a longing moan. Had it really only been a few days since they'd last kissed?

'You have nothing to apologise for. Now...' He put his hands on her shoulders and gently pushed her away.

Maria gasped when he went down on one knee and presented her with a small ring box with a white-gold band inside. 'I love you, Maria. Have loved you since the moment I met you. I realise we are already married, but I never gave you a ring. So I guess my question is—do you want to turn this into a real marriage?'

Maria nodded, a lump clogging her throat and rendering her unable to answer as tears of joy stung her eyes. Rafael smiled as well, taking her shaking hand into his and pushing the ring onto her finger. It fit perfectly.

'I guess this explains the small part of your fortune that you didn't donate,' she said in jest, as there was no doubt in her mind how expensive this piece of jewellery must have been.

But Rafael only laughed, pulling her back into his embrace. 'The money already arrived? I'm glad.' He paused, kissing the top of her head. 'I asked Sebastião to transfer everything to you. This money has been lusted after for long enough. It is time it went to something productive.'

Maria smiled into the crook of his neck, breathing in the scent that had been missing from her life for the last week. One that she never wanted to go without.

'I guess that means you need your job back? Because

there is no way I'm letting you stay here for free,' she said, joining in as Rafael began laughing.

'I was hoping you hadn't filled that vacancy yet,' he replied.

Maria nodded, cherishing this nearness to her husband—her real husband, finally.

There were many things still to discuss, but those could wait for a few days as they enjoyed their closeness in earnest. They would do this together, that was the only thing that counted. Everything else they would figure out with time.

EPILOGUE

'I REALLY WISH you would let me do this.'

Maria ignored her husband's concerned tone as she put a box down on the exam table, resting one hand on the top of the closed flaps while the other one came to rest on her large belly.

'Rafa, you have stuff going on in the clinic, and I still need to pick up animals whenever they call me, pregnant or not.'

Rafael scowled at her, an expression so full of love that Maria's insides melted. She smiled at him, then grabbed his hand and placed it where hers had just been. 'I know it's your job to worry, but keeping our tiny one safe and sound is my number one priority, okay? I would never do anything that would put us in danger, you know that.'

Ever since their reconciliation, Rafael had got progressively more relaxed when it came to the different dangers his family posed. They had sent a few more private eyes, photographers and lawyers to them to threaten them to release the funds but had eventually given up when they realised that Rafael had given his fortune away to charity.

A charity that he had since taken a larger role in. With the money at hand, they had expanded the building to add more pens and new exam rooms so they could increase their operations. Together they had hired more vets for domestic pets and vet surgeons to help with the injured animals that came in as deforestation efforts in the rainforest increased at a concerning pace.

Rafael had taken on the role of head vet, managing all their newly hired staff and coordinating the daily work that needed to be done—something Maria was eternally grateful for, because it left her plenty of time to look after the animals without having to worry about the clinic.

When she had agreed to marry Rafael out of desperation, she had never dreamed that her charity would look like this. The promised money was supposed to keep them going, but now they had made something to be proud of—and Maria's heart almost burst at the thought that she had done all of this together with her husband, the love of her life.

'Where is Mirabel? I didn't see her back at the house.'

Rafael laughed, the scowl on his face transforming into a bright smile that made her knees wobbly. 'She's cleaning out the pens. When I picked her up from school, she said she wanted to come hang out here.'

'What? She's not spoiling Mamãezinha and her daughters rotten? What have you done to my niece?' Maria shook her head, thinking about the stray cat that had become a new addition to the family—to the great displeasure of Alexander the Great Dane, who now had rivals to his affection.

Her chest expanded with joy and pride she couldn't put into words. Ever since Rafael had taken a more active part in Mirabel's life, her niece had come out of her shell, showing more interest in the world around her and especially in the animals they had in their care.

He had filled a void left by her brother, and Maria would never be able to express how thankful she was. He'd done it without hesitation, embracing Mirabel as his own.

'Speaking of pens… Did I show you the latest pictures of Lia?' she asked.

His eyes widened, his earlier reprimand all but forgotten. When he stepped closer, the familiar scent of lavender drifted towards her and she couldn't help the smile spreading over her face. The moment was one of pure perfection, the like of which she hadn't thought she would ever get to experience.

When he had first arrived in Santarém, Maria hadn't believed that the love of her life had just walked in. Yet here he was, eyes bright and gentle as he swiped through the images to check on the ocelot he had rescued so many months ago. The institute in Manaus sent her regular updates to let her know how their foundling cat was doing.

She added, 'They will try to re-wild her in the next couple of weeks. Maybe if you are up for a little babymoon we could fly down there and wish her farewell. They were able to release the monkeys into the wild already, so chances are we can find them back in Manaus.'

His eyes were still focused on the screen of her phone, and it was clear that her words hadn't found any purchase in his mind.

'She looks so big,' he whispered, and the awe lacing his voice made her chuckle.

Though they worked together a lot more these days, she still forgot sometimes that he wasn't familiar with the kinds of animals she treated every day.

'They grow that large, you know,' she teased him, and yelped when he shot towards her, hauling her into his arms.

Exactly where she belonged.

* * * * *

THE SECRET
SHE KEPT FROM
DR DELGADO

LUANA DaROSA

MILLS & BOON

For my mum,
who had to go through motherhood
mostly on her own and yet never gave up.

CHAPTER ONE

'WHAT DO YOU MEAN, he said *no*?'

Even though fury thundered through her at the news she had just received, Celine immediately regretted raising her voice. When it came to Darius, her fuse these days was rather short.

'I don't know what else to tell you.'

The voice on the other end of the phone belonged to Sebastião, a lawyer Celine had hired on the recommendation of Rafael, her brother-in-law.

'We tracked him down, sent the papers to him in Peru and now his lawyer just got in touch with me, saying that his client won't sign the papers like that.'

'I haven't seen this man in six years. How can he *refuse* to sign the divorce papers?' Nearly six years ago, Celine had made a grave mistake—she'd trusted her boyfriend enough to let him talk her into marriage. His mother, who held the visa for herself and Darius, had decided that it was time for them to leave Brazil. Darius had been in the final year of med school while Celine had just finished veterinary school. They had been seeing each other for two years, and the conversation around marriage had come up before. So when he'd asked her to get married so he could stay with her, she hadn't hesitated to say yes.

And then he'd left for Peru to sort out his return to

Brazil with a new visa—and let her know only two days after his departure that he wouldn't be coming back and that she shouldn't contact him any more.

'I'm trying to dig into this issue with a Peruvian colleague. Clearly, our threatening letter didn't inspire any action.' Sebastião went quiet for a moment before he spoke again. 'Why wouldn't he want to sign the papers? Because of Nina?'

'Nina? No, he doesn't know he has a daughter. And now I'm not sure I want to tell him about her either.' When his message arrived that he wasn't coming back, she had tried everything to contact him despite his request not to do so. Celine had called, texted, written letters and tried to get friends to deliver messages for her—had redoubled that effort when she'd realised she was pregnant. But the other side of the line stayed quiet.

'What do we do next?' Impatience strained her voice. She had finally summoned the courage to ask for a divorce, burying the last remnants of her love for him, and now he *refused* to let her go? When he wasn't even in the country?

'You can still sue for divorce. It will just take longer. The court will assign you a date to speak in front of a judge, and that's when Darius will need to defend his refusal.' Sebastião paused as Celine sighed, frustration bubbling in her chest.

'All right, thank you, Sebastião. I appreciate your help. Please let me know what I can do to get done as fast as possible.'

'I'll be back in touch soon. Hang in there. We'll get this sorted.'

Celine hung up the phone, collapsing onto the chair in the kitchen. She'd been pacing up and down when Sebastião had called her. Exhaustion clamped its iron fist around her chest, making her feel wearier than she had in the last couple of weeks.

What had driven her to seek a divorce after six years of silence? She'd given up hope ages ago, focusing on her daughter and building a life for her—a life she was proud of, despite the struggles of a single mother.

The answer to her question strolled in through the front door. Her sister, Maria, looked at her with raised eyebrows. 'Who ruined your day?'

Celine put her phone on the table and leaned forward, burying her face in her hands as she let out a long groan. 'Take a guess.'

'What happened?' Maria sat down in the chair next to her.

You happened, Celine thought, but didn't let those words pass her lips. It wasn't Maria's fault that she had found someone to share her life with. For the longest time the Dias sisters had shared this house, working alongside each other in their animal rescue and shouldering care for their children together.

Celine had been overjoyed when Maria found Rafael to fill a gap in her life she'd seen more clearly when things were quiet around them. It was their partnership that shone a glaring light on the problem she hadn't been dealing with in the last six years.

'Apparently Darius doesn't want to get divorced,' she said as she dropped her hands from her face.

Maria sucked her breath in. 'You spoke to him?'

'No. His lawyer spoke to my lawyer. Now we have to go to court to get this whole thing sorted out.' She sighed again, her eyes dropping to her hands splayed out on the table.

Maria frowned, leaning closer to pat her sister on the arm. 'We'll get through this. So the selfish jerk added another few months to the dissolution of your marriage. We've come so far, we can do this.'

Something inside Celine bristled at her sister's words. Though she had thought worse things of him, hearing someone else call him selfish set a deep-seated defence instinct loose in her. Even years later, the fragments of the relationship they had shared roared to life at the most unexpected times.

It wasn't as if her sister was wrong. What else could you call a man who ran away from the woman he had just married?

'Maybe this is just not worth the effort. I don't plan on getting married ever again, and I don't have time to think about men. Thanks to you, our charity has a shot at the future again.' Though she meant to sound cheerful, Celine couldn't keep the bitter edge from her voice. Before her sister had met Rafael, the two of them had run their animal charity together. Though that dream had always been more Maria's than Celine's. No, she had come here because of the heartache Darius's sudden desertion had caused her.

With Rafael to support Maria now, Celine had to admit that her role had significantly diminished, and she was more of a consultant than anything else.

'Don't give up, Cee. He doesn't get to hold you to this marriage when he isn't even a part of your life.' Maria crossed her arms in front of her chest and huffed out an annoyed breath. 'Men are twisted.'

'Oh, look who's talking—with your perfect husband and cute baby.' Celine mustered a laugh when a faint blush streaked over her sister's high cheekbones.

The door opened again and, as if summoned, Rafael stepped in, looking at them with a smile on his face. He was carrying a car seat in his hand, and the second Celine saw the sleeping face of her niece all the anger and frustration sitting in her chest melted away. Rafael set their daughter down and laid a hand on Maria's shoulder, giving it a gentle squeeze as he brushed a kiss on the top of her head.

This was why she wanted a divorce. She wanted a shot at *this*.

'Speak of the devil,' Celine said, but returned the smile her brother-in-law gave her.

'Ah, if you are at the part of your evening where you gossip about me, I think that's a good time to call it a day—or I will never get her out of here.'

Maria laughed and got up from her seat. They both bade her goodnight, and as Maria grabbed the baby carrier from the floor Rafael turned around to look at her.

'Oh, I almost forgot. Someone came by this morning to see you, but you weren't in.'

Celine furrowed her brow, thinking. She hadn't received any kind of message from her patients. While Rafael and Maria worked mainly in their vet clinic, Celine spent a lot of time travelling from place to place, tending to larger livestock in the area. This meant unpredictable work hours and that she might not be around for regular visits to their clinic. But who would even seek her out like that?

'Did they say what they wanted? I haven't received any calls.'

Rafael shook his head. 'No, he just asked to speak to you but wouldn't say anything else. I told him to try his luck in the evening.'

'Did he leave a name?' Who would have reason to visit her unannounced?

Rafael looked away for a second. 'Sorry, I didn't ask for the name. We were busy with an emergency when he came in. I just told him to come back in the evening.'

'I see, thanks for letting me know.' Celine saw them out and closed the door behind them, thinking about the mysterious visitor Rafael had mentioned. Her patients' owners never came to visit her here.

Was it someone unrelated to her work? That wasn't much more likely either. She travelled so much for work, Celine didn't really have friends in town that would just drop by to see her.

A knock on the door pulled her out of her contemplations, and her gaze darted around for a second. Had they left something behind?

'I don't see anything lying around,' she shouted as she moved to open the door. 'What do you—'

Her brain stopped working mid-sentence as she stared into a face from the past that had been haunting her for the last six years.

'Darius…'

A whirl of different emotions tore through Darius as he sat watching the house where his estranged wife lived. When he'd come here to talk to her, he hadn't imagined being stuck in his car, watching her from afar as he contemplated what to tell her.

Can we please not get divorced for another three months because I need the visa for my job?

That wasn't going to win him her favour—and he really needed her to help him. Not that he had any favours left with Celine. But he needed to ask her anyway, even though he suspected she would send him packing and all his plans for a future in Brazil would collapse with that.

Not that he didn't deserve it. The pain of leaving Celine all those years ago had left a hole in his chest that had never closed in the years he'd spent away.

He'd left Brazil intending to come back as soon as he had sorted his spouse visa out, but when he'd told his mother about it she had revealed the real reason they had left. She had initially claimed that it was because of an advantageous business deal back in Peru. After his father's sudden death over twenty years ago, his mother had founded Delgado Cosmetics to keep her and her son fed. Though she'd initially worked out of their small kitchen, the brand had gained acclaim for its high standard in skincare and had become popular in Brazil—which had been the reason for their move there.

But apparently after years of success, the sales had waned, leading to his mother making riskier investments and borrowing money from people she shouldn't have. The result had been her fleeing the country from her creditors, and telling Darius that he too was in great danger if he returned to Brazil as the people she had got involved with would not shy away from hurting him—or his new wife, were they to ever learn about that connection.

Fearing what the loan sharks would do to Celine, he had kept quiet, even though it had torn him up inside.

Darius sat up when the door opened and two shadowy figures walked out, waving at the woman standing against the light of her house. Celine.

He gritted his teeth when a flood of ancient emotions broke through parts of the dam he'd erected inside of him to stem any feelings that lingered for this woman. He'd spent a lot of time shutting them away, never to think about them again—but now the culmination of his dreams depended on their marriage. Would she agree to stay married to him just for a while? Would she even hear him out?

The chances were slim, but Darius had to try.

He watched the two people get into their car and drive off. Taking deep breaths, he forced himself into motion, getting out of his car and crossing the short distance between the street to the small building nestled against the back of the main house—the vet clinic her parents had run before they'd retired.

He'd been surprised to learn that she had returned to Santarém to be a part of the charity her family had been running for decades. Her sister, Maria, had been the one with the dream to take it over, but when Darius and Celine had spoken about their future together, Santarém had never once come up. His estranged wife had even said that she wanted to distance herself from the charity to give her older sister the time in the spotlight she deserved.

Had she come back because of him? Because his absence had rendered their future plans obsolete?

Nervous energy trickled through him when he stood in front of the door, staring at a worn wooden plaque with her family name engraved on it. Dias.

He swallowed the lump building in his chest as he raised his hand and knocked on the door. Behind it, he heard her muffled voice calling out, and then the door flew open again. 'What do you—'

The words stopped as she stared at him—in confusion at first. Clearly, he wasn't the person she'd expected on the other side. No one really expected their long-estranged husband to suddenly show up one evening.

The moment understanding dawned on her face and

he saw the pain flicker alive in her eyes he felt his breath leave his body as he sensed her agony in his own bones.

'Darius…' She said his name with a mixture of emotions too complex to unravel. Hurt—so much of it—wrapped itself around each syllable. But as her voice cracked, a sense of long-forgotten longing seeped through as well, matching the ancient memories resurrected in his own chest.

'Hey, Cee.' He didn't know what else to say. He'd flown here from São Paulo, where he worked as the head physician for one of the premier football clubs of the Brazilian league, and had agonised over what he would say when they finally met face to face.

But nothing had prepared him for the visceral reaction that erupted through him as he saw her stand in front of him. Six years had taken the budding beauty he'd seen in her and honed her into a woman so stunning he couldn't understand what she'd ever seen in him.

For a second her features remained soft, reminiscent of the love they'd once shared, and all the memories of their relationship came rushing back into the space between them. Darius felt a tug on his hand, calling it upwards to touch her cheek. But the moment was fleeting. Not even a heartbeat later, her expression changed into one hewn out of stone.

'You'd better be here to sign those divorce papers,' she said, her voice coated in ice so tangible his skin prickled.

'Yes, that's why I'm here. I just wanted to talk to you first.' This was the truth he was willing to go with. She hadn't asked if he wanted to sign the divorce papers *right now*. And he was going to sign them as soon as the current football season was over and he could convince the team's owners to sponsor his visa.

A subject he needed to broach with her today.

'*Now* you want to talk? After six years of silence and missed phone calls, you want to have a normal conversation like nothing ever happened?'

Darius bit his lip to stop the sigh building in his chest from escaping. He knew when he'd first arrived that this conversation wouldn't be an easy one, especially remembering one trait they had in common, which had also fuelled the fire of their relationship—they could both be incredibly stubborn over the most minute things.

'We're already not having a normal conversation, and I don't know when I gave the impression that I thought any of this was ordinary,' he replied through gritted teeth. 'If you give me some of your time, maybe I can start grovelling so you can finally find some closure. I'm not here because I want you back.'

He didn't know if it was necessary to state this, but he wanted to ensure that this question was out of the way. While his heart was pounding against his chest from being so near to the woman he'd desired so fiercely, he knew he couldn't have her—didn't want to either. Though he'd believed he had good reasons to stay away from her—his mother's lies around her financial problems only exposed with her death—he'd been a coward for leaving and he couldn't forgive himself for that.

And, by the look on her face, she wasn't close to forgiving him either.

'I certainly hope so. I'd have to call someone if you told me this is some strange romantic gesture.'

'Maybe if I can have some of your time...' Darius left the rest of the sentence unsaid, daring to meet her gaze. He couldn't help but marvel at the amber of her eyes that was only interrupted by smatterings of dark dots, almost as if they were trying to form a constellation in her iris. Darius had spent countless hours looking into those eyes, counting the little flecks.

'I can't talk here,' she finally said, her gaze darting over her shoulder for a second. 'How long are you going to be here?'

Darius paused, hope blossoming in his chest. This wasn't a hard no. He might be able to convince her—to apologise for lacking the courage a real husband needed.

'I'm on leave for the next week. The team is finishing up the Copa América, so they are training with the national team.'

'The Copa? What are you—' Steps shuffling on the far side of the house interrupted her. Celine looked back again before taking a step forward and pulling the door closed behind her. 'I'm driving to a farm tomorrow to examine some livestock. You can come with me, and we can talk in the car.'

'Are you with someone?' The question flew from his mouth before he could contemplate how it was really none of his business, yet the edge in his voice shook him on a deeper level. While they were technically married, Celine had, of course, moved on with her life.

Was that why she had sent him the divorce papers? Because she wanted to get married to someone else? The thought caused a dissonance within him he didn't want to inspect closer. Darius had been the one to leave— regardless of the good reasons he'd had, he'd left her to pick up the pieces on her own.

'What if I am? My *husband* hasn't really been in the picture for the last six years.' She gave voice to the inner monologue in his brain when he'd asked the question.

He shook his head, not wanting to delve into this topic.

The fury boiling in his veins stemmed from ancient affection that needed to remain long-forgotten for them to have a somewhat civil discussion. Darius wasn't here because of love. Though he'd never been able to bury his feelings for Celine, he was here to save his dream and give her—and himself—some closure.

He owed her the truth, no matter how painful it was.

'I'll come with you,' he said with a nod, not wanting to let the olive branch she extended go. This might be the only chance he had to tell her why he'd left and how he needed more time before he signed the papers.

'I'm leaving early tomorrow. Be here at six and we can talk. Stay in your car until you see me walk towards mine, then meet me there. I don't want anyone to see you loitering around my house.' Her voice was still frosty, but beneath the hurt he could glimpse the Celine who had agreed to marry him so they could be together—even though he'd learned that things weren't as simple as that.

She was still so much like the person he'd fallen in love with. It was hard to keep the old affection at bay. Darius reminded himself that he'd come here for a purpose, and it wasn't to fall in love again. No, he needed time to figure his life out, and he prayed that she'd grant him that time.

Three months until the season ended. That was all he needed.

CHAPTER TWO

CELINE TOOK A sip of her coffee, hoping that it would stave off the dread pooling in the pit of her stomach. Last night's surprise visitor had shaken her to her core, leaving her with a deep sense of inner turmoil that had kept her awake for a considerable portion of the night.

Darius was back—and he wanted to talk.

It was something Celine had wanted for many years, longing to get some sense of closure after what had happened. Because he'd been staying in Brazil under his mother's visa, he'd had to leave with her even after they'd got married so he could reapply for a spouse visa. Though it had been hard to say goodbye, she'd known it would only be for a few weeks before he'd return and no one could take him from her again.

The last thing she had expected was for Darius to be the one to end their relationship. His message had been vague, telling her he no longer wished to come back, but didn't explain why. Didn't give her an opportunity to fight for him either.

And another four weeks later Celine had received news that changed her life—and made Darius's departure that much more painful.

The thought of Nina brought the nervous energy to a boil. Darius didn't know he had a five-year-old daughter. That was something she would have to bring up with him. His reaction would tell her everything she needed to know about who he'd become in the last six years.

Though Celine had always remained light on the details, she'd told Nina that her father was away, and that he wouldn't be around. She would need to tell her about him too. How would she even go about having such a conversation? Before she could mention Darius's reappearance to their daughter, she needed to understand why he'd chosen to come back into her life rather than just signing the papers.

'Good morning, Mãe.' Celine looked up from her coffee as her daughter walked into the kitchen. Still wearing her pyjamas, she rubbed one hand over her eyes, lids still heavy with sleep.

'You're up early, *amor.*'

Nina only shrugged, then climbed onto the chair next to hers before putting her hands on the table and resting her head on top of them.

'Are you hungry?' Celine asked, then got up when her daughter nodded.

She grabbed a bowl from the cupboard and poured cereal into it. 'I'm off to vaccinate some livestock. They have a lot of animals to get through, so I'm starting early. Tia Maria will be over in a moment to watch you before taking you to kindergarten.'

She put the bowl of cereal in front of her daughter and grabbed the soy milk from their fridge, giving the carton a swift shake before pouring it out. Nina grabbed the spoon and dug in, filling the kitchen with the sound of quiet chewing.

With her daughter somewhat distracted, Celine stepped to the window and peered outside to see a car pull over, and Maria step out of it. But there was another car parked further down that she didn't recognise. Its windows were tinted, so she couldn't see who was sitting in it either. Was that Darius?

She turned away when her sister opened the door, letting herself in with her own key. 'Good morning, sweetie,' she said before her eyes found Celine.

Her eyebrows shot up. 'You okay?' she asked, clearly seeing something in her face that Celine didn't want her to see.

'Yeah, all good. Just a long day ahead of me and not looking forward to it,' she said as an excuse and, before Maria could ask anything else, she rushed over to the door, shouldered her bag and grabbed her keys. 'I'm off, my sweet. Your aunt will take you and your cousin to school today, so don't dally with your breakfast.' She hurried over to kiss Nina on the top of her head then left, slamming the door just a bit too hard.

She felt bad keeping Darius's presence from her sister, but she needed time to process it herself. Over the last few years Maria had been invaluable, keeping her sane throughout her unexpected pregnancy and taking care of Nina whenever she needed her to. Celine tried to give back to her sister as much as possible, spending time in the clinic whenever she could—less since Rafael had arrived.

That was a debt she didn't know how to repay.

When she reached her truck she threw the bag in the back seat and looked over her shoulder towards the house. The window in the kitchen was lit, but she didn't see Maria standing at it, watching her. Good. She didn't want to have the Darius conversation yet. Not when she herself was trying to figure it out.

Her eyes flitted to the unknown car and, as if he'd been waiting for some sort of signal, Darius emerged from it and strode towards her, the car lights flashing as he locked it with a remote. Celine's stomach gave a pitiful rumble as he came closer, his gait enough to elicit memories of a marriage that had lasted only a few days. If only the years had been unkind to him, she thought as she raised her chin. But whatever life he had lived in Peru had clearly done him well.

While the old sneakers and the worn-out jeans were appropriate attire for their morning outing, the expensive watch and light brown hair styled to perfection gave away the success he'd found as a person. Hair that was short on the sides and longer on top, begging to be ruffled through with longing fingers.

'Buenos dias,' he said when he got into the passenger seat of her car. And along with the perfect picture of masculinity and poise came the subtle scent of pine and spices, transporting her thoughts to the last place she'd smelled that combination—wrapped up in Darius's arms on the night of their courthouse wedding as they'd made love for the first time as a married couple.

Bad. This was very, *very* bad. He was the one who'd run away from his responsibilities after asking her to marry him. She should not be indulging any old memories of a time when their love was real—when she'd thought nothing could defeat them because she would have never believed Darius to be the one to break them apart.

'Darius.' She gave a curt nod and bit her lip as her traitorous body reacted to his proximity as if he had some kind of magnet that overpowered her free will with a mere glance.

'That's what you drive around in the countryside?' she

said as she eyed his expensive car, imagining it covered in mud after a few hours driving around rural Brazil.

'It's a rental car. What do you expect? At least it's better than the club car I drive in São Paulo,' he replied.

'Club car?' Celine shook off the tension gripping her chest, focusing on what he had just shared. Though the urge had been strong, she had used every ounce of stubbornness within her to resist stalking her estranged husband on the internet, knowing heartache was all it would bring her.

A stranger might as well have stood in front of her, that was how little she now knew the man she had married. A tingling sensation flowed from her hands down her arms and into her belly, pooling there in a coil of warmth and nervous energy.

This was so not happening to her. This was the man who had left her pregnant and alone mere days after marrying her, not once answering any of the hundreds of her calls or texts. There was no way the thing stirring right behind her belly-button was genuine attraction. It had to be some old memory that was now rearing its head at the sheer familiarity his presence brought back into her life.

'I'm the head physician for a *futebol* team in São Paulo,' he said, bringing her back to her question.

She stuck the key into the ignition but stopped midturn to look at him. 'You finished med school in Peru?'

A line appeared between his brows. 'Yes, of course. Why do you sound horrified at that?'

'Because...' Her voice trailed off as she searched for the right words. 'You left. You ran from your responsibilities, from your wife, and then what? You just moved on with your life and finished med school?'

The words came forth without a filter and Celine didn't

dare to look at him, afraid of what she might see in his face. She started the truck instead and began the journey to the farm. At least driving gave her a good excuse to keep her eyes off him.

'Cee, I—how do you expect me to respond to that? I'm sorry for what I did, and I'm not asking for your forgiveness. The way I hurt you—it's unforgivable. But I mean to look you in the eye when I apologise. You need to see that I mean it, that it's not just empty words.' From the corner of her eye she saw his chest rise and fall with a great heave, speaking of the effort this apology had taken from him.

Good. It wouldn't be a genuine apology if he wasn't struggling with it.

'Why?' It was the one question burning on her tongue, one word with so many answers outstanding.

Darius heaved a great sigh, his head dipping down as he rubbed his hands over his eyes. The weariness in his features was new. During their student romance he'd been the daring one, always looking for their next adventure, while Celine tempered his wilder ideas.

Something had happened to him that had forced him to leave. The naïve, hopeful part of her heart that still remained intact had clung to that narrative in her darkest hour, shielding her from the potential truth that he had never really loved her.

But what would have been so bad that he couldn't tell her?

They drove past lush green fields, a few of them fenced, with grazing cows and alpacas that had ventured far enough for one to see from the side of the road. Most of the landscape here was dedicated to grain farming to keep the population of livestock fed. The surroundings weren't quite the same as the dense trees of the rainforest that wound itself through the land alongside the Amazon River. But, unlike her sister, who was at home in the forest and dedicated their animal charity to the animals who lived there, Celine preferred the structure and schedule of the farm over the chaos of the wild.

The familiar view was a comfort to her as the silence in the truck grew longer.

Finally, Darius took a deep breath and said, 'My mother…she was sick, though I only learned that once I told her I was planning to go back to Brazil and be with you. She'd forced us to leave the country under…other circumstances, but in the end she wanted to be back in Peru for her health.'

The sign pointing at the road to the farm popped up on the side, a wooden plaque that welcomed everyone who drove by in big cursive letters. This was usually when the excitement to see everyone on the farm grew the closer Celine got. But it was as if her mind hadn't registered the sign, focused too much on her estranged husband sitting next to her and finally revealing the truth.

Darius too noticed the sign, glad that they would soon arrive. His eyes kept darting to Celine, but with her gaze trained on the road it was hard for him to gauge her reaction.

The truth—the entire truth—clung to his lips, but when he willed himself to say the words they wouldn't come to him. His mother had been sick, that *was* the reason she had wanted him to stay in Peru with her. But what had kept him there had been the web of lies she'd spun around him. The potential threat to Celine had been too great a risk for him to take.

Darius knew she deserved to know the truth, yet still he hesitated. Would she even believe him? The optics weren't in his favour, and if he put himself in her position he wasn't sure if *he* would believe his story either. After all, outwardly, his mother had been a successful businesswoman.

Would Celine judge him for believing his mother? Though he had acted on what he'd thought was true information, he couldn't deny the hurt he had caused. How could he ask for forgiveness when he himself struggled with what he had done? The guilt of his abandonment sat deep in his heart, but he didn't dare to let her see it.

No, the truth would only soothe his own guilt. It wouldn't give her anything. Better to let go of her, of the idea of their marriage, and carry the truth in his heart. He had nothing to gain from disturbing her again, of telling his side of the story. What if she did forgive him? Darius couldn't let her waste her time with him, not when his judgement and decision-making had been so wrong in the past.

What if he'd got other things wrong?

Celine didn't reply to his response, instead driving in silence until the tiled roofs of buildings appeared on the horizon as they approached the top of the hill where the farm was located. Several white-walled houses dotted the landscape, each one a different size to fit its purpose. They kept heading up the dirt road until they came to a halt in front of what could only be the main house.

Celine pulled the handbrake up, taking the key out of the ignition, but remained in her seat. Finally, she turned her head to look at him, her expression veiled. 'Your mother was sick?'

'She was, yes,' he said, and his heart rate took a tumble when he looked at her.

'And…' She hesitated, a hint of something intangible weaving itself through that word. Her throat bobbed as she swallowed before she continued. 'And you thought you couldn't tell me that?'

'What? No, I—'

'Then *why* did you not tell me? Why did you let me believe it was my fault? Why did you not pick up the phone?'

The last words weren't much louder than the others, but the pain in them amplified their sound as if a thunderstorm had struck right next to him. Her hurt cut him to the bone, leaving him stunned and staring at her with wide eyes.

'Celine, I thought we could—'

She cut him off again when she realised he wasn't giving an actual answer. 'There was a time when you'd tell me anything, but when it actually counted you couldn't open your mouth. Did you think I wouldn't understand? You thought so little of the woman you married?'

Her eyes swam with unshed tears, squeezing his chest so tight that all the air fled his lungs. His lips parted, but no words formed in his mind. Everything he had in him focused on the torment etched in her face. Darius had known this conversation would be painful. His chest tightened, the truth wanting to spill out into the open. But he couldn't let it out—not when it was only going to serve him. He'd do it if it were for her, but she would only see it as another excuse, another reason why she should never have married him.

'Cee…'

'Why, Darius? You had six years to think about this. By now you should have an answer to—'

He was the one to interrupt this time. 'You don't know *everything* that happened, Celine! I had good reasons to keep things from you.' He swallowed the lump in his throat, his mouth dry from the effort it took him to keep his voice from cracking. 'The truth won't change anything between us because you already decided how you want to see me. Anything I have to say in my defence is futile, is it not? So let's just both agree that I messed up this marriage, and then we can start finding our way towards a divorce.'

Celine blinked twice, the mist in her gaze dissolving. Movement in front of them drew their attention away from this intense moment that had been in the making for years. A short woman opened the front door, waving with a big smile on her face.

Celine returned the wave with a plastered-on smile before looking back at Darius, the disquiet in her eyes setting off alarm bells in his head. 'I hoped you'd have enough respect for me to at least tell me the truth. But you're right. All I want is you out of my life.'

He opened his mouth, but Celine shook her head. 'Juliana is waiting for us.'

Darius gave a curt nod, then looked around and jumped out of the car, opening the hatch to take the heavy-looking bag.

'What are you doing?'

He glanced at the contents of the bag through the half-open zip. 'This looks like vaccinations. I'm a doctor. I know how to administer vaccinations.'

Celine snorted at that, and the sound hit him in a different, softer part of his chest. For a moment she looked almost exactly like he remembered her, even-tempered

until someone or something slipped past her defences—
to find an adorable goofball.

'You're a *human* doctor. We're vaccinating cows today.'
Scepticism laced her voice and raised Darius's competi-
tive spirit.

'So a slightly bigger mammal. I think if you show me
how and where to poke the needle, I'll be more help than
hindrance.' He crossed his arms, nudging his chin forward in a challenge he knew she couldn't refuse. Six years
might have passed—and maybe too much bad blood to
repair their relationship—but he still knew this woman.

Her eyes narrowed, a dangerous sparkle entering those
endlessly deep amber eyes. Then she turned around to
face the woman approaching them.

'Juliana, good to see you,' she greeted her, stepping
forward to give the woman a quick hug. 'This is Darius,
my assistant.'

Juliana turned to Darius and held her hand out. The
quick but firm handshake was enough to feel the calluses
along her palms, a subtle but powerful sign of how much
work she put into her farm. And from the grin spreading
over her face, a similar understanding passed through her.

'I see you're a man who doesn't shy away from hard
work,' she said with a nod, and Celine raised one of her
eyebrows but didn't say anything.

'We're ready to get some cattle vaccinated. Are they
in the barn?'

Juliana nodded, waving them along. 'Glad to see things
are going better for you two now that you can afford some
help. You won't have to spend all day here,' the farmer
said, getting only a grunt back from Celine.

Better? Had she been in trouble? Darius furrowed
his brow but said nothing, letting his gaze drift when he

caught her glaring in his direction. Maybe if she thought him distracted she would let her guard down around Juliana.

He spotted the beginning of the fence denoting Juliana's property but, as his gaze followed it, it vanished behind the horizon, hinting at the vastness of the fields. Both alpacas and cows were grazing on green fields, the fragrance of fresh grass and dried hay enveloping them with every step. Brazil's humidity was much more oppressive out here, and it would only get worse with the rising sun.

'I want you to look at one of our horses as well. My daughter says there is an issue with Roach's foot. He's not lame, but she says she feels *something* when they ride,' Juliana said, and Celine nodded.

'Llamaste cucaracha a tu caballo?' Darius asked, his mouth faster than his brain.

The woman looked at him with raised eyebrows before looking back at Celine, who had a barely noticeable smirk on her face. 'Darius is from Peru, but he speaks Portuguese. He's surprised you would name your horse after an insect.'

'Ooh,' Juliana said, waving her hand dismissively. 'My daughter named the horse. It's from a video game or a TV show. I can't remember.'

Darius followed behind the women, shaking his head at the slip-up. He was more on edge than he had let himself believe if he lapsed into Spanish like that. Though he'd grown up speaking Portuguese, they'd always spoken Spanish at home, so much that people could still detect the hint of an accent if they listened closely.

They arrived at the largest of the several barns strewn around the property. The wide doors were already open and the sound of cows shuffling and mooing mixed with the smell of hay as they stepped in. Inside, the barn was divided into several pens in which the cows lived, each box large enough to accommodate several more than were currently inhabiting them.

A smile tugged on Celine's lips when he glanced over at her as she stepped closer to one pen and laid her hand on the wide forehead of a brown cow. Her fingers rubbed through the hair and the animal inclined its head to nuzzle closer at the affectionate touch.

Darius couldn't help but smile as well, the constant pulse of guilt fading away for a few moments as he observed the joy her work brought to her—wishing that he could have been there as she'd grown into her role as a veterinarian. The regret of missed opportunities came up his throat like bitter bile as another fragment of the life he'd lost came to life in front of his eyes.

Without the machinations of his mother, he might never have left and they would have had a chance at a genuine marriage. It was easy to blame his mother. He had only found out after her death that the loan sharks threatening her and her loved ones had been in her imagination—a ruse to keep him in check. But Darius needed to remind himself of the part he himself had played. After all, he'd chosen to leave—he'd been misled, but he'd left.

They stopped in front of a pen populated with calves. Some eyed them as they approached, but most remained with their heads down, nipping at the hay covering the ground.

'These are all?' Celine asked Juliana, who nodded.

'Yep, impressive, isn't it?' The woman sported a proud grin, eyeing both Darius and Celine as she waited for confirmation.

'You know how I feel about your gorgeous animals, Jules,' Celine said with a laugh.

She reached up to the door of the pen and undid the latch, pulling it open and waving Darius along with her. 'I'll give them a quick exam followed by their vaccine. This shouldn't take too much time. Darius—' She pointed at the bag hanging from his shoulder.

'Come find me at the house once you're done,' Juliana said, leaving them with a wave.

Darius took the bag, placing it on a small table to the side that looked like it had been brought in for this specific occasion. When he went to open the zip Celine moved next to him and bumped him with her hip to move him out of the way.

Her scent enveloped him for a fraction of a second, drowning out the surrounding sounds and smells as awareness rushed through him. Old memories flashed through his mind, the same scent of spice and something primal cradling him to sleep as he'd held her against him.

But the look she gave him now as she glared over her shoulder was nothing like the ones she used to give him. The light and gentleness had been replaced by an impenetrable brick wall that he couldn't see beyond. Darius used to know exactly what she was thinking… Before his life had been upended by his mother's lies.

Before he had left.

They vaccinated the calves and Celine didn't find anything of note that warranted alerting Juliana. All her new calves were happy and healthy. What she noted though was Darius through the entire process. His eyes had grown large when she had prepared the vaccination gun.

Clearly he had expected cattle to be vaccinated just like humans, each one getting their own syringe.

But with a farm the size of Juliana's that endeavour would take several days if they had to go through all the resident animals. To be time-efficient, large animal vets instead used an apparatus that would fill a syringe with a predetermined amount of medication and a mechanism to change the needle after every shot.

Despite his claim in the car, Darius wasn't able to assist her with vaccinating the animals, though he did a tremendous job in calming the little calves as she worked her way through them. Watching him rub each calf behind its ears before they moved onto the next one while whispering encouragements to them ignited a warm and fuzzy feeling in the pit of her stomach that Celine was too scared to examine any closer.

Heat rose in her body as she watched him, a flame she hadn't felt flicker inside her since the day he'd left. The familiarity of it was almost enough to lure her back into his arms. How could she be angry at a man who treated animals with such respect and empathy?

By remembering that he had left her and his child with only a message to let them know they would never see him again. Her chest squeezed tight when Nina came to her mind. She needed to tell him about his daughter, but fear surged through her veins when she thought about mentioning her. Their lives had been just fine without him. True, Santarém had never been the place she'd envisioned growing her family, but with the amount of help her sister had given her from the day she'd learned she was pregnant, she couldn't just up and leave because she felt like it.

Celine needed to know why he was here—and why he refused to sign the divorce papers.

'You handled the calves well for a people doctor,' she said, even though a myriad different words formed in her throat. But his bright eyes were so disarming she forgot about her apprehension for a few heartbeats.

'Is there something going on in the medical community that I'm unaware of? Are medical doctors and vets at war?' His tone was playful as he walked to the table with her bag on it, packing up the instruments she had used to examine the calves.

Celine didn't reply and watched him instead, her eyes gliding down to those hands that had once held her so tight—made her feel so safe. How could all of that have been an illusion dreamt up by a love-addled young adult?

'You still haven't told me why you're here,' she said when they remained quiet.

Darius rustled around the bag, his eyes trained on his hands. The sound of the zip filled the air, only stressing the silence rather than masking it.

'Let me preface everything by acknowledging how much pain I caused you when I left. Nothing I can say will make it better, but I'm willing to put in the work to rebuild your trust.'

Celine furrowed her brow, her arms crossed. 'Trust? Darius, I will *never* trust you again, so don't waste both of our time. What I want is for you to sign these divorce papers and get the hell out of my life again.' She bit her lip when her voice trembled, cursing herself for showing such fury in front of him.

Memories of their relationship flashed through her mind whenever she let her thoughts wander. Things had been so much easier six years ago when they were in love.

Ever the romantic, Celine's younger self knew she was meant to marry Darius and couldn't believe how lucky she was that she'd got to meet the love of her life at twenty-one without even trying.

'What if I told you I want to move back to Brazil for good?' he asked, and Celine stared at him as her pulse took a traitorous tumble at his words.

'What do you mean?'

He was coming back? A familiar heat rose through her body and to her cheeks at that information, leaving her at a loss for words. Why would she care if he was back? He had left her broken, unable to pick herself up. Unable to…move on, because how could she explain that she was stuck in a marriage that had lasted a few days total?

It was the reason Celine had waited so long to ask for a divorce. Her broken-down marriage had become a shield behind which she hid from any attention when her heart remained too broken to consider someone else by her side.

'That's the reason I came to see you. I'd been here a few weeks when my lawyer called to let me know that some papers had arrived—your divorce papers.' He zipped the front pockets of the bag closed and shouldered it again, looking at her expectantly when she didn't move. 'Should we go and see Cucaracha?'

'Oh…' Hearing the name of Juliana's horse snapped her back into reality and she nodded, walking out of the barn and to the stables a few metres further along.

'Why didn't you sign?' That was the question causing the lion's share of unease pooling inside of Celine. Why was he here instead of in his lawyer's office, signing the papers and finally letting her go?

'The club offered me the job under the condition that I start right away. It's a temporary contract, as their head physician had to leave somewhat abruptly. They said they wanted me, but they couldn't afford to wait for the visa process, not with the Copa ending so soon and their players coming back to the club.' He paused when they got to the stable and pushed the door open for them to enter.

'How does that concern me asking you to sign the divorce papers?'

She stopped in front of Roach's box, turning to look at the horse, her question to Darius forgotten. 'Hey, buddy. What's up with you today?' she greeted the animal, reaching over to her bag, still hanging from Darius's shoulder, to retrieve some treats.

She held her palm out flat, rubbing the ridge of Roach's nose as he snapped up the treats with a satisfied snort.

'There should be a black case in the bottom of the bag. Can you dig it out?' Celine unlatched the gate as Darius put the bag on the floor to find the requested item. She pulled the gate shut behind her, taking the case from him when he reached over to hand it to her.

Inside were all the tools she needed to inspect Roach's hooves. Darius leaned over the gate, watching as she tied the horse's halter to a hook on the wall and pulled one of his back legs off the floor, holding it between her thighs as she bent over it.

Celine put the open case on the floor, grabbing the clinch cutter and a compact hammer to straighten the nails with which a farrier had attached the horseshoe to the hoof. She grunted when the last nail came out and the shoe dropped onto the floor.

A tingling sensation crawled down her spine, and when she looked up she caught Darius staring at her with a soft expression, a slight smile pulling at his lips. The look on his face evoked more memories of a time long gone, when they were still in love.

'What?' she said, irritated at the heat rising to her cheeks. There should be no such reaction to him. Had her body already forgotten what damage he had wrought on her heart and soul?

'You're a farrier too?' he asked, and Celine wasn't sure if that was awe that she heard in his voice.

'It's sort of part of a large animal vet's training and sort of not. We speak a lot about different hooves, but the work of a farrier is an entirely different discipline. When I returned to Santarém the opportunity to work with the farmsteads in the area came up, which excited me more than the exotic animal work Maria does. So I took the time to apprentice with a farrier three years ago.'

She paused, putting the clinch cutter and hammer down, grabbing the hoof pick instead and started cleaning up the dirt and debris on the hoof in slow and precise downward strokes.

'I'm glad you get to do what you always wanted. You didn't seem to be enthusiastic about the rescue work, so I was worried you'd been forced into it when I realised you were back in your hometown,' Darius said from above her, renewing the heat that had just cascaded through her body.

He remembered that? Celine had never planned to come back to Santarém, not when she'd still thought that she and Darius would have a future together. But then he'd left, and shortly after she had learned of her pregnancy, and all her plans had been in pieces. At Maria's urging she'd come back to Santarém, so she could raise her child with the help of her sister. But she had never wanted to work at their family charity the way her sister had.

Why did Darius care at all about that? She didn't get to voice the question when she spotted something on Roach's hoof. With another grunt, she squeezed the hoof, some liquid coming to the surface from the area where the soft tissue of the hoof met the hard horn.

'Looks like we have a hoof abscess…' Celine mumbled, dropping the pick and grabbing the hoof knife instead to cut away at the excess sole as she narrowed down the location of the abscess.

It must be small, for Juliana hadn't mentioned anything about Roach avoiding standing on that leg. He didn't show any visible signs of discomfort, but that was difficult to tell with prey animals. Their natural inclination was to hide any pain, or they'd be left behind.

'Can you see if I brought any bandages? Antiseptic would be ideal, but I'll take any.' She didn't want to drain the abscess if they couldn't bandage Roach properly.

Darius's head disappeared as he ducked down to rummage through the bag, coming back up holding a large roll of bandages in a plastic bag.

Celine nodded with a smile. 'Okay, come in here. I'm going to cut a drain so the pus can flow out. We need to pack and bandage the hoof afterwards, so nothing gets into the wound.'

She dropped the hoof knife into the case, picking up a much smaller paring knife and squeezed the hoof again to see where to cut. Roach snorted above her, his tail swooshing back and forth as she worked on the hoof.

'Woah there, buddy. It's all good. You are doing so great. Just a bit longer and then you'll feel as good as new,' Darius mumbled above her, and Celine could feel the tension in the horse's body subsiding, making him more agreeable to her touch.

She swallowed the dryness spreading through her mouth, pushing away the unwanted sparks jumping around in her stomach. Now was not the time for her body to react to things her mind had already ruled out. The unbidden awareness of his presence was nothing more than a relic of their shared past—one she would soon be done with.

'All right, we're almost done here. Can you cut me a large length of the bandage?' she asked, passing him the scissors from her tool case.

'Well done, champion,' Darius said to Roach before he stepped back and cut the bandages to size, handing one to Celine each time she asked for it.

A few minutes later Roach's wound was dressed and they were on their way back to the main house.

'Thanks for your help back there. That would have been more difficult without you,' she said as she sent him a sideways glance.

The way he had soothed Roach when she was working on him had set off a different heat inside her, one that gently radiated inside her chest rather than the flashes of hot fire she'd tried her best to suppress all day. Though both were inappropriate and unwelcome.

'Glad I could help. I can see how treating animals is extra challenging. At least a human can tell you where it hurts. Here you had to rely on the intuition of Roach's rider to understand that something was off.' His fascination sounded genuine as he spoke, drawing her gaze back to him.

She slowed down her pace as she looked him over, seeing something akin to anguish in his eyes that drew her back to their discussion before she had checked on

Roach's hoof. There was a reason he'd come here rather than let his lawyer do the talking.

'Why are you here, Darius?'

He stopped, forcing her to turn mid-step so she could keep looking at him.

'I came here as the spouse of a Brazilian citizen so I could start working straight away. I cannot get divorced because that would mean deportation.'

Celine blinked several times as his words sank in.

'You did *what*?'

'I need three months to show the team I'm the person they want for the job. Once the season is over, I can go back to Peru and apply for a work visa.' He sighed, his fingers grasping the strap of her bag so tightly she saw the whites of his knuckles appear. 'Please give me three more months, and then I will sign any paper you want.'

No. The word clung to her lips the moment Darius uttered that ridiculous request, fury and hurt blooming in her chest and drowning out the gentle warmth she had sensed there just moments ago. But, despite her vehement reaction, she couldn't say or do what she wanted in this very moment, acting on years of abandonment issues he'd caused in her. Because this wasn't just about her and how much she wanted Darius to leave her alone.

This was also about Nina, who had never met her father.

How would she be any better than her brother, Daniel, who had walked out on his daughter—Celine's niece Mirabel, who lived with Maria and her husband—if she didn't consider this opportunity for Nina? No matter how she felt about Darius, wouldn't it be good for her child to have her father in her life?

'Is your plan to stay in Brazil long-term?' she asked,

wanting to know more about his plans before she committed to anything.

Telling Darius that he had a daughter would be an incredibly difficult conversation, one she'd been having in her head since he'd shown up at her door.

Celine had tried to inform him about being pregnant, but he had never picked up her calls, nor reacted to a single plea to phone her back. She could have texted him about it, but she hadn't wanted to. The news that they had created a life on their wedding night should come from her lips and not from a cheap text message.

But he hadn't picked up the phone, hadn't called her back, so she had never told him about their child.

Darius hesitated before he nodded. 'Yes. I want to work for this team.'

The conviction and passion entering his eyes as he spoke were almost enough to let her forget about the anger pumping through her veins, because it reminded her so much of the man she'd fallen in love with. If they hadn't been together, he'd been near a screen watching *futebol*. He'd expressed no interest in playing the game himself, happy enough being on the sidelines, and under any other circumstances Celine would have been glad that he'd found a career that let him do just that.

If he weren't the last person she wanted to see right now.

'Why did you choose to work for a Brazilian team?' she forced herself to ask. She was not entirely convinced of his good intentions, but for the sake of her—*their*—daughter, she had to try.

'Why I…' He stopped, head tilted, as he looked at her. 'Cee, I work for Atlético Morumbi.'

Her eyes rounded as the name unearthed a memory.

Weeknights and weekends spent in their favourite bar in Manaus, surrounded by people wearing the black and white stripes of Morumbi. Discussions about how the new team manager had turned the team around and was bringing them to glory. Whispers in the dead of night of his dream to work with the team. She'd been excited for him back then, thrilled about the idea of living in São Paulo and building their careers there.

'Your father would be proud of you.' The words slipped past her lips unbidden and before she could give them more consideration. Though she had never met his father, as he had passed away long before they'd met, she knew from Darius that his father had played a role in his interest in Brazilian *futebol* even before the Delgado family had arrived from Peru.

'I…hope so,' Darius huffed, the rawness in his eyes so unexpected that her breath caught in her throat.

This side of him was too close, the vulnerability of the moment drawing her in. Because, deep down inside, she had never believed that her estranged husband was a bad person. But he had made a mistake she could not forget or forgive.

'You understand why I can't let this go, then? Why I had to come back here when I got the offer?' he asked, his voice a plea that sent a cold shiver down her spine.

She understood why he'd come back, and through the hurt his presence stirred in her Celine couldn't help but find a kernel of sympathy for him. There were a lot of things that she could be angry about regarding Darius, but following his dream wasn't one of them.

A sharp whistle tore through the air, and they both whipped around to see Juliana standing on her porch, waving at them. Celine shot a look at Darius and nodded to acknowledge what he had said, then started walking to where the farmer stood to give her a report on her animals.

'I'll come back tonight to drop off the pain medicine for Roach. The abscess was small and your kid caught it early. He should make a full recovery,' Celine said as she handed her the rest of the bandages.

'She's got that intuition from me,' Juliana said, pride puffing her chest. 'If yours and mine stay on the same trajectory, we'll be establishing a dynasty.'

A stone dropped into the pit of Celine's stomach. The perfectly innocent words turned her blood to ice, and she didn't dare look at Darius to see if he had understood what she had said.

'Sorry, Jules. We have to run to the next appointment, but I'll see you in the evening when I drop off the medicine.'

She didn't wait for the woman to reply, walking towards her truck and flinging herself into the driver's seat, the motor already running by the time Darius climbed into the passenger seat.

CHAPTER THREE

THEY'D DRIVEN BACK in silence, Celine still reeling from the request Darius had made of her. Three months. That was how long he wanted her to wait before he signed the divorce papers. Three months and then he would be out of her hair for ever. Except he wanted to stay in Brazil, and if he stayed here then maybe her daughter could finally have a father.

She had told him she needed to think about his request and invited him to come back the following day. The moment Celine stepped through the door she called Maria, who arrived twenty minutes later with a bottle of wine.

Pouring each of them a glass that contained a bit more wine than necessary, Celine plonked down on one of the kitchen chairs. Her geriatric Great Dane, Alexander, shuffled over to where the sisters were sitting, laying his large head on Maria's lap, and she scratched him behind the ear.

'You traitor,' Celine huffed as she took a big swig of her wine.

'Aww, did you miss me, Alexander?' her sister cooed, looking down at the dog with a familiar smile. Then she trained her eyes on Celine. 'So, what is the emergency?'

Celine took a deep breath, the wine already hot in the pit of her stomach as she searched for the courage to say the words she'd been carrying around in her chest the entire day.

The wine burned as she took another sip, setting the glass down with much more force than necessary. 'Darius showed up at my door last night,' she said, and Maria's eyes widened.

Stunned silence enveloped them for a few heartbeats, the soft breathing of their dog the only noise vibrating through the tiny kitchen. Then Maria's gaze flicked to the stairs at the far end of the room, past the living room.

'Where is Nina?' she asked, her voice tense.

'At a sleepover, thank God.'

'Did she see him?'

Celine shook her head. 'No. I stepped outside when he knocked on the door so she wouldn't overhear us.'

'Oh, wow…' Maria reached for her glass of wine for the first time since they'd started talking, rolling it around in one hand while the other still petted the dog's head on her lap. 'So…'

'Why did he come?' Celine finished her sentence.

'Yeah. I can't imagine he would show his face after all this time just to sign the divorce papers in person.'

Celine sighed into her glass, which was now almost empty. 'No, of course not. This man could not pick up the damn phone six years ago when I, *his wife*, needed to tell him about *our* daughter.'

'So what miracle brought this useless man into your life again?'

Even though Celine herself had called him much worse, her eyes shot up at her sister's description of Darius. Words of defence came to her lips, but she swallowed them with the last bit of wine remaining in her glass.

Darius had hurt her terribly, done the exact opposite

of what he was supposed to do as her husband. Instead of struggling through everything—including his mother's sickness—together, he had shut her out and remained in Peru with no explanation. He *was* useless, yet Celine's immediate reaction had been one of defence.

He was *hers* to call as she pleased, no one else's. A tiny and yet intrusive thought that nestled itself inside her brain without permission. She should not feel possessive about Darius, the way she felt right now. It should not matter what Maria wanted to call him.

Yet it did.

'Apparently, he's been here for a while for work,' she said instead, willing her voice to remain neutral.

'Wait, here? In Santarém?'

Celine shook her head. 'He's working in São Paulo as the head physician for a football club.'

'He still became a doctor after he ran off?' The incredulous tone in Maria's voice hit another vulnerable spot inside Celine's chest that she didn't dare to examine too closely because she again wasn't wrong.

The way Darius had left didn't spark a lot of confidence in his reliability. Yet she knew this was what he'd dreamt of doing. Being the physician for Atlético Morumbi was the culmination of hard work and dedication, showing his tenacity and devotion to his dream. Even with all the hurt floating in the space between them, she couldn't deny him that credit. No, she only wished he had applied that same grit to their marriage.

'Okay, lay off him a bit, please.' The words shot out of her mouth before Celine could even contemplate their origin, yet alone decide if she wanted to say them.

Where was this sympathy coming from? After all the absent years with missed anniversaries, birthdays and major life events, she shouldn't even give him the time of day, yet alone defend him in front of Maria, who'd been the one to pick up the pieces when he'd left.

Her sister seemed to share the same thought, for a line appeared between her brows as she scrutinised her. 'Why?'

A question that expanded the size of the lump inside her throat. Because she didn't know why. The defensive feeling made no sense to her, yet it overpowered everything else and welled up strong enough that she had to say something about it. There was one reason—the only reason Celine was even talking about this whole charade as if she *might* agree to it.

'Because if Darius wants to stay in Brazil permanently, then that's a chance for Nina to finally have her father in her life. Six years late still seems better than not at all.' She had to try to put her complicated feelings for her estranged husband aside for the sake of her daughter— their daughter.

Maria frowned, closing her long and delicate fingers around her wineglass for the first time. The white-gold wedding band on her left hand caught the dim light of the kitchen and sparkled, and Celine caught her breath. The sight crushed her deeply wounded heart as longing surged within her.

What Maria had found in Rafael… Celine had once believed herself and Darius to be just like that. Now she knew better, but that didn't stop the longing from rearing its demanding head whenever she saw her sister and brother-in-law around the vet clinic. She was so happy for them, and after how hard Maria had fought to keep their animal charity going she deserved every chance of happiness she set her heart on.

But it still stung seeing every day what she couldn't have. Not that she had looked very hard. Her job meant she travelled for several hours, sometimes days, to get to the remote farms scattered across central Brazil. But even though there had been opportunities to meet someone else, strangers she met on the road or people associated with the farms she serviced, there hadn't been anyone else—ever.

None of the people she met had ever inspired her to sort out the divorce until Maria had brought Rafael into their lives and reminded her of what life could be like with that one person by her side.

And now Darius—the man who was supposed to be that person to her—was back, and that longing that had been quietly brewing inside her chest had burst alive with an unexpected ferocity that left her almost paralysed with fear.

'How do you know Darius wants to be involved?' her sister asked.

'I don't know that he will. But I've decided to give him the three months that he needs…and I will give him the choice to get to know his daughter in that time. The alternative is to leave and never show his face in my life again.' She'd had it all planned out on the way back from Juliana's farm. She would give him three months, but he'd also get a choice. He could get to know his daughter, or he could leave and never come back.

'Have you told Nina already?'

Celine shook her head. 'No, I haven't told her yet. I want to talk to him first and only if he agrees will I bring it up with her. I don't want to get her hopes up, just for him to say no.'

'That won't be a comfortable conversation… He won't

be happy about you keeping this to yourself for so long,' Maria mumbled into her glass as she took another sip.

That was something Celine had thought about as well, but she'd ultimately decided that she could weather his anger because he only had himself to blame. She'd *wanted* to tell him, had tried many times to reach him, until the strain and heartbreak of his abandonment had become too much and she'd given up trying. Darius had every opportunity to be in his daughter's life early on, and he'd made his decision by not answering her messages.

Maria shook her head and then laughed, the sound laced with the same incredulity Celine felt herself. 'Sounds like you've got your work cut out for you. I guess that means I have to make nice with Darius when he finally shows his face again.'

The displeasure in her sister's voice was apparent and, in this moment, she loved her for that. Because Maria understood what the idea of finally giving Nina access to her father meant to her.

'I've invited him here tomorrow to talk. We'll see how it goes after that.' Celine sighed, dropping her forehead into her hand and rubbing her temple with her thumb and index finger.

This would be painful for everyone involved.

Nervous energy pooled in the pit of his stomach when Darius arrived the next day around noon. Celine's message had given him no further sign of her decision.

Celine hadn't said no, which meant that his dream yet lived. Darius was so desperate to make this work, he was willing to promise her the stars and the moon if she only gave him three more months. Though the more likely wish she'd have for him was to never see his face again.

Something he was willing to give her as well, though the thought that this might be what she asked for turned the sensation circulating around his stomach into solid ice, sending chilled waves through his body with every beat of his heart.

Seeing her again and spending the better part of his day with her yesterday had shaken him to his very foundation, leaving him adrift as he searched for something to ground himself, to remind himself of his true purpose for being here. When they had first started seeing each other Celine had woven a spell around him he'd thought to be no more than the exaggerated memories of a teenage boy's first love.

Yesterday had shown him that the spell was still very much in place, drawing his eyes to places he couldn't touch—his mind to places it didn't belong.

Attraction had sparked back to life as easily as if they had spent days apart rather than years. That was how natural it had felt to Darius to share the same space with her again. If he spent any more time near her, he might actually start to believe that reconciliation could be in the cards for them.

Something he knew to be impossible. While his body might still react to Celine all these years later, he knew better than to let himself walk down that path. He couldn't possibly hope for redemption after all he had done. It didn't even matter if she ever forgave him. He himself could not forgive how little courage and trust he'd shown when faced with the lies of his mother.

Celine deserved to be set free to find a man worthy of her affection. All he needed from her was three months.

Darius glanced at himself in his rear-view mirror, frowning at the dark bags underneath his brown eyes.

The marks looked almost blueish against his dark brown skin, the agony that had robbed him of most of his sleep plainly written on his face. With a huff he got out of his car, taking a deep breath to steel himself as he walked the short distance to her house and knocked on the door. He heard muffled footsteps from the other side, and even though he had mentally prepared himself to see her again his breath still caught in his throat when she stood in front of him.

Instant awareness overloaded his system, his thoughts becoming clouded by the pull of remembered desire that screamed at him to grab her by the shoulders and kiss her, just to get one more taste from the lips he'd starved himself of for so many years.

Something wet and cold touched his hand, breaking their transfixed gazes as Darius looked down. An enormous hound sat next to Celine, his height reaching way past her hips even while sitting down.

'Well, hello,' he greeted the dog, who stared at him with calm but watchful eyes.

'This is our family dog, Alexander,' Celine introduced him, scratching a spot between his ears.

Darius couldn't help but chuckle at the name. 'I always find it strange when people give their pets people's names.'

'People don't have the monopoly on names,' Celine said as she stepped aside, inviting him into her home.

Memories of two nights before flashed up in his mind, when she had stepped outside and closed the door behind her. Had it been her dog that made the sound that prompted her to close the door?

He looked around, searching for clues that someone else lived here with Celine. The rustic wooden table in the kitchen had four chairs around it, but there were no indications that lunch had been served, making it hard to judge how many people might have eaten here.

The living room unfolded on the other side of the open-plan space, with a cosy three-seater couch that had a plaid blanket draped over its back. Bookshelves lined the walls, but the only titles he could make out from where he was standing were thick veterinary textbooks.

Darius's gaze drifted further along and landed on a small shoe rack that was tucked away in the corner that held shoes of two wildly different sizes. The larger, more practical ones seemed to be Celine's, but the smaller ones...

'And for you it's Alexander the Great Dane.' His head whipped around to look back at Celine, who had crossed her arms and stared back at him with a stubborn glint in her eyes that he remembered well.

'Alexander...the Great Dane.' He repeated those words, his tone laced with amusement as he beheld the dog. 'Did you or Maria come up with this name?'

'Actually, it was—' She interrupted herself, her eyes going wide, and Darius could almost sense the piece of information she was intentionally withholding from him. It stung a lot more than he'd thought it would, even though he knew he didn't deserve her confidence or her trust.

His eyes darted back to the shoe rack, wondering what those small shoes meant. These were clearly children's shoes. Something trickled down his spine, settling in his stomach in an uncomfortable sensation. Had Celine found the person she wanted to start a family with, and those were the shoes of her child?

The thought rose in him like bile, leaving a bitter taste in his mouth that he had no way to justify. He couldn't possibly be angry at her for moving on from their relationship. He had, after all. When he'd worked for a football team in Peru there had been many times when he'd taken women to his room after an away match, either to celebrate or to blow off steam—depending on the team's results.

True, he'd let no one get further than a few nights with him if they *really* got along well, but he'd always been upfront about the fact that he wasn't available. So why would it hurt to imagine Celine in the arms of someone else?

His gaze flickered over her fingers, which she had entangled in front of her. There wasn't a ring on her finger, nothing indicating someone else in her life except for the shoes. Even the rest of the living area and kitchen were conspicuously empty of anything that could point towards the life she led.

'Who named the dog?' he finally asked, even though he had convinced himself a second earlier that he wasn't going to ask. It was none of his business.

'Maybe we should sit. I want to discuss what you asked me about yesterday.' Celine pointed towards the chairs around the dining table and pulled one out to seat herself.

Darius followed her, pressure building in his chest as if someone were sitting on his sternum. Each step he took, it became harder to breathe. She had deflected his question. So there was definitely someone else in her life. Which meant that she didn't want to wait another three months for him to achieve his goals. And why would she? Clearly her life had turned out just fine without him.

'I didn't know how much I was asking of you when I presented you with my idea yesterday,' he said, trying to get ahead of the rejection.

But Celine shook her head, her fingers once again intertwined in a strangely nervous manner that gave him pause. Why was *she* nervous? He was the one putting his life's dream in her hands.

'When you told me you'd come back to Brazil using our marriage, I wanted to outright reject you. Because I thought if you could come back here and not let me know, not pick up the phone again, that you hadn't changed at all. Indeed, if I had never sent those divorce papers you wouldn't even have come here, would you?'

She paused to look at him, her voice so brittle that a lump appeared in his throat. Because, from his expression alone, she knew the truth. When Darius had come back to Brazil he had wrestled with the idea of reaching out to her to explain himself. But fear had always paralysed him, stopping him from making a decision.

'I thought about reaching out, but the reasons for calling you after so long seemed so self-serving. I thought you'd have moved on a long time ago and the only reason I would break the silence would be to assuage my guilt.' The words left his lips more evenly than he felt, something he was grateful for.

Celine took a couple of deep breaths while spreading her fingers wide in front of her, before pressing her palms onto the wood of the dining table. 'At least you got some of it right. I had moved on and definitely didn't need to know you had used our farce of a marriage to get back into the country.'

Her barbed words hit their mark with expert precision, but he steeled himself not to show the hurt on his face. Celine still hadn't said no and she was going through an awful lot of trouble just to tell him she didn't want to help him. No, he was certain she was going to agree to his proposed plan. She just needed to name her conditions—

something Darius wasn't concerned about. If it meant he could stay here and convince the team that he was worth keeping for the next couple of seasons, then he would pay any price. Nothing meant more to him than that.

Celine sighed, shaking her head as she understood what he was hoping. 'Okay, so you know I didn't ask you here to say no. I'm willing to help. But you just need to know something before we continue.'

Darius nodded. He'd known she would have a counter-offer when he'd proposed his idea yesterday. Celine had always been the one to plan things, needing to know all the details and how things were going to be before she agreed to anything. In fact it had surprised him she'd even agreed to marry him, knowing nothing more than that he needed her if he wanted to stay in Brazil—something that was true again six years later.

'I...' Her voice trailed off, her tone becoming thick with an emotion he couldn't quite decipher. She cleared her throat and when she met his gaze again he took in a sharp breath at the depth of conflict swirling in her amber eyes.

'Cee, what is it?' His hand was halfway across the table in an instinct to comfort her—an instinct he'd believed long dead. Could this still be about his request? What would put her in such a state of nervous anguish?

'I have a daughter. Her name is Nina, and she was the one who picked the dog at the shelter. Maria and I share custody because Mirabel and Nina keep fighting over who he belongs to.' Her laugh was noticeably tense.

Darius's hand froze in the air and a moment later he retracted it, placing it back in front of him. So Celine had a child. But why was she telling him?

Something deep inside him stirred, a strange premonition that made his blood run cold as he put together the splintered pieces of the conversation, along with her inexplicable nervousness when she was the one holding all the cards in this deal.

There was no way that the idea rising in him, squeezing all the air out of his lungs, could be true. It just couldn't be, because there was *no way* Celine would have kept this a secret from him for six years.

But why else would she bring up her daughter in this discussion, unless…

'Celine…' he said, his voice as thick as hers had been just a few moments ago. 'What are you trying to tell me?'

His breath trembled when she looked at him, hurt mixing with remorse as she sucked her lower lip between her teeth, her chin shaking with her own unsteady breathing.

'Four weeks after you told me you wouldn't come back I realised I was pregnant, and I had her and raised her on my own.'

CHAPTER FOUR

THE SILENCE BETWEEN them was deafening, and Celine didn't dare to breathe as she waited for his reaction. She'd known it would be bad from the moment she'd realised she would have to tell him—to give him the choice of being in their daughter's life.

Her brother, Daniel, had left her and Maria high and dry, and while for her sister the betrayal had meant that the charity she worked so hard for had come to the brink of collapse, it had hit Celine differently. She too had fond feelings for the charity, but it wasn't what she spent most of her time working on. No, Daniel leaving had left their relationship shredded to ribbons—a bond between the two siblings that had previously been ironclad. Or at least she'd thought that until the moment he had dumped Mirabel at this house and left to run after his mistress.

The situation had been hauntingly similar to the one with Darius, where she had tried calling, sending texts and asking friends to deliver messages if they ever saw him. Just to get some closure.

But she had to admit to herself that she had never been important enough to either of them to be accorded that respect. Even now, Darius was only here because he needed to defer their divorce, that she had been waiting too long to file—putting her life on pause for a man she wasn't even sure she wanted any more.

A ragged breath left Darius's mouth, then another as he looked around the room, his eyes snagging on the subtle details around them—indications that a child lived here with her.

'You...' He paused, staring towards the door, where Celine spotted some of Nina's shoes stacked next to her own. 'I...have a daughter?'

An avalanche of emotions rippled across his face. Too many for Celine to pinpoint exactly what was going on in his head. He probably didn't know either. How was he supposed to react to the news of the child they had made together?

She swallowed, considering her next words. Though, from where she was standing, she felt justified in laying the blame at his feet, she didn't want to overwhelm him with that now, when he was processing a far more important piece of information.

'You do. I tried to get in touch with you in every way possible. But when calls and texts went unanswered I assumed you weren't interested in me or her.' This time she could identify the emotion in his expression—shame.

That took her by surprise. She had expected anger towards her, or the indifference she'd believed he felt when he hadn't replied to her messages. Celine had prepared herself for those, steeled her will against the blame she'd believed he would hurl at her.

But his expression was one of shock...and guilt.

'Dios...' he whispered as he scrubbed his hands over his face, threading his fingers through his short hair.

Celine wanted to give him some space to process everything and sort through his thoughts, but she needed to get this off her chest too. The effort to speak up about this after so long had her trembling and if she didn't say everything at once she feared they would have to repeat the same conversation many times over.

'I'm willing to give you the time you need, and I want to offer you something more. A choice.' She paused to take a breath as Darius's wary eyes darted back to her. 'I'm telling you all of this because I want Nina to know her father. I *want* you in her life—I've always wanted that. But if you want to be a part of her life, you need to be in it for good. If you can't promise that, then leave and send me the papers when you're done. If you do—'

Darius shot up from his chair, his hand pressed flat onto the table between them and his expression thunderous. 'You don't need to finish your sentence. There is no way I'm walking away from my daughter when I already missed so much of her life…'

There was a pause—an incomplete sentence that Celine really wanted him to finish. The information omitted—the *why* around missing the first five years of his child's life—had tormented her for just as long.

Pushing those overwhelming thoughts away, she forced herself to nod. 'Okay, that's good. Then we have an agreement. You can meet Nina, and we'll tell her you're her father.'

Darius blanched, something she understood well as an icy chill pooled in the pit of her stomach. She knew her daughter well, knew that the question of where her father was had been on her mind, even at such a young age.

'What does she know about me?' he asked, picking up her strand of thought.

It almost made her smile how he could still guess her thoughts by the expression on her face alone. When they had been together, their non-verbal communication had been good enough to have entire conversations without saying a word.

'She knows she has a father and that he's been away.' Celine chose her words carefully, both now and whenever she spoke to Nina about her absent father. 'Whenever she had questions about you, I tried to answer them to my best ability without assigning any blame. Regardless of what you did to me, I never made her aware of my feelings about you.'

Darius started pacing in the small kitchen, his eyes darting around as he processed the magnitude of the news she had shared with him. Though she couldn't really blame him, the constant steps were ratcheting up her own nerves.

Being near him was bringing back so many feelings from the past that Celine fought hard to push them back down into the pit they had crawled out of. She couldn't afford to think about Darius the way she used to, *especially* not if he was about to become a constant in her life—her daughter's life—again.

The hurt of his abandonment still burned beneath her skin. Or was the heat coming from somewhere else— somewhere she didn't dare to look at?

'Do you want to see a photo of her?' she blurted out to distract herself from the torrent of emotions bubbling up in her chest.

Darius froze mid-stride, turning his head towards her with wide eyes that showed a mixture of longing and shock. The latter she could understand all too well, but it was the rawness of the former that made her heart skip a beat. He *really* was excited to know more about her. Had he already embraced the instant bond of parenthood that had sprung to life when she had revealed the news about Nina to him?

Celine grabbed her phone off the table and opened her camera roll to the latest photos of Nina, taken last weekend at Mirabel's birthday party, where she had insisted on dressing up like an extravagant princess and promptly dropped a slice of cake onto her puffy dress. Though instead of crying, as Celine had expected, Nina had simply dusted herself off and continued eating with a raised chin.

Her estranged husband stepped closer as she turned the phone around for him to see the image, then grabbed it with a soft reverence, as if he were handling Nina herself. He fell back onto the chair, as if his legs could no longer carry him.

'She is...*preciosa*,' he breathed, and the awe lacing his voice made her smile.

'She is very lovely, yes,' she replied, and the smile spreading over his lips when he looked up at her was so full of warmth and love that her breath caught in her throat as her heart sped up.

'When can I meet her?' he asked, bringing up the question Celine didn't have an answer to, because how did one set up a meeting between a long-estranged father and a daughter he never knew he had?

Celine searched within herself for an answer to the question she'd asked herself all day. She didn't know what to do about them meeting. Because she genuinely wanted the two to get to know each other, but every time she imagined it her heart stopped with fear of the inevitable fallout. What if he didn't stay true to his word and left again? She couldn't stand Nina suffering the same abandonment her cousin Mirabel had.

Yet even though Daniel had failed to appear in her life

again, Celine could see how happy her niece was despite all that had happened to her. Maria had become a new mother to her, Rafael stepping into the father role for both her and Nina. They had forged their own happy ending, with both Dias sisters and Mirabel accepting reality for what it was and taking the bad with the good.

'How do I know you won't leave again?' she asked, wanting to hear the words so she could remind him of them if things went wrong.

He lifted his head to meet her probing gaze. 'I promise you I want to be a part of her life and I will never abandon her.'

'Your promises haven't meant much in the past,' Celine said, suppressing a wince when his expression crumpled.

'My word is all I have to offer, Celine.' She watched as his hand scrubbed over his face, a heavy sigh dropping from his lips. Celine knew she would let him meet Nina, *wanted* it even. But that didn't mean the protectiveness within her was easily overcome. It didn't change that she'd had to go through the birth on her own. The long nights that had followed the equally long days leading up to Nina's first birthday that she had had to struggle through by herself, feeding her child while also working to keep a roof over their heads.

Celine couldn't have done it without her sister, but it should have been Darius who shared the burden with her.

She had to remind herself that it wasn't about her feelings for him, but rather Nina getting to know her father. Even if he didn't stand by his commitment to be her father, they would be fine. They had been so far, and they would find a way to heal again. The reward of Nina having her father in her life for ever was worth the risk of it going bad. Rip it off like a plaster, she told herself. Nothing she could do would prepare Nina for this meeting, so she might as well dive in headfirst.

'I asked Maria to take her for a few hours so we could talk in private,' she said, then she took her phone out of Darius's hands. 'I'll text her and let her know she can bring her back now.'

Darius's nerves were jangling, each sensation magnified to such an extent that he wasn't sure he would ever feel normal again. His thoughts were racing, everything inside of him reeling at the news Celine had dropped on him out of nowhere.

He was a father. Nearly six years ago, on their wedding night, they had made a child.

Nina.

When Darius had come here to ask for his estranged wife's help, this hadn't been on the cards at all. A child? With Celine? There had been a time when that had been his dearest wish, wanting nothing else than to grow a family with her. Now it was this tension-filled moment as he sat opposite the woman he had married six years ago, who was staring daggers at him from across the table.

Darius wanted to be angry with her, and a part of him believed himself betrayed out of the first five years of his daughter's life, years filled with importance and influence that she'd had to live without him—that *he'd* had to live without knowing *her*. But he couldn't let the fury bubbling in his veins show. Not when he had only himself to blame.

He had made the choice to stay in Peru, to not follow through with their plan of getting a spouse visa so he could return to Brazil. When he had told his mother that he was going back to Brazil to be with Celine, she had revealed the severity of her sickness—along with the debt she had incurred in Brazil trying to save her failing business. She had told him she wanted him to be a part of Delgado Cosmetics, even though he'd shown no interest in it.

But when she'd revealed what kind of people she had borrowed money from—the threats they were sending her—he knew he had to help her, especially because the cancer was progressing so fast. How could he have turned away when she had done so much for him?

Leona Delgado had lifted herself out of poverty so she could give Darius a good life. What had started out as a small stall in a weekly farmers' market in Manaus where she sold homemade skincare and make-up products had become a skincare company that was known for its high quality and humble beginnings right in their kitchen.

From there, his mother had reached for more, worked harder than anyone to bring them out of poverty and into a place where she could pay for his education and give him a better life than she'd had.

It was only after her death that he'd discovered her deception—that the threat to him and his wife didn't exist. That he hadn't had to stay away to keep Celine safe… To think that he could have returned then, explained himself and asked for her forgiveness… He would have had an extra year with his daughter, one more birthday that had come and gone without her knowing him.

The decision not to get in touch with Celine after he'd learned the extent of his mother's lies sat in the pit of his stomach like an ice-coated boulder. He had wanted to, but whenever his hand gravitated towards his phone he'd stopped and examined his feelings. Wanting to reach out just to explain his side of things wasn't a good enough reason—it needed to be more than just him trying to rid himself of the guilt he carried around.

But he'd suspected she had moved on, that she had found someone far more worthy of her affection than him. His selfishness had inflicted enough pain in her life—so he'd chosen to stay away for good. Until the divorce papers had arrived, opening a door that couldn't be closed any more. They would be in each other's lives until their last days.

The phone on the table vibrated and his heart skipped a beat when Celine grabbed it, reading the message she'd received.

'She says they're finishing up lunch and then she'll bring her over. Won't be longer than half an hour,' she said, her voice wavering.

His pulse rate raised, and he forced himself to breathe. He didn't know the first thing about being a father—or what to expect from his daughter. He swallowed the lump of anxiety forming in his throat, then he said, 'Can you tell me more about Nina? What is she like?'

Darius prepared himself to be laughed at, as he wasn't sure this question even made sense. She was five, after all. The realisation of how little experience he had with children flooded his stomach with dread. Would Nina realise he had no idea what it meant to be a parent and reject him for his clumsy attempts?

But Celine didn't laugh. She turned a thoughtful gaze towards him, and the smile that spread over her face was so gentle and warm he forgot to breathe for a few heartbeats.

'She's the best. Her current obsession is dinosaurs, so everything needs to involve dinosaurs somehow. She's about to start school next February, and even though that's still more than half a year away, she is so keen that she's already picked out her school bag and pencil case and everything.' Celine paused with a smirk. 'All also covered in dinosaurs, so I hope this particular interest lasts her a while.'

Celine's phone vibrated again, and his stomach dropped when she said, 'She's outside.'

She got up and strode towards the door, her hand stopping on top of the door handle as she hesitated. Darius's heart was pounding so hard he was worried it would escape his chest.

'You're sure about this?' he forced himself to ask, even though he didn't want her to reconsider.

She gave a short laugh. 'No, but I know that has everything to do with me and not her.' Celine threw him a look over her shoulder. 'She deserves to know her dad. My personal feelings don't matter.'

And with that Celine opened the door. A smile immediately spread over her face, and she crouched down, opening her arms. *'Oi, filha,'* he heard her say, and then a small figure stepped into Celine's open arms, throwing her slender arms around her neck.

Darius held his breath as he looked at his daughter, the onslaught of emotions too much for him to process. The moment Celine had told him about Nina a bond sprang to life within him that now firmed into a solid attachment of affection and the need to protect her.

Her hair was the same dark brown as Celine's and tied up in a bun on each side of her head, and she was wearing a grey shirt with a little T-Rex printed on it. But when she turned her head he took in a sharp breath as his own brown eyes stared at him.

'We have a visitor here today,' Celine said in a quiet

voice, wrapping her hands around their daughter's arms and pushing her away so she could look at her. 'Remember when I told you that your father lives in a different country and that's why he's not here?'

Her voice was gentle and there was no accusation there, yet her words hit him like a punch in the gut. She had been forced to have this conversation with their daughter when he hadn't even known that she existed. He pushed the anger down, not wanting Nina to see anything about his inner thoughts on his face. There was already some reluctance in her stance.

Nina only nodded, her eyes darting between Celine and him.

'Well, he's finally back in Brazil and he's come over to meet you. Would you be okay with that?'

Nina remained quiet, her gaze now focused on Darius as she scanned him, an understanding in her eyes that he would have thought to be beyond the comprehension of a five-year-old child. He didn't know what to do. Was he supposed to go over and say hello? Stay where he was and let her approach him?

Celine made that decision for him when she got up, her hand wrapped around Nina's. She looked at the door, giving a short nod, then closed it before taking a step back towards him.

Nina immediately stepped behind her mother, hiding behind her legs and peering at Darius with a wary expression. His heart was racing, so were his thoughts as he struggled to come up with something—*anything*—to say that would have meaning. Words that would soothe the years he'd spent not knowing she existed. That would show her and Celine how much this moment meant to him. How sorry he was.

'Do you want to say hello to your father, Nina?' Celine asked, looking over her shoulder down to her daughter, who was clinging to her leg with fierce little hands.

Her eyes were as round as saucers, then she squeezed them shut and shook her head. 'Uh-uh,' he heard her say, her grip on her mother's trousers so tight that her knuckles were turning white.

Celine clicked her tongue with a shake of her head, her hand resting on Nina's head and patting her. 'Are you sure? He came a long way to see you.'

Nina shook her head even more furiously, and the pressure in his chest built so much that he felt his heart crack. Her reluctance was understandable since he was no more than a stranger to her, but that didn't make it any easier to deal with.

'Okay, you don't have to.' Celine got on her haunches again, looking at Nina. 'Why don't you go up and get ready for a nap? I'll be with you in a moment.'

Darius watched with mixed feelings as Nina—his daughter—turned away from him with wide eyes and then scurried out of view and up the stairs.

Celine looked after her with a sigh, then shook her head before addressing him. 'We'll try again tomorrow. She wasn't expecting that and just needs some time to process.'

She grabbed her phone and held it out to him. 'Give me your number, and I'll text you the details for tomorrow. Might be easier on her if we go somewhere she likes, so she feels more at ease.'

Darius nodded, typing his number into her phone, and then stood up with the heaviness of a hundred boulders falling into the pit of his stomach. How was he going to win Nina over when he knew nothing about her or being a father?

The dark cloud these thoughts caused followed him as he bade Celine goodnight and made his way back to his hotel two towns over.

CHAPTER FIVE

OVER THE NEXT WEEK Nina slowly warmed to the idea of having her dad in her life and it made Celine breathe easier. In retrospect, she thought she might have handled the initial meeting better and given her daughter more forewarning of who she was about to meet. Though Darius had put on a brave face when he'd left, she could tell he'd been crushed by Nina's reaction.

But now, a week after Darius's sudden reappearance and his introduction to their daughter, Nina was daring to get closer to him and showing more interest in him. The concept of a father was still new for her, having only ever experienced it second-hand through encounters with her friends' families.

Today they had decided to go to the weekly farmers' market held in Santarém's town square—on the urging of Maria. She and Rafael enjoyed diving into the different stalls that came to the town, sampling every single thing and talking to everyone about the latest gossip.

Celine had never felt the same connection to the town and its people the way Maria did, and she understood why. Her sister was more sociable, attending all of the town meetings and keeping them informed about the happenings in town. She also spent way more time maintaining their home and spent more time put. Celine was more on the road than she was at home, as her patients needed her to go to them. Unlike Maria, the people she had bonded with were the farmers she worked with. Like Juliana and her wife, who had jumped at the opportunity to get rid of all their toddler gear once they'd got close enough to hear about Celine's situation.

She let her eyes drift in search of the familiar blonde hair but couldn't detect her in the crowd. Since the farms were in remote locations, many of her clients would come to Santarém on weekends to enjoy some time away from work.

'You want a hot chocolate? In this weather?' Darius's voice filtered over to her, and she watched with a small smile as he bent down to Nina, who nodded enthusiastically.

'It's never too warm for hot chocolate,' she replied with a grin that melted Celine's heart.

Watching the two interact with each other was a lot more heart-warming than she'd thought it would be—and it tied the knot of complex feelings towards Darius even tighter. The largest part of her was still angry at him, furious that he had left, that he had never answered a single phone call or text message.

But beneath the surface was an ever-increasing heat bubbling up inside of her. Each time she caught the tendrils of warmth—flashes of attraction and longing—she forced them back down into non-existence. The attraction had clicked back into place the moment they had sat in her truck together, with his scent mingling in her space and his smile bringing a wobble to her knees. His faults notwithstanding, the man she had married was still remarkable and stupidly handsome, to the point where she cursed him for it. Letting Darius back into her life was one thing but being attracted to her soon-to-be ex-husband was a complication Celine didn't need. No, it had been too easy for him to abandon her, and one week was not enough to prove himself worthy.

She pushed the thoughts away when the pair came strolling back to the picnic bench she sat on. Darius sat down opposite her, and Nina, to her surprise, slipped into the space next to her father.

He set down a cup in front of her that Celine eyed suspiciously. The walk from her house to the town square had been quiet and pleasant, feeling reminiscent of a time when they had loved nothing more than to spend time with each other. It had been like Celine had slipped into a vision of what her life would have looked like if they had stayed together, had raised Nina together and planned their weekends like a real family would. Like Maria and Rafael did…

The thought had freaked her out so much she'd needed some distance from Darius, so she had sent him with Nina to Emanuel's stand to get them a beverage.

'What is this?' she asked as she grabbed the cup. It was warm, and the scent of coffee wiggled its way through the closed plastic lid and up her nose—along with another, more subtle fragrance.

'It's a cappuccino but, instead of cocoa powder, I asked them to put on a sprinkling of cinnamon.' He flashed her a grin when her eyes widened. 'Ah, so you still like it? I wasn't sure and this little one says Tia Maria is not impressed with your coffee.'

Celine's eyes darted to Nina. 'Your *tia* said she doesn't like my coffee? Is that true?'

Nina giggled into her hot chocolate, amused by her mother's faux outrage. 'She says it tastes like dirty water.'

'Nina!'

Darius laughed, the rumble of his voice so deep and clear that it floated through the air between them, vibrating through her skin and settling into the pit of her stomach—which was already performing loops from being so close to her estranged husband and the unwanted attraction rearing its head.

'Well, I think what—'

Nina's delighted squeal interrupted whatever Darius had been about to say, and she waved her hand at someone behind Celine. Both her parents looked over, and Celine locked eyes with her sister just as Nina threw her tiny arms around Mirabel. Despite their age difference, the cousins had grown accustomed to each other's company when she and Maria had lived together in the small house she now occupied with Nina.

'Well, that's her gone for the rest of the afternoon,' she said and couldn't stop a groan dropping from her lips.

Darius raised his eyebrows. 'What's wrong?'

'I should have figured Maria would come here today. Now she's going to think all sorts of nonsense because she saw us together.'

'But she's also seen me come to your house this week,' he said. 'What's different about today?'

Celine snorted as she considered her answer. A part of her didn't want to go into any details. Not with him, not when he had hurt her so much that the memory alone pushed the air out of her lungs. But the constant fight against her attraction for Darius was wearing her down, the restraints easing as the days went by. The part of her that remembered what his arms felt like around her yearned for one last taste. Especially when those arms had only grown stronger in the past six years, she thought as her eyes took in the muscles peeking out of his T-shirt.

There was no chance of a reunion for them, she already knew that. There were too many open questions for her to be comfortable with him, but daydreaming didn't ever hurt anyone, right?

'They had their big romantic moment here at the farmers' market, where they presented themselves to the entire village as a couple,' she said, pushing the unwanted thoughts aside to focus on their conversation. Better she shared this little titbit rather than voice the other things popping into her head.

Celine wasn't going to rehash any of his past mistakes with Darius. Not only was it necessary for them to have a cordial co-parenting relationship, she also simply didn't want to know. There was no way he could say anything that would make her forgive him.

Celine had moved on with her life, from the idea of being married to Darius—she wanted the real deal. And that wasn't going to be Darius again. Not when he had trusted her so little that he couldn't even tell her his mother had been sick.

No, there was more behind his disappearance than he let on. Instead of coming clean, Darius was choosing to keep more secrets from her. Celine tried not to care. If they had been truly meant for each other, then things would have happened differently all those years ago. He would have trusted her.

But he hadn't, and Celine found the longer she thought about it, the less she wanted to know why—or the cage around her memories and feelings for him might grow even weaker, leaving her exposed and broken once more. If she had learned anything from being married in name only for six years and then watching Maria struggle through issues with Rafael, it was that someone who truly loved her would have stayed with her—or at least told her the truth.

Darius hadn't done either, and she needed to remind herself of that more often. Because the smile that lit up his face as his eyes drifted towards her daughter melted her heart so much it fell out of its beat. The scene that she had dreamt about for so long had suddenly appeared in front of her, but it was all wrong. The trust was gone, no matter how enticing the picture he now painted was to her.

'She had to introduce her husband to the entire village?' His voice had an incredulous edge that Celine understood far better than he would ever realise.

'Well…kind of? Santarém is so small, there aren't even a thousand people living here. That means everyone becomes *família*, and if someone new wants to join, they have to prove themselves.'

Darius nodded, his eyes darting over to Emanuel's stall. 'That explains the frosty look I received from that guy.'

'Did he give you grief?' Celine's eyes narrowed on the coffee shop owner, who was too busy serving his next customers to notice anything.

'You don't sound so appreciative of that,' he replied.

Her eyes snapped back to him at his words, rounding at the huskiness she heard in his voice. 'Maria loves them, but I prefer for people to stay out of my business.'

'You're not close to the villagers, then?'

The question gave her pause, for it highlighted a truth within her that everyone else around her seemed to be aware of, but nobody really wanted to address. Yet it had taken Darius one interaction to see through the complex web of relationships that kept this town going.

'Maria spends a lot more time at the clinic and with the people of Santarém. My job has me driving around to farms all week, so by default I don't get to spend a lot of time around them. I'm far closer to people like Juliana because I see them more often than the villagers,' she said, hinting at the obvious answer to the far more complex question of how she felt about Santarém.

Because the truth was something that she closely guarded—that she had come here out of necessity more than desire, and that she missed living in Manaus. A part of her wanted to leave and pick up the city life again, but not only would she be uprooting Nina's life, she also owed her sister too much to just leave now that everything was more stable. Maria had dropped everything to help her when Nina had been born, spending nights with her so that Celine could get some sleep. Though her role in the clinic had diminished since Rafael had arrived, she couldn't abandon her sister's dream when Maria had saved her in her time of need. There was a debt she needed to pay back and she would not abandon her duties as a sister for some misguided ideas about the freedom of city life.

'I see,' Darius replied in a tone that she knew far too well and that hadn't changed in the last six years. He knew her answer was evasive—but he wasn't supposed to know that.

She didn't have time to come up with a retort as he said, 'You came here because you needed help, and I wasn't around any more.'

Celine started at the sudden vulnerability in his expression, at the admission of guilt that she saw in his features. Over the last week she had sensed regret in some of his words, but none had been so evident as what he had just said.

'I…' Her voice trailed off as she tried to find the right words to say. His behaviour in the last week had not at all been what she had expected. She'd thought he would justify his absence, find excuses and argue with her. Enough time had passed for her to replace the loving and kind image she had of Darius with one built from hurt and anger over his abandonment of her, of the daughter he had never known.

But now her heart was softening as she saw the version of her husband that she had fallen in love with all those years ago.

'Yes, I came here because I didn't want to be alone. But now that she's older I—'

The clattering of plates interrupted her, followed by a loud shriek laced with terror.

'Álvaro!' The shouts came from where the food stalls stood, and Darius scanned the crowd that was forming around a man lying prone on the ground. A woman was kneeling next to him, and another woman sat on the ground, slumped against a food truck.

Darius surged to his feet, the conversation with Celine all but forgotten in the face of the medical emergency. He pushed some onlookers aside, then knelt next to the man named Álvaro. His face was a ghostly white, his hands and legs twitching involuntarily, his eyes closed but moving back and forth under his lids. Behind him Darius heard the soft moans and hisses from the other woman. Did they have some altercation? He looked back at the man in front of him. There were no obvious marks of an injury, but rather the signs of a seizure.

'What are you doing?' A middle-aged woman looked at him with confusion, and from the frantic look in her eyes he guessed she must be related to the patient—but he didn't have time to contemplate that. Not while Álvaro was having a seizure. He quickly glanced at the watch on his wrist, memorising the minutes and seconds so he could time the seizure.

'It's okay, Magda. He is a doctor.' Celine's voice drifted towards him, and he looked up. 'Did anyone already call emergency services?' she asked, looking at him.

Darius looked at his watch again, then up. 'If the seizure lasts less than five minutes, we don't need to declare it an emergency.'

He moved to the other side of the patient and pushed the man onto his side, pulling his arm underneath him at an angle that would ensure Álvaro wouldn't hurt himself while having a seizure. When he had ensured that the patient was in the recovery position, he got to his feet again.

'Does he have any existing condition that cause seizures?' he asked, looking at Magda, who shook her head as a sob escaped her throat.

'No, nothing of the sort. He has diabetes but never anything like this,' the old woman replied, kneeling on the ground next to her husband. 'What's wrong with him?'

Darius frowned as he crouched down as well to be eye to eye with Magda as he explained. 'See the twitching of his arms and legs? That's most likely because he's having a grand mal seizure. It comes in different stages. One of them is the slackening of muscles followed by tensing, as you can see here. The first symptom is usually a change that we call aura. Did Álvaro complain about sensing something strange? A smell or a taste that was agitating him?'

Magda's eyes rounded as she listened to his explanation and then she looked down, both of her hands resting on Álvaro's side. 'He didn't enjoy the coffee we got at Emanuel's, which is strange because that is his favourite part of the farmers' market. Just now we got his soup, and that's when it started. He threw the soup at poor Bruna while she was cutting up my sandwich...'

She looked over her shoulder to the woman slumped against the wheel of the food truck, a pained expression on her face. When his eyes dipped below to where one hand was clutching her arm, he noticed the cloth Bruna was pressing against her forearm that was slowly turning red.

Darius looked up and caught Celine's eyes on him. A pang of heat sliced through his chest at the concern etched into her features and he pushed it away. Now was not the time.

'It's been almost a minute since Álvaro went down. Can you alert me when five minutes have passed? I must check on Bruna over here.' Magda nodded, and he turned to look at the woman's injury. He crouched down in front of her and she opened her eyes when she felt his hand on her shoulder. 'Bruna, I'm Dr Delgado. Can I have a look at that wound?'

Bruna nodded, and Darius noted her pain-glazed eyes as her eyelids fluttered open and closed again. With delicate hands he prised Bruna's fingers away from her arm, then unwrapped the cloth. He swallowed the hiss rising in his throat, needing to project calmness so his patient wouldn't panic at any outward sign.

'I have to inspect the cut. This will be uncomfortable and I'm sorry for that,' he said to prepare her for his probing fingers.

The cut went along the upper side of her arm, he noted with relief. Though it was long, it wasn't deep and a few stitches would see Bruna as good as new. Had the cut been on the other side, it might have hit the radial artery and caused far more blood loss than presented here.

'I have good news for you. Though painful, this cut is shallow, and it avoided any major blood vessels. We'll be able to stitch you up here if I can find everything I'm looking for. Do you have any fresh towels in your truck that we can use to staunch the bleeding while I look for the first aid kit?'

Bruna opened her mouth but a low voice from behind interrupted her. 'Take this,' Emanuel, the coffee shop owner, said as he handed Darius a fresh hand towel that he carefully draped around the wound and pressed down on it for a few moments. The bleeding would not stop on its own, the gash too wide to knit itself back together, so until he could stitch it they needed to apply constant pressure.

He looked at Emanuel with a grateful smile. 'Can you keep pressure on the wound while I look at Álvaro?' The man nodded, then took Bruna's arm between his two hands and pressed down on the makeshift bandaging.

When Darius raised his head he saw Celine kneeling beside Magda, who whispered encouragement into her husband's ear. He glanced at his watch—three minutes and twenty-three seconds—then at Álvaro. The muscle spasms were less pronounced now, the rapid movements of his eyes gone, and when Darius reached out to feel his pulse it was slowing down—along with his breathing. Then Álvaro's mouth fell open, releasing a sigh that Darius felt in the depth of his bones.

'Magda,' he called out to get the attention of the old woman. 'The seizure is over, and Álvaro should wake up in a few moments. He might not remember that he had a seizure, and he will definitely be confused. It's best that you take him home to rest. Once he feels a bit more stable, you should call your general practitioner and discuss what happened. Your doctor will refer him to the right specialist for treatment. Did you come here by car?'

Darius looked around. They had walked here, and he hadn't seen any cars parked along the side of the road. Santarém was so small, he didn't think anyone would ever bother to drive here. Confirming his suspicion, Magda shook her head.

'We live just down the road from here,' she said, pointing at the principal road that wound itself alongside the town square.

Darius looked at Celine with a frown. 'I would drive them, but I have to take care of Bruna. She needs stitches for the cut on her arm.'

'Rafael will drive them home. He already left to fetch his car.' A familiar voice drifted towards his ears, and Maria appeared in front of them. She had her arm wrapped around the shoulder of an older girl—her niece Mirabel—and held onto his daughter's hand with her other one.

Darius's eyes rounded as a lump appeared in his throat. He'd been expecting to come face to face with Maria eventually and had steeled himself for whatever she would hurl at him. During the early days of his and Celine's budding relationship her sister had been fiercely protective of her, scrutinising his intentions on more than one occasion.

Whatever she had to say to him would have to wait for another time. With Álvaro's taxi sorted, he had to find everything he needed to stitch a wound, along with a sterile environment. He couldn't perform any medical procedure out here in the open.

'Do you have a local GP here?' he asked, hoping a fellow medical doctor would help him out in this situation.

But Celine shook her head. 'The GP is one village over.'

The sigh building in Darius's chest caught in his throat when an idea dawned on him. He didn't need to be in a *medical* practice. A cut on a human was surely treated similarly to a cut in a different mammal. 'You have iodine solution, sterile needles, forceps and thread in your clinic?'

Celine's eyes rounded when she followed his request. 'You want to stitch her up in the clinic?'

'It's mostly the same process. Do you use nylon sutures?'

She nodded, then got to her feet. 'I'll go ahead and prep a room. Can you and Emanuel see if Bruna is strong enough to walk?'

Darius nodded, then squatted back down as Nina approached them, opening his arms to give the girl a quick hug and a kiss on her forehead. 'I'm not going to be long, my sweet,' he said to her with a smile as she scurried back behind her aunt's legs.

Darius wished he had the time to look around and take in the clinic as a whole. Throughout their relationship he had heard so much about the animal charity that the Dias family ran here on the edge of the rainforest. But he couldn't take even a moment for himself when his patient was still in pain and losing blood.

Celine awaited him at the front door, ushering him through the reception and into one of the back rooms. As he stepped through the door, he already noticed all the necessary equipment laid out in a portable tray—gloves, sutures, vacuum-sealed needles and forceps, a bottle of iodine solution and the roll of bandages. He almost had to laugh as he looked at the assortment of tools.

'You had all of this already?' he asked, looking at Celine.

She nodded. 'Yeah, Maria uses all of this in her work every day. I don't really get to do a lot of stitching on the farms. Livestock usually don't cut themselves very often, and if they do, the farmers are well equipped to take care of that themselves.'

'Our work isn't really that different,' he said, then he sat on the stool next to Bruna, pulling the gloves on his hands. 'The only thing we can't do here is numb your skin before we stitch it. Unfortunately, the medication animals and humans use is different in that regard. But we have given you some pain meds. They won't help with the immediate pain, but they will take the edge off once you rest. I will try to be as fast and precise as possible, okay?'

Bruna nodded, and then winced when he unwrapped the hand towel that had soaked up quite a bit of blood on the way to the clinic. He held out the towel in an almost automatic gesture, being used to having an assistant helping him with any procedures the players on the team went through. But before he could get up to dispose of the towel himself, Celine grabbed it and threw it in a bin marked as a biohazardous waste.

Darius nodded, grateful for her assistance, then grabbed the sponge lying in the shallow bowl on the tray and cleaned the area around the cut. Bruna winced again, but held still as he continued and washed away all of the debris. As he prepped the needle and sutures, popping the forceps out of their sterile packaging and threading the nylon, Celine's hand appeared on Bruna's shoulder to give it a reassuring squeeze.

'Okay, I'm going to start now.' Her breath left her body in shaking trembles as Darius poked the needle through the skin then gathered both sides of the cut to align them for suturing.

To help her with the pain, he worked as fast as he dared without compromising the quality of his work—something that was harder said than done. Though he had trained in a hospital and done countless sutures in his time there, it had been a few years since he'd had to stitch someone up. Though his football players lived a dangerous life on the pitch, their injuries were often torn muscles and ligaments, not knife wounds.

As he focused on the stitches, Celine said softly, 'You're doing great. We're more than halfway through with the sutures. A bit more and then you can go home. Rafael is already waiting to take you.'

Warmth pooled in the pit of his stomach, radiating through his body in gentle tendrils as he listened to his wife as she calmed Bruna. In the first years of their relationship he had often fantasised about what it would be like to work together. Though their patients were vastly different, the empathy and diligence they needed to show them remained the same.

'Can you hand me the bandages?' he asked, then started wrapping the freshly stitched wound after brushing it with some iodine solution to keep any infection at bay.

He gently tapped Bruna's arm when he was done, drawing her gaze towards him. 'Okay, we are all done here. This should heal just fine, but since we used nylon sutures you need to have them removed. I suggest you get in contact with your GP and schedule an appointment so they can have a look at it.'

Bruna looked at him with wide eyes. 'You're not going to be here?'

'No, I'm just visiting,' he said with a shake of his head.

A knock sounded, and Rafael poked his head into the exam room. 'We're all set here?'

Celine nodded, then helped Bruna off her chair and ushered her through the door and into the care of Rafael.

Silence settled between them that was only interrupted by Celine shuffling the used equipment around. Darius cleared his throat as tension rose in his body.

'Thanks for setting all of this up,' he said, then took a step forward and handed her the things on the tray.

Celine gave a quiet laugh and when she looked back at him his breath caught in his throat at the sight of her. Her eyes were gentle, filled with an emotion that he couldn't quite pinpoint. All he knew was that the apprehension he'd seen was gone, melted away and replaced by something warm. Affection? Or was that what he wanted to see?

'I have to give thanks. I don't know what we would have done without you today.' She hesitated, flipping the used forceps in her hand, then she continued. 'I was impressed with your quick thinking and your care for Bruna and Álvaro. Seeing you work was…nice.'

His heart accelerated at her words, and without conscious input he took a step forward. The warm tendrils that had been sweeping across his body intensified, flaring to life in a blaze that set his blood to a boil.

He wanted to touch her so badly, wanted to press her against the wall and cover her body with his. The last few days had not only shown him how much of his daughter's life he had missed, but also how much of their married life had slipped through his fingers.

Celine watched him with wary eyes as he stepped closer, though something was different about her stance. The high walls he'd sensed around her in every interaction they'd had this week—they seemed lower. All because she'd watched him help the villagers? Any doctor would have done the same as him.

He hadn't seen that side of her ever since he had come back into her life a week ago, and it was so mesmerising that he forgot where he was—forgot what kind of relationship they had now, where the touches he'd once shared with her were now inconceivable. Instinct—or habit, Darius wasn't too sure—took possession of his motor functions as he leaned forward and kissed her on the cheek.

His hand settled down on her hip for a fraction of a second, then he stepped back, fishing his car keys out of his pocket. 'I have to go check on Álvaro. But I'll see you at your place?'

'I'll see you at your place.'

Celine hadn't registered his departing words, too stunned by the sudden kiss he had given her on her cheek—and what that small gesture had done to her.

A cascade of heat had rippled through her body, starting at her cheeks and tumbling all the way down to her stomach, where it settled in her core. Even now, as she sat on her couch and watched Nina flip through a book illustrating all the wild animals of the rainforest, she felt a tingle where his lips had brushed her skin.

An unwanted and unbidden reaction to what had no doubt been an innocent gesture that Darius hadn't thought through. That it rattled her to her very core was a problem Celine needed to examine on her own, not daring to speak to anyone about how the touch had made her heart beat faster—how that traitorous voice inside her was calling for more.

This could not be happening. These…feelings could not re-emerge from the place she had banished them to when Darius had decided not to come back to her. Six years ago, she had taken the love for her husband—the emotions that had been shredding her insides with the grief of his abandonment—and had put them in a locked box so she could move on with her life.

Now he was back, and not only was his scent alluring and his lips as soft as she remembered, he had also slotted into her life almost as seamlessly as if he had belonged with her all this time. The picture of the family she had wanted them to be, had dreamed of as they'd got married in a rush, was the reality that was unfolding in front of Celine now. Watching him work had only reaffirmed the thoughts in her head. His compassion and care for Bruna and Álvaro had touched a part inside of her that had remained dormant ever since he had walked out on her.

Celine had to admit that she had held onto the idea of her marriage miraculously mending itself for far too long, unwilling to admit that the family she had dreamt of when they had fallen in love was nothing more than an idle dream of a foolish woman in love.

When Maria had found love with Rafael, Celine realised she had been holding onto nothing but a figment of her dream. A made-up lie she had been clinging onto because she hadn't wanted to admit that she had married a man who had then betrayed her—a marriage that was holding her back from finding the one person who would be hers unquestioningly, the way Rafael belonged to Maria.

Darius was not this person. He couldn't be, despite his undeniable allure, bringing her back into his orbit. When he had elected not to return, he had irrevocably shattered Celine's trusting nature and the scepticism that had sprung to life had her rejecting any kind of closeness before it could get serious.

A problem she would have to figure out once she met the man who was meant for her. That part of her life would have to wait for another few months until she could finally get divorced and settle into a co-parenting routine with Darius. Right now, she wasn't comfortable leaving him and Nina on their own. But the day would come when she could at least trust him this far, and that day would give her the freedom to pursue other romantic interests.

Now she just needed to douse the fire that sparked to life whenever he was near her. No big deal. Darius meant nothing to her, after all. If he did, she wouldn't be fighting so hard to divorce him.

A knock on the door spooked her out of her thoughts. Celine jumped to her feet and opened the door. Her heart skipped a beat and then resumed its life-giving rhythm with increased speed as she looked into the gorgeous face of her estranged husband, his sculpted jaw and high cheekbones begging her to brush her fingers over them— his mouth twisted in a small smile that she wanted to kiss off his lips.

No big deal at all.

'Hey,' he said, his voice low enough to make her skin tingle. She remembered those deep tones, relishing them whenever he had hummed his desire into her ear as he pushed into her, and she...

'Are you okay? Will you let me in?' Darius's voice drifted through the memory surfacing in her mind, setting off both flames of need and alarm bells within her.

She blinked several times, struggling to chase the vision away, and stepped aside. As he walked past her, his scent crept up her nose, making it so much harder to keep that iron grip on her feelings for this man.

'Um…yeah, of course.' All of her senses were hyper-aware of Darius's proximity.

What was happening to her? Darius had left her when she'd needed him the most, when she had agreed to marry him so he could stay in the country. There was too much bad blood between them for her to ever forget that. It didn't matter that he set her heart racing. That didn't change what had happened between them. So how come she couldn't shake these feelings that were re-emerging without her consent?

It was just like Darius to reappear just as she was ready to move on.

'I wasn't sure how long it was going to take you, so I already fed Nina,' Celine said, gesturing towards the dining room table and stepping into the kitchen as he sat down. 'But I have some snacks around, since I'm sure you must be hungry after all of this.'

She didn't wait for a reply, but rather opened the fridge and retrieved a small container with some egg-shaped pastries in it. She fished four of them out, putting them on a plate and shoving them in the microwave.

Her heart was in her throat when she looked at him, the feelings she had been battling rising once more, and the look he gave her made her catch her breath. The same intensity—the same war—was happening in his eyes.

Celine opened her mouth, the tension between them

growing as they silently stared at each other, and acted on the need to break the quiet—and hopefully the tension with that. But before she could speak, Darius cleared his throat.

'What is that?' he asked, nodding his chin towards the microwave.

Celine followed his gaze and looked through the glass of the microwave, watching the food rotate. 'Nina had a little party in kindergarten, so I made some *coxinhas* for it last week.'

A strange expression flitted over Darius's face, one she wasn't able to read, but it set her heart pumping, anyway. Something about it was so soft, so delicate.

'You made *coxinhas*?' he asked, an incredulous edge to his voice.

Celine crossed her arms, leaning her hip against the kitchen counter as she levelled a challenging stare at Darius. 'Don't sound so surprised,' she said, narrowing her eyes at him.

Darius raised his hands in defence. 'I mean no offence, *senhora*. I'm sure I'm simply misremembering all the instant ramen that we used to eat at your place.'

She huffed, her lips parting in a reply that was interrupted by the ping of the microwave. Celine stared at him for a moment, then turned around and took the plate out of the microwave, setting it in front of him. Then she plopped down on the chair across from him, her eyes darting between him and the plate of food.

'Lucky for you, I had to learn how to feed myself more nutritious things than instant ramen.' Though she framed it as a point of contention, that wasn't actually how she felt about it. During veterinary school, anything that had been cheap and easy had been preferable as she didn't have a lot of time to invest in cooking. Not that she was very good at it. Her mother had gone to the trouble of teaching her the Dias family recipes, and ever since Maria moved out she'd had to learn how to cook rice without burning it. 'Edible' was a compliment in Celine's books.

When she had told her family that she was pregnant, her parents had wanted to defer their retirement in Switzerland, but both Celine and Maria had insisted that they stick to their plans. They had worked tirelessly to support their animal sanctuary, sacrificing holidays, gifts and other luxuries so they could help the animals that couldn't help themselves.

They had come back to Brazil when Nina had been born, meeting their second grandchild after Mirabel, her brother's daughter, who now lived with her sister after Daniel had run away with his mistress to build himself a new life.

Even though she had Maria to lean on, Celine had to figure out so much of motherhood on her own—struggling from mistake to mistake. She would have given anything to have her husband at her side as she'd celebrated Nina's first birthday, or when she had spent sleepless nights as her first teeth grew.

Darius reached for the plate in front of him, taking one of the *coxinhas* into his hand and taking a big bite out of the fried dough ball—a Brazilian speciality her mother had taught her, where they made a savoury chicken filling and stuffed it in a dough that got fried in hot oil for a couple of minutes to give it a crispy golden finish.

Her heart leapt when he closed his eyes, savouring the taste of her food. It was a small gesture, one that shouldn't mean anything to begin with, yet it somehow did.

'How is Álvaro?' she asked to distract herself from the rising desire in her body.

Darius looked at the half-eaten dough ball in his hand. 'He's okay, all things considered. There's no way of telling what caused the seizure. It could be an underlying condition that has just lain dormant within him like epilepsy. Or it could be something more acute, like a tumour or cancer.'

Celine frowned at that. 'Poor Álvaro. He used to run the auto repair shop in town before his son took over just two months ago as he finally retired.' She paused, a smile spreading over her lips despite the bad news for the villager. Watching Darius work with dedication and skill was something she hadn't really experienced in their time together at university.

'We were lucky you were around. Your second chance brought you here and might have saved two lives,' she said before she could consider her words, the underlying meaning not lost on her. Celine shocked herself as she looked inward, finding her words ringing true. Despite her heartache, the missed dreams and broken promises, she was glad he was here with her.

His head snapped up at her words, his eyes locking onto hers as they rounded. 'Second chance? What—'

A shrill beep interrupted his words, and Celine immediately jumped to her feet to reach for her phone on the counter. 'This is my emergency alert. Clients know to send me a message so I get notified day or night. It's foaling season right now, so it's difficult to predict when they might need me.'

Unlocking her screen, she scanned the message, a deep frown on her face. 'The waters on one of Juliana's mares broke ten minutes ago and there's no sign of the foal.'

'Ten minutes? That doesn't seem too long. I thought babies can stay in the birthing canal up to thirty minutes. Is there that much of a difference in horses?' Darius got to his feet as well.

'The time itself is not critical. But because it takes me some time to get there, they know to alert me early. I'd rather drive up and have wasted my time than risk the health of an animal. Especially if it's Juliana asking for my help...' Her mind switched to work mode, looking around the room to find what she needed. Her eyes stopped at Nina. She was thankfully still dressed from her earlier outing, and her overnight bag was leaning against the door, already packed for exactly this sort of situation.

'*Bebê*, please put on your shoes. I have to drop you off at your *tia*'s house because I need to go to work.' Her daughter looked up at her, the drowsiness in her eyes breaking Celine's heart. This situation happened a lot more often than she liked, her need for flexible hours meaning that Nina often needed to go to Maria's place if Celine was called to an emergency. But that usually happened when she hadn't had a full day of activities that left her drained and tired. 'You can have a sleepover with Mirabel,' she added to cheer her up.

Footsteps shuffled behind her, and Celine turned around to see Darius approaching with a hesitant expression on his face that flipped her stomach inside out. Was he going to offer what she thought? She really hoped he didn't, for she didn't know how to have this conversation while sparing his feelings.

'I can watch her if you need to go,' he said, the eagerness in his eyes breaking her heart. He wanted to spend some alone time with his daughter, an idea that both excited and terrified Celine. For the longest time she had been the only parent in Nina's life, and the thought of having another parent now to offload some responsibilities—to lean on when she needed to—was a novel experience that she didn't quite feel comfortable with yet. Just as she wasn't comfortable with the idea of leaving her daughter with the man who had walked out on them.

'Darius…' she began, and the way his eyes shuttered, she knew he understood what she was about to say. 'I just don't feel comfortable with this right now. She has only known you for a week, and I want to give all of us a bit more time before I leave her alone with you.'

Hurt rippled over his expression, and she felt the pain in her own chest as disappointment entered his eyes. Disappointment she could understand very well. One of her favourite things in this world was to hang out with Nina on the couch, watching whatever was on television and holding her close. Those were moments she wanted her daughter to have with her father, but it was still early days and there was a lot of trust to regain before Darius could have these moments with Nina.

Yet still the hurt in his eyes was unbearable, and in an attempt to wipe it away she said, 'Why don't you come to Juliana's farm with me? You were an immense help last time, and depending on how difficult this case is, I could use the extra hands.'

He lifted his brows, clearly surprised by her offer. Hell, her offer surprised *her*. It had slipped out unbidden when the pain in his eyes had become too much for her to withstand. But there was more to it than that, a strange excitement to have him by her side as she worked. A feeling she didn't dare to look at too closely, for she knew that only heartbreak would wait for her at the end of this path.

Despite that though, she smiled when he nodded and stuffed the rest of the dough ball into his mouth.

CHAPTER SIX

THEY ARRIVED AT the farm ten minutes later, with Celine rushing down the empty country road. He had watched as she'd packed her truck with the speedy efficiency of someone who had been through this sort of crisis a hundred times in her life. The first time he had been allowed to watch her work had already been a privilege, and he was strangely giddy that an opportunity had come up again so soon. But he realised why Celine had offered to take him with her—or at least he thought he knew.

She wasn't comfortable with him watching their daughter on his own. Though he understood her hesitancy, what puzzled him was the tension snapping into place between them every time they met. It had happened suddenly at the beginning, with Darius dismissing his own feelings for her—writing them off as an anomaly. He'd thought they would fade away as they interacted with each other, once they understood what kind of relationship they wanted to have now that they were co-parents.

His feelings had not faded, but rather grown with an intensity that made him balk. No, grown wasn't the right word. He recognised these feelings, knew them as he knew the back of his hand—like he knew what bones were in that hand, what their names were. What was blooming inside his chest was the tiny kernel of affection for Celine that had never died, despite his multiple attempts to smother it.

Darius had felt responsible for his mother's wellbeing since he was twelve, when an accident had killed his father, and the bond between them had only deepened over the years. Without his father or any siblings, they'd only had each other.

He now knew that his mother had kept him trapped at her side with the only bond she knew would get him—family. Darius had been raised to believe that his family would be worth any sacrifice, any hardship. It was something he still believed to this day, though the definition of family had changed. Blood relations had little to do with who he now considered his family. Especially when his mother had fabricated the evidence that had kept him away from Celine—making him believe he'd stayed away for her sake. He'd had to choose between one family or the other, his choice having consequences through the years.

No wonder she didn't trust him alone with their child. He still had a lot of work to do to regain the trust that he had broken. And the first thing he needed to do was push those re-emerging feelings back down and never let them see the light of day.

No, it was what came with that attraction, that desire, that he must suppress if he wanted that dynamic to work. Darius had already lost five years of his daughter's life. He wasn't going to miss any more of it just because he couldn't control the fire erupting in his veins every time he came close to his estranged wife. Reconciliation couldn't factor into any of his decisions.

His goal was to get to know his daughter, repair the trust between them enough so Celine would be willing to let Nina out of her sight without worrying too much and, once he had secured his contract with the team, he would be able to finally give her the divorce she wanted. Set her free.

The thought twisted his stomach, and he swallowed the wince that it brought to him. The pangs of jealousy he felt whenever he pictured Celine moving on from him were not only pathetic, they were also inappropriate. They hadn't been husband and wife for a long time—for as long as they had been married, he realised with profound sadness.

Darius found himself at a crossroads again, knowing he could only choose one side—and it had to be his daughter. If he lost Nina again just because he was chasing some remembered feelings for her mother, he would never forgive himself.

'What's the game plan?' he asked when she hopped out, grabbing the bag of supplies she had tossed into the flat bed of the truck.

'Game plan?' Celine looked at him with a raised eyebrow.

'Sorry, sports metaphor. How are we going to treat the horse?'

She chuckled at that, a sound so lovely and bright that his blood heated, the urge to fold her into his arms and never let her go surfacing with an unexpected ferocity. 'You call a treatment plan a game plan?'

'I work with professional athletes. They appreciate when I speak their language.' He shot her a grin as he added, 'You're just jealous that you don't know how to speak horse.'

'Excuse you, but I am fluent in horse. Clearly you don't remember how I treated Roach's abscess when there were little to no symptoms. How else could I have known that?'

Celine narrowed her eyes at him, then started towards the stables.

As he closed the door with a thud, Juliana's head appeared out of one of the enclosures and she waved them towards her. Darius met Celine's eye and she nodded. Gone was the soft expression their joking had put on her face, replaced with a compassionate determination that was the essence of her professional persona.

'Thank you for coming so fast,' Juliana said as Celine stepped into the enclosure. 'I think the foal is not sitting right in the birth canal.'

Worry laced the farmer's voice, her deep care for her animals tangible. She stepped aside to grant Celine admission, and Darius chose to stay outside and give her enough space to work, ready to help if she needed him.

Celine set the bag down and pulled on a pair of latex gloves that reached all the way up to her shoulders. He watched with intent as she stepped up to the mare and stroked her nose as she whispered words Darius couldn't quite hear from his vantage point.

'We'll get you and your foal sorted, lovely,' he heard Celine say as she walked over to her bag and grabbed her stethoscope, holding it against the horse's abdomen and listening with closed eyes for a few moments.

'The foal is still alive, that's good news. You were right to call me when you did, Jules.' She nodded at the other woman, then joined her at the back of the horse to inspect the progress of the birth.

Darius had to resist the urge to ask about what was happening when Celine's face scrunched into a frown of concentration. As if she heard his silent plea, she said, 'It looks like this is the face of the foal. It's almost in position, but not quite. How long has it been since the waters broke?'

'We're almost at thirty minutes,' Juliana replied, and Celine frowned.

She flicked her wrist around to look at her watch, frowning even deeper. Then she lifted her head, looking straight at him. 'Can you give me an update on time every five minutes? We need to work fast but carefully if we want this foal to be birthed alive.'

Darius stood up straight. He hadn't expected to become a part of the procedure. 'Okay,' he said as he looked at his own wristwatch, the situation strangely familiar to the one with Álvaro earlier this morning.

Celine nodded, a grateful smile on her face. 'Juliana, please get your front-loader in here. I need to give her an epidural so we can lift her legs up without her kicking and then shift the foal.'

The farmer nodded and left the stable to retrieve the machinery Celine had requested.

Celine almost laughed at Darius's shocked expression. Though most of the theory of illness and complications were the same—a human baby couldn't spend prolonged time in the mother's birth canal, same as a foal—how they resolved the problems were much different when dealing with a being that weight half a ton.

'You can't do a C-section? Is that even a thing with horses?' he asked.

'You can perform a C-section on a horse, yes. But we can't do it here. There's another farm twenty minutes from here that has a surgical facility they let me use from time to time, but we wouldn't be able to get there on time.' She looked at the horse, Rosalie, shaking her head. 'This is the best option we have to get mum and foal through this alive.'

The sound of an engine cut through the silence of the stable and Juliana appeared in a green front-loader. She stopped in front of the open enclosure, then lowered the mechanical arm of the vehicle and drove forward. Once positioned right about Rosalie, the arm came down some more before the engine noise died.

Celine stood, everything for the epidural ready in her hands and pockets. 'Grab that rope there and tie it on a loose loop around her waist,' she said to him, her chin pointing towards a coil of thick rope lying on the floor.

As he moved to do that, she grabbed a footstool from the side. Standing on top of it, she looked down at the horse, her fingers gliding over her spinal cord as she counted the vertebrae. When she found the spot she was looking for, she caught Darius's eyes and he held the loose end of the rope.

He immediately looked down at his watch. 'Four minutes and thirty-six seconds.'

'We're good on time, then.' She nodded, then pointed at her bag. 'There are some hair clippers at the bottom, Darius. Please hand them over.'

As her estranged husband dug for the clippers she carried around in her supplies, Celine was overcome with an odd sense of closeness. Though she had only asked him to join her to spare his feelings, she was now glad that she had. Juliana was well versed in being her assistant whenever she was treating larger animals and, even though she had never worked with Darius before, their non-verbal communication was still as good as it had been in their early relationship. Living apart for the last six years had somehow not hurt their connection—it had hurt her heart, though.

When he handed her the clippers she shaved a small patch of hair away, then took the syringe of lidocaine and inserted the needle under the horse's skin to numb the area. Darius's hand was by her side before she could even voice her request, taking the used syringe from her fingers and popping it into a small container inside her bag for biohazardous waste.

'There's a small bottle of saline solution in one of the smaller pouches. Get me that and, while I set the needle, prep another syringe with eight millilitres of lidocaine for the second dose,' she instructed Darius, who handed her the bottle of saline before turning back to the bag to see to her other request.

He might not be a vet but, as a medical professional, he still understood all the jargon she was throwing at him. A fact that she was grateful for as they worked through this high-pressure situation. With a shake of her head, Celine forced herself to focus, unscrewing the bottle and placing a small drop of saline on top of the spinal needle. She palpated the horse's vertebrae again, then inserted the needle in between the space, all the way down through the skin into the spinal cord.

The drop of saline disappeared down the needle, telling her that she had reached where she was supposed to be. When she looked up, Darius was already standing next to her, the lidocaine she had asked for in his hand.

'Thanks,' she said with a smile, then took the syringe and inserted it into the spinal needle, counting beneath her breath to ensure she wasn't pushing the medication in too fast. Once it was administered, Celine removed the syringe and the spinal needle, stepping down from the stool and dragging it back to the side of the enclosure.

'Time?' she asked, and Darius flicked his wrist.

'Eight minutes and two seconds.'

'The epidural takes six minutes to kick in. Once the six minutes are up, we will lift her then settle her back down.' She walked over to Rosalie, palpating her abdomen. 'She is still having strong contractions. I'm positive if we can right the position of her foal, we will be able to birth it. Get ready with the front-loader, Jules,' she said, then positioned herself behind the mare, watching her tail twitch back and forth.

The seconds ticked by slowly and Celine suppressed the nerves rising within her. Though she had been in this situation many times, each foaling was different. There was no one solution. No, each treatment plan was unique to the horse she worked with, and so there was a large margin for error. Confident as Celine was in her abilities, such tricky births could go either way.

An arm wrapped around her shoulders, the strong hand landing on her upper arm as Darius pulled her closer to him in a reassuring gesture. His other hand remained at his side, rising occasionally for him to look at his watch.

He radiated warmth into her body where her side touched his, the knot between her shoulders slowly relaxing as his thumb grazed over her arm in a calm and reassuring rhythm that instantly set her at ease—way more than his touch should. But her nerves were so fried, the day such a whirlwind of different emotions, culminating in the emergency delivery of a foal, that she couldn't spare the mental and emotional energy to contemplate why his body pressing against hers was flooding her with warmth and tranquillity the way little else could do in this situation.

So Celine let herself lean into the touch, cherishing the moment for what it was and resisting attributing any deeper meaning to it. Darius knew how stressful these treatments could be, was a doctor himself, so he was providing her with support in a difficult professional setting and nothing else. The heat pooling within her stomach was from exertion, not from his scent drifting up her nose and filling her head with old memories of other times they had pressed their bodies against each other.

His hand fell from her arm when the mare's tail went limp, and all three of them sprang into action. Juliana, who was already sitting in the front-loader, looked at her, and Celine nodded, giving her the signal to lift the arm of the machine in a controlled but fast motion, pulling the mare's legs up into the air. A loud whinny echoed through the stables, one that was picked up by several other horses as they whinnied in solidarity with their friend.

Celine pointed towards the mare's head, and Darius moved, laying his hand on her neck and stroking up and down.

'I have her legs secured,' she shouted as she held onto either side of Rosalie. 'Let her down slowly.'

Juliana did so, lowering her down centimetre by centimetre until her hooves were back on the floor. As she did so, Darius moved to untie the rope and drag it out of the way while Celine inspected the foal's progress. 'It seems to be in the right position now, but she may need some more help,' she said as she moved away from the back and palpated the abdomen again. 'With her next contraction, let's do manual traction to help the foal further along.'

Juliana nodded, then moved to the other side, placing her hand to mirror Celine's.

'Darius, I need you to stand behind Rosalie. Should the foal come fast, you need to ease it onto the floor. There are some disposable aprons and another pair of gloves in my bag.'

Celine thought he was going to balk at the idea of catching the foal but, to her surprise, he simply nodded then put on the apron and gloves before positioning himself behind the horse. Over the last week, she had thought many times that he would shirk away from difficult tasks or conversations, find the easy way out instead. That was what he had done six years ago, so she had no reason to believe this time would be any different. But at every single opportunity Darius had surprised her, standing his ground and facing any difficulties head-on. Had she been misjudging him all this time, letting the hurt he had inflicted on her blind her so much that she couldn't see the change in him?

Was it time to give him another chance?

The sensation of her side pressed against him, his arm around her shoulder as if it belonged there, surfaced in her mind, and she pushed it away as Rosalie's abdomen tightened. 'She is about to contract, Jules,' she said, and the other woman grunted. As they felt the spasms they pushed the foal along to re-enter the birth canal.

'I can see something... Hooves?' Darius didn't sound sure, so Celine walked over to him, letting out a sigh of relief when she saw a pair of hooves and, further down, the small nose of the foal.

'Graças a Deus,' she whispered her thanks, then reached inside to wipe the membrane and other fluids from the foal's mouth to make it easier to breathe. 'With the next contraction, I will pull enough so the head gets out. Once that's done, the hardest part is over and we just need to help Rosalie get over the finish line.'

He nodded, and she raised her eyebrows in question as a grin tugged on his lips. He leaned forward, his mouth close enough that, even in the heat of the stable, she could feel his breath grazing her cheek. 'Thanks for the sports metaphor,' he said, then retreated a step.

The shiver rising through her was the last thing she needed right now. She placed her palm flat on the mare's abdomen again, waiting for signs of the next contraction.

'Here she goes,' she whispered to herself, then removed her hand and reached to grab the already visible hooves to pull in time with the contraction.

Celine grunted as she pressed her feet into the floor, regulating her strength as she helped Rosalie with this tricky birth. Too much force could tear the umbilical opening in the abdominal wall, but too little wouldn't help the foal progress through the birth canal. She just needed to get the head out and the rest would follow.

'There we go,' she huffed, her hands dipping down behind the ears and helping the rest of the head out and into the air.

She looked up, her hand open to request a towel, but, before she could even voice her wish, a soft towel hit her outstretched palm. Her eyes rounded. How could he have known she needed a towel? She was covered in amniotic fluid and bits of the membrane that had surrounded the foal—none of which particularly bothered her since it came with the job. The towel in her bag could have easily been for her, yet he had somehow picked up that she needed it for the foal.

Five more minutes and two more contractions and the

foal was born, Darius standing next to her and helping her catch the young horse, placing it on a pile of straw behind its mother.

'Get behind the boundary now, *amor*,' she said, half distracted as she rubbed the towel all over the foal to get the fluids off and encourage breathing. 'Her maternal instincts can kick in just like that, and she'll go from docile to aggressive.'

Darius stared at her for a second, then walked across the enclosure and back behind the wooden half door that kept him separate from the mare while Celine began a thorough check on foal and mare.

Amor. The word had shocked Darius to his core, setting his heart at a pace that it could not sustain as he walked out of the horse box as she'd requested. Celine had seemed distracted, the fifty minutes they'd spent birthing this foal leaving her skin with a sheen of sweat and other stickier things that he for one couldn't wait to wash off in a long and hot shower.

Juliana had hovered around, following the inspection closely, though if Celine looked tired then the farmer had looked downright exhausted as she had swayed on her feet. Celine had noticed it too, for she had dismissed the woman. The two women seemed to share a close rapport that he meant to ask Celine about. Though all the football players on his team were technically his patients, he considered some of them also his friends. Maybe the same could be true for the owners of the livestock that Celine treated.

While all of this had been happening Darius's mind was reeling, the word of affection so casually spoken finding its way into his heart and bringing back the emotions that he had spent so much time locking up. Watching her work had filled him with awe, her compassion and decisive action were traits he'd always admired in her.

Now he sat on the floor outside Rosalie's box, his back leaning against the wood. He looked up as Celine stepped out, closing the door and pulling the gloves and apron off to reveal the clothing beneath free of any stains. She shot him a quick smile, then walked across the stable to where a sink stood tucked away. When she came back a couple of minutes later, her face and hands were wet as she slid down onto the floor next to him. The look she shot him was veiled, not betraying any of the thoughts in her mind.

Was she thinking about what she had said, the way he was? Or didn't she even realise that with one tiny word she had set his mind spiralling, trying to find meaning in something that didn't mean anything?

So he said the first thing that came into his mind. 'I thought you had brought me with you out of pity, but turned out you really needed some extra hands.'

Celine closed her eyes, her head falling back as she took a couple of deep breaths. Without opening them again, she said, 'I can always use extra hands when handling livestock and larger animals, so your help was welcome. But… I *did* invite you to lessen the blow as well.'

That confession didn't surprise him much, as he had sensed it the moment the invitation had left her lips. He wasn't offended by it, but rather intrigued. 'You still care enough about me to spare my feelings.'

A fact she couldn't deny. Why else would she have even hesitated a second to enforce a reasonable boundary around who got to look after her child? Or was there a hidden desire to spend more time with him alone?

The dark blush rising to her cheeks confirmed his suspicion that she herself had realised there was a deeper meaning in why she hadn't simply sent him home when she'd got the emergency call.

'And what about it?' Celine lifted her head again, her eyes fluttering open to look at him with the same unreadable expression. 'I care about the father of my child, have done so since she was born.'

He held his breath as she spoke, expecting her to throw his abandonment of her in his face—even though he would have been on the next flight back had he known back then that she was pregnant. Hadn't he admitted to enough fault at this point?

Darius would regret leaving for the rest of his life. Because of the five years of his daughter's life that he'd missed, yes. But also because he had left the one woman he had ever loved. Because he had unwittingly let her struggle through years of single motherhood when he could have been there to help.

'I didn't mean it like that,' he said, hoping his appeasing tone would lower her hackles. 'I'm glad I was here to help. Not sure how you would have done it with just Juliana here.'

Celine shrugged, clearly not as concerned as he had been about the help she'd needed. 'Usually, her wife or her older kids will help during foaling season. I've also been able to ask Rafael for assistance.'

'Rafael is Maria's husband? The one who drove Álvaro and Bruna home?'

She nodded, a small smile the only sign of her warm feelings towards the man, and even though Darius knew it was completely irrational, a pang of jealousy rose in his chest that he willed away with a few breaths.

'Maria and Mirabel used to live with us before she got

married to Rafael, so childcare used to be a lot easier. I just had to knock on the door and let her know I was on the way out.'

He searched his memories for the name Mirabel, finally stumbling upon it. 'She's your brother's daughter. Why is she living with Maria?'

Celine huffed at that, a laugh laced with a deep hurt that radiated from her like a sizzling flame, making him turn his head back to her to watch her expression. There was a strange resignation in her eyes, as if she had answered the question he'd asked her too many times.

'Daniel almost brought our family charity to its knees when he fell in love with the wife of our biggest benefactor. They ran away together, we don't even know where.' She paused, voice frosty as she added, 'He didn't care enough to take his daughter with him. Maria took Mirabel in, treats her like her own daughter. So does Rafael. Daniel shouldn't have left, but that little girl got the family she deserves.'

Tension snapped into place between them as he sensed the hidden meaning behind her words. Was that message aimed at his shortcomings? Darius knew that words alone would not be enough to convince her of his intentions, but he had not relied solely on words. No, he had stuck around, spent a week in Santarém so he could get to know his daughter, tried to become a part of her life.

'I wouldn't have left had I known about Nina,' he said, his voice low as he steeled himself for her rebuttal.

But her smile was soft and sad as she looked at him, a sigh falling from her lips before she said, 'I know you would have stayed. If you had done a worse job of cutting me out of your life, you might have heard about her. I certainly didn't *want* to raise her on my own.'

The gentleness was unexpected, hitting him in a low place and pushing the air out of his lungs. He'd prepared himself for her fury, knew how to withstand it. But this resigned regret was something wholly new to him and he didn't know how to process that.

'Was it hard for you to do it on your own?' It was a question that had been occupying his thoughts for a long time. Though he hadn't meant for her to go it alone, that was still how it had happened.

Celine considered, then gave a small nod. 'Her birth was tough. I had to learn everything on my own. That's actually how I met Juliana. She and her wife were at one of the birthing classes. When they told me they run a farm a few kilometres away from Santarém, I couldn't believe my luck. We became friends and working partners that day.' She paused, the warm feelings for Juliana clearly written in her face. 'The next low point was Nina's first birthday. I was by myself, didn't want Maria to make a big deal out of it because…a first birthday is something for the parents to celebrate. Nina doesn't remember anything about that day. That was a moment for me… For you.'

Darius's throat tightened at the melancholy in her voice. How could he ever give her those moments back? 'I'm sorry, Cee…'

It was Celine's turn to shift her gaze forward to scrutinise the wall in front of them.

He traced the soft shape of her jaw with his eyes, his gaze gliding down to her neck and resisting the urge to bury his face there to drink in more of her scent. God, even after six years, she was still the most stunning woman on the planet. How could he have walked away from her? Looking back at his choices, the sacrifices his mother had demanded in the name of family seemed too much to ask of anyone.

And as if she was picking up traces of his thoughts, she turned her head towards him again, a plea written in her amber eyes. He knew what she was about to ask even before she said the word.

'Why?'

Darius had known that the small amount of information he'd given her when they'd come to this farm the first time around would not appease her. She needed the whole story—even though there were so many whys to cover. So many things he didn't want to say.

Darius took a deep breath. He'd been steeling himself for this moment and had decided over the last week that if she wanted to know, he would tell her the truth. If it had been just about getting a divorce, he wouldn't have needed to expose himself like that, let her see his failure as a husband. But there was more at stake now. They had a daughter and, because of that, they would be a part of each other's lives for ever.

'When my mother said we had to leave Brazil, she made it sound like this was her choice, and that Brazil had just outlived its usefulness for our family business,' he said, his voice steady even though his heart was pushing against his chest.

'Her cosmetics brand was quite popular when I was a teen. Every girl in my class had a different colour of Delgado lip gloss so we could compare.' Celine chuckled at the memory. 'I was very starstruck to know that you were her son.'

'Her brand's sales had been in steady decline, with fewer and fewer stores picking up new products and shipments—to the point that she announced we were leaving, as there would be more favourable market conditions back in Peru.'

Celine nodded. 'I know this part of the story, Darius. You asked me to marry you so you could stay with me— to be together and make our own family. Only you never came back.'

Darius swallowed, his throat tightening as he considered the next part of the story. 'When we arrived in Peru, I started my application for a spouse visa. I told my mother that I was leaving, and…that was when she told me we'd *fled* Brazil because some shady creditors were after her when she'd defaulted on her business loans.' He paused, the memory of that conversation rising in his mind's eye. 'Along with a terminal diagnosis.'

Celine's eyes widened at that, her lips parting in a sound of surprise. 'Leona died?'

He nodded, the grief in his chest so heavily intertwined with the fury and regret her lies had inflicted on him that he couldn't feel one without the other. 'She had liver cancer, the slow kind that takes years but has a low survival rate. She pressured me into staying, told me I was the only one who could help her fix the business—that I would need to be the one to continue the Delgado legacy.'

He sighed, hardly able to believe how much he had sacrificed for his mother in her dying days, believing that what she'd told him was the truth. 'She said that I couldn't go back to Brazil, that the people she'd borrowed money from would be after me, and that they would be after you too. When she learned I had married you, she seemed genuinely concerned for your safety. So she convinced me to stay, to help her with the business and then find someone to run it since I had my mind set on being a doctor.'

As he spoke, his gaze dropped to the floor, his vision

blurry as he struggled to keep his tone even. The words had tumbled out as if he had been desperate to say them after all of these years. Darius wasn't looking for forgiveness, hadn't even planned on telling her as much as he already had. She would think him an idiot to have believed his mother's words so readily.

The rustling of straw drew his gaze, and he looked straight into Celine's eyes, his breath shuddering at the warmth he found there. She had shifted closer to him, her hand on his knee in silent encouragement. He couldn't help but smile, the touch radiating comfort through him.

'She told you I would be in danger if you came back here?' she asked, her voice soft and even.

'Yes. She showed me the communication she'd had with these loan sharks—people she'd turned to after the banks wouldn't give her any more money. There I saw they knew my name, your name and people in our circle, along with threats of harm. I was...shocked to learn that my mother was involved with these people.'

He laid his hand over hers, curling his fingers around it as he continued, finally revealing the truth. 'So I cut off contact, too scared that something might happen to you. But when I started digging into the problems in the business, I encountered...inconsistencies in her story. Things didn't add up, but every time I confronted my mother she would deny it, or change the subject. I could see how hard chemotherapy was hitting her, so how could I push her?'

Darius swallowed, thinking back to how much time he had spent going over the mountain of documents associated with the Delgado brand, and how much money she had sunk into a failing business, not willing to give up. 'Then she died, and I gained access to some documents she had been hiding until the very last day. There were no loan sharks, only legitimate banks and private investors demanding their money back. She had forced us to leave Brazil to escape them, knowing that they couldn't touch her in Peru. All the messages and emails she'd shown me had been fabricated, the people behind them no more than ghosts. I found out I had given up the most precious thing in my life because of my mother's lies… and I couldn't even confront her about it.'

The sound of him swallowing was audible in the silence. Celine still held his hand, her chest rising and falling in an even rhythm as she looked at him, none of her thoughts written on her face. He didn't know if she believed him, wasn't sure he would have believed someone if they had told him that story.

'Why did she lie?' she asked, giving voice to a question he'd spent countless hours contemplating.

'My father was the primary breadwinner. Before his death, making skincare products had been nothing more than a hobby for her. When he passed, she became responsible for both of us. She worked so hard to achieve success, I don't think she could let it go. Not without knowing that someone else would take care of what she'd built over the years.' He paused to sigh. Darius had no way of knowing if his theory was correct. A part of him believed his mother had misled him for her own gain, but another part couldn't see her acting in her self-interest like that. For his own peace of mind he needed to believe that she'd had good reasons, even if he couldn't understand them.

He continued. 'I think her diagnosis scared her, and I was the only person she thought could help her. That doesn't make it right, and I also don't mean that as an excuse. The choices I made were mine, even if based on lies.'

Finally, a frown tugged on her lips as she said, 'You should have told me...'

He huffed a bitter chuckle. 'I know that now. But back then I was too scared they would find you if I gave you any details—didn't know that none of this was real. I was worried that if I told you, you'd try to help.'

It was Celine's turn to chuckle, but there was no trace of bitterness in her voice. 'I probably would.'

Darius found it in himself to laugh, the weight of this secret he'd been carrying around lifted. Regret still burned in his veins whenever he thought of the chances he'd lost because he had been too blind to see. But he knew there was no point in wallowing in what was lost. All that was left to do was to move forward, to be a father to his daughter.

His grip tightened around her hand. 'I'm not asking you to forgive me. But I need you to know that I'm sincere when I say that I want to be a part of Nina's life.' He hesitated as an idea formed in his head. 'The summer holidays start next month, right? Why don't you and Nina visit me in São Paulo? A little family holiday, if you will.'

A part of him thought he was moving too fast, that Celine would push him back. She didn't trust him yet, at least not enough to leave Nina in his care without her supervision. But, to his surprise, she nodded, turning her hand around so she could return his squeeze with one of her own.

'Let's do that. These are the last days of foaling season, so I can take some time off. It'll be good for Nina to see where you live and get comfortable spending time in the big city,' she said, and Darius's heart leapt at that. There was nothing more exciting than the thought of having his daughter visit him.

Maybe one thing was equally exciting, a little voice whispered as his fingers grazed her palm and noticed the tiny shudder running through her body.

The glint in his eyes was so alluring, the warmth in them inviting her to lose herself by just staring into them for the rest of eternity. Each stroke of his fingers against her palm sent fire through her veins, setting every centimetre of her skin alight until she could no longer suppress the shivers that shuddered through her.

Celine stared down at her hand, willing it to let go of him, but it was no longer hers to command.

She was still reeling from what he had told her, the agony in his voice as he'd told her the truth something she would remember for a long time. He'd left because he'd been led to believe staying would put him in danger—would put *her* in danger. Celine tried to put herself in that situation, tried to understand what her reaction would have been, and with each new scenario that unravelled in her head, she came to the same conclusion.

She would have told him, risks be damned. Maybe that would have been dumb, but Darius had been the love of her life. Her other half. How could she not have trusted him with this information? She could understand his decision—and learning the truth set her heart at ease. But that he hadn't trusted her with this showed their marriage had been doomed to fail from the very beginning.

'I believe you, Darius,' she said, giving him a small smile that threatened to spill over into a larger one when she saw relief wash over his features. 'And I decided to move on from what had happened between us when you first met Nina. I figured we wouldn't be good co-parents if I held so much negativity for you in my heart.'

Her eyes dipped low when he swallowed, watching his throat bob, and on the way back up her eyes stopped on his lips, remaining there. The heat already circulating through her body gathered into a tight cluster in the pit of her stomach that gradually dropped lower, setting her core on fire and summoning the ghost of pleasure she'd found lying beneath those skilful lips.

'You are as kind as I remember, Cee,' he said, then lifted both of their hands to the lips she had just been fantasising about and blew a soft kiss onto her skin. 'I will not let this second chance go to waste.'

Her hand lingered against his lips, the feel of them so hauntingly familiar on her skin, the pleasure they could give one she had gone without for years—all her energy going into raising her daughter. She hadn't realised how much she had missed small affections like this. How big a gap Darius had truly left in her life. Not only as the father of her child and as her husband, but...as a friend. As a lover.

A slight tremble shook her hand as she extended her fingers towards him. He inhaled a sharp breath when her fingertips brushed over his lips, then wound their way over his jawline to his cheekbone, tracing the powerful line. Her body was no longer hers to control, each action coming from a place of need that she had ignored over the years—the person embodying all of that desire absent from her life.

But now he was right here, and the feelings she had been pushing away with such force over the last week burst back to life at that tiny brush of his lips against her flesh. A touch she wanted more of—all over her body.

Celine leaned forward, her face now close enough for their noses to touch. 'Maybe we can be friends again,' she whispered, shuddering as his breath swept across her heated cheeks.

'I would like that,' he replied, voice thick with the same desire and anticipation that had been rising in her ever since he'd stepped back into her life.

'But we need to stop with this,' she said, making no attempt at stopping at all.

'Yes, that would be wise.' In contrast with his words, his hands moved up to her face, cupping each side and then pulling her down, closing the remaining space between them.

The kiss was unexpected, its power shaking her to her core. Her hands went up to his chest, winding themselves into the fabric of his shirt and clinging onto him as if to ground her in this moment. A familiar taste filled her mouth as his tongue swept over her lips, then entered her with a soft groan that vibrated through her skin.

Need she had been suppressing broke free like floodwater from a dam, flooding her system and wiping away the doubts and worries that surrounded her relationship with Darius. The only thing she could focus on was the heat, the feeling of profound familiarity as his hands brushed down her sides, gripping her and making her forget where she was and who she was with—the clarity of knowing what to expect from this kiss chasing away any doubts.

Celine shuddered when his arms wrapped around her, one hand pressed against the small of her back, the other one on her chest and pushing her down until she lay on the floor—Darius's familiar weight between her legs. His hip pushed against hers and she writhed against his hardness.

With his scent filling her nose and his lips working their way down her neck, she couldn't remember the reasons she'd wanted to keep him at arm's length, thought herself silly to deny herself the pleasure of this man when he knew exactly how to touch her—how to drive her wild.

The loud creak of iron hinges swinging open ripped through the luscious cloud Darius had woven around her, and she straightened herself with a start. The sudden return to reality doused her like a bucket of ice water, and she pushed her husband off her.

Her head whipped around to see Juliana walking towards them. By the time the farmer arrived in front of Rosalie's enclosure, she and Darius had climbed to their feet and righted any items of clothing that had shifted.

Celine's pulse hammered in her throat as she looked at Juliana, the other woman's smirk telling her she knew exactly what had been going on.

'You're back early,' Celine said, though she didn't know how much time had passed. Once the mare had birthed the placenta and she had given them another check-up, she had retreated from the box. She had told Juliana to come back in three hours as that would be enough time to ensure the placenta had been delivered and observe any side-effects from the difficult birth.

'It's been almost four hours,' Juliana said, and from the corner of her eye she saw Darius look at his wristwatch and heard him utter a low curse in Spanish.

'Well...' Celine hesitated, searching for the right words. Her brain was scrambled with all that had happened in the last few hours, and it took her far too long to remember the reason she had been lying on the floor of her client's stable to begin with.

'Rosalie is all good. She birthed the placenta. The foal is a bit rattled but breathing and taking milk. The worst is behind us. I'll come back in a couple of days to check on them.' She looked at Juliana, a silent plea in her eyes to not say anything else, and, to her eternal relief, she did just that, giving her only a nod.

Celine grabbed her pack off the floor, hoisting it onto her shoulder, then dared a quick glance at Darius. His expression was unreadable, the flames she had seen in his eyes gone and nothing but some redness around his mouth betraying what had just gone on between them.

CHAPTER SEVEN

THE NERVES THAT had been fluttering in his stomach for the last couple of hours flared into a raging fire as the status of the flight from Manaus changed to 'Arrived'.

With the Copa América having played its final game last week, his team had come back to São Paulo to get ready for the next season of the Brasileirão—the most prestigious national league of Brazil. Though there wouldn't be any matches for another three weeks, the players were back on their usual training schedule so they would be ready for the first rounds. Having spent so much time playing for the national team, a few players needed extra care to avoid injury, so Darius had been watching them train every day.

But more than once these past two weeks, Celine had sneaked into his mind, the memory of their kiss in the stables popping up out of nowhere and robbing him of his composure. The kiss had been the final concession he'd made, the last battle he'd lost against the resurgence of his feelings for Celine—his wife.

Though he knew now that this had been one of the dumber mistakes he had made in recent weeks. Darius didn't know what it was about that night that had prompted him to share his story with her, but he had told her—and she had understood. Forgave him, even. It was that last part that made the thought of reconciliation so tangible, the way forward seemingly less daunting. The kiss had only helped to illuminate the path towards a happy ending for their marriage. An ending where they would become the family both of them had always dreamed of. All the elements were already there, they had to simply reach out and grab it.

Yet every time that thought arose, Darius batted it away, pushing it down and into obscurity, only for it to bounce back up into his consciousness. There was no way towards reconciliation, no matter what his brain conjured up in idle moments. His priority was his daughter and forming that relationship, not running after the wife he had been tricked into forsaking.

What had happened at Juliana's farm was a lapse of judgement and could never happen again—even though he yearned to have another taste of her, not having known that was the last time they would kiss. Just like he hadn't known six years ago... Would he ever have enough of Celine?

The way his pulse sped up when he saw her step through the doors told him the answer was probably no.

Celine and Nina were scanning the crowd, looking for him, and when their eyes locked on him both their faces lit up with smiles that kicked his heart into overdrive. Instead of lusting after the woman he couldn't have, he should be thankful that a mere visit caused such a joyful reaction in them.

Nina broke into a sprint as she saw him, leaving her mother behind as her tiny legs carried her over to him. Darius crouched down, extending his arms to sweep her into a hug that immediately set him at ease, dousing any nerves that were bubbling in the pit of his stomach.

This was why he had to keep his distance. Anything that threatened the relationship he was building with Nina was off-limits—that included his own feelings for her mother. He would not risk any more. What if they reconciled, and it didn't work out? It would devastate Nina. Their relationship had only just formed, his young daughter becoming more comfortable with him each time they saw each other.

'Darius!' she yelped with a giggle as he picked her up off the floor, heaving her onto his hip, and praying his face didn't show the stab of disappointment on hearing his name. He had no right to demand to be called Pai— Dad. Yet a part of him hoped she would say it every time they spoke.

'Hola, mi princesa preciosa. Cómo estás?' he said, earning himself a puzzled look from his daughter.

'Que?' she asked, though her attention was immediately drawn to the balloon he was holding by a string. 'Is that for me?'

Before he could answer, Celine stepped up to them, dragging a suitcase behind her. 'He asked you how you are, *filha*.'

'Oh.' Nina's lips rounded as the sound escaped her mouth, her eyes still snagging on the balloon. Whatever her mother had said had gone in one ear and out the other.

Darius laughed at that, then handed his daughter the string before he set her down on the floor. Then he turned to Celine, his hand going up to her arm and greeting her with a kiss on her cheek. Only when his lips brushed her skin did he realise that the way to greet someone that was ingrained in South American culture maybe hadn't been the best move with all the unresolved feelings floating around between them.

He sensed the rippling of her muscles under his finger-tips, but she didn't reveal anything and just smiled at him.

'Let me get that for you,' he said, reaching for her suit-case to distract himself from the heat rising in his chest—heat he had banished to the far corners of his being, which had no business re-emerging at this moment.

He led them through the airport to the car park, loading everyone into the car and driving them to his apartment in the heart of São Paulo. Both Nina and Celine stared wide-eyed as they drove through the city, pointing at the high-rise buildings reaching into the sky—including the one Darius lived in.

By the time he had ushered them into his apartment and given them the tour of his two-bedroom penthouse, Nina had made herself comfortable on his couch and promptly fell asleep on his lap. As he stroked her soft hair and looked down at her tranquil face, his heart was about ready to burst with the unconditional love that had grown tenfold ever since he'd heard about his daughter.

A soft chuckle from Celine tore him out of his obser-vation, and he raised his eyes to meet hers. 'She was up at five packing her little backpack for her trip to see you,' she said, melting his heart even further.

'She was excited to see me?' His voice was low, al-most not daring to ask that question. Ever since he had become a part of Nina's life he had braced himself for the inevitable rejection, that Nina would decide that his effort was too late.

His thoughts must have shown on his face, for Celine scooted closer on the couch, laying her hand over the one that had been stroking Nina's hair. 'Relax, Darius. She's comfortable with the idea of her father being in her life.'

He mustered a half smile at her words, the worry still

eating at his insides. Everything between them was so fresh, so…fragile. Just one more reason to keep his and Celine's relationship on a strictly co-parenting level.

'I didn't know I could love someone so much,' he said, his voice quiet with wonder and reverence.

Celine nodded, understanding exactly what he meant. 'I know. I grew attached to her as she was growing inside me. But nothing compares to that moment when they put her in my arms for the first time.'

'Should I put her in bed?'

She looked at the clock hanging from his wall. 'What's the plan for today?'

'I thought we could go to Paulista and have a walk there since it's Sunday. Have lunch at the Japan House and check out the street stalls.'

'Um… You'll have to repeat that because I'm not sure what you just said.' Celine looked at him with a furrowed brow, her head slightly tilted.

'You've never been to São Paulo?' he asked and chuckled as she shook her head. 'Paulista is the main shopping street and it's usually busy with traffic—except for Sundays. Every Sunday, the city shuts down traffic to the street and it turns into a large pedestrian area with food stalls, street music and other smaller attractions.'

'Oh…that sounds quite nice. I think she'll enjoy that.' Celine glanced at the clock again. 'We'll let her sleep for an hour. She was up much earlier than she usually is.'

Darius nodded, then scooped his sleeping daughter into his arms and walked to the bed he had put together for her. Tucking her in, he stooped to kiss her on the forehead, then left the room and pulled the door closed behind him—only to find the couch where he had left Celine empty.

He turned around, and then laughed when she walked back towards him with two cups in her hand. 'Maybe you should take a nap too, if you were up so early,' he said as he took the cup of coffee from her, settling back down on the couch.

Celine shrugged one shoulder, then closed her eyes and savoured the mouthful of coffee with a soft moan that sent his heated blood in entirely the wrong direction. 'Coffee is better. I don't think I could sleep later if I take a nap now.'

'I'm sure we'll find something fun to do once Nina is in bed for the night.' The words flew out of his mouth before he could reconsider them, going against everything he had told himself in the weeks leading up to their visit.

Celine's eyes rounded, clearly not oblivious to the sexually charged subtext in his words. Silence spread between them, the tension snapping into place so tight he felt a tiny breeze could crack it.

Though two weeks had passed, they hadn't spoken about *the kiss*. Darius had left early the next day, needing to get back to São Paulo as training sessions had started again, and Celine hadn't brought it up either. All their texting up to this point had been about the logistics of getting here.

He watched the rise and fall of her chest as she took some breaths, tension mingling with the hunger slumbering inside of him, making him want to reach out and grab the release he saw right in front of him.

Celine stared at Darius, her heart beating in her chest in an erratic dance as she waited for him to say something—though what exactly she wanted him to say, she wasn't sure. Wasn't quite certain what to say in this situation either.

That their kiss had haunted her ever since it happened? That the phantom of his lips sneaked onto hers every time she had an unguarded moment, yearning for them to find an excuse to be together again? No, late night impromptu kisses were off the menu. Because, even though Nina's liking of Darius was almost infectious, Celine couldn't forget what had happened between them. He'd explained the situation to her, and she understood and had meant it when she'd said she was ready to move on.

But when she had decided to move on, she hadn't meant to fall straight back into the patterns of their old relationship. Her goal was still to get a divorce, so she could finally find her missing piece. Even though her heart was currently trying to convince her that Darius might just be that person she was looking for, it was not possible.

Even if she could ever overcome the wounds his abandonment had caused her, sitting in his apartment in São Paulo, she realised their lives weren't compatible any more. She needed to be in Santarém to help her sister with the charity while Darius had built his career here.

The kiss had been a mistake. A delicious, mind-blowing mistake which had been on her mind ever since it had happened—and filling her with feelings she had believed long forgotten.

Celine bit back a sigh as she realised they would have to get it over with right now, while Nina was still sleeping.

'You want to talk about it?' she forced herself to say, reading the message in his eyes.

His eyes narrowed on her. 'Do you?'

She couldn't stop the laugh rising in her throat. 'No… but I think this week will be awkward if we don't.'

Darius huffed a laugh at that, some of the tension between them softening at the sound, and Celine found herself smiling as well—remembering how much she had loved his laugh.

'Life has been a lot less…fun without you.' The words had formed in her head as she relished his laugh, its timbre drawing out all the cherished memories of what they had shared in their relationship, with Darius clowning around so much that she couldn't even remember how she used to have fun without him.

His expression softened, warmth warring with an ancient pain that she knew all too well.

'I mean, it's not like I haven't enjoyed life, don't get me wrong. My life has been great,' she quickly added, cringing at how defensive the words had come out.

'Tell me more about it,' he said, his coffee mug dangling from his hand in a gesture so casual that it clashed with the intensity in his gaze. Was he trying to seem nonchalant?

Celine paused, then asked, 'Tell you about what?'

'The last few years. Tell me what I missed.'

'What an…incredibly broad question.' She smirked at him but didn't get the laugh she had been aiming for to cut the tension. No, Darius levelled a smouldering look at her, his dark eyes ablaze with a fire of unknown origin that brought heat to her own cheeks.

A smile appeared on his lips. 'Humour me.'

'Well…' She paused, casting her mind back. 'When I announced I was going back to live in Santarém with my sister, it was an enormous shock to my parents, Maria and the faculty, who thought I was going to stay there to work at the institute for veterinary medicine in Manaus. I didn't tell my sister I was pregnant until I'd been back at home for a few weeks.'

Celine had known that Maria would return and take

over the charity from their parents so they could finally ease into their long-awaited retirement in Switzerland.

'And then life in Santarém was much how I remembered it growing up. It was good for Nina to have her aunt and uncle around to give her the attention she needed. And once her cousin Mirabel came to live with us, the two developed an unlikely friendship.' Celine laughed. 'Our working theory is that Nina simply has an old soul.'

Darius laughed, the sound passing through her with a soft shudder that raised the hairs along her arms. 'I can see that, though my experience with five-year-old children is very limited.'

'With Maria's own child in the mix, it'll be interesting to see how she acts as an older cousin.' Nina had already shown great care and gentleness with her newborn cousin Sam, doting on her whenever they went over to Maria's place to visit.

'How well do you get along with your brother-in-law?' He smiled when Celine shrugged her shoulders.

'We hired Rafael when we opened the vet clinic to help cover the costs of the charity after losing our biggest donor to my brother's foolishness. Turns out, Rafael's family is semi-famous, making him the heir to a small fortune.' She paused, considering how much of Maria's story she wanted to tell. 'He grew very attached to Santarém, offered to help and, in the process, they fell in love.'

She looked down into her mug, the light brown liquid making small waves as she swirled it around. 'His arrival made me even more obsolete. Before that, I already didn't have much to do with the charity, other than helping Maria whenever she needed a second opinion. But I've been more of an advisor than a vet to our...her charity. When Rafael started, his interest in furthering the cause became apparent in an instant, so now what small role I had in my family legacy is now gone too.'

Celine's own words hit her with an unexpected ferocity. She blinked several times as emotions she hadn't realised she'd been carrying around welled up. She had always known that she and Maria hadn't been equals in their charity, but Rafael's presence showed her just how much she had detached herself from it.

Darius sensed the thoughts rising in her head, for he put his own mug down on the coffee table and closed some of the distance between them by scooting closer. He didn't touch her, yet his presence was enough to summon warmth to ease away the darkening clouds gathering inside of her.

'Do you regret not playing a larger part in your family charity?' he asked, voicing the nebulous question that had been dancing along the edges of her mind for quite some time, but Celine had been too scared to ever acknowledge it.

Discomfort clawed at her, and she closed her eyes, the breath she took filled with the scent of pine and spice, bringing memories of a simpler time, when they had both been happy with each other.

'No, I don't,' she finally said, her voice barely above a whisper. 'If you had stayed, I think our lives would not have taken us back to Santarém, and that wouldn't have been the worst thing.'

She didn't mean it as an accusation, yet hurt flashed in his eyes at the mention of the life they'd never got the chance to live. It was a thought they both needed to get comfortable with. It was easy to get wrapped up in the disappointments of their past, dream of the what-ifs and how they would have grown closer as a family. But what they needed to think about was the present, and what their relationship needed to be if they wanted to be the best co-parents they could be.

To do that, Darius needed to stop looking at her with those blazing brown eyes, because every time she gazed into them she got lost. But instead of pushing away and extracting herself from his aura, Celine leaned in as she asked, 'If you could go back and make a different choice, would you?'

'Yes.' That was all he said. *Yes*. No elaboration, no recapping of the past mistakes, no additional context to add to that word. Because he didn't need to. The gravel in his voice was all the context she needed to understand the deep regret that accompanied the decision he'd made all those years ago.

Celine held her breath when he reached out, taking hold of her hand and intertwining their fingers. 'I know there's no way back, and I'm not suggesting we should pick things up where we left them. We have a child now, and whatever she needs must come first.' He placed her hand on his chest, covering it with his own, and his heart-beat pulsing beneath her palm sent a shiver down her spine. 'It wasn't my plan to kiss you. I don't know if these feelings are old or new, but the moment got away with me.'

Was this moment getting away with them too? Celine took in a shaky breath, wanting to snatch her hand back, but his warmth radiated through her skin, filling her with a tingling sensation that she hadn't felt in six years. It was the feeling that she wanted to find, the emotion Maria and Rafael got to experience every day—but *not* with Darius. It *couldn't* be him, because how was she ever to trust him again?

'The adrenaline was pumping pretty hard through our veins, so I think we can forgive ourselves for that slip-up,' she said, though the lack of conviction was clear in her voice. She knew intellectually that it had been a mistake, but her heart was saying something else.

Darius's hand dropped from hers, but Celine kept hers pressed against his chest where he had placed it, his strong heartbeat filling her brain with a luscious fog that she was not ready to let go of just yet. His breathing was steady but his eyes darkened as they locked onto hers. A hungry spark flashed in them that turned her core into molten lava.

Then he lifted his hand and slipped it over her neck, cradling the back of it. 'I don't think I ever got over you, Cee,' he said, his voice low with the same desire she'd heard in it two weeks ago.

Everything inside of her wanted to give in, to lose herself in this sensation and to forget her doubts, forget about how he fitted into her life. She swallowed the lump in her throat, her voice breathy as she said, 'Me neither.'

'I tried to move on—tried to find a way forward. But no one has ever caught my attention the way you have.' His thumb grazed over her earlobe, leaving sparks in its wake and filling her head with fantasies of his lips on hers, her neck, her thighs…

'We need some closure,' she replied, grabbing at that word that coalesced in her mind. Because it was not rekindling but closure that was happening between them. Their relationship had ended so abruptly. Of course there were some unresolved feelings.

Darius's thumb slowed at that. 'Closure?'

'We both know there is no path forward for our marriage, Darius. So we need to…have it out and find some closure.'

He stilled, his hand on her neck still sending ripples of desire through her that she tried to douse with logic. The flames in his gaze were banked, the emptiness that filled his eyes so stark that she regretted saying those words. Her hands shot up to his face to cup it, bringing him closer to her as her mind blanked—her only concern to wipe the hurt from his expression as she pulled him into her arms.

Darius stiffened then relaxed against her, his lips replacing his hand on her neck. Goosebumps prickled along her arms and legs as his breath swept over her skin.

'I don't think this is how I will get closure,' he mumbled, his lips brushing over her neck with every word and sending heat lancing through her body.

The world around her faded away, narrowing down to that spot where his lips pressed against her flesh. No other sound or scent or sensation could penetrate that hyper focus, leaving her shivering with need for Darius.

'Darius…' she huffed out as his hands wrapped around her waist, squeezing tight before finding their way upwards—exploring. His name was a plea on her lips and he growled near her ear, his own desire for her taking form.

Then his hands stilled, his muscles tensing underneath her hands as they roamed up his back. She lifted her head to look at him.

Before she could say anything, Darius leaned back, his body no longer in her space, as he said, '*Hola, bella durmiente*. Did you have a nice nap?'

CHAPTER EIGHT

NINA HAD INTERRUPTED them at the wrong time—or was it actually the perfect time? Darius wasn't sure, but he didn't have the mental space to consider what had gone on between him and Celine when their daughter had stepped into the living room. From the look on his wife's face as he had backed off, he could tell that the thought of Nina walking in on this situation had horrified her.

Was Celine right about gaining closure? His mind told him yes, that he was looking exactly for a way to finally move on from her. But that thought didn't reach his heart, which yearned to pull her into his arms and never let her go again. Did it even matter what he wanted? Clearly Celine was ready to put the final notice on their marriage, as she had presented him with divorce papers and spoke of closure. Then why did she keep reaching for him?

After their unceremonious interruption Celine had whisked Nina away to get ready, and they'd spent the rest of the afternoon walking down Paulista Avenue, stopping at various shops and musicians and for one unbelievably delicious ice cream. He'd watched Celine as much as his daughter, enjoying the wonder and excitement in their eyes whenever they spotted something.

By the time they had eaten and were ready to go home, Nina had been so exhausted that Darius had carried her on his back. Now they were back at his place, Nina standing on her feet with her eyes half closed, and Celine looking fairly similar, though he knew from her expression that she tried her best not to show it.

'How about you two get comfortable in your room? We have a whole week's worth of fun activities stacked up, so no need to push so hard,' he said, crouching down in front of his daughter to give her a hug and a kiss on the forehead as the little girl leaned against her mother's legs for support.

He looked up, meeting Celine's equally tired eyes. 'Do you need any help?' he asked, looking back at Nina.

Celine shook her head, then put her hand between their daughter's shoulder blades and pushed her towards the open door of their room. 'Say goodnight to your father, *filha*,' she said as they crossed the threshold.

Nina turned around, giving him a small wave as she said, *'Buenas noches.'*

Darius's eyes widened at her use of Spanish, his native tongue, and kept frozen in place as he stared at the closed door. He'd occasionally sprinkled some Spanish into their conversation, pointing at different things and saying the right words. Not to teach her his language, but to evoke the idea that there was more to her than what she had learned so far. Though Brazil had become his chosen home, and he spoke Portuguese like a native, he was still a Peruvian man, making his daughter part Peruvian.

Maybe further down the line he could help her learn Spanish. The idea warmed him, as did any that involved a future where he was more involved with Nina...and with Celine.

He gave weight to the thought, his mind turning back to the moment they had shared earlier today. He'd spent the time they were apart steeling his resolve, telling himself that there was no path back to where they had been. But the path he was looking onto right now was not the old one that they had walked together before. No, what unfolded in his mind's eye was something completely new, a world full of possibilities that he wanted to reach out and grab with both hands. A reality where they had both learned what they wanted in life, had grown into the people they needed to be, and had then found their way back to each other.

A picture so sublime, so full of love, that Darius immediately pushed it away.

No, he *could not* fall for his wife again. Though he knew his heart, knew that he would never make the same mistakes again, he didn't want to risk anything that could jeopardise his relationship with his daughter. How could they even be together when their lives had grown in such different directions?

Darius let himself fall onto the couch, unbuttoning his shirt and exposing his chest to the chill air in his apartment. His mind was too busy for him to even contemplate sleep, so he lay there in silence instead, his eyes roaming over the dark ceiling as if it had the answer to his problems written on it.

Celine opened her eyes with a frustrated sigh, her hand groping for her phone on the nightstand. She turned on the screen, sighing again when she looked at the time. She'd spent two and a half hours trying to fall asleep, with no success at all. Her thoughts were too loud, her heart racing whenever she thought of how they had spent the day together.

She had rarely seen Nina happier than she'd been today.

Having grown up in Santarém with the same people surrounding her every day of every year, her daughter had been excited to explore the city, pointing her finger at every new and exciting thing, asking a million questions as the day went along. Questions that Darius had been more than happy to answer.

Watching them interact, seeing Nina cling to Darius's side at every opportunity, twisted her heart the way nothing else had in the last few weeks. Somehow they had become the family Celine had already dreamed they would be, yet something was missing…something crucial that she needed to complete the picture. That special person in her life to complete her.

The person she'd thought Darius would be when they had met all those years ago.

Quietly, so as not to wake Nina, Celine climbed out of bed and walked towards the door, opening it slowly and closing it behind her with just as much caution. She had to blink a few times to adjust to the light in the living room, the lights of the city filtering in through the large windows. Looking up, the sky was black, the stars she was used to seeing in her remote village wiped away by the brightness of the city itself, millions of people going about their lives.

The day had shown her the appeal of the city life, everything one could ever want at arm's reach, and she'd enjoyed the fantasy of building her own life here. Closer to Darius.

A shiver shuddered down her spine, and she turned away from the window—and stared right into Darius's eyes. He was sitting on the couch, the shirt he'd worn earlier hanging from his shoulders. Her eyes glided downwards, drinking in his exposed chest and abdomen, her fingers prickling at the thought of exploring every plane, ripple and muscle in painstaking detail.

'You're up late,' he said as he straightened himself, giving her an even better view of his body. Her mouth went dry at the sight of it, wetness pooling in other parts of her body.

'Couldn't sleep,' she replied, her breath hitching when he got up in a smooth motion, reminiscent of the wild cats they sometimes treated in the clinic. Watching them stalk up and down their enclosure was a terrifying and impressive sight.

Just like Darius as he walked up to her. Her skin tingled as his eyes swept over her.

'What's keeping you up?' he asked as he approached, her eyes dragging down his body the same way he had checked her out just a moment ago and liking what she saw. *Really* liking what she saw.

His unbuttoned shirt fully exposed his upper body, muscles rippling as he walked, but her gaze dipped further down—following the dark trail of hair as it vanished in his waistband.

He stopped his prowl as he came to a stop in front of her, forcing her to lift her chin to look at him. His eyes were dark, smouldering with a fire that she had seen earlier today—when she had told them they needed distance. Closure. This was the exact opposite of that, yet Celine couldn't fight the attraction. Didn't want to fight it either.

'You,' she breathed, knowing she shouldn't say that, for it stoked the flames in his eyes even higher.

His hand reached out to her, his knuckles brushing over her bare shoulder and down her front, where her peaked nipples were already straining against the silken fabric of her nightdress. She inhaled sharply when he swept over the hardened peaks, his touch no more than a whisper, yet the sensation exploded through her.

'That's funny,' he said, his head coming down towards hers until his lips were right next to her ear. 'You were keeping me up too.'

'Oh, yeah?' Her hands, no longer under the control of her mind, slid up to his chest, feeling the strong muscles flex underneath her fingertips. Pushing further up, she caught the edges of his shirt and flicked the fabric off his shoulders and down his arms before linking her fingers behind his neck.

Darius chuckled, slipping his hands out of the cuffs. The shirt fell onto the floor and, not even a heartbeat later, his hands were back on her. One pressed against the small of her back, eliminating any space between them. The other one cradled the back of her head, pulling her face towards his.

His lips brushed over hers in a gentle kiss that was enough to send a flood of heat through her core, shivers clawing down her back. She dug her fingers into his shoulders, a low moan leaving her lips when he pulled away ever so slightly.

'I cannot resist you, Celine,' he whispered against her lips, his breath as heavy as hers, each inhale an almost insurmountable feat while their mouths were apart. 'I tried for weeks to forget what you mean to me. Ignore the pull I sense whenever I see you. But I cannot.'

'Darius…' Her eyes fluttered shut when he kissed her again, the gentleness gone and replaced by an urgency that spoke of the restraints he had put himself under—restraints she, too, had practised whenever they had been near each other.

His tongue darted over her lips, then dipped into her

mouth as they deepened the kiss, his scent and touch and heat an explosive concoction that robbed her of any clear thought. All she could focus on was the ache building in her core, the flames lapping at her thighs, lancing through her body and driving her desire for him higher and higher.

'Say yes, *amor*,' he said, leaving her mouth to nibble at her earlobe before trailing further down her neck. 'Say yes to me, to us. If the last weeks have shown me anything, it's that you and I belong together.'

Her breath left in a shudder, the onslaught of sensation too much for her to think straight. She should say no. Their relationship was not one to be rekindled. Her heart had barely healed, the shock of seeing him so unexpectedly ripping all of her wounds open again.

Yet he had owned his mistake from the very start, explained his side. She understood why he had left, even though she still disagreed with the way he had handled everything. Would she have done anything different if she'd believed him in danger?

Celine wasn't certain. Six years ago, she would have done just about anything to keep him safe—including getting married to him so he could stay in Brazil. But she couldn't say yes, not to a future with him still as her husband. The trust in him was too far gone.

'Say yes, Celine. I promise you, I will never hurt you again.' He slid his mouth over hers again, brushing her lips in a gentle kiss that exploded tiny fireworks in her stomach that roared into a fire when his hand slipped under the seam of her nightdress, his nails grazing over her thighs.

Her head fell backwards when his lips brushed over the hollow of her throat, his mouth leaving a burning trail of kisses down to the centre of her breasts while his fingers on her thigh were drawing lazy circles on their way inward.

Her own hands began to wander, roaming over his back in a desperate search for purchase as waves of anticipation and need crashed through her, turning everything inside of her upside down. His scent was so familiar, the brushes of his fingers something she had been yearning for ever since he had left—unable to find anyone like him again.

Celine shuddered when his fingers brushed against the gusset of her underwear, and that was when she cracked wide open, the walls she had built tumbling down as the desire to be with this man overwhelmed her, leaving no room for logic or argument. There was just the passion that was passing between them with every swapped breath.

'Yes,' she breathed, the word hanging in the air.

Darius's hands stilled, his lips stopping their march down her body to come back to her face. His dark gaze bored into hers, then his lips parted in a smile so stunning and genuine that it robbed Celine of her remaining breath. It was just as well, because that meant the yelp she let out was a quiet one as he hoisted her upwards.

She wrapped her legs around his waist to keep her balance as he braced his hands on her butt and walked her towards his bedroom.

Yes. A thrill of triumph had raced through his body at that one syllable that made the hidden desire in his heart he had been denying for the last few weeks an actual reality.

Darius had watched her as she'd stepped out of the room, hard an instant later as his eyes were drawn downwards where the diaphanous fabric swished against the peaks of her breasts. Those feelings came over him unbidden, his control over them wearing thin, and he had feared that the moment would come soon when he wouldn't be able to help himself.

It would have been so easy to forget about it if she hadn't kissed him too. Or kissed him back today. Or if she had simply said no, he could have turned his back and walked away. But now Darius realised he was in way too deep and there was no way out. He *wanted* to be with his wife. Not just in bed, not just this one night or this week they spent together. He wanted her back for good.

For the first time in years his heart felt light, and he could breathe easy again. All thanks to this woman who had her legs wrapped around his waist, her wetness pronounced enough that he could feel it through the barrier of fabric on his skin. The sensation only tightened his erection, and he lengthened his stride, kicking the door shut behind him as they stepped over the threshold.

He dropped her onto the bed and watched from above as she stretched out on his sheets, drinking her in. 'You are stunning,' he whispered, his words prompting her to sit up so her legs were hanging off the bed.

His hand came up to her shoulder, intending to push her back down, but her fingers wrapped around his wrist to stop him. Her eyes were filled with unbridled desire that was reflected in his own. 'Stay right there,' she said, her voice low and full of promises that made him ache.

Then she released his wrist and placed her hands on his abdomen, wandering up towards his chest and caressing the skin there before coming back down, drawing circles as she went and leaving nothing but fire in her wake. He groaned in anticipation as her fingers slipped beneath his waistband, pulling at the fabric without releasing him. His eyes fluttered closed when her breath grazed over his skin and, a moment later, he shuddered when she pressed her lips just below his navel.

Then one of her hands moved to the front of his trousers and, with a flick of her fingers, his button popped open. A sigh fell from his lips as she pulled his trousers down, the discomfort from his trapped manhood subsiding and replaced with a sensation that bordered on discomfort in the most sensual of senses as Celine palmed his length through the fabric of his underwear.

'Celine...' Her name was a plea on his lips, though the edge in his voice left her undeterred from her path.

His hands came to rest on her shoulders, his fingers digging into her flesh as she pulled the remaining layer of fabric that lay between them away. He shuddered as she wrapped her fist around him and pumped in long slow movements, each one a delicious agony he hadn't felt in a long time.

This was almost too much, his muscles so tight under her touch that Darius thought he would explode if he didn't find release soon. That he would be so lucky to get a second chance, to have the opportunity to redeem himself—he hadn't dared to hope ever since he'd stepped back into her life.

And Celine had found it in her heart to see his sincerity for what it was as he'd finally shared the whole story of his disappearance. They would become the family they had always dreamed of.

Then her lips closed around him and his mind went blank, the leash on his passion broken by her touch.

Celine closed her eyes as she took him in her mouth, writhing at the groan that dropped from his lips. His hands, clinging to her shoulders not even a moment ago, roamed down her back, and he balled his fists into the fabric of her nightdress. He drew a muffled chuckle from her as he yanked on it, forcing her face away from him as he pulled it over her head.

When she tried to capture him again, he stepped backwards and then knelt on the floor. She looked down, and the intent and passion in his eyes caught her breath in her throat. Heat spread in a star shape through her body, rising to her cheeks in a faint blush and settling in her core that contracted in anticipation.

Darius grinned, a look she knew all too well. 'My turn now,' he said, voice filled with gravel that worsened the ache inside. All she could think about was to have him inside of her.

The fabric of her underwear grazed her thighs as he pulled it down, his breath cool on her heated skin as he put both of her legs over his shoulders. But then he took his time, kissing the inside of one knee and trailing his lips and tongue up before repeating the process on the other side. All the while Celine bucked her hips, her body having its own mind that she couldn't override.

All she wanted was his tongue right there where she had been aching for him for weeks.

'You evil, evil man,' she breathed out between clenched teeth as he kissed the apex of her thigh, just above the place she *really* wanted him to kiss.

The breath of his laugh skittered over her skin, raising goosebumps all over her flesh, and he stroked over her thigh, savouring the feel of it.

'Be patient, *amor*,' he whispered, his hand wandering further up to caress her stomach. 'We have the rest of our lives ahead of us.'

Did they, though? That thought managed to push through

the fog of lust his touch had elicited in her, drawing her attention to a place she didn't want to be in right now. She hadn't said yes to for ever, and Darius knew that. There was no *for ever* for them. If there was, he wouldn't have left. No, she had said yes to this moment. A night to forget her heavy heart, her hurt and her anger, and to just be with the man she had been craving since he'd appeared at her front door.

Thoughts of tomorrow could wait until dawn, she thought to herself. Then her mind was wiped of any thought, all of her attention homing in on where his tongue connected with her body as he parted her with a stroke.

'Oh, *Deus*...' Her breath was ragged, the heat inside of her an inferno, and she prayed that this would never stop. Because with each stroke of his tongue she came closer to the edge, came more *alive* than she had felt in a long time. It was as if the world had lost some of its splendour the moment Darius had left, and now her vision had turned into Technicolor.

Celine shuddered as he pressed his tongue flat against her. 'You are so exquisite,' he mumbled into her thigh before nipping at it, drawing another yelp from her that made her clasp her hands over her mouth, eyes wide.

Darius only smirked, the intent to hinder her being as silent as possible clearly written on his face. Yet he showed some mercy as he caught her eyes and said, 'Are you ready?'

The heat pulsing through her, release so close she sensed it at the edge of her mind, scrambled her brain. Only when he lowered his face again, with a hungry glint in his eyes, did Celine understand what he meant.

Sensation exploded through her as his tongue was

joined by his fingers, and she stretched her arms above her. Her fingers grazed over the sheet and she reached, desperate to close her hand around the pillow before Darius could make her...

Celine grasped the edge of the pillow between two fingers and pulled it down, slamming it down on her face as release barrelled through her with such intensity that even the soft cushion wasn't enough to fully absorb her scream.

Darius kept stroking her through the aftermath of her orgasm, and when she dared to lower the pillow again to gulp for air he stood in front of her with a devilish grin that squeezed her heart.

'I missed you,' she said, giving voice to the ache in her chest and the warmth in her body that was partially caused by what he had done, but also because of who he was—what he meant to her, back then and now.

The mischievous grin softened at her words, and the look in his eyes almost broke her heart all over again. The traitorous words hung on her lips, words she had said so many times and wanted to shout them again, but knew she couldn't—not when she still felt the pain of the scars he had left with his disappearance. Not when there was so much at stake between them. This night was all they could have.

This moment was so perfect Darius never wanted it to end. He stood in front of her and drank in all her naked glory.

He'd missed her too, and over the last weeks this had become abundantly clear to him. When he had still been trapped in a web of lies, he'd had to justify his abandonment to himself to not crack under the guilt, and once he'd seen what mistakes he'd made he didn't dare to intrude back into her life—not when he was certain that she would have moved on.

But as Darius climbed into bed with his wife the realisation struck that he had never stopped loving her. That throughout everything a part of his heart had remained locked behind the promises they had made to each other six years ago.

He pulled her into his arms, the soft kiss he breathed onto her lips now fuelled by passion, and a moment later she had him on his back while she straddled him. As his manhood strained against her he was cautious not to go too far and he reached for the drawer of his nightstand and pulled out a condom.

Celine watched with hungry eyes as he rolled it down, and as his hands settled back on her hips she leaned forward, kissing him.

Bright stars appeared in front of his vision as he dipped into her wet heat, the feel of her exactly like he remembered and yet so different at the same time. Her tongue darted into his mouth, her moans filling his ears as he held onto her hips, guiding her—or rather letting her guide him.

His breath mingled with hers as she bent down for another kiss, and Darius wrapped his arms around her, pulling himself up. His hand slipped between them to find the bundle of nerves to stroke in tandem with his thrusts.

Celine's breathing grew heavier, her breasts pushing against his chest. She let out a low moan when he dipped his head down and sucked one of her nipples into his mouth, rolling it over his tongue.

'Darius, please…' she huffed, her fingers clawing into his shoulders. 'Please, please, I am so…close.'

She waved her hand at something behind him, and he

stilled momentarily, a grin spreading over his lips as he understood. Grabbing her by the waist, he pulled Celine off him and then flipped her around so she was lying on her stomach. Her hands were already clasping the pillow, her chest heaving with each breath, and he knew her next orgasm was in sight.

So was his, but he couldn't resist taking a moment to stroke his hands down her back, her muscles smooth and defined, no doubt from how physically demanding her work was. A burden he planned on sharing with her going forward. How they would go about it, he wasn't sure, but he knew that he would move mountains to make it work with her this time around.

'Darius!' Her voice was a mixture of a plea and a demand, her tone surging straight to his groin, and as he reached around her to put his finger back where it belonged, he thrust into her again. Her hips moved in rhythm with him, her front pressing against his hand in a frantic chase to the finish line.

Darius heard the drawn-out moan swallowed by the pillow just as he felt her convulse around him. The second he rolled off her, he snaked his arms around her and pulled her back to his chest. He placed a kiss on the back of her neck, catching a whiff of her scent as he nestled his nose into her hair.

This moment was pure and undiluted perfection, he thought as he closed his eyes and relished the warmth of her body and the silken feel of her skin against his.

CHAPTER NINE

THE REST OF the week in São Paulo went by in a flash and by the end of it Darius had conjured up an image of harmonious family life that Celine so desperately wanted to believe. Everything she had ever wanted from her marriage with him was right there—days spent with their daughter, nights spent with each other, and everything in between filled with joy and laughter.

But she knew it wasn't real. Knew it because though she enjoyed being by his side, relished every touch and still shivered with need hours after they had made love to each other, she held her breath for the pain to catch up with her. And that was the big red flag in their relationship she couldn't ignore.

She wasn't relaxed, at least not entirely, always preparing herself for the inevitable end to the whirlwind rekindling of their attraction to each other. Attraction, *not* love. That was something she reminded herself of every time she fell asleep in his arms, his warmth surrounding her to a point where she could almost imagine a life like this.

Their lives were not the same, the paths they had taken too different. How could she leave Maria and her work at the charity behind when she owed so much to her sister? She wasn't free to leave Santarém, whether she wanted to or not.

Nothing about this week had been rooted in reality, and they'd have to talk about it. Something that was made infinitely harder as Darius hauled her into his arms every time they were alone. Though they hadn't really spoken about any of this, neither of them wanting to disturb this fragile framework they had created, they had at least come to a silent understanding that they would keep their hands to themselves in front of Nina.

'Are you all packed up?' Celine asked her daughter.

They sat around the dining table, with Darius having surprised her once more by whipping up a lavish breakfast for them for their last morning in São Paulo. Their plane was leaving later in the afternoon to take them to Manaus, where they would catch the next flight back to Santarém.

Nina nodded as she bit into the churro on her plate, the dusting sugar clinging to her mouth. 'Do we have to leave so soon?' she asked, the sadness in her voice stabbing at Celine's chest.

'You know Mummy has to work, *filha*. But we will be back soon, and Pai can come visit us too.'

A chill pooled in her stomach at the thought of having to return home, of leaving this perfect week of affection and fun behind her to return to what her life had been like before Darius had come back—even though she *knew* that this was the only way.

Nothing had changed that would make her believe this time around would be different. They were still the same people, and attraction could not sustain their relationship for long. The trust was too far gone, the risk of hurting Nina in the process too great. The best thing to do was to move on from this week, treating it as the closure she had wanted for them both. They might still be sexually compatible, but their past failings clearly showed that they were not meant for each other—no matter how wrong that thought felt.

But her daughter's words reminded her of another conversation they needed to have. One Celine was actually looking forward to among all the complicated emotions they had woven around each other. She reached her hand out and laid it on Nina's arm.

'Isn't there something you wanted to ask before we leave?' she prompted her daughter, who looked at her with a puzzled expression. 'Remember what you asked me before bedtime?'

Her heart had melted when Nina had whispered the question into her ear, both excited and anxious to deepen the relationship she had with her father—something that didn't really help with Celine's own complex feelings, but she would never discourage her daughter because of her own struggles.

'Oh, right...' Nina looked up to Darius, who wore a curious look on his face. 'Can I call you Pai like Mummy does?'

'Can you...?' Darius's voice trailed off, shock rounding his eyes at the question, and Celine had to bite back a laugh.

When Nina had asked her that question she'd decided that they should all have a conversation about it. When she'd first introduced her husband to their daughter, she had decided not to force or even encourage Nina to call him Pai. That needed to be something that came from Nina herself whenever she felt ready to call him by that title.

What she hadn't expected was the confidence and nonchalance her daughter showed when she asked—free from the emotional weight that came with such a question. No, all of the emotions landed on Darius's shoulders when he hadn't expected it. The mist in his eyes as he processed her question was the sweetest heartbreak Celine had ever experienced, and she had to reel in her own reaction. This moment was between father and daughter.

'I… Yes, of course, *princesa*. I would love nothing more,' he finally said, his voice strained with the held-back emotions she sensed bubbling beneath the surface of his words.

'Okay! Now, Pai… Will you come to the dog show next weekend?' Nina asked, pulling Celine out of her thoughts.

But, before she could say anything, Darius asked, 'Dog show?'

'Tia Maria's charity has a dog show where the dogs of the village compete for prizes. We get to pet all the doggies.' Nina's eyes sparkled. Even though she was often surrounded by very exotic and sometimes rare animals, her daughter preferred dogs over anything else.

The annual dog show their charity organised was one of her favourite times. Celine also had flat-out forgotten about it, her mind too preoccupied with the sudden appearance of her estranged husband—and the resurgence of unwanted emotions that were doing their best to cloud her mind.

'It's quite the affair in Santarém,' Celine added when she saw his brow rise. She wasn't sure if she would have invited him—had she even remembered. But, knowing how much it meant to Nina, she couldn't not invite him. 'You should come if your schedule allows. I know it's far, but it's a bit of a family tradition that we are all there.'

Truth be told, though she wanted Nina to see Darius often, she had been hoping for a break to cool her nerves around him. They had yet to discuss what had transpired this week, neither of them seemingly daring to say anything that might break whatever spell they had woven together.

Say yes to me, to us.

The words echoed in her mind, the rawness in his voice, as if his life had depended on her saying yes, etched into her memory. But were they both aware of what they had agreed to? Celine wasn't sure at this point. There was no way he'd thought they would try again, was there?

'I'd love to come,' he said, his smile, though directed at their daughter, sending sparks raining down her spine.

Nina smiled from ear to ear, the excitement of having her father at the dog show clear to anyone who looked at her, and Celine's heart twisted inside her chest. She wouldn't ruin this for her daughter by getting involved with Darius. Whatever had happened here in São Paulo would have to stay here, the memories of his touch all she would take with her.

Celine hadn't been joking when she had said that the dog show in Santarém was quite the affair. Darius sat on a bench some distance away from all the action as the Dias family set up everything for the dog show, with villagers and their pooches ready to help.

He'd asked several times if he could be of assistance, but Celine and Maria had waved him off multiple times— and ended up banishing him to this bench so he was no longer in the way.

'Ah, I see you got exiled as well. Welcome to the club.' Darius twisted around to see a man approaching and sitting down next to him. His face was familiar. He'd been the one to pick up Bruna after he had sutured her wound.

'You're Maria's husband?' he asked, and the man laughed before stretching his hand out to him.

'I used to be Rafael Pedro but nowadays "Maria's husband" is more popular,' he said as they shook hands.

'Darius Delgado,' he replied, and Rafael nodded, clearly aware of who he was.

'My reputation precedes me?' he asked with a smirk, earning him another laugh from Rafael.

'Don't worry, it's probably not as bad as you think. Though the sisters are tight, Maria is the one who needs Celine to talk her through things—not so much the other way around.' He shot Darius a knowing look. 'Doesn't mean they don't talk.'

Darius sighed, a heaviness settling into his chest that had been haunting him for the last week. Communication with Celine had been sparse, most of their messages revolving around Nina and the logistics of his visit. He knew that before he left to go back to São Paulo tomorrow, they would need to sit down and talk about a schedule. They'd been lucky that for the last few weeks he'd been off work with the Brazilian football league on break, but that was changing now and he wouldn't have the freedom to stay for as long as he wanted.

Though, instead of talking about schedules and flights, what Darius really wanted to do was to ask her to move to São Paulo with him. Move in *with* him, resume the life they had been living last week. The time they had spent together had been a vision of the future—or rather the present if they had made different choices in the past.

'So, is this where they banish the useless husbands to?' he asked in a joking tone that matched the slight smile he saw on the other man's face.

'Pretty much. Though, like most of the charity work,

this is Maria's brainchild and poor Celine gets roped into helping her. It's a strange situation that both are in.'

Darius's ears sharpened at that. Rafael was striking a conversational tone, but his words were weighed down with a meaning that went beyond the surface level. This man was trying to tell him something.

'What situation is that?' he asked point-blank.

'The charity is Maria's passion—has been since the day she was old enough to help her parents at the rescue. But the same isn't true for Celine. She seems to be happy to let Maria make the decisions and be the face of the charity while pursuing her own work with the farmers,' he said, his eyes drifting towards the two women, who were setting up the table with the prizes—several bags of dog food and a mountain of different toys.

Darius only grunted at the information, comparing it to his own observations. Celine had told him that as well, and hearing this hadn't surprised him. Though they were always pretty tight, their passions differed, with Maria far more invested in the family's rescue operations.

'She didn't come here of her own choice but out of necessity,' Darius said, fighting to keep the growl from his tone. Dwelling on his mistakes in the past would not help him now as he was trying to figure out where they stood in their relationship.

She had said yes, had given him everything he'd been yearning for since he'd seen her again, and that week together had been nothing short of a fantasy come to life. Had she understood what he'd been trying to tell her? That he wanted them to try and save this marriage?

He shot Rafael a sideways glance. Was that what this man was trying to tell him?

Sensing his gaze, Rafael nodded. 'Yes…she needed help,

and back then her parents, her brother and Maria were ready to support her with whatever she needed. I think this has instilled a sense of obligation in her, a loyalty to her sister. Maria has been relying less and less on Celine to run her charity, but keeps pulling her in—because she, too, doesn't want to give the impression that she's pushing her sister out just because I'm here now.'

Rafael raised his hand towards the two women. Maria had moved on to the middle of the park and was trying to get Alexander, the family's Great Dane, to engage with the obstacle course they had created. Nina and her cousin Mirabel were at her heels, laughing and clapping as the dog climbed up one of the ramps. Celine, however, stood a few paces back with her arms crossed in front of her.

'She doesn't want to be involved, but she can't say no because she thinks she owes Maria.' The thought sank into his consciousness, dropping far below the surface and settling in an uncomfortable pinch in the pit of his stomach. What exactly did that mean for them? Would she consider leaving?

Rafael nodded and said, 'Maria, on the other hand, feels obliged to involve her because it's the family legacy. For the longest time it's just been the two of them, raising their kids on their own.'

Darius turned his head, looking into the other man's hazel eyes. 'What's your point, Pedro?'

The man frowned, his eyes drifting back towards where both of their wives stood. 'My point is they are so stuck in this routine, and in assuming that what they are doing is what the other sister wants, that they cannot see a way out. Not without someone presenting a new…option.'

Darius followed his gaze, his eyes locking into Celine's at a distance. Her expression remained veiled for a few heartbeats, then she smiled at him with a small wave of her hand.

An option? Like coming back to São Paulo with him?

'I don't know if the option that I have is what she wants,' Darius said, his heart twisting at the mere thought of rejection.

But hadn't she said yes last week? He'd asked her to choose them, and every night she had ended up in his room, his bed, his arms.

Next to him, Rafael shrugged. 'I have my suspicions around that, but Celine is the only one who can tell you. She can't pick an option that she doesn't know about.'

Darius's eyes rounded, his head snapping back to Rafael as the words sank in. An option she didn't know about? He looked back towards Celine, then at Nina, who was holding Alexander's lead and encouraging him to jump through a hoop. Laughter echoed across the park when the Great Dane lay down instead, placing his large head on top of his paws with a yawn.

That was what he needed to talk about with Celine— he had to tell her how he felt, how his affection and love for her had never stopped but only slept, waiting for the right moment to reawaken.

The choice was hers—but he had to make sure she knew that he *was* a choice.

The turnout for the dog show this year was a lot higher than any of the other events Celine remembered—and she believed a large part of that had to do with the social media following their charity had attracted after a video of Rafael rescuing a mother cat and her kittens went viral.

Celine was glad of it as more people meant more donations, but she wasn't one to enjoy the spotlight. So, instead of being in there with Maria and the villagers, Celine chose to hover on the sidelines of the spectacle, observing instead of getting involved. Something she had done more and more with the arrival of Rafael and his taking up a larger role in the rescue.

The highlight of her day so far had turned out to be Darius and seeing him interact with Nina. Once the dog show had begun, Nina had taken her father by the hand and walked him through the family history of every single dog that was on the roster. And Darius had listened to her patiently, asked questions to keep her talking and interacted with the dogs she pointed out as if they were part of the audience rather than the show.

Not that the show was particularly strict. They called it a dog show, but it was really more an opportunity for the community to get together and shore up some donations for the charity.

She cast her eyes around. Darius caught her attention, standing some paces away with Nina on his shoulders, and the sight brought forward a deep yearning unlike anything she had ever felt. The desire for her own family stirred in her chest. An idea that could become a reality if she dared.

But, after a week apart, their week together seemed more like a dream than reality. Was it even possible to have what they'd had last week on a long-term basis, when their lives were so far apart from each other? Celine doubted it, not when her place was here, next to her sister, who still relied on her to help with the charity.

Could she trust Darius to treat her heart with more care this time around? Doubt remained embedded in her chest as she cast her eyes inward, believing this to be her answer. With a lump growing in her throat, she walked towards Darius. They needed to talk.

The smile he gave her as she came to a stop next to him threatened to break her resolve.

'You two having fun?' she asked, and smiled when Nina answered her question with a vigorous nod.

'Freya is still so agile,' Nina said, pointing at the dog now climbing a ramp.

'Anabel keeps her well exercised.' Freya's owner, Anabel, was walking alongside her dog, giving her directions through the obstacle course.

They watched the show in silence, Celine drifting closer to Darius. Even through the crowds comprised of both humans and animals she was still able to pick up his scent—the smell of spice so delicious she wasn't sure she would be able to give it up.

'Will you be there for dinner? I think we should talk,' she asked Darius, earning herself a sideways glance.

'I was about to say the same thing,' he replied, his expression not letting her see what thoughts lay beneath the surface.

'What do you—'

The screeching of tyres ripped through the air, all heads turning as a car lost control on the road running parallel to the little park. It spun around, smoke rising from where the tyres tried to grip the road, and then the side of the car crashed into the iron gate that marked the entrance to the park. Shouts of fright mingled with the barking of several dogs, everyone frozen into place as they watched the accident happen—everyone except Darius.

His hands closed around Nina's waist and he pulled her off his shoulders, setting her down on the grass. 'I have to go help them,' he said.

'I'll go with you, maybe you'll need some help,' Celine said.

He nodded, then pointed at the judges' table. 'Nina, go stand with your aunt and uncle. You'll be safe there, okay?'

Nina nodded, eyes wide in shock, then she ran over to where Maria was half standing from her chair, ready to intervene as well. Celine waved her sister off, then turned and followed Darius as he walked towards the car.

The driver's side had hit the iron gate, the car bending inwards where it had suffered the impact, and through the windscreen she could see two unconscious figures in the front seats.

'I'll have to check both of them through the passenger side since we can't move them safely.' Darius circled around to the other side of the car and pulled the handle. The door did not budge. He whispered a curse under his breath, his eyes casting about. 'Do we have any tools around to help us open the door? If we wait for them to wake up it might already be too late.'

'Oh, I have something,' she mumbled, to herself as much as to Darius, and pulled her key chain from the small bag hanging from her shoulder, unclipping one of the tools hanging from it and giving it to him.

The tool was made out of purple plastic, one side sloping down and the other side capped off with a black stopper. He took it in his hand, turning it around once. A line appeared between his brows, and he looked at her in a silent question. Celine took the tool back, uncapping it, and held it against the back window. Then she pushed a button on the side of the tool, releasing a metal pin.

Spider cracks appeared around the tool, webbing throughout the window. She looked back at Darius as she said, 'This is a tool to cut belts and break car windows in case I ever get stuck in a car.'

'I'll have to ask you about why you carry this around with you later on,' he said, then watched as she pushed against the window with some force, the glass giving in under her hand and spilling onto the back seat.

Celine reached through the window to the front of the passenger side, pulling at the pin to unlock the door. She breathed out a sigh of relief when Darius pulled the door open, kneeling in front of the still unconscious passenger. He held his ear close to her face, then pulled back.

'She's still breathing but not conscious,' he said, then stepped back to look at the driver, whose head was moving from one side to the other, seemingly conscious but not reacting to what was happening. 'We can't pull them out until the emergency services arrive to secure their necks and spines in case of any injuries.'

Celine nodded, then dialled the emergency number, the call going though almost immediately. She described the scene in front of her, approximating the age of the patients, then turned to Darius, who had just re-emerged from the vehicle, to ask if he had any more details to add.

'Both patients are breathing, one of them conscious and complaining of chest pain,' he said as she held the phone to his ear, then he nodded as the call disconnected. 'An ambulance is too far out so they are bringing in a helicopter.'

A low moan brought their attention back to the car. The patient on the passenger side had opened her eyes, staring dead ahead as she muttered something that neither of them could understand.

A pin on the passenger's sweater caught her attention. It was an enamel pin with three black dots on a yellow background. 'She's blind,' Celine said to Darius, who followed her gaze to the pin.

He went on his knees, leaning forward to place his ear right in front of her mouth. Then he looked at Celine over his shoulder, wearing a confused expression. 'She says Bella was with her.'

'Bella?' They both looked at the driver, who held his hand to his chest, a dangerous-sounding cough shaking his body.

Darius let out a low curse before leaning back into the vehicle. '*Senhor*, try to take deep, calm breaths. I suspect one of your lungs has collapsed, making it hard to breathe. The medevac is en route.'

As if to underline his words, the faint sounds of a faraway helicopter echoed over the constant mutter of the crowd that was standing several paces away, thankfully letting Darius do his work.

'Bella is…' the man tried to press out, then another coughing fit interrupted him.

Celine gasped when the pieces clicked into place. 'Bella is her service dog!'

And she had broken the window inward, right on top of where Bella had probably been on the floor.

She rushed to the rear door, pulling at the mechanical lock then yanking the door open. A quiet whine crept into her ears, too high to hear over the commotion. On the floor lay a Golden Retriever, Bella, with her ears close to her skull and her tongue flicking over her mouth nervously. The hi-vis vest was still attached to her body, her harness thrust to the other side of the car.

'Hey gorgeous,' Celine said in a low voice, the high-pitched whine coming from the dog a clear sign of distress. 'Let me check if you're hurt.'

back she saw it descending from the sky and landing on a free patch of grass a few metres away from them.

Rafael appeared behind her, crouching down next to her. 'This dog needs help?' he asked, immediately understanding the situation.

Celine nodded, thankful to have her brother-in-law nearby. 'I can treat her, but I can't carry her all the way back.'

Rafael pushed both of his arms under the dog, lifting her off the ground, and nodded towards the exit. Their clinic was luckily only a short walk away. Celine hesitated, looking at Darius, who got to his feet as two people hopped out of the helicopter.

'Are you okay here?' she asked, a strange part of her unwilling to leave him alone, even though she knew her help was needed elsewhere.

'I'll find out what hospital they'll go to so we can drive the dog once she is fit to go,' he replied, and that little word *we* made her heart skip a beat.

'I can stay if you need me. Rafael will be okay.' She didn't know why she had offered that, some impulse inside of her not wanting to be away from Darius.

He, too, seemed to have picked up on the subtext in her words, for he put his hand on her cheek and brushed a light kiss onto her lips, his eyes filled with affection. Her stomach twisted at the sight, her heart beating faster. He should not be looking at her like that—like they had a future.

'Go take care of Bella. I will be there as soon as I've seen the paramedics off.'

He dropped his hand to his side, then strode towards the two figures scurrying over from the medevac.

CHAPTER TEN

TEN MINUTES AFTER its arrival the helicopter had been airborne again, taking the two car crash victims to a nearby city. Darius had noted the name of the hospital and looked up the distance—a two-hour drive. Something to worry about once Celine had assessed the dog and how soon it would be able to travel.

After the helicopter lifted off a murmur had rippled through the crowd, who had all turned to look, some even holding their phones in front of them as if they were filming. Thankfully, Maria had shooed the crowd away after a few minutes, handing his daughter back to him and sending him to the house while she dealt with the unsettled villagers. A task he'd been all too happy to leave to her.

Hours had passed since then, enough time that Darius had made the decision to have dinner with Nina before putting her to bed.

Now he stood at the window, looking out at the clinic, where one lonely light was on. He'd seen Rafael leave almost two hours ago, making him think Celine had decided to treat the dog herself.

Darius's nerves were stretched thin, his heart beating inside his throat as he went over the words he wanted to tell her today. The ones he had said so many years ago, had repeated many times over before they'd got married.

A kernel of fear had nestled itself inside his heart this morning, growing larger with each passing minute that he waited for her. She had asked to speak to him tonight, though nothing in her expression had told him if it was the same thing he wanted to talk about.

They still hadn't agreed on how often he would come to visit, or if Nina would be permitted to visit him in São Paulo without her mother. Those were important things they needed to agree on.

But, equally, they hadn't spoken about what had happened between them in São Paulo—how they had slept with each other every single night. Celine had spoken of closure, of getting over what they had lost and moving on with their lives. He'd asked her to choose him, choose them, and he'd meant it. These had not been cheap words he'd spoken to get her into bed.

Darius was still in love with his wife, and tonight he would tell her.

He straightened his back when the light turned off, holding his breath as he saw a figure emerging from the building several minutes later, walking towards the house. A moment later, the door handle twisted and Celine stepped inside, looking as tired as he felt.

She looked at him, eyes wide in surprise. 'You waited for me?'

Darius furrowed his brow at her astonishment. 'I didn't think I should let Nina sleep here on her own.'

Celine's eyes darted around, scanning the kitchen and then the living room, stopping to inspect every trace he'd left in her house. 'You were alone with her?'

The sharp edge in her voice drove straight through his chest and into his heart, spearing physical pain through his body. After the last few weeks together, after what had happened between them in São Paulo, she *still* didn't trust him?

` 'Of course I was alone with her. She is my child, Celine.' The hurt her question had caused him wove itself through his tone, the words coming out in a low growl.

Celine clenched her jaw, a deep line appearing between her brows as she levelled a stare at him. 'I left her with Maria for a reason.'

'Your sister was too busy handling the fallout at the dog show, so she handed me *my* daughter to take her home.' Darius couldn't believe what he was hearing from Celine. What more would he have to do to show her he was serious about being a part of his child's life—that he would never let anything happen to her?

'I told you I'm not comfortable with you being alone with her at the moment. Why would you disrespect this one request?' She let out a bitter laugh, the sound so twisted that he could hardly recognise her. 'Oh, right, you don't take promises very seriously. That's on me for forgetting that.'

His stomach twisted, the pain lancing through him intensifying as her words sank in. Her barb struck true, hitting him in the one place she knew would hurt him beyond anything else. The need to turn around and leave bubbled up in him, turn his back before he could say anything unkind in return. He closed his eyes, taking a few deep breaths before facing her again.

He was no longer the man who would run from his wife, no matter what she had to say to him. Though the hope that had grown bigger and bigger each time she had returned to his room last week wilted at her harsh words—at the hurt that lay beneath them.

'Celine…this was an emergency. You, of all people,

should know that. I didn't take her because I wanted to go against your wishes. I took her because there was chaos at the park, and *I am her father.*' His last words came out thick with the hurt her words had caused him.

But from the way Celine crossed her arms in front of her, she wasn't seeing it his way. How was he supposed to have the conversation he'd been planning in his head? The fear clawing at him exploded through his chest, almost robbing him of breath.

If she didn't trust him alone with their daughter, what were the chances that she would invite him back to be her husband? Darius knew he had to say it, even though he saw his plans for their future together crumbling before him. He would regret it if he didn't. He took two steps forward, closing the space between them.

'The moment you told me about Nina my life changed for ever. A place inside my heart unlocked, flooding with joy and fear alike as I became a father in that moment— knowing I'm now responsible for her life, her wellbeing and her happiness.' His hand went up to his chest, clutching his heart. 'Even six years late, there isn't a greater gift you could have given me, Cee.'

Celine's lips parted to say something, a protest, going by the gleam in her eyes, but he continued. 'I know I hurt you, and I can't change that. But I showed you at every turn in the last few weeks that I *am* a changed man. I learned from my mistakes, and I'm not letting them get in my way any more.'

He heaved in a deep breath, steeling himself for the one thing he had to say to lay it all out—and then the ball would be in her court.

'Celine…' His voice was thick with the joy and pain that combined themselves into a deadly cocktail inside his heart. 'I love you. What else do I have to do to show you I've changed—that I'm worthy of your trust?'

Celine's eyes rounded, his words driving the air out of her lungs. The words she had been dreading to hear—*longing* to hear in the safety of her dreams—crossed his lips and were now floating in the space between them. Along with the question Celine had been too afraid to address.

A part of her knew that her reaction to him being alone with Nina was unnecessary, caused by the fierce protectiveness she felt towards her daughter. She did what she had to do to protect Nina, to make sure Darius coming back into her life was not something that she would come to regret—that would cause her any heartache. If that meant Celine was the one who had to bear the heartache then this was a price she was willing to pay.

'I can't trust you, Darius. I can't *love* you, not after everything that happened,' she said, her voice shaking with the pain her own words were inflicting on her.

'Why not?'

The defeat in his face almost undid her, tears she quickly blinked away threatening to fall.

'Because you left when I needed you the most. That your reasons were noble doesn't help with the scars that your actions left on me.' Her lower lip trembled as she struggled to keep her voice steady. 'Coming back and proving your trustworthiness when things are easy is not enough to show me you've changed.'

The words tasted bitter in her mouth as she questioned the truth of her own argument. She meant what she said, but the origin of her words was a place of fear and hurt—a place she shouldn't be making permanent decisions from.

Yet that was all that was in her right now, raging like an inferno as his declaration of love rippled through her.

'In order to prove to you I have changed I need to find you when you're down?' he asked, incredulity lacing his words.

She swallowed the lump in her throat as she forced the next words out of her mouth. 'There is nothing you can do to change my mind.'

Silence stretched between them, and a part of Celine prayed he would leave—the way he had left six years ago. She wanted to curl up into a ball and let the agony of this moment settle in her.

I love you. The words echoed through her, finding purchase in her own heart, where the words were reflected back at him. But she couldn't say it, wouldn't risk it. Not when Nina had finally got the chance to have her father in her life.

Celine's feelings would always come second.

Darius's face showed the pain her words caused in him, and she had to clench her teeth to stop herself from reaching out to wrap him in her arms. He swallowed, then he said, 'Then why did you say yes?'

Her breath stuttered in her chest, the moment when she had given in to him appearing in her mind's eye—a memory that hurt as much as it soothed her. Because for those seven days their lives had been perfect, their minds and bodies and hearts in sync, and, for a brief moment, Celine had believed that she could do this. Could have her husband back.

But that had been nothing more than an idle fantasy.

'I didn't think you meant it when you asked me to say yes to us. We were both caught up in the moment. After what happened between us at Juliana's farm, I thought we both just needed to…get things out of our system.' The truth was blurred though, her words only partly ringing true in her ears. She had wanted to believe that he'd meant what he said, but that also struck so much fear in her heart that she'd immediately retreated—treating their week together as just sex.

'I meant it…' he whispered, his words trailing off and stretching into silence between them. 'I meant all of it. Every kiss, every touch. Everything I did was to show you I'm here for good.'

She took another trembling breath, shaking her head. 'I think it's best that we focus on our relationship as co-parents.'

Darius's eyes shuttered at her words, the pain she'd seen but a second ago gone, replaced with a stony expression that wouldn't let her see what lay behind. He silently stalked past her, stepping into the kitchen and grabbing the stack of papers she had shoved between the fridge and the microwave, intending to deal with them later.

He dropped the stack onto the kitchen table, and her heart sank when she realised they were their divorce papers. Then he grabbed the pen that hung from a magnet on the fridge door. The rustling of paper filled the silence between them, the only interruption the scratching of a pen on paper. After what felt an eternity, Darius stood up straight again, putting the pen back onto the fridge.

Celine took a step back when he grabbed the papers and pushed them into her hands.

'There you go, Celine. You are officially done with me,' he said, some of the pain slipping through his icy exterior. 'I'll be in touch about Nina.'

And then he walked through the door and out of her life again, the gap he was leaving yawning open within her.

CHAPTER ELEVEN

DARIUS'S HEART TWISTED inside his chest as he pressed the call button, knowing that in a few seconds he would see—

Celine's face appeared on his phone, a searing pain stabbing through him at the sight of his lost love. Her mouth twitched when she saw him, as if she was fighting down a smile.

He'd returned to São Paulo to lick his wounds and patch himself back up—a task that took a lot more effort than he had energy for. His only relief from it was his daily phone calls with his daughter. Though they came with the drawback of having to see Celine first, constantly re-opening the wound.

'Hey, Darius,' she said, the tone of her voice unusually lacklustre.

He opened his mouth to say something, to ask her how she was or what she had been up to, *anything* to bring some kind of normality back into their relationship as parents. But, before he could find the right words, Celine's phone twisted and Nina popped up on his screen, a small smile on her face.

'Hola, mi princesa hermosa,' he said, her face easing the dark clouds gathering in his head.

'Hi, Dad! I'm at my *tia*'s house.' She grabbed the phone from where Celine had put it, panning the camera around to show him the interior of Maria's house—including Rafael, who lay on the couch with his baby sleeping on his chest.

Darius glanced at the clock on his phone, then he asked, 'Are you over there for dinner?'

'I'm having a sleepover with Mirabel because Mummy is working...' His ears sharpened as her words trailed off, his daughter's voice gaining a strange quality.

'What's wrong, princess? You usually like sleepovers with your cousin.'

'Mummy has been working a lot lately, and I miss having her home.' She paused, her big brown eyes almost round as she stared down at the phone screen. 'I miss you here too.'

Tears suddenly spilled over her cheeks, and Darius's heart shattered again into the thousand pieces it had been in when he had left Santarém to come back to São Paulo. Helplessness flooded him as his daughter sobbed, her words no longer intelligible.

'*Bebê*, don't cry. I'm going to come and visit you in two weeks and we'll have lots of fun together, I promise.' Nina's tears continued and, a moment later, Maria popped into the frame, scooping Nina into her arms.

'Hang on a second, Darius,' she said, and he watched helplessly as she cut the time with his daughter short.

The angle of the camera changed, giving him a view of the ceiling. Then a familiar face appeared on the screen. Rafael smiled at him, a sympathetic look on his face.

'*Oi, cunhado,*' he said, then adjusted the phone so Darius could see the baby lying on his chest.

His choice of word sent a stab through him. 'Brother-in-law no more, Pedro. I signed the divorce papers before I left.'

Rafael chuckled as if he had just made a funny joke, and Darius's temper flared. Wasn't it enough that his daughter was crying for him without him being able to do something about it? Now this man was laughing at what was the most miserable time in his life?

'Sure, if you want to reduce it to a piece of paper, I guess we can agree,' he said, and Darius thought he saw a flash of regret in Rafael's eyes.

'Listen… I don't know what Celine told you two about what happened, but I honestly don't want to get into any of that. All I want is to talk to Nina,' he gritted out through his teeth, reminding himself to stay calm. Maria and Rafael had nothing to do with his foul mood, so he shouldn't let it show so much.

'She'd rather stay with you than here with us. It seems she got used to having you around.' The baby—Sam, if he remembered the name right—coughed, her eyes opening for a fraction of a second before fluttering shut again. Rafael's hand came down on her back, rubbing up and down.

Envy came out of nowhere, spearing through him with a flashing heat that left him without words. Before he'd gone to Santarém to talk to Celine—to ask her not to divorce him just yet—he hadn't known what was missing in his life, but now that he knew what having his wife and daughter felt like it was as if he was walking through a world of muted colour. *He* wanted to be the man to lie on the couch with his sleeping baby on his chest, and it didn't make sense to him that he wasn't. Not when he had done everything he could.

Rafael seemed to read his thoughts from the expressions flitting over his face, for he gave him a crooked smile. 'Here's the thing, Delgado. I was in a similar position a year ago, running away from the woman I loved because I convinced myself that she would be better off without me.'

Darius straightened at that, his brow furrowing. He'd never heard that part of their story before. Whenever Celine had spoken about them, it sounded like love at first sight, with both being exactly what the other one needed—the way it had been with them when they'd first met.

Except Darius wasn't running away. Sure, he'd left, but not without asking her to reconsider. Not without telling her how he felt.

'I didn't run,' he said, reinforcing that thought, but Rafael only chuckled at that.

'Then why aren't you here fighting for her?'

His eyes widened at that question as he struggled to come up with an answer. Fight for her? But she...

'She asked me to leave. What else was I supposed to do?'

'Did you give her the choice to come with you?'

'I...' Darius's voice trailed off as he cast his thoughts inward, remembering that fateful night that now lay a few weeks back. He'd been so sure of his feelings back then, convinced that she felt the same. Had been devastated to find out she didn't. A lot of things had been said that night, most of them hurtful, but...

'No, I didn't. She came back after treating the dog and when she realised I had been alone with Nina she accused me of disrespecting her request. Things escalated from there, and then I...told her I loved her.' Hadn't that been clear enough in his intentions?

Rafael nodded, the smile gone and replaced with an expression of deep sympathy. Whatever had gone on between him and Maria had been bad enough for him to understand his pain. Though even then they had got to the other side, were living a life he *dreamed* of living.

'How?' he asked, completely out of context, yet his brother-in-law somehow knew what he meant.

'I fought for her. Our lovely Dias sisters have been through a lot, Delgado. First Celine was forced to come back to Santarém so your daughter would have a family, then their brother almost doomed the charity to financial ruin with his decision, abandoning his daughter to their care.' He paused when his baby hiccupped, gently patting her back. 'All of their experiences makes them fiercely protective, and they will...test you. Unknowingly, but they do.'

Darius stayed quiet, staring at the man on his screen as he considered his words, when Rafael added, 'Give her the choice to come with you. She loves you too. Anyone with eyes knows that. But she's not someone to walk towards the unknown. Celine likes to have a plan.'

Darius laughed at that—at the truth that smacked him in the face. Celine had *always* been a planner. He'd seen it first-hand so many times during their university days. Though he had told her he loved her, he had not given her a choice like Rafael had suggested.

'Let me ask you the same question that a friend of mine asked me a year ago when I was on the brink of giving up on Maria. What would happen if you showed up now and painted a picture of your life together? How would it be?'

There was a lot of history in Rafael's love story he didn't know, and a part of him wanted to dig deeper into that, but now was not the time. His gaze drifted around the room, imagining what his apartment would look like if they were here with him.

His spare room would become Nina's room, while Ce-

She leaned in and palpated the dog's legs, stomach and back as well as she could from her position. 'I don't feel any bumps or abnormalities. Let's see if you can walk.' Celine grabbed the dog by her vest and pulled, hoping that the strict training of a service dog would kick in and she would move despite her fear.

Bella did so, and when she stepped onto the floor she immediately raised her left hind leg, keeping her weight off it as she stepped forward. Celine went back onto her knees, casting her eyes skyward. The sound of helicopter blades filled the air now, its arrival imminent. She wrapped her arms around Bella, lifting the dog with a grunt, putting her down in front of the passenger side door.

She looked over her shoulder, searching the crowd, and lifted her hand when she locked eyes with Rafael, waving him towards her.

'Can she understand me?' she asked Darius as she looked at the woman, who was still staring ahead without any further reaction.

He nodded, so Celine said, 'I freed Bella from the car. She has an injury on her leg, but she seems otherwise well. I'm a vet, so I will take her to my clinic to get treatment. Once that's done, I'll drive her to the hospital.'

The woman's eyes rounded and, sensing her owner's distress, Bella limped forward and wedged her head in her hands. 'I can't be without her,' the woman said, voice hoarse.

'They can't treat her leg at the hospital, *senhora*. Please trust me with her, and I will return her to you as soon as she is patched up. She's limping and in pain, let me help her.' The sounds of the helicopter had swelled to a loud roar that swept over the village, and when Celine looked line would sleep in his bed every night—wake up next to him every day. There would be a space for Alexander in the corner of the living room, where the sun glowed in the morning to warm the old Great Dane. He'd be off to work at the stadium, and Celine... She could have the freedom to pursue the veterinary work she was passionate about without having to worry about her sister needing her.

Didn't she want to break free of that, anyway? Every time they had spoken about it, she had said as much.

'I have to go,' Darius mumbled as the pieces clicked into place.

She had said no because she didn't have all the information—didn't know what she could choose. Celine would never choose the unknown when she believed her responsibilities would tie her to Santarém. But that was because both sisters were so used to relying on each other, they couldn't imagine either of them not *wanting* that.

Rafael shot him a big grin. 'Ah, I know that expression all too well. See you in a bit, Delgado.' He raised his hand in a short wave, then the call disconnected.

Darius jumped to his feet, his eyes drifting to the overnight bag that he had never unpacked after getting back to São Paulo—as if he'd known he'd be needing it soon.

The sun had just crept over the horizon when Celine arrived at Maria's house. A peek through the window showed no sign of the family being up, so she let herself in with the copy of their key. Toeing off her shoes, she walked down the corridor and into the open-plan kitchen, finding the space devoid of anyone—which was just as well.

Ever since Darius had left after their argument, Celine had immersed herself in her work to keep her mind from spinning out of control. The more time she spent moving, the less space to think about what he had said—what *she* had said to him. The look of hurt in his eyes was one she wouldn't forget.

Things were difficult with Nina now too. Though Darius had only been a part of her life for two months now, her daughter had got so used to having her father around that his prolonged absence was causing her to act out. With half the country between them, he could only visit every other weekend and during school breaks. With his career being the reason he had returned to Brazil in the first place, she didn't think he would give it up to come and live in the countryside—where jobs for physicians specialising in athletes were arguably obsolete.

And Celine couldn't leave either. Though the family charity was not a cause that was close to her heart, she had seen how much Maria had put into this place, had put into helping her with Nina as well when she had been a baby. There was no way she could leave her sister now, when Maria had done so much for her.

Celine shook her head, trying her best to shoo these thoughts away. She turned towards the kitchen counter, grabbing some coffee and a mug from the cupboard, and made to set the machine up. She needed to wait until the children woke up.

'Would you mind making one for me as well?'

Celine almost dropped the mug she was holding when her sister's voice filtered through the air out of nowhere.

She whirled around, scanning her surroundings, when she saw her sister's hand appear over the back of the couch. Breathing out a laugh, Celine stepped closer to the couch. Maria lay on it with her baby on her chest. Sam had her big eyes wide open, her tiny fist resting against her lips, while her sister had her hands resting on the baby's back. Dark brown circles spread under Maria's eyes as she slowly blinked the weariness away.

'Rough night?' Celine asked, circling around the couch to sit down on the other end.

'Samara is teething, which means she likes to sleep in thirty-minute increments.' Maria sighed, looking down at her baby.

Celine blew out a breath, nodding. 'Teething is not fun. Frozen chewing toys helped a lot with Nina. It supposedly feels nice on the gums.'

'How was work?' Her sister's eyes drifted closed but, from her breathing, she could tell she was still listening.

'Good. I'm making the rounds to vaccinate all the livestock that was recently born as well as some minor surgeries that I've been putting off for a while. One of Juliana's horses keeps developing an abscess in its hoof and I can't quite figure out why.' Work had been a godsend in the last weeks, keeping her out of the house and out of her head.

She'd taken on a lot more than she usually would, her need to escape her own thoughts driving her to spend long hours on the road for consultations and checkups across several farms.

Her absence seemed to have been noted by Maria, for she said, 'I haven't seen you around in the clinic for a while.'

Guilt stabbed through Celine. She'd hoped that her busyness wouldn't be noticed, as it would lead to a lot of questions she didn't really want to answer. Though she feared if she owed anyone some answers, it was Maria. She'd been the one taking care of Nina whenever she needed to work late at night.

'I'm sorry. I'll try to be around more. I know I've been

taking advantage of your kindness by leaving Nina with you while I…' Her words drifted off into nothingness, and Maria opened her eyes.

'It's not necessary, Raf and I get it,' she said, and though warmth radiated from her eyes, the words landed in her stomach like lead. 'You helped me out a lot these last few years to keep our…no, *my* dream alive. But now that you're using it as an excuse, I feel it's my duty as your sister to let you go.'

'Let me go?' The lump appearing in her throat turned her voice hoarse. The exhaustion from working all night crept into her bones, settling with a heaviness that she struggled to shake. Was this the right moment to have such a conversation?

Maria seemed to think so, for she went on. 'I know you feel you owe me a debt of gratitude and that you have an obligation to this family—to what our parents built. But…you've given enough. You don't need to let him go.'

Her weariness turned to ice as her sister said those words. 'This is about Darius? I don't want to talk about him.'

Their argument was the reason she was feeling so hollow—why she had to bury herself in work. Anything to gain a reprieve from the thought of him, of what she had walked away from.

'You chose to involve me in this by using me as an excuse. Nina cried again during her call with Darius. And don't pretend like you haven't been crying either. Why are you so set on making your lives miserable? Because he made a mistake six years ago?'

Celine leaned back as her sister rounded on her. The ferocity in her words was unexpected, so was the sting they brought to her chest. Despite her young age, Nina could sense something at odds between her parents, and she knew from her sister that she often cried because she missed him. But that wouldn't be different if she had said the words back.

'This isn't just one mistake, Maria. How would you feel if Rafael had run away after marrying you?' she asked, then cursed under her breath when a grin spread over her sister's face.

'Ah, so you remember Rafael running away after I told him I loved him. Do you also remember all the speeches you gave me about the true nature of my feelings for him?'

Celine did remember that. When Maria and Rafael had gone through their time of crisis, it had been Celine who'd pushed her sister towards the man, believing in the love story she'd seen unravel in front of her eyes. Maria had never been happier than the moments she had spent with Rafael.

But Darius wasn't coming back.

'He signed the divorce papers.'

'But you didn't send them to the lawyer.'

Another truth that sank to the bottom of her stomach, bubbling there with the rest of them and painting a picture that Celine didn't want to be confronted with—couldn't look at, for it revealed the mistake she had made that evening when Darius had told her he loved her.

She should have said that she loved him too. Her heart, her soul, every hair on her body belonged to him—had belonged to him since they'd first got together.

'I can't ask him back. How would that even work, with him living so far away? He won't want to give up his work, and I...' Her eyes widened in surprise as she realised what Maria had said, why she had told her she was no longer needed at the clinic.

Her sister swallowed, the first sign of nerves she'd seen in her since the conversation had started. 'Go home and sleep on it, Cee. I'll keep Nina here for the day. Figure out what you want—and then go get him back.'

It was a possibility she had never taken into consideration—or, rather, she had never *let* herself consider it. Because if she thought about leaving Santarém behind Darius would have had a clear shot at her heart. But fear and past rejection had clouded her mind, rendered her immobile and unable to accept that he *had* changed—and that she needed to be brave enough to trust him again.

Celine loosened a deep breath, then got to her feet. Her thoughts were still jumbled, but a plan had formed. Maria was right. She and Rafael had gone through a crisis, and it had only made their relationship stronger. She could have that too. Celine only needed to be brave.

By the time Celine pulled her car over on the street in front of her house, she was ready to book a flight to São Paulo to talk to Darius. The week they had spent together there kept replaying inside her head, the memories some of the happiest she had. What if it was time to leave, and the pain that thought caused had been one of the factors to push him away?

What if he *was* her missing piece, the person to complete her? Not the Darius she had married, but this version—the one who had to struggle before finding his way back to her? What if their timing had just been wrong?

She jumped out of her car, her strides widening as urgency bubbled up in her, when an unfamiliar car caught her attention. A man stood next to it, his face shadowed by the half-light of dawn. Celine froze, then turned to look at him with wide eyes. She didn't know if it was instinct or fate that told her who stood there, but when she realised it was Darius she broke into a run.

Her husband caught her as she threw herself at him, pressing his face into the side of her neck and whispering her name against her skin. Her hands roamed up his back, clinging to him.

'Cee—' he began, but Celine interrupted him as she slid her lips over his, swallowing the rest of his words with a kiss that shook her knees.

'Forgive me,' she huffed when their mouths parted, her eyes still wide with astonishment. 'I got scared, and I lashed out.'

'Celine…' The gentleness in his voice, along with the warmth radiating from his gaze, tore a sob from her throat when she saw nothing but forgiveness coming from him.

'I understand,' he whispered against her cheek, his lips brushing over her skin and causing a shiver to claw through her. 'I got upset, and I ran away again. *I* need to be the one to ask for forgiveness.'

Celine immediately shook her head and wrapped her arms around his torso to pull him closer. 'The week in São Paulo with you was the happiest I've ever been, but I was too scared to accept that, too tied up with everything here to see clearly.'

'But now you do?' he asked and when she nodded into his chest he pushed her away.

His hands came up to her face, cupping it from each side, his thumbs brushing over her cheeks. 'Then say yes—to *everything* this time. Say yes to us, our marriage, our family…our life together in São Paulo.'

His voice was deep and warm, her eyes fluttering

closed as she imagined what their life would be like if she said yes. There he was, her missing piece, and she would never let go of him ever again.

'Yes.'

EPILOGUE

CELINE BREATHED IN the humidity surrounding her. The scent of the Amazon River mingling with the rainforest crept up her nose and gave her a strange longing. It had been a year since she'd left Santarém behind. She hadn't missed it, yet being back gave her a sense of nostalgia that pulled at her heart.

In the last year her life had developed in ways she couldn't have imagined. If anyone had told her that she would reconcile with her estranged husband after finally sending him divorce papers, she would have laughed in their face. But there he was, standing right next to her with his arm wrapped around her waist.

'Mirabel!' Nina shouted when she spotted her cousin. She glanced upwards, looking at her father, who nodded, and off she went to greet Mirabel.

Behind her they spotted Rafael, who waved at them as they picked their way through the gathering crowd. 'The dog show is becoming larger every year,' Celine said when they got close enough to hear each other, then she hugged her brother-in-law.

'I know. Maria says she's excited, but the amount of stress happening at home paints a different picture,' Rafael replied with a twinkle in his eyes, then he looked her up and down. 'You look well, Cee.'

Celine smiled, the genuine concern in her brother-in-law's expression warming her heart. 'So do you. I missed your face.'

'We miss you around here. Let me get Maria. She'll want to say hi before the show starts.' Rafael nodded towards Darius, then made his way to the judges' table, where Maria was setting up the scorecards.

Celine shivered when her husband's breath grazed over her cheek as he leaned into her. 'He has no idea, does he?' he asked, to which she huffed a laugh.

'Nope. But Maria will see it the second she spots me.' Nervous energy bubbled up within her.

After leaving to be with Darius in São Paulo, Celine had spent the first few weeks at home, getting herself and Nina settled into their new life. After reaching out to her old friends at the veterinary institute in Manaus, recruiters had started calling her, offering her partnerships at different practices or staff to start her own business. None of them had seemed right, until the offer she'd ended up accepting had landed in her inbox. Someone at the veterinary university in São Paulo had heard she'd moved there and offered her a teaching position. With Darius still working full-time as the head physician of Atlético Morumbi, the flexibility teaching at the university promised had been too good to pass up.

Plus, Professor Dr Dias-Delgado had a nice ring to it—though outside of Darius no one took the trouble to say her full title.

Since then they had another big change in their lives, one neither of them had expected.

'Oh, my God!' Maria knocked the wind out of her lungs when she threw herself at her sister in a tight hug. Next to her Celine heard Darius chuckle as he let go of her hand to give the sisters some space for their hug.

Maria planted both of her hands on her shoulders and pushed her away, looking her up and down. Then she turned her head and looked at Rafael with narrowed eyes. 'Why didn't you tell me she was pregnant?'

His eyes widened, then they dropped to her stomach that showed a small but clear bump. 'I…' he began, but Maria had already turned around to haul her into another hug.

'Why didn't *you* tell me?' she asked, the unbridled joy in her sister's eyes exactly the reaction she had wanted to see.

'I wanted to surprise you,' Celine replied, then reached out to pull Darius closer, his hand coming to rest on her stomach. 'We had another…accident, but as it turns out it was something we had both been thinking about.'

Darius moved his thumb over her stomach and smiled when their eyes met. 'This time we're doing it together— all the way.'

* * * * *

COMING SOON!

We really hope you enjoyed reading this book. If you're looking for more romance be sure to head to the shops when new books are available on

Thursday 28th September

To see which titles are coming soon, please visit

millsandboon.co.uk/nextmonth

MILLS & BOON®

Coming next month

HER OFF-LIMITS SINGLE DAD
Marion Lennox

This was not sensible—not sensible in the least. There was no need at all for her to stay with Rob for a moment longer. She was this man's tenant and a colleague, and that was all. She lived at the far end of the house. She needed to keep some distance.

But distance had never been Jen's strong suit.

Maybe it was her childhood, absent parents who'd appeared sporadically, causing her to cling fiercely, to take what she could because she'd known they wouldn't be there the next day.

Maybe that was why she'd jumped into all sorts of disastrous relationships—okay, Darren hadn't been the first. Jump first, ask questions later. Take people at face value because looking forward didn't change a thing.

And here it was, happening again. This man had so much baggage—impossible baggage—yet here he was, looking down at her, smiling, and here was that longing again—for closeness, for warmth, for connection.

Her friend Frankie might have poured a bucket of cold water over her, she thought, demanding, "Will you ever learn?" But right now...

Right now Rob was reaching down to help her up. His

hands were strong and warm, and his smile was oh, so lovely.

Maybe this time…

What was she thinking? It was too soon—way, way too soon.

But that smile… She had no hope of fighting the way his smile made her feel.

And he tugged her a little too strongly, or maybe she rose a little too fast, and all of a sudden she was very, very close.

Here comes another catastrophe! She could almost hear Frankie's inevitable warning.

But Rob was right here, and she could feel his warmth, his strength… His lovely hands were steadying her, and he was still smiling.

She was lost.

Here I go again.

She could hear her brain almost sighing in exasperation, but did she care?

Not tonight. Not when he was so close.

So, she thought blindly as she felt the warmth of his chest, felt his hands steady her. Catastrophe, here I come.

Continue reading
HER OFF-LIMITS SINGLE DAD
Marion Lennox

Available next month
www.millsandboon.co.uk

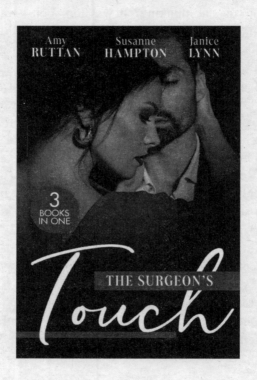

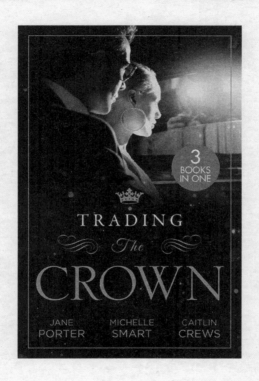

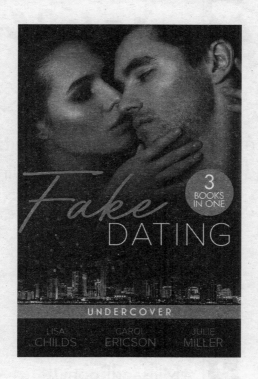

MILLS & BOON

THE HEART OF ROMANCE

A ROMANCE FOR EVERY READER

DERN
Prepare to be swept off your feet by sophisticated, sexy and seductive heroes, in some of the world's most glamourous and romantic locations, where power and passion collide.

ORICAL
Escape with historical heroes from time gone by. Whether your passion is for wicked Regency Rakes, muscled Vikings or rugged Highlanders, awaken the romance of the past.

ICAL
Set your pulse racing with dedicated, delectable doctors in the high-pressure world of medicine, where emotions run high and passion, comfort and love are the best medicine.

Love
Celebrate true love with tender stories of heartfelt romance, from the rush of falling in love to the joy a new baby can bring, and a focus on the emotional heart of a relationship.

ire
Indulge in secrets and scandal, intense drama and sizzling hot action with heroes who have it all: wealth, status, good looks…everything but the right woman.

OES
The excitement of a gripping thriller, with intense romance at its heart. Resourceful, true-to-life women and strong, fearless men face danger and desire - a killer combination!

To see which titles are coming soon, please visit

millsandboon.co.uk/nextmonth